UNDER WESTERN EYES

JOSEPH CONRAD, born as Józef Teodor Konrad Nałęcz Korzeniowski in the Russian-occupied Polish Ukraine on December 6, 1857, was involved in the causes of nationalism and politics from his birth. The cause of Polish freedom was directly inherited from his father and from the two families of his parents. After going to France at the age of sixteen, he soon became entangled in the causes of Royalism and Carlism there and in Spain. After he took to sea in 1878 he came to see the workings of imperialism, revolution, and conquest in the countries of the East, in the Congo, and in Latin America. After he adopted British residence and became a British subject, he saw the events of English and European politics at closer range; and in the last years of his life he again defended the cause of Polish nationalism. Though it was his life at sea or in the East that produced books like *Almayer's Folly* (1895), *The Nigger of the "Narcissus"* (1897), *Lord Jim* (1900), *Victory* (1915), and *The Rescue* (1920), the problems of modern politics and revolution claimed him for the writing of three of his most searching books: *Nostromo* (1904), *The Secret Agent* (1907), and *Under Western Eyes* (1911), novels that now stand as classics of their kind in twentieth-century literature. Nine of Conrad's shorter *Tales of Heroes and History* have already appeared in Anchor Books. *Under Western Eyes* now joins *The Secret Agent* in the series to show Conrad at his most powerful as a dramatist of modern history. Conrad died in England on August 3, 1924.

UNDER WESTERN EYES

by
JOSEPH CONRAD

"I would take liberty from any hand as a
hungry man would snatch a piece of bread . . ."
Miss Haldin

WITH AN INTRODUCTION BY
MORTON DAUWEN ZABEL

ANCHOR BOOKS
DOUBLEDAY & COMPANY, INC.
GARDEN CITY, NEW YORK

UNDER WESTERN EYES was originally published by Harper
& Brothers in 1911. The Anchor Books edition is published by
arrangement with Doubleday & Company, Inc.

Anchor Books edition: 1963

INTRODUCTION

I

Late in 1907 Conrad, now fifty and in his thirteenth year as a published author, began the writing of a new novel—the book that was not to appear until four years later as *Under Western Eyes*. He was at this time crossing the decade of his severest tests in authorship, and of problems that mark the years between 1902 and 1912 as a crucial phase in his career. Such tests had never been lacking in his writing life, but once the impulse of what he called his "first" or "Malayan phase" was spent, and once he had completed the series of tales and novels, culminating in "Typhoon" and "Falk," that had derived from his life at sea, they took on a new and formidable appearance.

His early stages in his art, however persistent in labor and accomplishment, had been anything but easy. It took him five years, between the ages of thirty-two and thirty-seven, to complete *Almayer's Folly* before it was published in 1895. *The Rescue*, begun in 1896, proved so baffling that he abandoned it after more than three years of struggle and did not return to it, as to an unsettled account in his conscience, until seventeen years later. His doubts in conceiving and finishing *Lord Jim* run through the letters he wrote during the year of its writing, and even after its appearance in 1900. His work in the shorter forms of fiction veered between the almost spontaneous exhilaration that produced his masterpieces in these forms and the profound uncertainty that yielded his mistaken efforts. Critical recognition had come to him early but practical success lagged to the point of bringing him to desperate crises in his financial prospects. When he arrived at a virtual point of rupture in his relations with William Blackwood of Edinburgh, the publisher who had done most to advance his literary fortunes in the early years, he felt that his struggle at "labouring against an anxious tomorrow, under the stress of an uncertain future," had brought him to a crisis more forbidding than any he had yet faced.

Yet against these hazards he had carried to completion a remarkable body of work in a short space of years—four novels, two book-length collaborations, four long tales, eight short stories—which testifies to the sustained energy, the sometimes astonishing intensity of excitement and labor, that had impelled him. "Youth" had been written in three weeks; "Heart of Darkness" in about three months; *The Nigger of the "Narcissus"* in less than six; *Lord Jim*, once its tentative beginnings were past, in about twelve. The long-stored, long-meditated years of his youth and sailing life; the restraints he had put on his imagination until the hour of his first effort at writing a novel struck in 1889; his three decades of dramatic encounters in Poland, in Russia, in France, in the East, and on the high seas—all these had combined to produce a succession of tales that make Conrad's first decade as a published author one of the most productive in modern literature. He had kept his mind and nerves steadily on the stretch. He had reaped a swift harvest from his past. Neither his personal responsibilities nor his creative need had allowed him to rest. The cumulative strain and tension of his work were bound to arrive at a point of snapping—of a radical climacteric in his imaginative life; and by Conrad's own account that point came in 1902.

"I don't mean," he wrote fifteen years later, "to say that I became then conscious of any impending change in my mentality and in my attitude towards the tasks of my writing life. And perhaps there was never any change, except in that mysterious, extraneous thing which has nothing to do with theories of art; a subtle change in the nature of the inspiration; a phenomenon for which I cannot in any way be held responsible. What, however, did cause me some concern was that after finishing the last story of the *Typhoon* volume it seemed somehow that there was nothing more in the world to write about."[1] Few writers have escaped such moments of spent energy or impasse, and Conrad was still to meet more than one of them before his life ended. But several circumstances combined to make the crisis of 1902 particularly significant in his career.

The East and the sea had already given him the most powerful tales he was to write on these subjects. For the moment their force had been exhausted. Blackwood, having published four of the best of these works, had found them too unprofitable to make it possible for him to agree to a financial scheme Conrad had proposed to him as a means of future support. ("He was very kind but told me plainly that I was a loss to the Firm. That's hard enough to hear at any time.") The sting of this refusal, the momentary sense of failure it brought to Conrad ("I admit that after leaving you I remained for some time under the impression of my 'worthlessness'"), caused him to write the most serious defense of his work and aims that he had yet attempted—crucial even beyond the credo he had written in 1897 as his preface to *The Nigger of the "Narcissus,"* because this time it came in the face of a direct challenge to his personal fortunes and future. It was more than a defense. It was a stubborn affirmation of his vocation and of his pride as an artist and a moral dramatist. "I am conscious of having pursued with pain and labour a calm conception of a definite ideal in a perfect soberness of spirit. . . . I have nothing but a faith—a little against the world—in my reasoned conviction. . . . Now my character is formed: it has been tried by experience. I have looked upon the worst life can do—and I am sure of myself, even against the demoralising effect of straitened circumstances. I know exactly what I am doing. . . . I want

[1] "Author's Note" to *Nostromo*, dated 1917, in *Conrad's Prefaces to His Works* (London: J. M. Dent & Sons, 1937), p. 85.

to make good my contention that I am not writing 'in the air.' It is not the haphazard business of a mere temperament. . . . Therefore I am emboldened to say that ultimate and irretrievable failure is *not* to be my lot. . . . My work shall not be an utter failure because it has the solid basis of a definite intention. . . ."[2]

It was in this conflict of self-doubt and enforced resolution that Conrad lived out the year 1902, and its acuteness, already evident in so many of the past phases of his life, was to persist in a renewed form in the years that lay ahead. He pressed on with the completion of "The End of the Tether," the last tale he wrote for Blackwood, even after most of the manuscript of its first draft had burned one night when the lamp on his writing table exploded. He saw the publication of the *Youth* volume and told Edward Garnett he was "overcome" by the appearance of the "three-headed monster in the green cover. I hate the sight of the thing." He assembled the four stories of the *Typhoon* volume for Heinemann and said he was "ashamed of them all; I don't believe either in their popularity or in their merit. . . . My mind is becoming base, my hand heavy, my tongue thick—as though I had drunk some subtle poison, some slow poison that will make me die, die as it were without an echo." Such were his private comments on some of the finest tales he had yet written or was ever to write.[3]

[2] Conrad to William Blackwood, May 31, 1902, in *Joseph Conrad: Letters to William Blackwood and David S. Meldrum*, edited by William Blackburn (Durham, N.C.: Duke University Press, 1958), pp. 152–56. Conrad's situation in 1902, also traced in the letters included in *Joseph Conrad: Life and Letters*, edited by G. Jean-Aubry (Garden City, N.Y.: Doubleday, Page & Co., 1927), and in *Letters from Conrad, 1895–1924*, to and edited with introduction and notes by Edward Garnett (Indianapolis, Ind.: The Bobbs-Merrill Co., 1928), and other records, is most closely documented in the letters to Blackwood and Meldrum.

[3] Letters to Edward Garnett of November 27, 1902, and June 10, 1902, in *Letters from Conrad, 1895–1924*, pp. 186–87, 183–84.

But another ferment was working in his mind. Black-wood's rebuff, the prolonged strain of the past five years, recurring ill health and domestic worries that prolonged themselves into 1903, apparently joined with the sense that he had run out of his material to compel Conrad toward a different subject matter, a new direction in his work, an attack on themes more closely actual and contemporary than those of his exotic or maritime tales. The drama of modern life, modern politics, the social crisis and the future of nations, was in the air. Novelists like his friend Wells and various popular entertainers were making a success of it. Newspapers were full of the unease of the world that lay behind the outward shows and successes of imperialism or *ententes*. The Russian novelists were seizing the public attention in Constance Garnett's translations, and though Conrad expressed himself as "think[ing] but little" of these books, they must have struck his old memories of his Polish youth and its tragedy with the impact of a profound hereditary recognition. A part of his personal life and inheritance that was older and more deepseated in his mind than anything he had experienced at sea or in the East was stirred to action in him. Whatever attempts he had made to come to grips with the problems of modern history in "An Outpost of Progress," "Heart of Darkness," and the abandoned *Rescue* were now feeling the claim of a more pressing actuality.

Imperialism, autocracy, nationalism, and revolution had been living presences to Conrad in more than the news of the day. They were conditions of his intimate history and personal knowledge. He now sensed himself to be at the edge of a new and bolder undertaking in his art. His "so strangely negative but disturbing mood" having "lasted some little time," there strayed into his mind the "first hint" of a new book "in the shape of a vagrant anecdote completely destitute of valuable details"—a memory of having heard "in 1875 or '6, when very young, in the West Indies, or rather in the Gulf of Mexico," the "story of some man who was supposed to have stolen single-handed a whole lighter-full of silver, somewhere on the Tierra Firme seaboard during the troubles of a revolution." Now, "twenty-six or seven years afterwards," he "came upon the very thing in a shabby volume picked up outside a second-hand bookshop." The germ of a new book was in his hands; and though he could scarcely have anticipated it at the moment, its writing was to involve him in almost two years of unremitting labor that resulted in the "most anxiously meditated" of his novels, and in "an intense creative effort on what I suppose will always remain my largest canvas."[4]

Early in 1903, on an undated Thursday, he wrote in a letter to John Galsworthy that "with my head full of a story, I have not been able to write a single word—except the title, which shall be, I think: *Nostromo* . . ." Twenty months later, on September 1, 1904, he announced, again to Galsworthy, "Finished! finished! on the 30th in Hope's house in Stanford in Essex"; and two days later, in letters to Garnett and William Rothenstein, that the completion of the book was "a fact upon which my friends may congratulate me as upon a recovery from a dangerous illness," and that "What the book is like, I don't know. . . . Personally I am not satisfied. It is something,—but not *the* thing I tried for. There is no exultation, none of that temporary sense of achievement which is so soothing. Even the mere feeling of relief at having done with it is wanting. The strain has been too great, has lasted too long. But I am ready for more. I don't feel empty, exhausted. I am simply joyless,—like most men of little faith."[5]

"I don't know whether I really felt that I wanted a change, change in my imagination, in my vision, and in my mental attitude," he recalled in 1920; "I rather think

---

[4] "Author's Note" to *Nostromo* in *Prefaces*, p. 85; and to *The Secret Agent*, 1920, *Prefaces*, p. 105. For a further note on Conrad's derivations in *Nostromo*, see supplementary note 4 at the end of this volume.

[5] The letters to Galsworthy are in Jean-Aubry's *Life and Letters*, Vol. I, pp. 308, 332–35; those to Garnett and Rothenstein, pp. 335–36. Conrad's following remark is in his "Author's Note" to *The Secret Agent* in *Prefaces*, p. 105.

that a change in the fundamental mood had already stolen over me unawares." The change, though not radically discontinuous with the mood and impetus of certain of his earlier works, was to remain with him for almost a decade. Though interrupted by recurrences to his more familiar maritime or Eastern subjects, it was to sustain him through the writing of three of his most ambitious and searching books between 1903 and 1910, and to produce, in *Nostromo*, *The Secret Agent*, and *Under Western Eyes*, the works that give him his major rank among the political novelists of the twentieth century.

II

"Books have their fate," Conrad said in one of his early essays, "and it is very much like the destiny of man. They share with us the great incertitude of ignominy or glory—of severe justice and senseless persecution—of calumny and misunderstanding—the shame of undeserved success." Nor can they rely on "the formulas of art" for assurance against these hazards of chance or fortune, for such formulas too "are dependent on things variable, unstable, and untrustworthy; on human sympathies, on prejudices, on likes and dislikes, on the sense of virtue and the sense of propriety, on beliefs and theories that, indestructible in themselves, always change their form—often in the lifetime of one fleeting generation."[6]

The fate of Conrad's own books supports his contention. From early neglect to later success; from public admiration for the romantic glamour and atmosphere of his exotic or maritime tales to a lingering public indifference to the serious values that were masked by these; from the impatience of careless readers to the respect of his fellow artists and to a gradually insistent critical esteem, the fortunes of his art during the past seven decades describe the

[6] "Books" in *Notes on Life and Letters* (Garden City, N.Y.: Doubleday, Page & Co., 1921), pp. 3–10. The essay was first published in *The Speaker*, July 15, 1905.

destiny of his resolutely individual talent and of the risks to which it was fated. Some of his tales were admitted to the rank of modern classics as early as half a century ago, but certain others—among them some of his most serious achievements—have had to wait much longer for the turn of taste or of events that had to appear before they won their hearing and a measure of justice.

The tales of Conrad that have remained most widely read during the past sixty years happen to be those he wrote early or late in his career. *Almayer's Folly, The Nigger of the "Narcissus," Lord Jim,* "Youth," "Heart of Darkness," and "Typhoon" were all completed by 1902, in his first eight years as a professional writer. *Chance, Victory, The Shadow-Line, The Arrow of Gold, The Rescue,* and *The Rover,* the novels that won him public success in the last decade of his life, came after 1913. But between these two groups of tales he wrote the series of novels that may be called the works of his middle period —books that deviated from the maritime, exotic, or romantic scenes of his more popular fiction by addressing themselves to the drama of modern society and politics. These novels show not only some of his most serious subjects but some of his most ambitious art; and if their value was largely neglected at the time of their appearance, it has been made unmistakable by the events and crises that have followed them in the twentieth century. *Under Western Eyes* was a failure when it was first published in 1911 and must still be one of his least-read novels. But it profits by the irony of circumstance more than any of the others, and it is without question one of the books that must be read by anyone concerned to know Conrad's art in its full dimensions and resonance. Today, even after so many novels have been written on its subject, and when the developments of Russian and international history have made its drama more familiar to Western readers than ever before, it shares with its two immediate predecessors in Conrad's canon the stature of a classic drama of modern history and one of the few English books of the century that calls for a rank among its Russian and European companions.

Nostromo, appearing in 1904, and variously rated by critics as his most difficult or perplexing book and as "one of the great novels of the language," gave Conrad, in its complex drama of civil war, revolution, and rival moralities in the South American state of Costaguana, his first full test as a dramatist of politics and statecraft. *The Secret Agent* of 1907 is now readily recognizable as a pioneer in its genre—the tale of political intrigue, espionage, and moral anarchism in modern Europe which has become a typical mode of fiction in our age of *Machtpolitik,* scientific violence, and "international evil." *Chance,* the book that turned the tide of Conrad's fortunes when it ran serially in the *New York Herald* in 1912, though not a political novel, combined its maritime theme with a drama of modern finance, ethical confusion, and social persecution in which Marlow, the narrator Conrad had created to tell the tales of "Youth," "Heart of Darkness," and *Lord Jim,* reappeared to manipulate, in the history of Flora de Barral, one of his most intricate tales of moral duplicity and alienation. All three of these novels are radically and recognizably Conradian in their subjects and craftsmanship. All of them develop themes and motives that were essential to his work from its beginnings. But *Under Western Eyes,* as Conrad himself admitted, has a personal relevance that gives it a special interest among his books. Its subject—Russian character, despotism, and revolution—is one with which, as a Pole whose nation and family had suffered under the heel of Russian imperialist occupation, he was sooner or later bound to come to terms in his art. And beyond this it forms, along with *The Secret Agent,* his most serious effort to describe the forces at work in the body politic of modern Europe. It also serves as his closest link with the Dostoevskian tradition in Russian fiction—a tradition which, though he persistently repudiated it and professed himself both baffled and repelled by it, opens a radical question of temperamental affinity and influence in his work. And lastly the book presents a theme which, however remote from the public interests of fifty years ago, has become of absorbing concern to the West during the past four decades, and never more so than at the present moment.

The novel fell almost completely flat in England and America, but in Europe and Russia it won serious attention. It was translated into Russian (by E. Pimenova, for the house of Polza) as early as 1912, and numerous editions were printed before 1917; and while it has not been possible to trace its recent fate there—the recent editions of the *Great Soviet Encyclopedia* do not mention either *The Secret Agent* or *Under Western Eyes* in describing Conrad as a "bourgeois decadent" who abandoned true social subjects in favor of the exotic and the subjective— it must still be the book by which Conrad is best known to such Russian readers as have access to his work. The present time of crisis between Russia and the West has given it the force of a prophecy; and an age that has been bred on such classics as *Virgin Soil, Crime and Punishment,* and *The Possessed,* and that has found images of its ordeal in books like Kafka's *The Trial,* Koestler's *Darkness at Noon,* Orwell's *1984,* as well as in the tales of Sartre, Camus, Graham Greene, Aldanov, Victor Serge, Schwarz-Bart, and a host of other recent novelists of ideological conflict and political terror, must encounter *The Secret Agent* and *Under Western Eyes* with the shock of recognizing novels which, written well in advance of the wars and crises of the twentieth century, have become appallingly corroborated by the events of contemporary history.

The present writer has found himself returning to *Under Western Eyes* during the past thirty years as often as to any of Conrad's books, and discovering in it a force and achievement that only two of his other novels and three or four of the tales rival. This may be a matter of personal taste, but it has been supported by several of Conrad's distinguished readers. Ford Madox Ford once said that for himself the book was "in a long way the greatest—as it is the latest—of all Conrad's great novels"; and André Gide, who on first making its acquaintance in 1917, admired its "prophetic reflections about the Russian soul," continued to read and ponder it, saying of the theme it shares with *Lord Jim* that "there is no more pathetic subject for a novel," and finding in it a reflection of his own persistent concern with "that *irresponsible act* of the hero, to redeem which his whole life is subsequently engaged." The English critic V. S. Pritchett has said that the novel has become "more and more suggestive to the contemporary reader," and another, F. R. Leavis, has rated it one of Conrad's best—"a most distinguished work," which "must be counted among those upon which Conrad's status as one of the great English novelists securely rests."[7] More

[7] Ford Madox Ford in *Return to Yesterday* (London: Victor Gollancz, 1932), p. 193; André Gide in *Journal* (Paris, 1941), 13 décembre, 1917, p. 641, and 23 février, 1930, p. 971 (as here translated by Justin O'Brien in *Journals* [New York, 1948, 1949], Vol. II, p. 219; Vol. III, pp. 94–95); V. S. Pritchett in *The New Statesman and Nation* (London), July 15, 1950, pp. 72–73; F. R. Leavis in *The Great Tradition* (1948), pp. 219–22. [Gide adds to his comment of February 23, 1930: "Much interested by the relationship I discover between *Under Western Eyes* and *Lord Jim*. (I regret not having spoken of this with Conrad.) . . . For the thing that leads to the heaviest responsibility is just the *irresponsibilities* in a life. How can one efface that act? There is no more pathetic subject for a novel, nor one that has been more stifled in our literature by belief in Boileau's rule: that the hero must remain, from one end to the other of a drama or a novel, 'such as he was first seen to be.' "]

Since the present essay on *Under Western Eyes* was first published in 1951 a number of studies of the novel have been made: among them Douglas Hewitt's in *Conrad: A Reassessment* (1952), pp. 80–88; Robert F. Haugh's in *Joseph Conrad: Discovery in Design* (1957), pp. 119–35; Albert J. Guerard's in *Conrad the Novelist* (1958), pp. 218–53; and Eloise K. Hay's in an as yet unpublished doctoral thesis on *The Political Novels of Joseph Conrad*, Radcliffe College, 1961. Other comment has appeared in more incidental form in other recent criticism. The present study appears in a revised and expanded version from that which appeared as an introduction to the novel in 1951 (New York: New Directions) and as an essay in the author's *Craft and Character* (New York: The Viking Press, 1957).

recent studies have given it increasing attention and a major place in his achievement. And Conrad himself had a special feeling for his effort "to capture the very soul of things Russian," and one of the last projects of his life was to make a play out of the novel under the title he originally gave it, *Razumov*.[8]

To these opinions there has been a certain amount of critical dissent, and it is possible that at a first reading or casual glance the reader will find that the book, especially in its second and third parts, shows Conrad at his densest and most discouraging. Yet there can be little in modern fiction more acutely conceived and written than its first and final parts; and while it must be allowed that between these there are stretches of dramatic indirection, calculated delay, and psychic or moral dissection that are likely to put any reader's patience to a test, the narrative repeatedly rises to points of extraordinary intensity and in the end achieves a depth of penetration, of cumulative effect and resonance, that brings it into the company of the most memorable books of its period and certainly of Conrad's own finest powers. Even its attenuations put less of a strain on credulity or attention than many distinguished modern books do; and one can only advise the reader to stay with the book, to keep his patience alert, and to see what becomes of the novel's long-drawn tensions. He is likely to find himself rewarded with a remarkable experience in fiction, and to discover a reason in Conrad's method which, though it may not be as compelling as in some of his shorter tales, will have much to say about the kind of art Conrad here practised at its maturity and about the difficult theme of conscience and retribution with which the novel deals. If *Nostromo* shows a larger vision and a more comprehensive conspectus of history, and *The Secret Agent* a more sustained focus of tragic action and irony, it may be argued that *Under*

---

[8] The play, sketched and apparently partly written, was never finished. For a further note on it and Conrad's other plays, see supplementary note 8, where a French film version of *Under Western Eyes* is also described.

Western Eyes combines these elements in the proportions that make it finally more penetrating, more akin to a classic tradition in European fiction, than either of its companion books. And if the ominous test of Dostoevsky's novels looms behind it, it is for the Western reader to decide what *Under Western Eyes* does to bring an acuteness of moral concentration and insight to bear upon its Dostoevskian subject and even, perhaps, to refine upon and rival it.

III

The writing of the book, as so often with Conrad, gave him severe difficulties. The prolonged ordeal of *Nostromo* in 1903–4, though it did not baffle him as *The Rescue* had done or involve him in an unexpected elaboration of his subject as in the case of *Lord Jim,* had drained him of strength, and it was almost eighteen more months before he ventured on a new novel. Meanwhile he wrote a number of essays, among them his first and most important treatise on politics, "Autocracy and War," in 1905. He turned to the writing of his sketches of sea life, largely at Ford Madox Hueffer's prodding, and by 1906 had accumulated enough of them to publish *The Mirror of the Sea.* He wrote "Gaspar Ruiz" as a pendant to *Nostromo* in 1905, and later in the same year he significantly tackled the themes of modern political intrigue and anarchism that resulted in the two slight but premonitory tales of "An Anarchist" and "The Informer."

By these steps he brought his political subject out of its Eastern and South American settings and closer to contemporary Europe and England. The compelling need of dealing with the forces of contemporary history which had counted in the shaping of *Nostromo* was obviously becoming more insistent in his thought. Early in 1906 his chronic sense of feeling "powerless in an exhaustion of thought and will" was alleviated by a vacation in southern France at Montpellier—a change that not only proved more successful than a trip to Capri in the previous year but that also gave him hints that were to contribute, years later, to *Victory* and the French historical dramas of his final years. He was soon able to begin a new book. "A few words uttered by a friend in casual conversation about anarchists or rather anarchist activities" combined with his memory of the "blood-stained inanity" of the "already old story of the attempt to blow up the Greenwich Observatory" in 1894 and with some other "not very recondite" sources to shape a drama of London espionage in his mind. In "a matter of about three days" its plot was decided; and in an unusual stride of steady application the novel of *The Secret Agent* was completed by early November.

The Secret Agent, which derived in large part from London itself—"the vision of an enormous town . . . a monstrous town more populous than some continents"—is one of the most concentrated of Conrad's books and his most sustained feat of "ironic method." It undoubtedly acted as a resolving test of his political insight. Less nebulous or remote than the Eastern dramas of *The Rescue* and *Lord Jim*, less riddled by complex plotting and dramatic diffusion than *Nostromo*, more convinced in its action and language than "An Anarchist" and "The Informer," it concentrated his political imagination more effectively than anything he had yet written. Though it carries some effects of the *tour de force*, it shows what was for Conrad an unusual excitement and movement of inspiration. "All of a sudden I found myself stimulated. . . . It was at first for me a mental change, disturbing a quieted-down imagination, in which strange forms, sharp in outline but imperfectly apprehended, appeared and claimed attention as crystals will do by their bizarre and unexpected shapes." It gives the impression that Conrad was now more forcibly propelled toward the drama of Europe than ever before, and toward the more intimate treatment of it that was soon to come.

Having completed the novel he found himself again spent, "horribly seedy and depressed." Another vacation in Montpellier was undertaken in December 1906. He wrote "Il Conde," worked on "The Duel," and cast about in the lore of Napoleonic history. He also began to struggle with a longer project, the novel *Chance,* whose germinal idea had first come to him as early as 1898. But *Chance* at this point was spurred by no such impetus as had produced *The Secret Agent,* and proving intractable throughout 1907, it was finally put aside, to remain unfinished for another five years. During the Montpellier visit an alarming illness of the Conrads' son Borys took the family to a hydropathic cure at an old scene, Champel, near Geneva, which Conrad had visited in the nineties. At this distracted juncture he remembered "something told [him] by a man in Geneva many years ago," when he had gone to Switzerland on an earlier search for health and inspiration. Now, revisiting Geneva, he seized on the earlier memory and by January 1908 was at work on the novel that became *Under Western Eyes.* At that point he called it *Razumov* and his conception of it differed radically from the book he completed, after another series of delays and interruptions, two years later (on January 22, 1910, according to the date he wrote on the manuscript) and published on October 5, 1911, with its dedication to his American friend Agnes Tobin of San Francisco, "who brought to our door her genius for friendship from the uttermost shore of the West."9

The strands of suggestion and memory that combined in Conrad's shaping of his tale were thus both immediate and remote, and they included some of the most profound and deeply rooted emotions of his life. There was first the suggestion of Geneva itself, "the respectable and passionless abode of democratic liberty, the serious-minded town

9 On Agnes Tobin see supplementary note 9. The manuscript of *Under Western Eyes* is in the Keating Collection in the Yale University Library. It shows many revisions and some lengthy deletions of details and episodes before the novel reached its published form; there were other revisions between the serial and book form. The novel was first serialized in *The English Review* (London) and in *The North American Review* in America, December 1910–October 1911, before being published by Methuen in London and Harper & Brothers in New York in 1911.

of dreary hotels, tendering the same indifferent hospitality to tourists of all nations and to international conspirators of every shade": Voltaire's

> ville froide et fade, où tout est entamé,
> Où l'on calcule toujours, et ne sent jamais—

the city of Calvinist rectitude and Swiss sobriety which from the time of Herzen, Bakunin, and Kropotkin to that of Lenin and Trotsky had offered its impervious sanctuary to the exiles of Tsarist autocracy. There, perhaps in the quarter which, "on account of many Russians residing there, is called La Petite Russie," Conrad heard from his unknown acquaintance the hints of the story which served as his germ. (He was as avid as Henry James was for those chance suggestions that illustrate what James called "that odd law which somehow always makes the minimum of valid suggestion serve the man of imagination better than the maximum," although, as Graham Greene has pointed out, there is a striking difference between the germs Conrad seized upon, "remarkable as a rule for their anarchy" or "their ambiguity," and "those neat little dinner-table stories which set James off constructing his more intricate and deeper fictions, holding up his hand in deprecation to prevent the whole story coming out.")[10]

What Conrad remembered of the stranger's tale he heard in Geneva in 1895 must have fallen in with the mood that still possessed him after the writing of *The Secret Agent* and its two short companion pieces. That novel of intrigue, anarchism, and treachery in the London of the 1890's, with its plot of terrorists, bomb-makers, and *agents provocateurs* manipulated by an unnamed foreign power in the interests of inciting the western European nations to suppress the alien revolutionary groups to whom they gave asylum, was his first full portrayal of two of the

---

[10] Henry James, preface to *The Aspern Papers, etc.*, in the New York Edition of 1907–09, and in *The Art of the Novel* (1934), pp. 161–62. Graham Greene in *The Lost Childhood and Other Essays* (1951), p. 99.

evils he feared most profoundly in his life and age—the "plague spots" of radical socialism and anarchism that undermined the solidarity of European society, and the "ferocity and imbecility of an autocratic rule" that bred them. The shadow of the Tsarist tyranny and violence was already falling heavily across Europe. Nineteen hundred five was the year of the aborted Russian revolution that foreshadowed 1917. Nihilism, anarchism, and revolutionary terrorism had spread westward through the past five or six decades. The First International at The Hague in 1872 had brought to a head the conflict between the scientific socialism of Marx and the anarchist policy of Bakunin, resulting in the expulsion of the anarchists. The *Communist Manifesto* of 1848 and *Das Kapital* had descended and proliferated into a widespread lineage of tracts, texts, theses, programs of action, systems of organized protest, and crises of crime and persecution, extending across Europe and to both Asia and America. And from the time of Turgenev's *Smoke, Rudin,* and *Virgin Soil* or the novels of Dostoevsky, the modern novel had become increasingly concerned with themes of despotism, protest, and revolt. Conrad's friends Constance and Edward Garnett were busy in England translating and writing propaganda for the Russian classics, or mixing in the circles of refugees like Kropotkin, Stepniak, and other exiles from Russia. His collaborator Ford Madox Hueffer was involved in the socialist activities of the younger Rossettis and other sympathizers with Continental radicalism.

Twenty-five years before Conrad wrote his novel Henry James had dealt with the subject of revolutionary anarchism in *The Princess Casamassima.* That book, the first notable work of fiction in English on its theme and the most impressive novel of its kind to appear in England or America before 1900, was inspired by the radical activity of the 1880's; and Lionel Trilling[11] and others have shown in their studies of the book how closely its material

---

[11] In his introduction to the novel (New York: Macmillan Co., 1948), included in *The Liberal Imagination* by Lionel Trilling (1950), pp. 58–92.

tallies with such events as the Lyons riots of 1882, with a series of attempts to assassinate the rulers of Germany, Spain, Italy, and Russia, with the Phoenix Park murders in Ireland and the Haymarket Riots in Chicago, with dynamite conspiracies in England and Germany, and with the activities of such anti-scientific rivals of Marx as Bakunin and Johann Most. In Russia the "Socialist Revolutionary" Party and its terrorist Battle Organization were augmented by the student revolutionary groups that sprang up in the eighties and nineties. And against them stood the organized forces of Tsarist officialdom and the political secret police, the *Okhrana*. All these served to provide Conrad—as they were to provide many other novelists—with his situation and background. From their activities he fastened upon the episode of recent history with which his novel opens: "an event characteristic of modern Russia in the actual fact"—the "successful attempt on the life of Mr. de P——, the President of the notorious Repressive Commission of some years ago, the Minister of State invested with extraordinary powers."

The novel—of which Conrad was later to say that "I was induced to write" it "by the rubbishy character of stories about Russian revolutionists published in magazines"—thus hinges on an occurrence which had only recently shaken Europe and figured in the world's news. "De P——" was the celebrated Viatscheslav Konstantino-vitch Plehve, whose assassination took place in July 1904. Born in 1846 of Lithuanian stock, educated in Warsaw and at the University of St. Petersburg, he had ascended by carefully calculated stages from assistant Solicitor-General to become the director of the Russian state police, Secretary of State, member of the Council of the Empire, and eventually in 1902 Minister of the Interior. He had attracted the favor of Alexander III for his work in investigating the assassination of Alexander II; had earned the hatred of Poland, Lithuania, and Finland for his ruthless "Russification" of those subject provinces; had manipulated pogroms against the Jews and persecutions of Armenians in the Caucasus; was credited with being accessory to the Kishinev massacres; opposed Witte's policy of commercial development in Russia along European lines because it tended to further both a dangerous proletariat and a prosperous middle class; and in time became the fanatical archetype of the autocratic principle and an arch-villain in revolutionary history. Long plotted by the Battle Organization, his murder was finally brought off by a bombing as he was driving to the Petershof to make his regular report to the Tsar, and it made an enormous impression on all strata of Russian society and throughout Europe. The assassin indicted and executed for the murder, Sasonov, enacted a role comparable to that of Victor Haldin in Conrad's story.

Plehve's assassination involved another person who became notorious in Russian revolutionary history. This was Azeff, one of the most notorious of the police spies and double agents of the time who, double-dealing as revolutionary conspirators and as tools of the Tsarist police, became a familiar product of the politics of despotism. From the time of Vidocq and Balzac's Vautrin they had figured in modern European intrigue, but Azeff achieved a special celebrity. Born of poor parents in 1869, he absconded from Russia with some stolen money at the age of twenty-three; went to Karlsruhe in Germany (like Stuttgart, Baden, and Geneva, one of the centers of Russian conspiracy abroad); joined there a group of Russian student-revolutionists among whom he appeared as a student of engineering; and at the same time offered his services as a spy to the Russian state police. Thus while, as a member of the Socialist Revolutionary Party and head of its terrorist section, he was instrumental in plotting the assassination not only of Plehve in 1904 but of the Grand Duke Sergei in 1905 and of Dubasov, Governor-General of Moscow, in 1906, he simultaneously remained the best-paid and most valued secret agent of the *Okhrana*.

His double life was symptomatic of the fantastic world he lived in. The drawn battle between the Tsarist state and the revolutionary anarchists was little less deadly than the rivalries within each of these bodies. State officials were willing to see their rivals assassinated and their policies discredited by terrorist outrages. Frequent atrocities increased the importance of the *Okhrana*. A police spy against whom suspicion might be directed by one set of officials could find patronage in another set. Official intrigue, time-serving, and opportunism taxed the wits of vested authority quite as much as its declared enemies did. And against these tangled lines of a corrupt officialdom stood the equally tangled loyalties and intrigues within the revolutionary circles themselves, riddled by sectarian careerism and rivalries through which a conspirator like Azeff might pick his way if he possessed a sufficient genius for duplicity. The situation was as typical of the deadly world of Tsarist politics as it was later to become of Soviet and Praesidium machinations; and it took the stubborn persistence of V. L. Burtzeff, editor of the revolutionary historical review *Byloye* (*The Past*), to track Azeff's treachery down by extracting the truth about it from a disappointed ex-director of the Police Department, Lopuhin, and exposing the sordid case in the pages of his journal. Whereupon Azeff, his dual standing as terrorist and spy shattered, had to flee Russia and go into hiding in Germany, where he lived incognito on a false passport as an apparently respectable citizen and member of the Berlin Stock Exchange in the company of his mistress Madame N—— (known also as "La Bella Heddy de Hero"), until, to his horror, he was arrested in 1914 by the German authorities as "a dangerous revolutionary, anarchist, and terrorist, who, according to the international police conventions, was to be handed over to the Russian authorities at the end of the War." He was thrown into the Moabit Prison, but was released on the outbreak of the Bolshevik Revolution in 1917, was given a minor post in the German Ministry of Foreign Affairs, and died in Berlin in 1918. His onetime notoriety was to become obscured after his death by a proliferation of men of his type among the spies, double agents, and *intrigueurs* of our time, but during his life his name became a legend and Azeff himself a classic model of political duplicity.

It is not to be assumed that Conrad took the career of Azeff as a model for his story of Razumov. The two characters are quite different. But there is a strong possibility that Conrad followed Burtzeff's exposure of Azeff while he was writing his novel. It took place in 1908 while *Under Western Eyes* was in its first stages; it became headlined in the news of the day; it had a direct connection with the Plehve murder of 1904 which Conrad explicitly incorporated into his story; and before the novel was finished it had already become the subject of learned scholarship in France and Germany.[12] And Conrad had already fixed upon the police spy and *agent provocateur* as a radical symptom of the whole sinister machinery of European corruption and Russian duplicity. The hero of *The Secret Agent*, Mr. Verloc, was precisely such a character in the squalid circles of London anarchist life and activity, simultaneously employed by a foreign embassy (unspecified but obviously Russian) to foment public outrages among his confederates, and accepted as a fellow conspirator by the gang he harbored in the back room of his shop in Soho. A similar type appears in the police agent Servin of the story "The Informer," whose exposure brings confusion to all his confederates in the house they have used as their headquarters in Hermione Street, London. There is also the different but related figure of the anarchist victim in Paul, the modest workingman engineer in the story called "An Anarchist," who becomes ruined as much by his exploiting radical friends as by the police machinery of Paris. As Henry James, in *The Princess Casamassima*, shows his hero Hyacinth Robinson becoming fatally involved in the anarchist machinations of Paul Muniment, of the ambiguous dilettante-radical Princess, and of the great mastermind Hoffendahl, so Conrad shows both his squalid Verloc and his high-minded Razumov trapped by the treacheries and furtive guilt into which the dupe or

[12] On Azeff and his career see supplementary note 12, where the contemporary investigations to which Conrad may have had access are also described.

the willing self-deceiver falls when he trafficks with the
evil genius of despotism or anarchy.

IV

But Conrad, in treating this subject, unquestionably felt
the force of it more intimately and personally than James
could have felt it. The subject was part of his life and
memory; it had conditioned his experience from his childhood; and no distance he put between himself and the
country of his birth or the empire that occupied it could
possibly have effaced his memory of them. Politics, nationalism, the forces of imperialism and rebellion, were the
first and deepest part of his inheritance; and few novelists
in English—perhaps none—could have brought a more tenacious sense of those forces to their work and art.

He was a Pole, born in the Russian-occupied Poland of
1857 as the son of one of the most spirited participants
in the Polish National Committee, and with a profound
fear of Russian autocratic power in his blood. Three of his
uncles had been killed or exiled during the Polish rising
against Russia in the 1860's, and his father, Apollo Nałęcz
Korzeniowski, poet, translator, patriot, and member of the
"Red" or extremist wing of the Polish cause, had been arrested by the Russian authorities in 1861 for his part in
the illegal National Committee and in framing its seditious
mandate against the occupying powers. With his wife
Evelina Bobrowska, named in the penal document as his
fellow exile, he was sentenced to deportation in a remote
province of Russia, the Government Vologda. Their five-
year-old son accompanied them into this exile in May
1862. Both of Conrad's parents later died as a result of
their hardships soon after their return to Poland—the
mother in 1865, the father in 1869—leaving Conrad an or-
phan at the age of eleven, bereft of his immediate family
by the repressive hostility of the Tsarist autocracy. The
stamp of that tragedy was never effaced from his mind or
emotion.

Thus Conrad brought into his early manhood two

strains of his native inheritance—the patriotic and nationalistic ardor of his father's nature and the more conservative
"land-tilling gentry" temper of his mother's people, the
Bobrowskis. And while he was to become confirmed in the
conservative leanings of his mother's family, now represented by his uncle Tadeusz Bobrowski who soon took
over the guardianship of the young Conrad, he carried
into his mature life a divided allegiance. One side of his
nature was ardent, excitable, strenuous, adventurous, self-
willed, and haunted by the memory of his father's and his
country's dedication—it was the side that led to his first
youthful ventures of bravado, Carlist enthusiasm, amateur
seamanship, and reckless living in France and Spain between 1874 and 1878. The other side of his character was
incurably committed to caution and doubt, a somber pessimism, fearing violence, fanaticism, anarchy, and Slavic
instability, all of them symptoms of the autocratic or revolutionary extremism which both Russia and the Polish
nationalist enthusiasm came to represent in his mind, and
which eventually led him to seek his future in western
Europe and finally in the "sanity and method" of England
and her Merchant Service. "The obligation of absolute
fairness" which he claimed for the writing of *Under Western Eyes* was, as he said in his "Author's Note" to the
novel, "imposed on me historically and hereditarily, by the
peculiar experience of race and family. . . . I had never
been called before to a greater effort of detachment: detachment from all passions, prejudices, and even from personal memories." Those passions and prejudices were
personally present in his formative years in the characters
of his father and uncle. Apollo Korzeniowski and Tadeusz
Bobrowski conditioned in him a moral character whose
divided temper and conflicts of emotion were to remain
with him for life.

When Razumov, in *Under Western Eyes*, finds himself
caught in the trap of Haldin's act of violence and of his
own betrayal of the man who came to him for help, he
writes certain lines on a sheet of paper and impales them
on his bedroom wall with his penknife. They describe the

antagonism of forces which Conrad knew in his own history and define the reaction to which his deep-seated historical pessimism finally compelled him:

> History not Theory.
> Patriotism not Internationalism.
> Evolution not Revolution.
> Direction not Destruction.
> Unity not Disruption.

When he spoke of the novel in 1920 Conrad confessed that his "greatest anxiety" in writing it had been "to strike and sustain the note of scrupulous impartiality," and to obey his "primary conviction that truth alone is the justification of any fiction which makes the least claim to the quality of art or may hope to take its place in the culture of men and women of its time." He had claimed that justification for his work from its beginnings: the argument is expressed in the first two statements he wrote on his craft, his prefaces to *Almayer's Folly* in 1895 and to *The Nigger of the "Narcissus"* in 1897. But whatever the tests he had met, whatever the strains he had suffered, in writing his other books, they could hardly have equaled in emotional and intimate immediacy the challenge he faced when he wrote *Under Western Eyes*. The fear or suspicion of Russia he expressed in his letters; the fear of revolutionary zealotry he felt in his blood; the distrust with which he regarded political extremism or racial mysticism, whether Russian or Polish; his cautious view of all such excesses in thought or action—these were now subjected to the test of an aesthetic or moral justice more demanding than any he had yet confronted. He must have felt himself under the scrutiny of a judicious criticism in every line he wrote. In 1920 his final judgment on the novel and on the modern Russian history to which it refers—he is now writing three years after the Bolshevik revolution of 1917 —was emphatic:

> The ferocity and imbecility of an autocratic rule rejecting all legality and in fact basing itself upon com-

plete moral anarchism provokes the no less imbecile and atrocious answer of a purely Utopian revolutionism encompassing destruction by the first means to hand, in the strange conviction that a fundamental change of hearts must follow the downfall of any given human institutions. These people are unable to see that all they can effect is merely a change of names. The oppressors and the oppressed are all Russians together; and the world is brought once more face to face with the truth of the saying that the tiger cannot change his stripes nor the leopard his spots.

This is the Conrad who speaks in his own person, and in the simplified language of argument. When he wrote as a novelist he had another kind of truth to contend with, and his artist's doctrine of "the highest kind of justice to the visible universe" fell under the demands of a severer conscience, a more complex intelligence. It is these that give *Under Western Eyes* its moral and dramatic quality, its Conradian dimension. If there remain for some readers of the novel evidences of a prejudice that mars the ultimate or abstract justice of the tale, there can be no question that his consciousness of that prejudice is as intense in its pages as his struggle to redress it. One of Conrad's recent critics, Miss M. C. Bradbrook, writing in 1941, said that "No wonder the book was unpopular in 1911. It might have been equally unpopular in 1931, but at the moment its premises are familiar."[13] The remark has become even more to the point in the decades that have followed. And as for the charge that Conrad harbored an unbalanced "Russophobia," a comment E. M. Forster once made on him is also relevant: Conrad's "passions are intelligible and frank: having lived thus, thus he feels, and it is as idle to regret his account of Russians as it would be to regret Dostoevsky's account of Poles in *The Brothers Karamazov*. A philosopher would moderate his transports, or attempt to correlate them. Conrad isn't that type: he

[13] M. C. Bradbrook, *Joseph Conrad: Poland's English Genius* (1941), p. 9.

claims the right to be unreasonable when he or those whom he respects have suffered."[14] The effort to moderate or correlate exists in the book; Conrad himself boasted of it. But he was, in the end, writing a novel, not a treatise in scientific or historical impersonality. Had his moderation fully succeeded, he would not have achieved the book he wrote.

What he called a "senseless desperation provoked by senseless tyranny" epitomized for Conrad the Russian danger and its effects on the Polish cause that had led him to leave Poland in 1874 and to identify his personal fate with the West. Yet his divided allegiance between East and West, between the Slavic world and the European or English, remains basic to his tale and it was referred to explicitly when he decided on what he called its "awkward title." It became his special purpose to hold in double focus two views of the Russian fate—that of the Russians themselves (and the respect the book first won in Russia perhaps testifies sufficiently to his success on this score) and that of their alien observers who represent the standards of Western life. This alone, quite apart from its difficult moral theme, gives the work its characteristic Conradian complexity. It also gives it what no Russian novelist —except possibly a Turgenev or Tolstoy in the nineteenth century or a Pasternak in the twentieth—would be likely to give it: a quality of intense personal commitment combined with a severe discipline in moral and humanistic objectivity. A distinguished critic to whom I once gave the book remarked, after expressing some impatience with its method and construction, that its handling of Russians ("about whom," he allowed, Conrad "says many things that seem to me true and penetrating") has "a little the second-hand quality of most sketching of national types by foreigners." "Isn't it," he asked, "much more satisfac-

[14] E. M. Forster, "Joseph Conrad: A Note," in *Abinger Harvest* (1936), p. 136. This "note" is a review of Conrad's *Notes on Life and Letters* (1921), but it has a wider relevance to his work, and it includes some essential statements on Conrad and his art.

tory to read *The Possessed* or *Crime and Punishment?*"
Possibly in the interests of a final authority it is. Conrad,
as Thomas Mann once said, "is far from being the size of
Dostoevsky"; and it is both impossible and unnecessary to
read *Under Western Eyes* in the expectation of finding
another Dostoevsky novel in it, whatever its links with the
Dostoevskian art and subject matter. But Mann added that
though Conrad's "objectivity may seem cool," it is informed by "a passion—a passion for freedom," the "refusal
of a very much engaged intelligence to hang miserably
in the air between contraries."[15] The expression of such
a passion is never possible in a wholly engaged participant
or an undivided nationalist. And a foreigner may have a
contribution of importance to make in writing about another nationality. His outsider's point of vantage, if sufficiently informed by knowledge and sympathy, makes it
possible for him to add something of importance, in critical
insight and judgment, to a native tradition. Stendhal made
such a contribution in writing about Italians, James in
writing about the English and the French, Forster in writing about India, Lawrence in writing about Mexico or
Australia, Orwell and Koestler in writing about the Bur-
mese and the Russians. Conrad, divided between a reasonable fear of tyranny or fanaticism and the demands of the
justice to which his art committed him, achieved in *Under
Western Eyes* what is possibly the most searching portrayal of Russian character and history that has yet been
arrived at in a non-Russian novel. Perhaps only one other
in the past fifty years—*Darkness at Noon*—can be said to
rival it. Its justice is more than a matter of the detachment
or impartiality he claimed for it. It is a matter of the charity and compassion that have their origins in sympathy
and suffering.

[15] Thomas Mann, "Vorwort zu Joseph Conrads Roman *Der
Geheimagent*," a preface he wrote for the German translation
of *The Secret Agent,* included in *Die Forderung des Tages*
(1930), pp. 325–40; translated by H. T. Lowe-Porter in *Past
Masters and Other Papers* by Thomas Mann (1933), pp. 231–47,
here 238, 246–47.

V

But the book he wrote is, of course, more than a document on Russian character or history; more than an exemplum of his conviction that "the old despotism and the new Utopianism are complementary forms of moral anarchy." It is a novel whose subject and artistry are continuous with his other work; and the reader of *Lord Jim, Nostromo,* "Heart of Darkness," "The Secret Sharer," and *Victory* will soon realize that *Under Western Eyes* offers yet another version of the hero and moral drama that Conrad made his own. In fact, the novel shows his theme and method in essence, as well as the ordeal of doubt and creative intensity that had, by the time he wrote it, become habitual with him.

On January 6, 1908, he wrote a letter to his friend Galsworthy in which he described his first steps in the writing of his manuscript:

"Et le misérable écrivait toujours."

He is writing now a story the title of which is *Razumov.* Isn't it expressive? I think that I am trying to capture the very soul of things Russian,—*Cosas de Russia.* It is not an easy work but it may be rather good when it's done. . . .

Listen to the theme. The Student Razumov (a natural son of a Prince K.) gives up secretly to the police his fellow student, Haldin, who seeks refuge in his rooms after committing a political crime (supposed to be the murder of de Plehve). First movement in St. Petersburg. (Haldin is hanged, of course.)

2d in Genève. The Student Razumov meeting abroad the mother and sister of Haldin falls in love with that last, marries her, and, after a time, confesses to her the part he played in the arrest of her brother.

The psychological developments leading to Razumov's betrayal of Haldin, to the confession of the fact to his wife and to the death of these people (brought about mainly by the resemblance of their child to the late Haldin), form the real subject of the story.

And perhaps no magazine will touch it. . . . Ah! my dear, you don't know what an inspiration-killing anxiety it is to think: "Is it saleable?" There's nothing more cruel than to be caught between one's impulse, one's act, and that question, which for me simply is a question of life and death. There are moments when the mere fear sweeps my head clean of every thought. It is agonizing,—no less. And,—you know,—that pressure grows from day to day instead of getting less.

But I had to write it. I had to get away from *Chance*, with which I was making no serious progress.[16]

Two years later, on December 23, 1909, we find him still laboring at the book and writing to Norman Douglas:

The novel hangs on the last 12,000 words, but there's neither inspiration nor hope in my work. It's mere hard labour for life—with this difference, that the life convict is at any rate out of harm's way—and may consider the account with his conscience closed; and this is not the case with me. I envy the serene fate and the comparative honesty of the gentlemen in gray who live in Dartmoor. I do really, I am not half as decent or half as useful. . . . All the same, don't give me up in your thoughts entirely. In the light of a "tormented spirit" I am not to be altogether despised.

It was another month before the manuscript was finished and almost two years before the novel reached book form, not under the title Conrad gave to Galsworthy but as *Under Western Eyes*—a change which, in indicating a shift of the post of observation from the hero to a disinterested spectator (the old English teacher of languages

[16] As given in *Joseph Conrad: Life and Letters*, by G. Jean-Aubry (1927), Vol. II, pp. 64–65. The letter following, to Norman Douglas, is in Vol. II, p. 105.

in Geneva who tells the story, partly from his own witness of it but largely from evidence gained from other characters or from Razumov's secret diary) and to a critical attitude alien and largely incomprehensible to the Russian, tells much about the narrative method Conrad had by this time made his own and outside of which he seldom trusted himself to work. It was, of course, more than a method. It was a temperamental necessity and compulsion. When Henry James described Conrad as "a votary of the way to do a thing that shall make it undergo most doing," and his method as "a prolonged hovering flight of the subjective over the outstretched ground of the case exposed,"[17] he put his finger on the radical factors that operate throughout Conrad's art at its best—its exhaustively empirical workmanship, the subjective commitment of its imagination, its intensity of scrutiny and analysis, and the origins of these in personal conditions of temperament and sympathetic intimacy that stamp it from beginning to end. If these factors sometimes betrayed him into an excessive identification of his emotion with his material in his weaker work, and if they produced at times an exaggerated solicitation of effect in his language and argument, their necessity to him is clear and their part in his originality is unquestionable. They, even more than his dramatic subjects, are the essential *donnée* of his work. Without them it would lack both its occasional weakness of control and its radical power.

Conrad's letter to Galsworthy shows that he first conceived the story in strongly active terms, embodied in physical encounters and external conflict of an almost melodramatic tendency. But what had already happened in the writing of *An Outcast of the Islands*, *Lord Jim*, and *Nostromo*, and what was to happen again in *The Rescue* and *The Rover*, happened in this case. The title was not the only thing that was changed. The plot was also transformed. Razumov and Nathalie Haldin never marry. They

[17] Henry James, "The New Novel, 1914," in *Notes on Novelists* (1914), pp. 314–61, here pp. 345, 348. The novel under discussion is *Chance*, Conrad's latest book at the moment.

never have a child who resembles the dead Haldin and thus "brings about" the "death of these people." And the "psychological developments" which Conrad planned as leading to the marriage and these deaths were altered to take a different direction. As in so many of his tales, the more Conrad pondered his theme, the more he came to grips with the shaping of it, the less he was able to adhere to an objective dramatization of it. What he retained was his initial episode—the assassination of Plehve by Haldin; Haldin's seeking refuge with Razumov; Razumov's betrayal of that trust to Prince K—— and General T——; Haldin's arrest and execution; and then the trap of official suspicion snapping down on Razumov when, resolving "to retire" into his solitude and win the University's prize that will rescue his life from its lonely nonentity, he finds his illusion of safety suddenly shattered by Councillor Mikulin's quiet and ominous question: "Where to?"

On that question the novel pauses and hangs. By the time Razumov reappears in Part II, we see what the question means. "Isolation and conscience are the dominant motifs in the novels of Conrad": the fact has been remarked by Mr. Pritchett and every attentive reader of the books. Razumov is to enact a drama that has already been played by Lord Jim, by both Kurtz and Marlow in "Heart of Darkness", by Decoud, Dr. Monygham, and Nostromo himself in *Nostromo,* by the young ship captain in "The Secret Sharer"; and it will be enacted again by Flora de Barral and Captain Anthony in *Chance,* by Axel Heyst in *Victory,* and by Tom Lingard in *The Rescue.* Geneva, where, unknown to the Russians among whom he is accepted as a fellow revolutionary and dedicated spirit, Razumov comes as a spy for Mikulin, becomes the stage for his test of conscience. There his ordeal of guilt, self-condemnation, and expiation will, by driving him to confession, first to Nathalie Haldin and then publicly to the revolutionists, and to the virtually suicidal disclosure of his part in Haldin's death, save him from the damnation of living his lie and his treachery.

In that drama of conscience all the exiles will play their

parts.[18] Their roles in Razumov's ordeal—at times so protractedly digressive, sometimes tangential or trivial, oftener unconscious, trusting, or confident—will embody and objectify the agonized movement of his mind from passivity to action, from a benumbed fatalism to expiatory truth. The fatuous philosophical pretensions of Peter Ivanovitch, the seedy dilettantism of Madame de S——, the devoted ardor of Sophia Antonovna, the dedicated zeal of Laspara, the cowed humility of Tekla, the anthropoid brutality of Nikita—all these lenses of delusion, vanity, self-deception, cruelty, and devotion in the cause will turn and refract the light of truth or falsehood on Razumov's agony of mind and conscience. All of them will serve to objectify or "transfer" the lie his treachery toward Haldin, his deception of Nathalie, and the unrealized egotism of his secret self have trapped him into living. They will reveal to him the "everlasting black hole of his life" into which, like the hero of *Lord Jim*, his ignorance or failure

---

[18] The novel offers a gallery of types and characters familiar in the literature and history of Russian life and politics, and comparisons can be made with those in the novels of Turgenev, Dostoevsky, Tolstoy, and in the biographies of revolutionary leaders. The reader of *Under Western Eyes* will find special interest in the literature of the Russian exiles, notably the memoirs of Alexander Herzen (*My Life and Thoughts*), Prince Peter Kropotkin (*Memoirs of a Revolutionist*), Stepniak (*Underground Russia, The Russian Storm Cloud,* and *The Career of a Nihilist*), as well as accounts of Bakunin and Ogarev. Especially relevant among books in English are Edward Hallett Carr's excellent account of *The Romantic Exiles* (1933) and his *Michael Bakunin* (1937), Edmund Wilson's *To the Finland Station* (1940), and George Woodcock's and Ivan Avakumovic's biography of Kropotkin, *The Anarchist Prince* (1950); there are numerous other accounts of Russian, anarchist, and communist activity in the past hundred years. Conrad's Peter Ivanovitch (obviously derived from Bakunin, with possible suggestions of the later Tolstoy), Madame de S——, Tekla, Laspara and his daughters, Yakovlitch, Ziemianitch, Kostia, Sophia Antonovna, etc., suggest their analogies in this literature and place the novel in a large context of historical and literary characters.

in moral courage forced him to jump. They will take him, step by step, on his downward journey into the "destructive element" of moral reality which, by destroying him, may finally save him. But most of all he will be condemned and saved by Nathalie herself. Her pure and credulous spirit—one of Conrad's exceptional successes among his portrayals of women—will drive him to self-condemnation and confession, to the test of honor that at last breaks and redeems him.

Razumov is what the Conradian hero invariably is: a solitary. He is the man designed by nature or circumstance to live not by the law of his kind but by self-law. Like Willems, Kurtz, Tuan Jim, Nostromo, Decoud, and Heyst, he is Conrad's version of the man—descendant of the self-willed heroes of Balzac, Stendhal, Turgenev, Dostoevsky, and Melville, and brother to those of Mann or Gide—who chooses or is compelled to live a life of egoistic self-regard or compulsive self-assertion: the existence *pour soi* or the fate of estrangement and isolation. As we are later told of Heyst, confirmed in his father's nihilism by the treachery he has encountered in human society, that "not a single soul belonging to him lived anywhere on earth . . . he was alone on the bank of the stream. In his pride he determined not to enter it"; so we are told of Razumov that "he was as lonely in the world as a man swimming in the deep sea. . . . He had nothing. He had not even a moral refuge—the refuge of confidence." And on the heels of that statement comes another no less terrifying: "Who knows what true loneliness is—not the conventional word but the naked terror? To the lonely themselves it wears a mask. The most miserable outcast hugs some memory or some illusion. . . . No human being could bear a steady view of moral solitude without going mad."

When, in one of the novel's greatest scenes, Razumov walks the wintry night streets of St. Petersburg, furious that Haldin has suddenly erupted into his lonely life of high resolve and secret ambition with his crime and his appeal, he stamps his foot in desperation upon the snow-sheeted ground, suddenly to discover that he has stamped the earth of Russia herself, "inanimate, cold, inert, like a sullen and tragic mother hiding her face under a winding-sheet—his native soil!—his very own—without a fireside, without a hearth!" He looks upward and "as if by a miracle" he sees "above his head the clear black sky of the northern winter, decorated with the sumptuous fires of the stars." He receives "an almost physical impression of endless space and of countless millions," of "an inheritance of space and numbers." His pathetic solitude and desperate egoism find refuge in the "sacred inertia" of the Russian earth, with its "guarantee of duration, of safety, while the travail of maturing destiny went on—a work not of revolutions with their passionate levity of action and their shifting impulses—but of peace." Without warning he finds himself standing "on the point of conversion"—"fascinated by its approach, by its overpowering logic." "Don't touch it," a voice cries within him, and another says "Haldin means disruption." And "like other Russians before him, Razumov, in conflict with himself, felt the touch of grace upon his forehead." But cutting across that sudden benediction there comes one of Conrad's most acute comments: "a train of thought is never false. The falsehead lies deep in the necessities of existence, in secret fears and half-formed ambitions, in the secret confidence combined with a secret mistrust of ourselves, in the love of hope and the dread of uncertain days." And presently, in the struggle to rationalize his confused impulses of treachery and self-justification, Razumov articulates another and even deadlier truth: "All a man can betray is his conscience." He will betray Haldin too, and later he will carry his deception to Geneva and the trusting soul of Nathalie; but he will be condemned to discover that it is the greater betrayal that tracks him down.

Though he does not yet know it, his existence has become committed to that implacable test of truth—committed by what Gide has called those fatal acts or unconscious treacheries for which "a whole lifetime, afterward, is not enough to give them the lie and to efface their mark." The novel becomes a drama of their consequences. There is no escape from them. As we watch the unfolding of Razumov's fate in Geneva—watch it through the shifting focus of the Russian eyes and the Western; follow it through Razumov's encounters with all the disclosures of delusion, conceit, sincerity, or honor in the characters who surround him; trace it through the splendidly imaged scenes that shift from the Haldin apartment to the Château Borel, from the promenade of the Bastions to Rousseau's island in the lake, from Razumov's tormented colloquies with Nathalie and the other exiles to his bitter vigils in the Rue de Carouge or on the bridge beneath which the water, "violent and deep," rushes headlong in "its vertiginous rapidity, its terrible force"—we see where that fate is leading him. It is carrying him remorselessly to the moment when his confession will break through his torment in the white boxed glare of the Haldin vestibule, thence into the storm-lashed streets of Geneva where the rain will wash him clean, and thus to Laspara's house where his guilt is made public and Nikita's brutal fist deafens him forever.

The prolonged attenuation and indirection of Conrad's narrative seems as if designed to put the reader's senses on the rack as much as Razumov's. The art and method of Conrad's work had by this time arrived at this almost excruciating refinement of sensory and moral impressionism, this extreme elaboration of the *progression d'effet*. But the process is continuously relieved and condensed in superb moments of imagery and action—moments that mount toward the novel's shattering climax and thus toward its bitter conclusion, poised between pathos and irony. The humanity of Conrad's pessimism insists on both. Razumov, deafened and crippled, lies at last in Russia, tended by the faithful Tekla and broken to the law of "unavoidable solidarity" which all of Conrad's estranged souls must finally sense or recognize—"the solidarity in mysterious origin, in toil, in joy, in hope, in uncertain fate, which binds men to each other and all mankind to the visible earth." Nathalie too returns to Russia to carry her faith into the ominous future of her country and the end that awaits her there. The truth that wrecked his life and the hope that sustains hers both offer the coldest of comforts to those who ask "from men faith, honour, fidelity to truth in themselves and others." But there is no other comfort possible—perhaps no comfort at all except in that "resignation, not mystic, not detached, but . . . open-eyed, conscious, and informed by love," which Conrad believed to be "the only one of our feelings for which it is impossible to become a sham." The "solidarity" he so insistently invoked as a mode of moral salvation offered little but this grim consolation to his skepticism; but that much it did offer, and on that principle of trust and sincerity he staked his personal and aesthetic faith. A more certain confidence lies with such characters as Sophia Antonovna and Peter Ivanovitch, and it is for her stubborn faith and his triumphant self-conceit that the novel's final touch of irony is reserved. "There are," said Conrad in *Typhoon*, "on sea and on land such men thus fortunate—or thus disdained by destiny or by the sea."

[handwritten margin note: Capt. McWhirr]

VI

In *Under Western Eyes* Conrad wrote a political novel which today, half a century after its publication, still stands as pre-eminent of its kind in English fiction and calls for a rank in European fiction as well. The literary genre of the political novel admits a large variety of content and method, and has perhaps never been very clearly defined; but Conrad's book is recognizably a descendant of the type classically established by Stendhal, Turgenev, Dostoevsky, and James, and prophetic, as much through its acumen of historical insight as through the accident of the contemporary events it foreshadowed, of the novels that were to come after it from writers like Malraux, Silone, Sartre, Koestler, Camus, Orwell, and Pasternak. Its continuing and increasing relevance to the twentieth century takes on the force of a compensation for the neglect to which it was treated on its first appearance in 1911. Its "precarious hold on life," for Conrad always a lurking fear

in his struggles as a novelist, has been proved mistaken by
the events and conflicts of our time. It has declared its
value as a drama of that "pursuit of happiness by means
lawful and unlawful, through resignation or revolt," which
he once defined as "the only theme that can be legitimately
developed by the novelist who is the chronicler of the
adventures of mankind amongst the dangers of the king-
dom of the earth."

It forms a judgment on modern history and on the
morality of political action; and on this score it constitutes,
even more specifically than *Nostromo* or *The Secret
Agent*, his commitment to a position on the future of Europe and the West. What that position came to be for
Conrad involves a consideration of his intelligence not only
as a man of historical vision but as a Pole and an exile
from Poland, whose life and thought were conditioned by
one of the most complex political and nationalistic situations of his age. He was thus involved "antecedent to
choice," long before he became a novelist. But it was in
his novels more than in his practical conduct or expressed
political convictions that he had to meet the test of what
his inherited situation imposed on him as a political thinker
and critic of history. *Under Western Eyes* necessarily became in his hands something more than a political argument, tract, or parable. It became a story of the soul of
man under tyranny and rebellion, the drama of a character subjected to the most searching tests of challenge,
moral probity, and self-knowledge to which the human
spirit can be exposed. It is finally in this drama that the
book achieves its essential strength as well as its continuity
with Conrad's work as a whole. The book remains a novel,
a work of human and moral relevance, well after its spe-
cific political reference is taken into account. But this is
not to minimize the urgency of that reference to Conrad
when he created the book, or to relegate to an incidental
role the problem he faced when he undertook to dramatize
its Russian (and by extension its European) subject—
cosas de Russia.

That problem—granting his prejudice and inherited

emotion regarding Russia—was less one of the "impartiality" to which he addressed himself than of an engagement in the Russian fate and drama: of entering that
drama not as a critic or observer—a man of "Western
eyes"—but as a participant and sharer in the Russian destiny. Had he failed to penetrate his subject in this way,
his novel would have failed in substance as much as in
art. But in spite of his use of the old English professor as
his narrator, with all its attendant emphasis on incompre-
hension and bafflement before the riddle of Russian character and psychology, the book finds its strength in its
penetration of the riddle, its distributed insight, and its
identification with its characters and their fate. Conrad,
like any valid novelist, had to become in some sense a
Russian to write the book, and it became his paradox as
the artist of his subject to convert his Polish life and inheritance into a means of that imaginative and moral authority.

We may agree with him when he said that he "had
never been called before to a greater effort of detachment: detachment from all passions, prejudices and even
from personal memories." The effort was doubtless acute
to the point of paralyzing his mind and hand. But it is not
detachment that finally counts in the strength the novel
achieves. It is sympathy, compassion, participation, insight. In these the novel met its test, and Conrad himself
one of the most severe personal and aesthetic tests of his
career.

It would not have required Conrad's personal temper,
so radically divided between a skeptical intellect and an
imperative human feeling, between moral pessimism and
a deep-seated racial and political emotion, to make that
text a complex one. This was a conflict that existed in all
his treatments of history.[19] Nor would it have required

[19] The larger outlines of Conrad's view of history are discussed
by the present writer in the introduction to a collection of nine
Tales of Heroes and History by Joseph Conrad (Anchor Books,
1960), where these stories are related to Conrad's political novels
as well as to his political ideas as they appear in his letters and

the presence in his immediate family of a collision between his father's romantic and patriotic idealism and his
uncle's conservative caution to bring the divided mind of
Polish nationalism home to him in an intimate form—
though that collision was one of the decisive factors in the
formation of his character. The conflict was an immediate
personal condition of his youth, but the division was a
larger fact in the mind and culture of his people. Poland,
possibly more consciously and acutely than the other nations of central Europe, is a traditional ground of the conflict. East and West, Slavophilism and "Westernism," a
precarious location between the rival powers of Russia and
Germany, an aristocratic and Catholic tradition joined
with democratic humanism and liberal impulse, a strong
conviction of a mystical and religious national destiny at
grips with a polity of ethnic necessity and pragmatic compromise—these factors have for three centuries formed the
condition of Poland's physical and historic entity, and
they continue to show themselves in the form of a major
European crisis down to the present moment.

When Conrad argued the cause of Poland and "Polo-
nism" in his essays at the time of the First World War he

---

essays. The latter include "Autocracy and War" (1905), "The
Shock of War" (1915), "To Poland in Wartime" (1915), "Poland Revisited" (1916), "The Crime of Partition" (1919), and
"A Note on the Polish Problem" (1916), all included in *Notes
on Life and Letters* (1921).

The evolution of the political novel from Stendhal and Dostoevsky to the present has been traced by various writers in
recent years—by, for one, Irving Howe in his study of *Politics
and the Novel* (1957), which includes a chapter on "Conrad:
Order and Anarchy." This is the most stimulating and suggestive
recent study of the genre in its European and American scope.
An early, but now very tentative and limited, treatment of the
subject was Morris Speare's *The Political Novel: Its Development in England and America* (1924); other recent studies
have been Joseph L. Blotner's *The Political Novel* (1955) and
W. M. Frohack's *The Novel of Violence in America* (revised
edition, 1957). There is a larger Continental literature on the
subject; Albert Camus' *L'Homme revolté* is a notable example.

defined his country as "the offspring of the West," as "universal" in its "sentimental attitude towards the Western Powers," as Latin, Western, and "humanistically" European in its roots, as a "racial unity" compressed between "Prussian Germanism on one side and the Russian Slavonism on the other," toward the first of which it felt "nothing but hatred," and toward the second "not so much hatred as a complete and ineradicable incompatibility." These have been the claims of Polish nationalism at various points of its modern history, and they remain its claims among the Western councils today; but the Polish situation has never been as simple as this. If its deprivation of independence and its partition among three imperial powers during the nineteenth century inflamed the cause of Polish nationalism to a pitch of passion and bred a *mystique* of cultural salvationism among its defenders, the opposite bent of self-criticism, ethnic necessity, and pragmatic compromise also existed. If "anti-Slavonism" and "Russophobia" had their adherents, so did the critical prudence that was induced by the need of survival among the powerful military oppressions that hedged the country in. The visionary Christian idealism—"*le messianisme polonais*"—of Mickiewicz, Malczewski, and the Polish romantics was reproved by realistic nationalists and historians: by, for one, the romantic poet Słowacki, whom Conrad's uncle Tadeusz Bobrowski once quoted to his nephew as having charged Poland with a morbid pride and persecutory bent: "a nation who consider ourselves great and misunderstood, the possessors of a greatness which others do not recognize and will never recognize."[20] Mystical dedication and realistic caution, the

---

[20] The letter, of November 9, 1891 is given by Jean-Aubry in *Life and Letters*, Vol. I, pp. 147–48; the original text appears in "Listy Tadeusza Bobrowskiego do Conrada," ed. Jabłkowska, *Kwartalnik Neofilologiczny*, Vol. III, pp. 110–11. This and other Polish letters and documents by Conrad, his father, his uncle, and others are to appear in a book on *Joseph Conrad's Polish Background*, by Zdzislaw Najder, announced for publication by the Oxford University Press, London, in 1963, which will be the

elation of a sacred martyrdom and the mortifications of
political and military defeat—these formed the opposing
elements of the Polish temper throughout its tragic ordeals
of the nineteenth century; and they came to Conrad in
the form of a direct challenge to his personal and political
identity. He was not alone in contending with that challenge. It is one of the radical facts in the arguments of
modern Polish intellectuals and cultural historians, and a
primary feature of it is Poland's division between the
claims of its Slavic and European elements.[21] But to
Conrad, in his exiled life and vulnerable conscience, the
challenge came in a particularly disturbing and sensitive
form. Reflecting a division within his own family, increasing as he matured in his own thought and sensibility, it
exposed him to what the exile from a persecuted country
is bound to feel—that he is open to the charge of deserting
a native trust and inherited obligation.[22]

---

most complete collection of these materials and the only comprehensive one in English.

See supplementary note 20 for further details on Polish scholarship and criticism on Conrad.

[21] The present writer is fully conscious of the fact that no
brief description of a nation or its ethnic, political, and moral
elements can be anything but a sketch, and thus inadequate. For
some of the historical works (in addition to the Conrad scholarship in Poland and elsewhere) upon which the above account
is based, see supplementary note 21.

[22] The word "guilt," often used in studies of this aspect of
Conrad's life and psychology, and encouraged by Joseph Morf's
study of his "Polish heritage" of 1929, is a decided simplification
of an elusive problem, though some element of "guilt," or at
least of acute moral sensitiveness, certainly figured in Conrad's
relations with Poland and his family. Several times in his career
the problem impinged on him severely. It did so at the time of
the First World War and can be sensed in the essays he wrote
on the Polish cause at that time; they are listed here in foot-
note 19. An earlier episode occurred in 1899 when Vincent
Lutosławski, following a visit to Conrad in England, defended
his exile from Poland and his service to "the cause of Poland"
abroad ("as loyally as those who stayed at home"), in an article

What this situation stimulated in Conrad—apart from any probing of his personal conscience to which he may have subjected himself or his sensitivity to the debates of his compatriots—was a profound sympathy with these divisions of mind or loyalty in other peoples: the men of his Eastern kingdoms in *An Outcast of the Islands*, *Lord Jim*, and *The Rescue*, the rival factions of Costaguana in *Nostromo*, even in the Russians whom he was bred to fear as Poland's traditional enemy and oppressor. When he expressed himself on Russia in his letters or essays it was invariably in terms of a convinced aversion, an open fear, or a contemptuous hostility. But it was part of his personal and Polish instinct, and most of all of his artist's intelligence, to know that Russia too was a sharer in the moral and political destiny of mankind; that its Slavic temper had a kinship with his own; and that what he and his people knew of moral and civil conflict had laid an even greater and more crushing burden on the Russian soul.

It was this burden that he had to deal with when he wrote *Under Western Eyes*—"this pitiful fate of a country held by an evil spell, suffering from an awful visitation for which the responsibility cannot be traced either to her sins or her follies." More portentously he could say of the

on "The Emigration of the Talents" in the Polish journal *Kraj*, published in St. Petersburg (March 1899). This essay was answered vehemently by Eliza Orzeszkowa in the April issue, accusing Conrad and other expatriates of desertion to more rewarding and lucrative fields, and supporting the protest of one of the journal's editors, Tadeusz Zuk-Skarszewski, in the March issue. This episode was dealt with by Jean-Aubry in his *Vie de Conrad* (1947; translated as *The Sea Dreamer*, 1957, pp. 237–38); by Jocelyn Baines in his book of 1960 (pp. 352–54); and at length by Józef Ujejski in his *O Konradzie Korzeniowskim* of 1936 (French translation as *Joseph Conrad*, 1939). An interesting speculation on the possible bearing of this episode on the writing of *Lord Jim* is given in an article by Eloise K. Hay, "*Lord Jim*: From Sketch to Novel," *Comparative Literature*, Vol. XII (Fall, 1960), pp. 289–309.

Tsarist autocracy (again in his essay on "Autocracy and War" in 1905): "this dreaded and strange apparition, bristling with bayonets, armed with chains, hung over with holy images; that something not of this world, partaking of a ravenous ghoul, of a blind Djinn grown up from a cloud, and of the Old Man of the Sea," which "still faces us with its old stupidity, with its strange mystical arrogance,"—the "decrepit, old, hundred years old, spectre of Russia's might [that] still faces Europe from across the teeming graves of Russian people." He could, even at the point of turning his indictment to the rival "enemy" of Prussianism, quote with approval Bismarck's "*La Russie, c'est le néant*"—a "*Néant* which for so many years had remained hidden behind this phantom of invincible armies"; but, more than a *Néant* or "empty void," a "yawning chasm open between East and West: a bottomless abyss that has swallowed up every hope of mercy, every aspiration towards personal dignity, towards freedom, towards knowledge, every ennobling desire of the heart, every redeeming whisper of conscience." We know too little about Conrad's actual reading of Dostoevsky to connect his aversion to the Russian novelist with this contempt of the Russian evil, but his reaction to *The Brothers Karamazov* when Edward Garnett sent him his wife's translation in 1912 put Dostoevsky down as an embodiment of all he despised or dreaded in the Russian mentality: "I don't know what D. stands for or reveals, but I do know that he is too Russian for me. It sounds like some fierce mouthings from prehistoric ages."[23] In Dostoevsky

[23] The quotations above are from "Autocracy and War" in *Notes on Life and Letters* (1921), pp. 83–114. The letter to Garnett is given in *Life and Letters* (1927), Vol. II, p. 140, and in Garnett's *Letters from Conrad* (London, 1928), pp. 260–61 (under the date May 27, 1912). The question of Conrad's possible derivations from or relationship to Dostoevsky has been touched on by various writers during the past four decades. Richard Curle touched on it in his early study *Joseph Conrad* in 1914 and again in *The Last Twelve Years of Joseph Conrad* (1928), pp. 28–29 and elsewhere ("I have an idea that his real

he evidently found in combination the elements he most feared in Russia and its history—its Panslavic messianism, its mystical illuminism, its contempt for subject peoples (Poland among them), its moral confusion and militant arrogance, its emotional excess and "convulsed terror-haunted" morbidity.[24]

But as if to restore a balance to this aversion he found in another Russian the virtue that indicts the Dostoevskian excess as emphatically as any indictment of his own. Inevitably that Russian was the one who most impressively embodied to the Western world the nobler soul and vision of his country—Turgenev. For Conrad it was Turgenev who created an art of "absolute sanity and the deepest sensibility, the clearest vision and the quickest responsiveness, penetrating insight and unfailing generosity of judgment, an exquisite perception of the visible world and an unerring instinct for the significant, for the essential

---

hatred for Dostoevsky was due to an appreciation of his power. . . . Dostoevsky represented to him the ultimate forces of confusion and insanity arrayed against all that he valued in civilization. He did not despise him as one despises a nonentity, he hated him as one might hate Lucifer and the forces of darkness."). Jocelyn Baines, in his *Joseph Conrad* (1960), has noted comparisons between *Under Western Eyes* and *Crime and Punishment*, including some verbal similarities, pp. 360–61, 370–71 ("It seems almost as if *Under Western Eyes* were a challenge to Dostoevsky on his own ground."). There are comparisons in Gustav Morf's *The Polish Heritage of Joseph Conrad*, numerous perceptive insights in Albert Guerard's *Conrad the Novelist* (1958), and other comments in the work of Polish scholars. Others appear in Eloise K. Hay's Radcliffe dissertation of 1961; and one of the earlier treatments of the problem was written by Henri Daniel-Rops in his essay on Conrad in his *Carte d'Europe* (Paris, 1928).

[24] Those concerned with Conrad's hostility to Russia may find interest in the condemnations of another vehement critic and accuser of Russia and the Russians, Karl Marx. Marx's letters on Russia at the time of the Crimean War (1853–56), written for the *New York Tribune*, have recently been collected as *Marx vs. Russia* (New York: Ungar, 1962).

in the life of men and women, the clearest mind, the warmest heart, the largest sympathy"; and whose characters were "human beings, fit to live, fit to suffer, fit to struggle, fit to win, fit to lose, in the endless and inspiring game of pursuing from day to day the ever-receding future"—"not strange beasts in a menagerie or damned souls knocking themselves to pieces in the stuffy darkness of mystical contradictions." The humane justice of Turgenev stood, among Conrad's models in his craft, as an example of the novelist's art at its finest—of its power to bring "all [its] problems and characters to the test of love." But whatever Conrad's repugnance or disclaimers, the "turmoil and darkness" of Dostoevsky's vision evidently had as much to say to the Pole's experience of excess and contradiction as Turgenev's classic balance did; and if a novel like *Under Western Eyes* is to be referred to a Russian precedent, it is as much to that of the "terror-haunted" Dostoevsky as to that of the "impartial lover of *all* his countrymen."[25]

It refers inevitably to both precedents, for it combines with its sense of human evil and corruption the necessity of sympathy—sympathy "with common mortals, no matter where they live," with the "multitude of the bewildered, the simple, and the voiceless"—which Conrad defined as the basis of the moral community to which all valid art is dedicated and of which he made a principle whenever he wrote his credo as a novelist. But an abstract or generalized sympathy, the "malady of the quotidian," is hardly possible for a realist or moral critic. When he came to write his drama of Russia Conrad put himself to the test of reconciling his effort at sympathy ("impartiality") with a realistic view of what the Russian threat to Europe involved. That view required both the practical judgment of a political realist and the humane objectivity of a historical intelligence. Being by nature a novelist and moral

[25] Conrad's essay on Turgenev, his single formal writing on a Russian author, was written as an introduction to Edward Garnett's *Turgenev: A Study* in 1917. It is included in *Notes on Life and Letters* (1921), pp. 45–48.

dramatist, he could fill neither of these offices—that of the scientific politician or that of the philosophic historian—with systematic logic or competence; and it has been possible for some critics to see in him a case of evasion or ambiguity in both these roles.[26] His real ground lay between them. For the extremes of the forces at work in the Russia he depicts—Tsarist tyranny and revolutionary brutality or fanaticism—he declares an equal indictment. It is in the sincere and distraught "souls," the idealists, dreamers, or characters of dedicated conscience, caught between these evils, that he establishes his true moral bearings and the ground of his most searching insight. And the circumstance that he brought to bear on these his personal experience of historical and political fact is what gives his novel its actuality, its dialectic substance, and its weight as a document on the crisis of his age.

The factor of "contradiction" which repelled Conrad in Dostoevsky was in truth a factor in his own sensibility and intelligence, rooted there fully as "historically and hereditarily, by the peculiar experience of race and family," as any "obligation of absolute fairness" he professed. To turn to evidences of it in his letters or personal statements is to find that he was as subject to conflicts of skepticism and partisan passion as any of the characters he created in his political novels. To Cunninghame Graham and his other Socialist friends in the nineties, as to his old Polish friend Spiridion Kliszczewski earlier, he could express a pessimism on political reforms or social programs amounting to a complete cynicism.[27] It was this tem-

---

[26] One of the perceptive studies of this problem appears in two essays by G. H. Bantock: "The Two 'Moralities' of Joseph Conrad," *Essays in Criticism,* April 1953, pp. 125–42; and "Conrad and Politics," *English Literary History,* June 1958, pp. 122–36.

[27] E. g.: "Disestablishment, Land Reform, Universal Brotherhood are but like milestones on the road to ruin." "Faith is a myth and beliefs shift like mists on the shore." "Socialism must inevitably end in Caesarism." "You want from men faith, honour, fidelity to truth in themselves and others . . . [this to Graham];

peramental disillusionment that led him to view later creeds or programs of political or revolutionary action with revulsion; and the forms such action took in his lifetime—imperialism, anarchism, militant nihilism or communism, power coalitions, the tactics of *Realpolitik*— gave him sufficient occasion for distaste and contempt, as the casuistry of "balances of power" among the Western nations gave him cause for alarm for the future of the West. But against his professions of indifference or disgust there played a tenacious sense that there is a social and political community in the affairs of men no less than a moral one, and that a man repudiates it at his peril.

The imperative for Conrad was specifically the Polish question, far beyond any loyalty he professed for England —his exile's fealty to an adopted nationality, usually conservative, conventional, and reactionary, which could nettle or disgruntle his liberal and skeptical English friends. When he wrote outside his fiction it was in the Polish cause that he centered his commitment. In his fiction the case was otherwise. Only once, in the story "Prince Roman" of 1911, did he employ the Polish subject there, and he employed it then in its traditional heroic form. But into his treatments of polity, honor, and political casuistry elsewhere—in South America, England, the colonial East, or Russia—he carried a critical insight which, however bred in his own native nationalism, could exercise itself more objectively, realistically, and far more searchingly than a situation personally prejudiced could allow. It may be true that in practical terms Conrad's political fiction, as has more than once been said, "finally

---

What makes you dangerous is your unwarrantable belief that your desires may be realized." "I look with the serenity of despair and the indifference of contempt upon the passing events. . . . there is no earthly remedy for those earthly misfortunes, and from above, I fear, we may obtain consolation, but no remedy. 'All is Vanity.'" These passages are from letters given in *Life and Letters,* Vol. I, pp. 79–86, and 268–70, 215–16, 221– 23, 229–30; the strain appears in many of Conrad's letters at this time and later.

solves nothing." It provides no prescriptions for actionable policy, party or sectarian maneuver, tactical action, or concerted protest. But it is doubtful if the serious political novel has ever provided these. They are not provided by Turgenev, Stendhal, Tolstoy, or Dostoevsky, or even by such later novelists as Malraux, Camus, Hemingway, or Pasternak, who have experienced political warfare and ideology in more immediate and physical forms. The fiction of political policy is the preserve of party journalists and propagandists. The serious novelist has a more vital and radical subject to contend with—not the tactics of power but the morality of power, of political responsibility, and of social intelligence; and from that obligation there is no shirking or evasion. It is an imperative continuous with a man's moral existence. Perhaps the two phrases in *Under Western Eyes* that are most likely to echo in the reader's mind as the focal epigram of the book are those that come at the end of Part I—Razumov's declaration to Mikulin that he intends "To retire," and Mikulin's sinister and comprehensive question "Where to?" In that defiance and reply Conrad, by means of an oral image as resolving as his great visual images can be, condensed not only this particular novel's radical issue but the issue of his own experience in social and moral engagement.

To its dramatization he brought a narrative method and a sequence of motifs that had by this time become his typical usages. There is, at the outset, Razumov's isolation, his secret illusion of his destiny, his ignorance of his moral identity. Abruptly there enters into his solitude the challenge, the test, that cuts across that illusion and puts it to proof—Haldin's confidence and appeal. There follows the derangement of Razumov's mind and purpose that invariably accompanies the collision of the secret self with external circumstance: his perception that his life and fate have become inescapably identified with Haldin's—the hallucination of walking across the man lying in the snow, the imprint of Haldin's outstretched body on his bed. Having resolved to betray Haldin to the police, he senses, even if dimly, that his youth is over, his young manhood

hurtled into the maelstrom of political and revolutionary
conflict, his "shadow-line" crossed: hearing Prince K——
murmur of "a quarter-life-size smooth-limbed bronze of an
adolescent figure, running," in General T——'s reception
room, "Spontini's. 'Flight of Youth.' Exquisite," he assents
faintly, "Admirable." Then comes the interview with
Mikulin which snares him as a spy for the official police;
then the bewildering shift to Geneva, wrenching him out
of his life's purpose, casting him into the company and
confidences of the exiles, exposing him to their challenges
of delusion or fidelity, hypocrisy or truth. Thus he goes on,
another trapped conscience, to enact his lie, his deception
of Nathalie, his recognition by agonized stages of her
dedicated sincerity and his own falsehood, eventually his
confession, the breaking of his will and body, and his final
return to Russia and to the living out of the remorseless
logic of his personal fate that awaits him there. The drama
recapitulates the logic of destiny that Conrad had already
traced in the lives of Almayer, Willems, Jim, Kurtz, Nostromo, Decoud; and the law which operates in it—that
"no man can escape his fate"—was to remain the law of
life that Conrad carried to the end of his career in fiction.
If that law became attenuated by sentiment or moral
compromise before the end, it found, in this novel, one of
the most rigorous and consistent embodiments that Conrad ever achieved; and here it arrived at a strength of
social and historical reference that brought it out of its
earlier remote or exotic versions into the full light and
actuality of a crisis that is a radical fact and test of the
twentieth century.

Under Western Eyes shows Conrad writing in the
strength of his sincerity and despair, his lacerating irony
and his passionate humanism. If the book lacks the
stronger intimacy of *Lord Jim* and "Heart of Darkness,"
the more complex reverberations of *Nostromo*, the ironic
tautness of *The Secret Agent*, or the overt symbolic dimension of "The Secret Sharer" and *Victory*, it shows his
power to memorable effect and ends by making its unquestionable impression of authority and justice. The jus-

tice with which it deals is painful and baffling, but his treatment of it, whatever its complexity of sympathy or insight, is not evasive, and the workings of truth and conscience are neither shirked nor disguised. Perhaps, as Mr. Pritchett has said, Conrad wrote the book "to bring a harder Western focus upon a theme of Dostoevsky." The book has, at any rate, the quality of translating the Dostoevskian vision and ethos into the terms of a moral necessity which the West, whatever its compromises or failures of principle, can never forget, and which it will forget now only at its peril. That Conrad should have been able to illuminate that necessity by means of a subject so deeply involved in his personal history, and to achieve in doing so a version of the Russian fate that calls for comparison with the art of the Russian masters themselves, testifies to the risks he was willing to take in his art and to the vision and insight that rewarded him. The novel, as strenuous in its craft as in the drama it describes, carries his reading of the human destiny to a pitch of sometimes unendurable intensity, and the judgment at which it finally arrives is as exigent and as stern in its conclusions as any we are likely to find in modern fiction. It proposes a major question to the age, and it leaves that question pending the moral decision of Europe and the West. The novel thus becomes more than an experience in the drama and craftsmanship of one of the most scrupulous and searching of modern novelists. It becomes an example and a portent for an era in history whose crisis Conrad, through his own experience of it and the severity of vision it yielded him, was able with a remarkable prophetic instinct to foresee.

MORTON DAUWEN ZABEL

1951–1961

AUTHOR'S NOTE

It must be admitted that by the mere force of circumstances "Under Western Eyes" has become already a sort of historical novel dealing with the past.

This reflection bears entirely upon the events of the tale; but being as a whole an attempt to render not so much the political state as the psychology of Russia itself, I venture to hope that it has not lost all its interest. I am encouraged in this flattering belief by noticing that in many articles on Russian affairs of the present day reference is made to certain sayings and opinions uttered in the pages that follow, in a manner testifying to the clearness of my vision and the correctness of my judgment. I need not say that in writing this novel I had no other object in view than to express imaginatively the general truth which underlies its action, together with my honest convictions as to the moral complexion of certain facts more or less known to the whole world.

As to the actual creation I may say that when I began to write I had a distinct conception of the first part only, with the three figures of Haldin, Razumov, and Councillor Mikulin, defined exactly in my mind. It was only after I had finished writing the first part that the whole story revealed itself to me in its tragic character and in the march of its events as unavoidable and sufficiently ample in its outline to give free play to my creative instinct and to the dramatic possibilities of the subject.

The course of action need not be explained. It has suggested itself more as a matter of feeling than a matter of thinking. It is the result not of a special experience but of general knowledge, fortified by earnest meditation. My greatest anxiety was in being able to strike and sustain the note of scrupulous impartiality. The obligation of absolute fairness was imposed on me historically and hereditarily, by the peculiar experience of race and family, in addition to my primary conviction that truth alone is the justification of any fiction which makes the least claim to the quality of art or may hope to take its place in the culture of men and women of its time. I had never been called before to a greater effort of detachment: detachment from all passions, prejudices and even from personal memories. "Under Western Eyes" on its first appearance in England was a failure with the public, perhaps because of that very detachment. I obtained my reward some six years later when I first heard that the book had found universal recognition in Russia and had been re-published there in many editions.

The various figures playing their part in the story also owe their existence to no special experience but to the general knowledge of the condition of Russia and of the moral and emotional reactions of the Russian temperament to the pressure of tyrannical lawlessness, which, in general human terms, could be reduced to the formula of senseless desperation provoked by senseless tyranny. What I was concerned with mainly was the aspect, the character, and the fate of the individuals as they appeared to the Western Eyes of the old teacher of languages. He himself has been much criticised; but I will not at this late hour undertake to justify his existence. He was useful to me and therefore I think that he must be useful to the reader both in the way of comment and by the part he plays in the development of the story. In my desire to produce the effect of actuality it seemed to me indispensable to have an eye-witness of the transactions in Geneva. I needed also a sympathetic friend for Miss Haldin, who otherwise would have been too much alone and unsupported to be perfectly credible. She would have had no one to whom she could give a glimpse of her idealistic faith, of her great heart, and of her simple emotions.

Razumov is treated sympathetically. Why should he not be? He is an ordinary young man, with a healthy capacity for work and sane ambitions. He has an average conscience. If he is slightly abnormal it is only in his sensitiveness to his position. Being nobody's child he feels rather more keenly than another would that he is a Russian—or he is nothing. He is perfectly right in looking on all Russia as his heritage. The sanguinary futility of the crimes and the sacrifices seething in that amorphous mass envelops and crushes him. But I don't think that in his distraction he is ever monstrous. Nobody is exhibited as a monster here—neither the simple-minded Tekla nor the wrong headed Sophia Antonovna. Peter Ivanovitch and Madame de S. are fair game. They are the apes of a sinister jungle and are treated as their grimaces deserve. As to Nikita—nicknamed Necator—he is the perfect flower of the terroristic wilderness. What troubled me most in dealing with him was not his monstrosity but his banality. He has been exhibited to the public eye for years in so-called "disclosures" in newspaper articles, in secret histories, in sensational novels.

The most terrifying reflection (I am speaking now for myself) is that all these people are not the product of the exceptional but of the general—of the normality of their place, and time, and race. The ferocity and imbecility of an autocratic rule rejecting all legality and in fact basing itself upon complete moral anarchism provokes the no less imbecile and atrocious answer of a purely Utopian revolutionism encompassing destruction by the first means to hand, in the strange conviction that a fundamental change of hearts must follow the downfall of any given human institutions. These people are unable to see that all they can effect is merely a change of names. The oppressors and the oppressed are all Russians together; and the world is brought once more face to face with the truth of the saying that the tiger cannot change his stripes nor the leopard his spots.

1920   J. C.

UNDER WESTERN EYES

PART FIRST

To begin with I wish to disclaim the possession of those high gifts of imagination and expression which would have enabled my pen to create for the reader the personality of the man who called himself, after the Russian custom, Cyril son of Isidor—Kirylo Sidorovitch—Razumov.

If I have ever had these gifts in any sort of living form they have been smothered out of existence a long time ago under a wilderness of words. Words, as is well known, are the great foes of reality. I have been for many years a teacher of languages. It is an occupation which at length becomes fatal to whatever share of imagination, observation, and insight an ordinary person may be heir to. To a teacher of languages there comes a time when the world is but a place of many words and man appears a mere talking animal not much more wonderful than a parrot.

This being so, I could not have observed Mr. Razumov or guessed at his reality by the force of insight, much less have imagined him as he was. Even to invent the mere bald facts of his life would have been utterly beyond my powers. But I think that without this declaration the readers of these pages will be able to detect in the story the marks of documentary evidence. And that is perfectly correct. It is based on a document; all I have brought to it is my knowledge of the Russian language, which is sufficient for what is attempted here. The document, of course, is something in the nature of a journal, a diary, yet not exactly that in its actual form. For instance, most of it was not written up from day to day, though all the entries are dated. Some of these entries cover months of time and extend over dozens of pages. All the earlier part is a retrospect, in a narrative form, relating to an event which took place about a year before.

I must mention that I have lived for a long time in Geneva. A whole quarter of that town, on account of many Russians residing there, is called La Petite Russie—Little Russia. I had a rather extensive connexion in Little Russia at that time. Yet I confess that I have no comprehension of the Russian character. The illogicality of their attitude, the arbitrariness of their conclusions, the frequency of the exceptional, should present no difficulty to a student of many grammars; but there must be something else in the way, some special human trait—one of those subtle differences that are beyond the ken of mere professors. What must remain striking to a teacher of languages is the Russians' extraordinary love of words. They gather them up; they cherish them, but they don't hoard them in their breasts; on the contrary, they are always ready to pour them out by the hour or by the night with an enthusiasm, a sweeping abundance, with such an aptness of application sometimes that, as in the case of very accomplished parrots, [one can't defend oneself from the suspicion that they really understand what they say] There is a generosity in their ardour of speech which removes it as far as possible from common loquacity; and it is ever too disconnected to be classed as eloquence. . . . But I must apologize for this digression.

It would be idle to inquire why Mr. Razumov has left this record behind him. It is inconceivable that he should have wished any human eye to see it. A mysterious impulse of human nature comes into play here. Putting aside Samuel Pepys, who has forced in this way the door of immortality, innumerable people, criminals, saints, philosophers, young girls, statesmen, and simple imbeciles, have kept self-revealing records from vanity no doubt, but also from other more inscrutable motives. There must be a wonderful soothing power in mere words since so many men have used them for self-communion. Being myself a quiet individual I take it that what all men are really after is some form or perhaps only some formula of peace. Certainly they are crying loud enough for it at the present day. What sort of peace Kirylo Sidorovitch Razumov expected to find in the writing up of his record it passeth my understanding to guess.

The fact remains that he has written it.

Mr. Razumov was a tall, well-proportioned young man, quite unusually dark for a Russian from the Central Provinces. His good looks would have been unquestionable if it had not been for a peculiar lack of fineness in the features. It was as if a face modelled vigorously in wax (with some approach even to a classical correctness of type) had been held close to a fire till all sharpness of line had been lost in the softening of the material. But even thus he was sufficiently good-looking. His manner, too, was good. In discussion he was easily swayed by argument and authority. With his younger compatriots he took the attitude of an inscrutable listener, a listener of the kind that hears you out intelligently and then—just changes the subject.

This sort of trick, which may arise either from intellectual insufficiency or from an imperfect trust in one's own convictions, procured for Mr. Razumov a reputation of profundity. Amongst a lot of exuberant talkers, in the habit of exhausting themselves daily by ardent discussion, a comparatively taciturn personality is naturally credited with reserve power. By his comrades at the St. Petersburg University, Kirylo Sidorovitch Razumov, third year's student in philosophy, was looked upon as a strong nature—an altogether trustworthy man. This, in a country where an opinion may be a legal crime visited by death or sometimes by a fate worse than mere death, meant that he was worthy of being trusted with forbidden opinions. He was liked also for his amiability and for his quiet readiness to oblige his comrades even at the cost of personal inconvenience.

Mr. Razumov was supposed to be the son of an Archpriest and to be protected by a distinguished nobleman—perhaps of his own distant province. But his outward appearance accorded badly with such humble origin. Such a

descent was not credible. It was, indeed, suggested that
Mr. Razumov was the son of an Archpriest's pretty daughter—which, of course, would put a different complexion on
the matter. This theory also rendered intelligible the protection of the distinguished nobleman. All this, however,
had never been investigated maliciously or otherwise. No
one knew or cared who the nobleman in question was.
Razumov received a modest but very sufficient allowance
from the hands of an obscure attorney, who seemed to
act as his guardian in some measure. Now and then he
appeared at some professor's informal reception. Apart
from that Razumov was not known to have any social relations in the town. He attended the obligatory lectures
regularly and was considered by the authorities as a very
promising student. He worked at home in the manner of a
man who means to get on, but did not shut himself up
severely for that purpose. He was always accessible, and
there was nothing secret or reserved in his life.

I

The origin of Mr. Razumov's record is connected with
an event characteristic of modern Russia in the actual fact:
the assassination of a prominent statesman—and still more
characteristic of the moral corruption of an oppressed society where the noblest aspirations of humanity, the desire of freedom, an ardent patriotism, the love of justice,
the sense of pity, and even the fidelity of simple minds are
prostituted to the lusts of hate and fear, the inseparable
companions of an uneasy despotism.

The fact alluded to above is the successful attempt on
the life of Mr. de P——, the President of the notorious
Repressive Commission of some years ago, the Minister of
State invested with extraordinary powers. The newspapers
made noise enough about that fanatical, narrow-chested
figure in gold-laced uniform, with a face of crumpled
parchment, insipid, bespectacled eyes and the cross of the
Order of St. Procopius hung under the skinny throat. For
a time, it may be remembered, not a month passed with-

out his portrait appearing in some one of the illustrated papers of Europe. He served the monarchy by imprisoning, exiling, or sending to the gallows men and women, young and old, with an equable, unwearied industry. In his mystic acceptance of the principle of autocracy he was bent on extirpating from the land every vestige of anything that resembled freedom in public institutions; and in his ruthless persecution of the rising generation he seemed to aim at the destruction of the very hope of liberty itself.

It is said that this execrated personality had not enough imagination to be aware of the hate he inspired. It is hardly credible; but it is a fact that he took very few precautions for his safety. In the preamble of a certain famous State paper he had declared once that "the thought of liberty has never existed in the Act of the Creator. From the multitude of men's counsel nothing could come but revolt and disorder; and revolt and disorder in a world created for obedience and stability is sin. It was not Reason but Authority which expressed the Divine Intention. God was the Autocrat of the Universe. . . ." It may be that the man who made this declaration believed that heaven itself was bound to protect him in his remorseless defence of Autocracy on this earth.

No doubt the vigilance of the police saved him many times; but, as a matter of fact, when his appointed fate overtook him, the competent authorities could not have given him any warning. They had no knowledge of any conspiracy against the Minister's life, had no hint of any plot through their usual channels of information, had seen no signs, were aware of no suspicious movements or dangerous persons.

Mr. de P—— was being driven towards the railway station in a two-horse uncovered sleigh with footman and coachman on the box. Snow had been falling all night, making the roadway, uncleared as yet at this early hour, very heavy for the horses. It was still falling thickly. But the sleigh must have been observed and marked down. As it drew over to the left before taking a turn, the footman

noticed a peasant walking slowly on the edge of the pavement with his hands in the pockets of his sheepskin coat
and his shoulders hunched up to his ears under the falling
snow. On being overtaken this peasant suddenly faced
about and swung his arm. In an instant there was a terrible
shock, a detonation muffled in the multitude of snowflakes;
both horses lay dead and mangled on the ground and the
coachman, with a shrill cry, had fallen off the box mortally
wounded. The footman (who survived) had no time to
see the face of the man in the sheepskin coat. After throwing the bomb this last got away, but it is supposed that,
seeing a lot of people surging up on all sides of him in the
falling snow, and all running towards the scene of the explosion, he thought it safer to turn back with them.

In an incredibly short time an excited crowd assembled
round the sledge. The Minister-President, getting out un-
hurt into the deep snow, stood near the groaning coachman and addressed the people repeatedly in his [weak,
colourless voice:] "I beg of you to keep off. For the love of
God, I beg of you good people to keep off."

It was then that a tall young man who had remained
standing perfectly still within a carriage gateway, two
houses lower down, stepped out into the street and walking
up rapidly flung another bomb over the heads of the
crowd. It actually struck the Minister-President on the
shoulder [as he stooped over his dying servant,] then falling
between his feet exploded with a terrific concentrated violence, striking him dead to the ground, finishing the
wounded man and practically annihilating the empty
sledge in the twinkling of an eye. With a yell of horror
the crowd broke up and fled in all directions, except for
those who fell dead or dying where they stood nearest to
the Minister-President, and one or two others who did not
fall till they had run a little way.

The first explosion had brought together a crowd as if
by enchantment, the second made as swiftly a solitude in
the street for hundreds of yards in each direction. Through
the falling snow people looked from afar at the small heap
of dead bodies lying upon each other near the carcases of

the two horses. Nobody dared to approach till some Cossacks of a street-patrol galloped up and, dismounting, began to turn over the dead. Amongst the innocent victims of
the second explosion laid out on the pavement there was
a body dressed in a peasant's sheepskin coat; but the face
was unrecognizable, there was absolutely nothing found in
the pockets of its poor clothing, and it was the only one
whose identity was never established.

That day Mr. Razumov got up at his usual hour and
spent the morning within the University buildings listening
to the lectures and working for some time in the library.
He heard the first vague rumour of something in the way
of bomb-throwing at the table of the students' ordinary,
where he was accustomed to eat his two o'clock dinner.
But this rumour was made up of mere whispers, and this
was Russia, where it was not always safe, for a student
especially, to appear too much interested in certain kinds
of whispers. [Razumov was one of those men who, living
in a period of mental and political unrest, keep an instinctive hold on normal, practical, everyday life. He was
aware of the emotional tension of his time; he even responded to it in an indefinite way. But his main concern
was with his work, his studies, and with his own future.]

Officially and in fact without a family (for the daughter
of the Archpriest had long been dead), no home influences
had shaped his opinions or his feelings. He was as lonely
in the world as a man swimming in the deep sea. [The
word Razumov was the mere label of a solitary individuality.] There were no Razumovs belonging to him anywhere.
His closest parentage was defined in the statement that he
was a Russian. Whatever good he expected from life would
be given to or withheld from his hopes by that connexion
alone. This immense parentage suffered from the throes of
internal dissensions, and he shrank mentally from the fray
as a good-natured man may shrink from taking definite
sides in a violent family quarrel.

Razumov, going home, reflected that having prepared
all the matters of the forthcoming examination, he could
now devote his time to the subject of the prize essay. He

hankered after the silver medal. The prize was offered by
the Ministry of Education; the names of the competitors
would be submitted to the Minister himself. The mere
fact of trying would be considered meritorious in the
higher quarters; and the possessor of the prize would have
a claim to an administrative appointment of the better sort
after he had taken his degree. The student Razumov in an
access of elation forgot the dangers menacing the stability
of the institutions which give rewards and appointments.
But remembering the medallist of the year before, Razumov, the young man of no parentage, was sobered. He
and some others happened to be assembled in their comrade's rooms at the very time when that last received the
official advice of his success. He was a quiet, unassuming
young man: "Forgive me," he had said with a faint apolo-
getic smile and taking up his cap, "I am going out to order
up some wine. But I must first send a telegram to my folk
at home. I say! Won't the old people make it a festive
time for the neighbours for twenty miles around our
place?"

Razumov thought there was nothing of that sort for
him in the world. His success would matter to no one. But
he felt no bitterness against the nobleman his protector,
who was not a provincial magnate as was generally supposed. He was in fact nobody less than Prince K——, once
a great and splendid figure in the world and now, his day
being over, a Senator and a gouty invalid, living in a still
splendid but more domestic manner. He had some young
children and a wife as aristocratic and proud as himself.

In all his life Razumov was allowed only once to come
into personal contact with the Prince.

It had the air of a chance meeting in the little attorney's
office. One day Razumov, coming in by appointment,
found a stranger standing there—a tall, aristocratic-looking
personage with silky, grey side-whiskers. The bald-headed,
sly little lawyer-fellow called out, "Come in—come in, Mr.
Razumov," with a sort of ironic heartiness. Then turning
deferentially to the stranger with the grand air, "A ward

of mine, your Excellency. One of the most promising students of his faculty in the St. Petersburg University."

To his intense surprise Razumov saw a white shapely hand extended to him. He took it in great confusion (it was soft and passive) and heard at the same time a condescending murmur in which he caught only the words "Satisfactory" and "Persevere." But the most amazing thing of all was to feel suddenly a distinct pressure of the white shapely hand just before it was withdrawn: a light pressure like a secret sign. The emotion of it was terrible. Razumov's heart seemed to leap into his throat. When he raised his eyes the aristocratic personage, motioning the little lawyer aside, had opened the door and was going out.

The attorney rummaged amongst the papers on his desk for a time. "Do you know who that was?" he asked suddenly.

Razumov, whose heart was thumping hard yet, shook his head in silence.

"That was Prince K——. You wonder what he could be doing in the hole of a poor legal rat like myself—eh? These awfully great people have their sentimental curiosities like common sinners. But if I were you, Kirylo Sidorovitch," he continued, leering and laying a peculiar emphasis on the patronymic, "I wouldn't boast at large of the introduction. It would not be prudent, Kirylo Sidorovitch. Oh dear no! It would be in fact dangerous for your future."

The young man's ears burned like fire; his sight was dim. "That man!" Razumov was saying to himself. "He!"

Henceforth it was by this monosyllable that Mr. Razumov got into the habit of referring mentally to the stranger with grey silky side-whiskers. From that time too, when walking in the more fashionable quarters, he noted with interest the magnificent horses and carriages with Prince K——'s liveries on the box. Once he saw the Princess get out—she was shopping—followed by two girls, of which one was nearly a head taller than the other. Their fair hair hung loose down their backs in the English style; they had merry eyes, their coats, muffs, and little fur caps were exactly alike, and their cheeks and noses were tinged a cheerful pink by the frost. They crossed the pavement in front of him, and Razumov went on his way smiling shyly to himself. "His" daughters. They resembled "Him." The young man felt a glow of warm friendliness towards these girls who would never know of his existence. Presently they would marry Generals or Kammerherrs and have girls and boys of their own, who perhaps would be aware of him as a celebrated old professor, decorated, possibly a Privy Councillor, one of the glories of Russia—nothing more!

But a celebrated professor was a somebody. Distinction would convert the label Razumov into an honoured name. There was nothing strange in the student Razumov's wish for distinction. A man's real life is that accorded to him in the thoughts of other men by reason of respect or natural love. Returning home on the day of the attempt on Mr. de P——'s life, Razumov resolved to have a good try for the silver medal.

Climbing slowly the four flights of the dark, dirty staircase in the house where he had his lodgings, he felt confident of success. The winner's name would be published in the papers on New Year's Day. And at the thought that "He" would most probably read it there, Razumov stopped short on the stairs for an instant, then went on smiling faintly at his own emotion. "This is but a shadow," he said to himself, "but the medal is a solid beginning."

With those ideas of industry in his head the warmth of his room was agreeable and encouraging. "I shall put in four hours of good work," he thought. But no sooner had he closed the door than he was horribly startled. All black against the usual tall stove of white tiles gleaming in the dusk, stood a strange figure, wearing a skirted, close-fitting, brown cloth coat strapped round the waist, in long boots, and with a little Astrakhan cap on its head. It loomed lithe and martial. Razumov was utterly confounded. It was only when the figure advancing two paces asked in an untroubled, grave voice if the outer door was closed that he regained his power of speech.

"Haldin! . . . Victor Victorovitch! . . . Is that you?

. . . Yes. The outer door is shut all right. But this is indeed unexpected."

Victor Haldin, a student older than most of his contemporaries at the University, was not one of the industrious set. He was hardly ever seen at lectures; the authorities had marked him as "restless" and "unsound"—very bad notes. But he had a great personal prestige with his comrades and influenced their thoughts. Razumov had never been intimate with him. They had met from time to time at gatherings in other students' houses. They had even had a discussion together—one of those discussions on first principles dear to the sanguine minds of youth.

Razumov wished the man had chosen some other time to come for a chat. He felt in good trim to tackle the prize essay. But as Haldin could not be slightingly dismissed Razumov adopted the tone of hospitality, asking him to sit down and smoke.

"Kirylo Sidorovitch," said the other, flinging off his cap, "we are not perhaps in exactly the same camp. Your judgment is more philosophical. You are a man of few words, but I haven't met anybody who dared to doubt the generosity of your sentiments. There is a solidity about your character which cannot exist without courage."

Razumov felt flattered and began to murmur shyly something about being very glad of his good opinion, when Haldin raised his hand.

"That is what I was saying to myself," he continued, "as I dodged in the woodyard down by the river-side. 'He has a strong character this young man,' I said to myself. 'He does not throw his soul to the winds.' Your reserve has always fascinated me, Kirylo Sidorovitch. So I tried to remember your address. But look here—it was a piece of luck. Your dvornik was away from the gate talking to a sleigh-driver on the other side of the street. I met no one on the stairs, not a soul. As I came up to your floor I caught sight of your landlady coming out of your rooms. But she did not see me. She crossed the landing to her own side, and then I slipped in. I have been here two hours expecting you to come in every moment."

Razumov had listened in astonishment; but before he could open his mouth Haldin added, speaking deliberately, "It was I who removed de P—— this morning."

Razumov kept down a cry of dismay. The sentiment of his life being utterly ruined by this contact with such a crime expressed itself quaintly by a sort of half-derisive mental exclamation, "There goes my silver medal!"

Haldin continued after waiting a while—

"You say nothing, Kirylo Sidorovitch! I understand your silence. To be sure, I cannot expect you with your frigid English manner to embrace me. But never mind your manners. You have enough heart to have heard the sound of weeping and gnashing of teeth this man raised in the land. That would be enough to get over any philosophical hopes. He was uprooting the tender plant. He had to be stopped. He was a dangerous man—a convinced man. Three more years of his work would have put us back fifty years into bondage—and look at all the lives wasted, at all the souls lost in that time."

His curt, self-confident voice suddenly lost its ring and it was in a dull tone that he added, "Yes, brother, I have killed him. It's weary work."

Razumov had sunk into a chair. Every moment he expected a crowd of policemen to rush in. There must have been thousands of them out looking for that man walking up and down in his room. Haldin was talking again in a restrained, steady voice. Now and then he flourished an arm, slowly, without excitement.

He told Razumov how he had brooded for a year; how he had not slept properly for weeks. He and "Another" had a warning of the Minister's movements from "a certain person" late the evening before. He and that "Another" prepared their "engines" and resolved to have no sleep till "the deed" was done. They walked the streets under the falling snow with the "engines" on them, exchanging not a word the livelong night. When they happened to meet a police patrol they took each other by the arm and pretended to be a couple of peasants on the spree. They reeled and talked in drunken hoarse voices. Except for these strange outbreaks they kept silence, moving on ceaselessly. Their plans had been previously arranged. At daybreak they made their way to the spot which they knew the sledge must pass. When it appeared in sight they exchanged a muttered good-bye and separated. The "other" remained at the corner, Haldin took up a position a little farther up the street. . . .

After throwing his "engine" he ran off and in a moment was overtaken by the panic-struck people flying away from the spot after the second explosion. They were wild with terror. He was jostled once or twice. He slowed down for the rush to pass him and then turned to the left into a narrow street. There he was alone.

He marvelled at this immediate escape. The work was done. He could hardly believe it. He fought with an almost irresistible longing to lie down on the pavement and sleep. But this sort of faintness—a drowsy faintness—passed off quickly. He walked faster, making his way to one of the poorer parts of the town in order to look up Ziemianitch.

This Ziemianitch, Razumov understood, was a sort of town-peasant who had got on; owner of a small number of sledges and horses for hire. Haldin paused in his narrative to exclaim—

"A bright spirit! A hardy soul! The best driver in St. Petersburg. He has a team of three horses there. . . . Ah! He's a fellow!"

This man had declared himself willing to take out safely, at any time, one or two persons to the second or third railway station on one of the southern lines. But there had been no time to warn him the night before. His usual haunt seemed to be a low-class eating-house on the outskirts of the town. When Haldin got there the man was not to be found. He was not expected to turn up again till the evening. Haldin wandered away restlessly.

He saw the gate of a woodyard open and went in to get out of the wind which swept the bleak broad thoroughfare. The great rectangular piles of cut wood loaded with snow resembled the huts of a village. At first the watchman who discovered him crouching amongst them talked in a friendly manner. He was a dried-up old man wearing two ragged army coats one over the other; his wizened little face, tied up under the jaw and over the ears in a dirty red handkerchief, looked comical. Presently he grew sulky, and then all at once without rhyme or reason began to shout furiously.

"Aren't you ever going to clear out of this, you loafer? We know all about factory hands of your sort. A big, strong, young chap! You aren't even drunk. What do you want here? You don't frighten us. Take yourself and your ugly eyes away."

Haldin stopped before the sitting Razumov. His supple figure, with the white forehead above which the fair hair stood straight up, had an aspect of lofty daring.

"He did not like my eyes," he said. "And so . . . here I am."

Razumov made an effort to speak calmly.

"But pardon me, Victor Victorovitch. We know each other so little. . . . I don't see why you . . ."

ᵼ "Confidence," said Haldin.

This word sealed Razumov's lips as if a hand had been clapped on his mouth. His brain seethed with arguments.

"And so—here you are," he muttered through his teeth.

The other did not detect the tone of anger. Never suspected it.

"Yes. And nobody knows I am here. You are the last person that could be suspected—should I get caught. That's an advantage, you see. And then—speaking to a superior mind like yours I can well say all the truth. It occurred to me that you—you have no one belonging to you—no ties, no one to suffer for it if this came out by some means. There have been enough ruined Russian homes as it is. But I don't see how my passage through your rooms can be ever known. If I should be got hold of, I'll know how to keep silent—no matter what they may be pleased to do to me," he added grimly.

He began to walk again while Razumov sat still, appalled.

"You thought that——" he faltered out almost sick with indignation.

"Yes, Razumov. Yes, brother. Some day you shall help to build. You suppose that I am a terrorist, now—a destructor of what is. But consider that the true destroyers are they who destroy the spirit of progress and truth, not the avengers who merely kill the bodies of the persecutors of human dignity. Men like me are necessary to make room for self-contained, thinking men like you. Well, we have made the sacrifice of our lives, but all the same I want to escape if it can be done. It is not my life I want to save, but my power to do. I won't live idle. Oh no! Don't make any mistake, Razumov. Men like me are rare. And, besides, an example like this is more awful to oppressors when the perpetrator vanishes without a trace. They sit in their offices and palaces and quake. All I want you to do is to help me to vanish. No great matter that. Only to go by and by and see Ziemianitch for me at that place where I went this morning. Just tell him, 'He whom you know wants a well-horsed sledge to pull up half an hour after midnight at the seventh lamp-post on the left counting from the upper end of Karabelnaya. If nobody gets in, the sledge is to run round a block or two, so as to come back past the same spot in ten minutes' time.'"

Razumov wondered why he had not cut short that talk and told this man to go away long before. Was it weakness or what?

He concluded that it was a sound instinct. Haldin must have been seen. It was impossible that some people should not have noticed the face and appearance of the man who threw the second bomb. Haldin was a noticeable person. The police in their thousands must have had his description within the hour. With every moment the danger grew. Sent out to wander in the streets he could not escape being caught in the end.

The police would very soon find out all about him. They would set about discovering a conspiracy. Everybody Haldin had ever known would be in the greatest danger. Unguarded expressions, little facts in themselves innocent would be counted for crimes. Razumov remembered certain words he said, the speeches he had listened to, the harmless gatherings he had attended—it was almost impossible for a student to keep out of that sort of thing, without becoming suspect to his comrades.

Razumov saw himself shut up in a fortress, worried, badgered, perhaps ill-used. He saw himself deported by an administrative order, his life broken, ruined, and robbed of all hope. He saw himself—at best—leading a miserable existence under police supervision, in some small, far-away provincial town, without friends to assist his necessities or even take any steps to alleviate his lot—as others had. Others had fathers, mothers, brothers, relations, connexions, to move heaven and earth on their behalf—he had no one. The very officials that sentenced him some morning would forget his existence before sunset.

He saw his youth pass away from him in misery and half starvation—his strength give way, his mind become an abject thing. He saw himself creeping, broken down and shabby, about the streets—dying unattended in some filthy hole of a room, or on the sordid bed of a Government hospital.

He shuddered. Then the peace of bitter calmness came over him. It was best to keep this man out of the streets till he could be got rid of with some chance of escaping. That was the best that could be done. Razumov, of course, felt the safety of his lonely existence to be permanently endangered. This evening's doings could turn up against him at any time as long as this man lived and the present institutions endured. They appeared to him rational and indestructible at that moment. They had a force of harmony—in contrast with the horrible discord of this man's presence. He hated the man. He said quietly—

"Yes, of course, I will go. You must give me precise directions, and for the rest—depend on me."

"Ah! You are a fellow! Collected—cool as a cucumber. A regular Englishman. Where did you get your soul from? There aren't many like you. Look here, brother! Men like me leave no posterity, but their souls are not lost No man's soul is ever lost. It works for itself—or else where would be the sense of self-sacrifice, of martyrdom, of conviction, of faith—the labours of the soul? What will become of my soul when I die in the way I must die—soon—very soon perhaps? It shall not perish. Don't make a mistake, Razumov. This is not murder—it is war, war. My spirit shall go on warring in some Russian body till all falsehood is swept out of the world. The modern civilization is false, but a new revelation shall come out of Russia. Ha! you say nothing. You are a sceptic. I respect your philosophical scepticism, Razumov, but don't touch the soul. The Russian soul that lives in all of us. It has a future. It has a mission, I tell you, or else why should I have been moved to do this—reckless—like a butcher—in the middle of all these innocent people—scattering death—I! I! . . . I wouldn't hurt a fly!"

"Not so loud," warned Razumov harshly.

Haldin sat down abruptly, and leaning his head on his folded arms burst into tears. He wept for a long time. The dusk had deepened in the room. Razumov, motionless in sombre wonder, listened to the sobs.

The other raised his head, got up and with an effort mastered his voice.

"Yes. Men like me leave no posterity," he repeated in a subdued tone. "I have a sister though. She's with my old mother—I persuaded them to go abroad this year—thank God. Not a bad little girl my sister. She has the most trustful eyes of any human being that ever walked this earth. She will marry well, I hope. She may have children—sons perhaps. Look at me. My father was a Government official in the provinces. He had a little land too. A simple servant of God—a true Russian in his way. His was the soul of obedience. But I am not like him. They say I resemble my mother's eldest brother, an officer. They shot him in '28. Under Nicholas, you know. Haven't I told you that this is war, war? . . . But God of Justice! This is weary work."

Razumov, in his chair, leaning his head on his hand, spoke as if from the bottom of an abyss.

"You believe in God, Haldin?"

"There you go catching at words that are wrung from one. What does it matter? What was it the Englishman said: 'There is a divine soul in things. . . .'? Devil take him—I don't remember now. But he spoke the truth. When the day of you thinkers comes don't you forget what's divine in the Russian soul—and that's <u>resignation</u>. Respect that in your intellectual restlessness and don't let your arrogant wisdom spoil its message to the world. I am speaking to you now like a man with a rope round his neck. What do you imagine I am? A being in revolt? No. It's you thinkers who are in everlasting revolt. I am one of the resigned. When the necessity of this heavy work came to me and I understood that it had to be done—what did I do? Did I exult? Did I take pride in my purpose? Did I try to weigh its worth and consequences? No! I was resigned. I thought, 'God's will be done.' "

He threw himself full length on Razumov's bed and putting the backs of his hands over his eyes remained perfectly motionless and silent. Not even the sound of his breathing could be heard. The dead stillness of the room remained undisturbed till in the darkness Razumov said gloomily—

"Haldin."

"Yes," answered the other readily, quite invisible now on the bed and without the slightest stir.

"Isn't it time for me to start?"

"Yes, brother." The other was heard, lying still in the darkness as though he were talking in his sleep. "The time has come to put fate to the test."

He paused, then gave a few lucid directions in the quiet impersonal voice of a man in a trance. Razumov made ready without a word of answer. As he was leaving the room the voice in the bed said after him—

"Go with God, thou silent soul."

On the landing, moving softly, Razumov locked the door and put the key in his pocket.

II

The words and events of that evening must have been graven as if with a steel tool on Mr. Razumov's brain since he was able to write his relation with such fullness and precision a good many months afterwards.

The record of the thoughts which assailed him in the street is even more minute and abundant. They seem to have rushed upon him with the greater freedom because his thinking powers were no longer crushed by Haldin's presence—the appalling presence of a great crime and the stunning force of a great fanaticism. On looking through the pages of Mr. Razumov's diary I own that a "rush of thoughts" is not an adequate image.

The more adequate description would be a tumult of thoughts—the faithful reflection of the state of his feelings. The thoughts in themselves were not numerous—they were like the thoughts of most human beings, few and simple—but they cannot be reproduced here in all their exclamatory repetitions which went on in an endless and weary turmoil—for the walk was long.

If to the Western reader they appear shocking, inappropriate, or even improper, it must be remembered that as to the first this may be the effect of my crude statement. For the rest I will only remark here that this is not a story of the West of Europe.

Nations it may be have fashioned their Governments, but the Governments have paid them back in the same coin. It is unthinkable that any young Englishman should find himself in Razumov's situation. This being so it would be a vain enterprise to imagine what he would think. The only safe surmise to make is that he would not think as Mr. Razumov thought at this crisis of his fate. He would not have an hereditary and personal knowledge of the means by which a historical autocracy represses ideas, guards its power, and defends its existence. By an act of mental extravagance he might imagine himself arbitrarily thrown into prison, but it would never occur to him unless he were delirious (and perhaps not even then) that he could be beaten with whips as a practical measure either of investigation or of punishment.

This is but a crude and obvious example of the different conditions of Western thought. I don't know that this danger occurred specially to Mr. Razumov. No doubt it entered unconsciously into the general dread and the general appallingness of this crisis. Razumov, as has been seen, was aware of more subtle ways in which an individual may be undone by the proceedings of a despotic Government. A simple expulsion from the University (the very least that could happen to him), with an impossibility to continue his studies anywhere, was enough to ruin utterly a young man depending entirely upon the development of his natural abilities for his place in the world. He was a Russian: and for him to be implicated meant simply sinking into the lowest social depths amongst the hopeless and the destitute—the night birds of the city.

The peculiar circumstances of Razumov's parentage, or rather of his lack of parentage, should be taken into the account of his thoughts. And he remembered them too. He had been lately reminded of them in a peculiarly atrocious way by this fatal Haldin. "Because I haven't that, must everything else be taken away from me?" he thought.

He nerved himself for another effort to go on. Along the roadway sledges glided phantom-like and jingling through a fluttering whiteness on the black face of the night. "For it is a crime," he was saying to himself. "A murder is a murder. Though, of course, some sort of liberal institutions. . . ."

A feeling of horrible sickness came over him. "I must be courageous," he exhorted himself mentally. All his strength was suddenly gone as if taken out by a hand. Then by a mighty effort of will it came back because he was afraid of fainting in the street and being picked up by the police with the key of his lodgings in his pocket. They would find Haldin there, and then, indeed, he would be undone.

Strangely enough it was this fear which seems to have kept him up to the end. The passers-by were rare. They came upon him suddenly, looming up black in the snow-flakes close by, then vanishing all at once—without footfalls.

It was the quarter of the very poor. Razumov noticed an elderly woman tied up in ragged shawls. Under the street lamp she seemed a beggar off duty. She walked leisurely in the blizzard as though she had no home to hurry to, she hugged under one arm a round loaf of black bread with an air of guarding a priceless booty; and Razumov averting his glance envied her the peace of her mind and the serenity of her fate.

To one reading Mr. Razumov's narrative it is really a wonder how he managed to keep going as he did along one interminable street after another on pavements that were gradually becoming blocked with snow. It was the thought of Haldin locked up in his rooms and [the desperate desire to get rid of his presence which drove him forward.] No rational determination had any part in his exertions. Thus, when on arriving at the low eating-house he heard that the man of horses, Ziemianitch, was not there, he could only stare stupidly.

The waiter, a wild-haired youth in tarred boots and a pink shirt, exclaimed, uncovering his pale gums in a silly grin, that Ziemianitch had got his skinful early in the afternoon and had gone away with a bottle under each arm to keep it up amongst the horses—he supposed.

The owner of the vile den, a bony short man in a dirty cloth caftan coming down to his heels, stood by, his hands tucked into his belt, and nodded confirmation.

The reek of spirits, the greasy rancid steam of food got Razumov by the throat. He struck a table with his clenched hand and shouted violently—

"You lie."

Bleary unwashed faces were turned to his direction. A mild-eyed ragged tramp drinking tea at the next table moved farther away. A murmur of wonder arose with an undertone of uneasiness. A laugh was heard too, and an exclamation, "There! there!" jeeringly soothing. The waiter looked all round and announced to the room—

"The gentleman won't believe that Ziemianitch is drunk."

From a distant corner a hoarse voice belonging to a horrible, nondescript, shaggy being with a black face like the muzzle of a bear grunted angrily—

"The cursed driver of thieves. What do we want with his gentlemen here? We are all honest folk in this place."

Razumov, biting his lip till blood came to keep himself from bursting into imprecations, followed the owner of the den, who, whispering "Come along, little father," led him into a tiny hole of a place behind the wooden counter, whence proceeded a sound of splashing. A wet and bedraggled creature, a sort of sexless and shivering scarecrow, washed glasses in there, bending over a wooden tub by the light of a tallow dip.

"Yes, little father," the man in the long caftan said plaintively. He had a brown, cunning little face, a thin greyish beard. Trying to light a tin lantern he hugged it to his breast and talked garrulously the while.

He would show Ziemianitch to the gentleman to prove there were no lies told. And he would show him drunk. His woman, it seems, ran away from him last night. "Such a hag she was! Thin! Pfui!" He spat. They were always running away from that driver of the devil—and he sixty years old too; could never get used to it. But each heart knows sorrow after its own kind and Ziemianitch was a born fool all his days. And then he would fly to the bottle. "'Who could bear life in our land without the bottle?' he says. A proper Russian man—the little pig. . . . Be pleased to follow me."

Razumov crossed a quadrangle of deep snow enclosed between high walls with innumerable windows. Here and there a dim yellow light hung within the four-square mass of darkness. The house was an enormous slum, a hive of human vermin, a monumental abode of misery towering on the verge of starvation and despair.

In a corner the ground sloped sharply down, and Razumov followed the light of the lantern through a small doorway into a long cavernous place like a neglected sub-

terranean byre. Deep within, three shaggy little horses
tied up to rings hung their heads together, motionless and
shadowy in the dim light of the lantern. It must have been
the famous team of Haldin's escape. Razumov peered fearfully into the gloom. His guide pawed in the straw with
his foot.

"Here he is. Ah! the little pigeon. A true Russian man.
'No heavy hearts for me,' he says. 'Bring out the bottle and
take your ugly mug out of my sight.' Ha! ha! ha! That's
the fellow he is."

He held the lantern over a prone form of a man, apparently fully dressed for outdoors. His head was lost in a
pointed cloth hood. On the other side of a heap of straw
protruded a pair of feet in monstrous thick boots.

"Always ready to drive," commented the keeper of the
eating-house. "A proper Russian driver that. Saint or devil,
night or day is all one to Ziemianitch when his heart is
free from sorrow. 'I don't ask who you are, but where you
want to go,' he says. He would drive Satan himself to his
own abode and come back chirruping to his horses. Many
a one he has driven who is clanking his chains in the
Nertchinsk mines by this time."

Razumov shuddered.

"Call him, wake him up," he faltered out.

The other set down his light, stepped back and launched
a kick at the prostrate sleeper. The man shook at the impact but did not move. At the third kick he grunted but
remained inert as before.

The eating-house keeper desisted and fetched a deep
sigh.

"You see for yourself how it is. We have done what
we can for you."

He picked up the lantern. The intense black spokes of
shadow swung about in the circle of light. A terrible fury—
the blind rage of self-preservation—possessed Razumov.

"Ah! The vile beast," he bellowed out in an unearthly
tone which made the lantern jump and tremble. "I shall
wake you! Give me . . . Give me . . ."

He looked round wildly, seized the handle of a stable-fork and rushing forward struck at the prostrate body with inarticulate cries. After a time his cries ceased, and the rain of blows fell in the stillness and shadows of the cellar-like stable. Razumov belaboured Ziemianitch with an insatiable fury, in great volleys of sounding thwacks. Except for the violent movements of Razumov nothing stirred, neither the beaten man nor the spoke-like shadows on the walls. And only the sound of blows was heard. It was a weird scene.

Suddenly there was a sharp crack. The stick broke and half of it flew far away into the gloom beyond the light. At the same time Ziemianitch sat up. At this Razumov became as motionless as the man with the lantern—only his breast heaved for air as if ready to burst.

Some dull sensation of pain must have penetrated at last the consoling night of drunkenness enwrapping the "bright Russian soul," of Haldin's enthusiastic praise. But Ziemianitch evidently saw nothing. His eyeballs blinked all white in the light once, twice—then the gleam went out. For a moment he sat in the straw with closed eyes with a strange air of weary meditation, then fell over slowly on his side without making the slightest sound. Only the straw rustled a little. Razumov stared wildly, fighting for his breath. After a second or two he heard a light snore.

He flung from him the piece of stick remaining in his grasp, and went off with great hasty strides without looking back once.

After going heedlessly for some fifty yards along the street he walked into a snowdrift and was up to his knees before he stopped.

This recalled him to himself; and glancing about he discovered he had been going in the wrong direction. He retraced his steps, but now at a more moderate pace. When passing before the house he had just left he flourished his fist at the sombre refuge of misery and crime rearing its sinister bulk on the white ground. It had an air of brooding. He let his arm fall by his side—discouraged.

Ziemianitch's passionate surrender to sorrow and consolation had baffled him. That was the people. A true

Russian man! Razumov was glad he had beaten that brute —the "bright soul" of the other. Here they were: the people and the enthusiast.]

Between the two he was done for. Between the drunkenness of the peasant incapable of action and the dreamintoxication of the idealist incapable of perceiving the reason of things, and the true character of men. It was a sort of terrible childishness. But children had their masters. "Ah! the stick, the stick, the stern hand," thought Razumov, [longing for power to hurt and destroy.]

He was glad he had thrashed that brute. The physical exertion had left his body in a comfortable glow. His mental agitation too was clarified as if all the feverishness had gone out of him in a fit of outward violence. Together with the persisting sense of terrible danger he was conscious now of a tranquil, unquenchable hate.

He walked slower and slower. And indeed, considering the guest he had in his rooms, it was no wonder he lingered on the way. [It was like harbouring a pestilential disease that would not perhaps take your life, but would take from you all that made life worth living—a subtle pest that would convert earth into a hell.]

What was he doing now? Lying on the bed as if dead, with the back of his hands over his eyes? Razumov had a morbidly vivid vision of Haldin on his bed—the white pillow hollowed by the head, the legs in long boots, the upturned feet. And in his abhorrence he said to himself, "I'll kill him when I get home." But he knew very well that that was of no use. The corpse hanging round his neck would be nearly as fatal as the living man. [Nothing short of complete annihilation would do. And that was impossible. What then? Must one kill oneself to escape this visitation?]

Razumov's despair was too profoundly tinged with hate to accept that issue.

And yet it was despair—nothing less—at the thought of having to live with Haldin for an indefinite number of days in mortal alarm at every sound. But perhaps when he heard that this "bright soul" of Ziemianitch suffered from a drunken eclipse the fellow would take his infernal resignation somewhere else. And that was not likely on the face of it.

Razumov thought: "I am being crushed—and I can't even run away." Other men had somewhere a corner of the earth—some little house in the provinces where they had a right to take their troubles. A material refuge. He had nothing. He had not even a moral refuge—the refuge of confidence. To whom could he go with this tale—in all this great, great land?

Razumov stamped his foot—and under the soft carpet of snow felt the hard ground of Russia, inanimate, cold, inert, like a sullen and tragic mother hiding her face under a winding-sheet—his native soil!—his very own—without a fireside, without a heart!

He cast his eyes upwards and stood amazed. The snow had ceased to fall, and now, as if by a miracle, he saw above his head the clear black sky of the northern winter, decorated with the sumptuous fires of the stars. It was a canopy fit for the resplendent purity of the snows.

Razumov received an almost physical impression of endless space and of countless millions.

He responded to it with the readiness of a Russian who is born to an inheritance of space and numbers. Under the sumptuous immensity of the sky, the snow covered the endless forests, the frozen rivers, the plains of an immense country, obliterating the landmarks, the accidents of the ground, levelling everything under its uniform whiteness, like a monstrous blank page awaiting the record of an inconceivable history. It covered the passive land with its lives of countless people like Ziemianitch and its handful of agitators like this Haldin—murdering foolishly.

It was a sort of sacred inertia. Razumov felt a respect for it. A voice seemed to cry within him, "Don't touch it." It was a guarantee of duration, of safety, while the travail of maturing destiny went on—a work not of revolutions with their passionate levity of action and their shifting impulses—but of peace. What it needed was not the conflicting aspirations of a people, but a will strong and one: it wanted not the babble of many voices, but a man—strong and one.

Razumov stood on the point of conversion. He was fascinated by its approach, by its overpowering logic. For a train of thought is never false. The falsehood lies deep in the necessities of existence, in secret fears and half-formed ambitions, in the secret confidence combined with a secret mistrust of ourselves, in the love of hope and the dread of uncertain days.

In Russia, the land of spectral ideas and disembodied aspirations, many brave minds have turned away at last from the vain and endless conflict <u>to the one great historical fact of the land</u>. <u>They turned to autocracy for the peace of their patriotic conscience as a weary unbeliever, touched by grace, turns to the faith of his fathers for the blessing of spiritual rest</u>. Like other Russians before him, Razumov, in conflict with himself, felt the touch of grace upon his forehead.

"Haldin means disruption," he thought to himself, beginning to walk again. "What is he with his indignation, with his talk of bondage—with his talk of God's justice? All that means disruption. Better that thousands should suffer than that a people should become a disintegrated mass, helpless like dust in the wind. Obscurantism is better than the light of incendiary torches. The seed germinates in the night. Out of the dark soil springs the perfect plant. But a volcanic eruption is sterile, the ruin of the fertile ground. And am I, who love my country—who have nothing but that to love and put my faith in—am I to have my future, perhaps my usefulness, ruined by this sanguinary fanatic?"

The grace entered into Razumov. He believed now in the man who would come at the appointed time.

What is a throne? A few pieces of wood upholstered in velvet. But a throne is a seat of power too. The form of government is the shape of a tool—an instrument. But twenty thousand bladders inflated by the noblest sentiments and jostling against each other in the air are a miserable incumbrance of space, holding no power, possessing no will, having nothing to give.

He went on thus, heedless of the way, holding a discourse with himself with extraordinary abundance and facility. Generally his phrases came to him slowly, after a conscious and painstaking wooing. Some superior power had inspired him with a flow of masterly argument (as certain converted sinners become overwhelmingly loquacious.)

He felt an austere exultation.

"What are the luridly smoky lucubrations of that fellow to the clear grasp of my intellect?" he thought. "Is not this my country? Have I not got forty million brothers?" he asked himself, (unanswerably victorious in the silence of his breast.) And the fearful thrashing he had given the inanimate Ziemianitch seemed to him a sign of intimate union, a pathetically severe necessity of brotherly love. "No! If I must suffer let me at least suffer for my convictions, not for a crime my reason—my cool superior reason —rejects."

He ceased to think for a moment. The silence in his breast was complete. But he felt a suspicious uneasiness, such as we may experience when we enter an unlighted strange place—the irrational feeling that something may jump upon us in the dark—(the absurd dread of the unseen.)

Of course he was far from being a moss-grown reactionary. Everything was not for the best. Despotic bureaucracy . . . abuses . . . corruption . . . and so on. Capable men were wanted. Enlightened intelligences. Devoted hearts. But absolute power should be preserved—the tool ready for the man—for the great autocrat of the future. Razumov believed in him. The logic of history made him unavoidable. The state of the people demanded him. "What else?" he asked himself ardently, "could move all that mass in one direction? Nothing could. Nothing but a single will."

He was persuaded that he was sacrificing his personal longings of liberalism—rejecting the attractive error for the stern Russian truth. "That's patriotism," he observed mentally, and added, "There's no stopping midway on that road," and then remarked to himself, "I am not a coward."

And again there was a dead silence in Razumov's breast. He walked with lowered head, making room for no one. He walked slowly and his thoughts returning spoke within him with solemn slowness.

"What is this Haldin? And what am I? Only two grains of sand. But a great mountain is made up of just such insignificant grains. And the death of a man or of many men is an insignificant thing. Yet we combat a contagious pestilence. Do I want his death? No! I would save him if I could—but no one can do that—he is the withered member which must be cut off. If I must perish through him, let me at least not perish with him, and associated against my will with his sombre folly that understands nothing either of men or things. Why should I leave a false memory?"

It passed through his mind that there was no one in the world who cared what sort of memory he left behind him. He exclaimed to himself instantly, "Perish vainly for a falsehood! . . . What a miserable fate!"

He was now in a more animated part of the town. He did not remark the crash of two colliding sledges close to the curb. The driver of one bellowed tearfully at his fellow—

"Oh, thou vile wretch!"

This hoarse yell, let out nearly in his ear, disturbed Razumov. He shook his head impatiently and went on looking straight before him. Suddenly on the snow, stretched on his back right across his path, he saw Haldin, solid, distinct, real, with his inverted hands over his eyes, clad in a brown close-fitting coat and long boots. He was lying out of the way a little, as though he had selected that place on purpose. The snow round him was un-trodden.

This hallucination had such a solidity of aspect that the first movement of Razumov was to reach for his pocket to assure himself that the key of his rooms was there. But he checked the impulse with a disdainful curve of his lips. He understood. His thought, concentrated intensely on the fig-ure left lying on his bed, had culminated in this extraordinary illusion of the sight. Razumov tackled the phenomenon calmy. With a stern face, without a check and gazing far beyond the vision, he walked on, experiencing nothing but a slight tightening of the chest. After passing he turned his head for a glance, and saw only the unbroken track of his footsteps over the place where the breast of the phantom had been lying.

Razumov walked on and after a little time whispered his wonder to himself.

"Exactly as if alive! Seemed to breathe! And right in my way too! I have had an extraordinary experience."

He made a few steps and muttered through his set teeth—

"I shall give him up."

Then for some twenty yards or more all was blank. He wrapped his cloak closer round him. He pulled his cap well forward over his eyes.

"Betray. A great word. What is betrayal? They talk of a man betraying his country, his friends, his sweetheart. There must be a moral bond first. All a man can betray is his conscience. And how is my conscience engaged here; by what bond of common faith, of common conviction, am I obliged to let that fanatical idiot drag me down with him? On the contrary—every obligation of true courage is the other way."

Razumov looked round from under his cap.

"What can the prejudice of the world reproach me with? Have I provoked his confidence? No! Have I by a single word, look, or gesture given him reason to suppose that I accepted his trust in me? No! It is true that I consented to go and see his Ziemianitch. Well, I have been to see him. And I broke a stick on his back too—the brute."

Something seemed to turn over in his head bringing uppermost a singularly hard, clear facet of his brain.

"It would be better, however," he reflected with a quite different mental accent, "to keep that circumstance (altogether to myself.")

He had passed beyond the turn leading to his lodgings, and had reached a wide and fashionable street. Some shops were still open, and all the restaurants. Lights fell on the pavement where men in expensive fur coats, with here and there the elegant figure of a woman, walked with an air of leisure. Razumov looked at them with the contempt of an austere believer for the frivolous crowd. It was the world—those officers, dignitaries, men of fashion, officials, members of the Yacht Club. The event of the morning affected them all. What would they say if they knew what this student in a cloak was going to do?

"Not one of them is capable of feeling and thinking as deeply as I can. How many of them could accomplish an act of conscience?"

Razumov lingered in the well-lighted street. He was firmly decided. Indeed, it could hardly be called a decision. He had simply discovered what he had meant to do all along. And yet he felt the need of some other mind's sanction.

With something resembling anguish he said to himself— "I want to be understood." The universal aspiration with all its profound and melancholy meaning assailed heavily Razumov, who, amongst eighty millions of his kith and kin, had no heart to which he could open himself.

The attorney was not to be thought of. He despised the little agent of chicane too much. One could not go and lay one's conscience before the policeman at the corner. Neither was Razumov anxious to go to the chief of his district's police—a common-looking person whom he used to see sometimes in the street in a shabby uniform and with a smouldering cigarette stuck to his lower lip. "He would begin by locking me up most probably. At any rate, he is certain to get excited and create an awful commotion," thought Razumov practically.

An act of conscience must be done with outward dignity.

Razumov longed desperately for a word of advice, for moral support. Who knows what true loneliness is—not the conventional word, but the naked terror? To the lonely themselves it wears a mask. The most miserable outcast hugs some memory or some illusion. Now and then a fatal conjunction of events may lift the veil for an instant. For an

instant only. No human being could bear a steady view of
moral solitude without going mad.

Razumov had reached that point of vision. To escape
from it he embraced for a whole minute the delirious purpose of rushing to his lodgings and flinging himself on his
knees by the side of the bed with the dark figure stretched
on it; to pour out a full confession in passionate words that
would stir the whole being of that man to its innermost
depths; that would end in embraces and tears; in an incredible fellowship of souls—such as the world had never
seen. It was sublime!

Inwardly he wept and trembled already. But to the
casual eyes that were cast upon him he was aware that he
appeared as a tranquil student in a cloak, out for a leisurely
stroll. He noted, too, the sidelong, brilliant glance of a
pretty woman—with a delicate head, and covered in the
hairy skins of wild beasts down to her feet, like a frail and
beautiful savage—which rested for a moment with a sort
of mocking tenderness on the deep abstraction of that good-
looking young man.

Suddenly Razumov stood still. The glimpse of a passing
grey whisker, caught and lost in the same instant, had
evoked the complete image of Prince K——, the man who
once had pressed his hand as no other man had pressed it
—a faint but lingering pressure like a secret sign, like a half-
unwilling caress.

And Razumov marvelled at himself. Why did he not
think of him before!

"A senator, a dignitary, a great personage, the very man
—He!"

A strange softening emotion came over Razumov—made
his knees shake a little. He repressed it with a new-born
austerity. All that sentiment was pernicious nonsense. He
couldn't be quick enough; and when he got into a sledge he
shouted to the driver—

"To the K—— Palace. Get on—you! Fly!"

The startled moujik, bearded up to the very whites of
his eyes, answered obsequiously—

"I hear, your high Nobility."

It was lucky for Razumov that Prince K—— was not a man of timid character. On the day of Mr. de P——'s murder an extreme alarm and despondency prevailed in the high official spheres.

Prince K——, sitting sadly alone in his study, was told by his alarmed servants that a mysterious young man had forced his way into the hall, refused to tell his name and the nature of his business, and would not move from there till he had seen his Excellency in private. Instead of locking himself up and telephoning for the police, as nine out of ten personages would have done that evening, the Prince gave way to curiosity and came quietly to the door of his study.

In the hall, the front door standing wide open, he recognized at once Razumov, pale as death, his eyes blazing, and surrounded by perplexed lackeys.

The Prince was vexed beyond measure, and even indignant. But his humane instincts and a subtle sense of self-respect could not allow him to let this young man be thrown out into the street by base menials. He retreated unseen into his room, and after a little rang his bell. Razumov heard in the hall an ominously raised harsh voice saying somewhere far away—

"Show the gentleman in here."

Razumov walked in without a tremor. He felt himself invulnerable—raised far above the shallowness of common judgment. Though he saw the Prince looking at him with black displeasure, the lucidity of his mind, of which he was very conscious, gave him an extraordinary assurance. He was not asked to sit down.

Half an hour later they appeared in the hall together. The lackeys stood up, and the Prince, moving with difficulty on his gouty feet, was helped into his furs. The carriage had been ordered before. When the great double door was flung open with a crash, Razumov, who had been standing silent with a lost gaze but with every faculty intensely on the alert, heard the Prince's voice—

"Your arm, young man."

The mobile, superficial mind of the ex-Guards officer,

man of showy missions, experienced in nothing but the
arts of gallant intrigue and worldly success, had been
equally impressed by the more obvious difficulties of such
a situation and by Razumov's quiet dignity in stating them.

He had said, "No. Upon the whole I can't condemn the
step you ventured to take by coming to me with your story.
It is not an affair for police understrappers. The greatest
importance is attached to . . . Set your mind at rest. I
shall see you through this most extraordinary and difficult
situation."

Then the Prince rose to ring the bell, and Razumov,
making a short bow, had said with deference—

"I have trusted my instinct. A young man having no
claim upon anybody in the world has in an hour of trial
involving his deepest political convictions turned to an illustrious Russian—that's all."

The Prince had exclaimed hastily—

"You have done well."

In the carriage—it was a small brougham on sleigh run-
ners—Razumov broke the silence in a voice that trembled
slightly.

"My gratitude surpasses the greatness of my presumption."

He gasped, feeling unexpectedly in the dark a momentary pressure on his arm.

"You have done well," repeated the Prince.

When the carriage stopped the Prince murmured to
Razumov, who had never ventured a single question—

"The house of General T——."

In the middle of the snow-covered roadway blazed a
great bonfire. Some Cossacks, the bridles of their horses
over the arm, were warming themselves around it. Two
sentries stood at the door, several gendarmes lounged under
the great carriage gateway, and on the first-floor landing
two orderlies rose and stood at attention. Razumov walked
at the Prince's elbow.

A surprising quantity of hot-house plants in pots cum-
bered the floor of the ante-room. Servants came forward.
A young man in civilian clothes arrived hurriedly, was

whispered to, bowed low, and exclaiming zealously, "Certainly—this minute," fled within somewhere. The Prince signed to Razumov.

They passed through a suite of reception-rooms all barely lit and one of them prepared for dancing. The wife of the General had put off her party. An atmosphere of consternation pervaded the place. But the General's own room, with heavy sombre hangings, two massive desks, and deep armchairs, had all the lights turned on. The footman shut the door behind them and they waited.

There was a coal fire in an English grate; Razumov had never before seen such a fire; and the silence of the room was like the silence of the grave; perfect, measureless, for even the clock on the mantelpiece made no sound. Filling a corner, on a black pedestal, stood a quarter-life-size smooth-limbed bronze of an adolescent figure, running. The Prince observed in an undertone—

"Spontini's. 'Flight of Youth.' Exquisite."

"Admirable," assented Razumov faintly.

They said nothing more after this, the Prince silent with his grand air, Razumov staring at the statue. He was worried by a sensation resembling the gnawing of hunger.

He did not turn when he heard an inner door fly open, and a quick footstep, muffled on the carpet.

The Prince's voice immediately exclaimed, thick with excitement—

"We have got him—*ce misérable*. A worthy young man came to me—— No! It's incredible. . . ."

Razumov held his breath before the bronze as if expecting a crash. Behind his back a voice he had never heard before insisted politely—

"*Asseyez-vous donc.*"

The Prince almost shrieked, "*Mais comprenez-vous, mon cher! L'assassin!* the murderer—we have got him. . . ."

Razumov spun round. The General's smooth big cheeks rested on the stiff collar of his uniform. He must have been already looking at Razumov, because that last saw the pale blue eyes fastened on him coldly.

The Prince from a chair waved an impressive hand.

"This is a most honourable young man whom Providence itself . . . Mr. Razumov."

The General acknowledged the introduction by frowning at Razumov, who did not make the slightest movement.

Sitting down before his desk the General listened with compressed lips. It was impossible to detect any sign of emotion on his face.

Razumov watched the immobility of the fleshy profile. But it lasted only a moment, till the Prince had finished; and when the General turned to the providential young man, his florid complexion, the blue, unbelieving eyes and the bright white flash of an automatic smile had an air of jovial, careless cruelty. He expressed no wonder at the extraordinary story—no pleasure or excitement—no incredulity either. He betrayed no sentiment whatever. Only with a politeness almost deferential suggested that "the bird might have flown while Mr.—Mr. Razumov was running about the streets."

Razumov advanced to the middle of the room and said, "The door is locked and I have the key in my pocket."

His loathing for the man was intense. It had come upon him so unawares that he felt he had not kept it out of his voice. The General looked up at him thoughtfully, and Razumov grinned.

All this went over the head of Prince K—— seated in a deep armchair, very tired and impatient.

"A student called Haldin," said the General thoughtfully.

Razumov ceased to grin.

"That is his name," he said, unnecessarily loud. "Victor Victorovitch Haldin—a student."

The General shifted his position a little.

"How is he dressed? Would you have the goodness to tell me?"

Razumov angrily described Haldin's clothing in a few jerky words. The General stared all the time, then addressing the Prince—

"We were not without some indications," he said in French. "A good woman who was in the street described to us somebody wearing a dress of the sort as the thrower of the second bomb. We have detained her at the Secretariat, and everyone in a Tcherkess coat we could lay our hands on has been brought to her to look at. She kept on crossing herself and shaking her head at them. It was exasperating. . . ."

He turned to Razumov, and in Russian, with friendly reproach—

"Take a chair, Mr. Razumov—do. Why are you standing?"

Razumov sat down carelessly and looked at the General.

"This goggle-eyed imbecile understands nothing," he thought.

The Prince began to speak loftily.

"Mr. Razumov is a young man of conspicuous abilities. I have it at heart that his future should not. . . ."

"Certainly," interrupted the General, with a movement of the hand. "Has he any weapons on him, do you think, Mr. Razumov?"

The General employed a gentle musical voice. Razumov answered with suppressed irritation—

"No. But my razors are lying about—you understand."

The General lowered his head approvingly.

"Precisely."

Then to the Prince, explaining courteously—

"We want that bird alive. It will be the devil if we can't make him sing a little before we are done with him."

The grave-like silence of the room with its mute clock fell upon the polite modulations of this terrible phrase. The Prince, hidden in the chair, made no sound.

The General unexpectedly developed a thought.

"Fidelity to menaced institutions on which depend the safety of a throne and of a people is no child's play. We know that, *mon Prince*, and—*tenez*—" he went on with a sort of flattering harshness, "Mr. Razumov here begins to understand that too."

His eyes which he turned upon Razumov seemed to be starting out of his head. This grotesqueness of aspect no longer shocked Razumov. He said with gloomy conviction—

"Haldin will never speak."

"That remains to be seen," muttered the General.

"I am certain," insisted Razumov. "A man like this never speaks. . . . Do you imagine that I am here from fear?" he added violently. He felt ready to stand by his opinion of Haldin to the last extremity.

"Certainly not," protested the General, with great simplicity of tone. "And I don't mind telling you, Mr. Razumov, that if he had not come with his tale to such a staunch and loyal Russian as you, he would have disappeared like a stone in the water . . . which would have had a detestable effect," he added, with a bright, cruel smile under his stony stare. "So you see, there can be no suspicion of any fear here."

The Prince intervened, looking at Razumov round the back of the armchair.

"Nobody doubts the moral soundness of your action. Be at ease in that respect, pray."

He turned to the General uneasily.

"That's why I am here. You may be surprised why I should . . ."

The General hastened to interrupt.

"Not at all. Extremely natural. You saw the importance . . ."

"Yes," broke in the Prince. "And I venture to ask insistently that mine and Mr. Razumov's intervention should not become public. He is a young man of promise—of remarkable aptitudes."

"I haven't a doubt of it," murmured the General. "He inspires confidence."

"All sorts of pernicious views are so widespread nowadays—they taint such unexpected quarters—that, monstrous as it seems, he might suffer. . . . His studies. . . . His . . ."

The General, with his elbows on the desk, took his head between his hands.

"Yes. Yes. I am thinking it out. . . . How long is it since you left him at your rooms, Mr. Razumov?"

Razumov mentioned the hour which nearly corresponded with the time of his distracted flight from the big slum house. He had made up his mind to keep Ziemianitch out of the affair completely. To mention him at all would mean imprisonment for the "bright soul," perhaps cruel floggings, and in the end a journey to Siberia in chains. Razumov, who had beaten Ziemianitch, felt for him now a vague, remorseful tenderness.

The General, giving way for the first time to his secret sentiments, exclaimed contemptuously—

"And you say he came in to make you this confidence like this—for nothing—*à propos des bottes.*"

Razumov felt danger in the air. The merciless suspicion of despotism had spoken openly at last. Sudden fear sealed Razumov's lips. The silence of the room resembled now the silence of a deep dungeon, where time does not count, and a suspect person is sometimes forgotten for ever. But the Prince came to the rescue.

"Providence itself has led the wretch in a moment of mental aberration to seek Mr. Razumov on the strength of some old, utterly misinterpreted exchange of ideas—some sort of idle speculative conversation—months ago—I am told—and completely forgotten till now by Mr. Razumov."

"Mr. Razumov," queried the General meditatively, after a short silence, "do you often indulge in speculative conversation?"

"No, Excellency," answered Razumov, coolly, in a sudden access of self-confidence. "I am a man of deep convictions. Crude opinions are in the air. They are not always worth combating. But even the silent contempt of a serious mind may be misinterpreted by headlong utopists."

The General stared from between his hands. Prince K— murmured—

"A serious young man. *Un esprit supérieur.*"

"I see that, *mon cher Prince*," said the General. "Mr. Razumov is quite safe with me. I am interested in him. He has, it seems, the great and useful quality of inspiring confidence. What I was wondering at is why the other should mention anything at all—I mean even the bare fact alone—if his object was only to obtain temporary shelter for a few hours. For, after all, nothing was easier than to say nothing about it unless, indeed, he were trying, under a crazy misapprehension of your true sentiments, to enlist your assistance—eh, Mr. Razumov?"

It seemed to Razumov that the floor was moving slightly. This grotesque man in a tight uniform was terrible. It was right that he should be terrible.

"I can see what your Excellency has in your mind. But I can only answer that I don't know why."

"I have nothing in my mind," murmured the General with gentle surprise.

"I am his prey—his helpless prey," thought Razumov. The fatigues and the disgusts of that afternoon, the need to forget, the fear which he could not keep off, reawakened his hate for Haldin.

"Then I can't help your Excellency. I don't know what he meant. I only know there was a moment when I wished to kill him. There was also a moment when I wished myself dead. I said nothing. I was overcome. I provoked no confidence—I asked for no explanations——"

Razumov seemed beside himself; but his mind was lucid. It was really a calculated outburst.

"It is rather a pity," the General said, "that you did not. Don't you know at all what he means to do?"

Razumov calmed down and saw an opening there.

"He told me he was in hopes that a sledge would meet him about half an hour after midnight at the seventh lamp-post on the left from the upper end of Karabelnaya. At any rate, he meant to be there at that time. He did not even ask me for a change of clothes."

"Ah violà!" said the General, turning to Prince K— with an air of satisfaction. "There is a way to keep your protégé, Mr. Razumov, quite clear of any connexion with the actual arrest. We shall be ready for that gentleman in Karabelnaya."

The Prince expressed his gratitude. There was real emotion in his voice. Razumov, motionless, silent, sat staring at the carpet. The General turned to him.

"Half an hour after midnight. Till then we have to depend on you, Mr. Razumov. You don't think he is likely to change his purpose?"

"How can I tell?" said Razumov. "Those men are not of the sort that ever change their purpose."

"What men do you mean?"

"Fanatical lovers of liberty in general. Liberty with a capital L, Excellency. Liberty that means nothing precise. Liberty in whose name crimes are committed."

The General murmured—

"I detest rebels of every kind. I can't help it. It's my nature!"

He clenched a fist and shook it, drawing back his arm. "They shall be destroyed, then."

"They have made a sacrifice of their lives beforehand," said Razumov with malicious pleasure and looking the General straight in the face. "If Haldin does change his purpose to-night, you may depend on it that it will not be to save his life by flight in some other way. He would have thought then of something else to attempt. But that is not likely."

The General repeated as if to himself, "They shall be destroyed."

Razumov assumed an impenetrable expression.

The Prince exclaimed—

"What a terrible necessity!"

The General's arm was lowered slowly.

"One comfort there is. That brood leaves no posterity. I've always said it; one effort, pitiless, persistent, steady— and we are done with them for ever."

Razumov thought to himself that this man entrusted with so much arbitrary power must have believed what he said or else he could not have gone on bearing the responsibility.

The General repeated again with extreme animosity—

"I detest rebels. These subversive minds! These intellectual *debauchés!* My existence has been built on fidelity."

It's a feeling. To defend it I am ready to lay down my life —and even my honour—if that were needed. But pray tell me what honour can there be as against rebels—against people that deny God Himself—perfect unbelievers! Brutes. It is horrible to think of."

During this tirade Razumov, facing the General, had nodded slightly twice. Prince K——, standing on one side with his grand air, murmured, casting up his eyes—

"*Hélas!*"

Then lowering his glance and with great decision declared—

"This young man, General, is perfectly fit to apprehend the bearing of your memorable words."

The General's whole expression changed from dull resentment to perfect urbanity.

"I would ask now, Mr. Razumov," he said, "to return to his home. Note that I don't ask Mr. Razumov whether he has justified his absence to his guest. No doubt he did this sufficiently. But I don't ask. Mr. Razumov inspires confidence. It is a great gift. I only suggest that a more prolonged absence might awaken the criminal's suspicions and induce him perhaps to change his plans."

He rose and with a scrupulous courtesy escorted his visitors to the ante-room encumbered with flower-pots.

Razumov parted with the Prince at the corner of a street. In the carriage he had listened to speeches where natural sentiment struggled with caution. Evidently the Prince was afraid of encouraging any hopes of future intercourse. But there was a touch of tenderness in the voice uttering in the dark the guarded general phrases of goodwill. And the Prince too said—

"I have perfect confidence in you, Mr. Razumov."

"They all, it seems, have confidence in me," thought Razumov dully. He had an indulgent contempt for the man sitting shoulder to shoulder with him in the confined space. Probably he was afraid of scenes with his wife. She was said to be proud and violent.

It seemed to him bizarre that secrecy should play such a large part in the comfort and safety of lives. But he wanted to put the Prince's mind at ease; and with a proper amount of emphasis he said that, being conscious of some small abilities and confident in his power of work, he trusted his future to his own exertions. He expressed his gratitude for the helping hand. Such dangerous situations did not occur twice in the course of one life—he added.

"And you have met this one with a firmness of mind and correctness of feeling which give me a high idea of your worth," the Prince said solemnly. "You have now only to persevere—to persevere." *(cf. scene in lawyer's chambers)*

On getting out on the pavement Razumov saw an ungloved hand extended to him through the lowered window of the brougham. It detained his own in its grasp for a moment, while the light of a street lamp fell upon the Prince's long face and old-fashioned grey whiskers.

"I hope you are perfectly reassured now as to the consequences. . . ."

"After what your Excellency has condescended to do for me, I can only rely on my conscience."

"*Adieu*," said the whiskered head with feeling.

Razumov bowed. The brougham glided away with a slight swish in the snow—he was alone on the edge of the pavement.

He said to himself that there was nothing to think about, and began walking towards his home.

He walked quietly. It was a common experience to walk thus home to bed after an evening spent somewhere with his fellows or in the cheaper seats of a theatre. After he had gone a little way the familiarity of things got hold of him. Nothing was changed. There was the familiar corner; and when he turned it he saw the familiar dim light of the provision shop kept by a German woman. There were loaves of stale bread, bunches of onions and strings of sausages behind the small window-panes. They were closing it. The sickly lame fellow whom he knew so well by sight staggered out into the snow embracing a large shutter.

Nothing would change. There was the familiar gateway

yawning black with feeble glimmers marking the arches of the different staircases.

The sense of life's continuity depended on trifling bodily impressions. The trivialities of daily existence were an armour for the soul. And this thought reinforced the inward quietness of Razumov as he began to climb the stairs familiar to his feet in the dark, with his hand on the familiar clammy banister. The exceptional could not prevail against the material contacts which make one day resemble another. To-morrow would be like yesterday.

It was only on the stage that the unusual was outwardly acknowledged.

"I suppose," thought Razumov, "that if I had made up my mind to blow out my brains on the landing I would be going up these stairs as quietly as I am doing it now. What's a man to do? What must be must be. Extraordinary things do happen. But when they have happened they are done with. Thus, too, when the mind is made up. That question is done with. And the daily concerns, the familiarities of our thought swallow it up—and the life goes on as before with its mysterious and secret sides quite out of sight, as they should be. Life is a public thing."

Razumov unlocked his door and took the key out; entered very quietly and bolted the door behind him carefully.

He thought, "He hears me," and after bolting the door he stood still holding his breath. There was not a sound. He crossed the bare outer room, stepping deliberately in the darkness. Entering the other, he felt all over his table for the matchbox. The silence, but for the groping of his hand, was profound. Could the fellow be sleeping so soundly?

He struck a light and looked at the bed. Haldin was lying on his back as before, only both his hands were under his head. His eyes were open. He stared at the ceiling.

Razumov held the match up. He saw the clear-cut features, the firm chin, the white forehead and the topknot of fair hair against the white pillow. There he was, lying flat on his back. Razumov thought suddenly, "I have walked over his chest."   *(or if he is dead)*

He continued to stare till the match burnt itself out; then struck another and lit the lamp in silence without looking towards the bed any more. He had turned his back on it and was hanging his coat on a peg when he heard Haldin sigh profoundly, then ask in a tired voice—

"Well! And what have you arranged?"

The emotion was so great that Razumov was glad to put his hands against the wall. A diabolical impulse to say, "I have given you up to the police," frightened him exceedingly. But he did not say that. He said, without turning round, in a muffled voice—

"It's done."

Again he heard Haldin sigh. He walked to the table, sat down with the lamp before him, and only then looked towards the bed.

In the distant corner of the large room far away from the lamp, which was small and provided with a very thick china shade, Haldin appeared like a dark and elongated shape—rigid with the immobility of death. This body seemed to have less substance than its own phantom walked over by Razumov in the street white with snow. It was more alarming in its shadowy, persistent reality than the distinct but vanishing illusion.

Haldin was heard again.

"You must have had a walk—such a walk . . ." he murmured deprecatingly. "This weather . . ."

Razumov answered with energy—

"Horrible walk. . . . A nightmare of a walk."

He shuddered audibly. Haldin sighed once more, then—

"And so you have seen Ziemianitch—brother?"

"I've seen him."

Razumov, remembering the time he had spent with the Prince, thought it prudent to add, "I had to wait some time."

"A character—eh? It's extraordinary what a sense of the necessity of freedom there is in that man. And he has sayings too—simple, to the point, such as only the people can invent in their rough sagacity. A character that . . ."

"I, you understand, haven't had much opportunity . . ." Razumov muttered through his teeth.

Haldin continued to stare at the ceiling.

"You see, brother, I had been a good deal in that house of late. I used to take there books—leaflets. Not a few of the poor people who live there can read. And, you see, the guests for the feast of freedom must be sought for in by-ways and hedges. The truth is, I have almost lived in that house of late. I slept sometimes in the stable. There is a stable . . ."

"That's where I had my interview with Ziemianitch," interrupted Razumov gently. A mocking spirit entered into him and he added, "It was satisfactory in a sense, I came away from it much relieved."

"Ah! he's a fellow," went on Haldin, talking slowly at the ceiling. "I came to know him in that way, you see. For some weeks now, ever since I resigned myself to do what had to be done, I tried to isolate myself. I gave up my rooms. What was the good of exposing a decent widow woman to the risk of being worried out of her mind by the police? I gave up seeing any of our comrades . . ."

Razumov drew to himself a half-sheet of paper and began to trace lines on it with a pencil.

"Upon my word," he thought angrily, "he seems to have thought of everybody's safety but mine."

Haldin was talking on.

"This morning—ah! this morning—that was different. How can I explain to you? Before the deed was done I wandered at night and lay hid in the day, thinking it out, and I felt restful. Sleepless but restful. What was there for me to torment myself about? But this morning—after! Then it was that I became restless. I could not have stopped in that big house full of misery. The miserable of this world can't give you peace. Then when that silly caretaker began to shout, I said to myself, 'There is a young man in this town head and shoulders above common prejudices.'"

"Is he laughing at me?" [Razumov asked himself, going on with his aimless drawing of triangles and squares.] And suddenly he thought: "My behaviour must appear to him strange. Should he take fright at my manner and rush off somewhere I shall be undone completely. That infernal General . . ."

He dropped the pencil and turned abruptly towards the bed with the shadowy figure extended full length on it—so much more indistinct than the one over whose breast he had walked without faltering. Was this, too, a phantom?

The silence had lasted a long time. "He is no longer here," was the thought against which Razumov struggled desperately, quite frightened at its absurdity. "He is already gone and this . . . only . . ."

He could resist no longer. He sprang to his feet, saying aloud, "I am intolerably anxious," and in a few headlong strides stood by the side of the bed. His hand fell lightly on Haldin's shoulder, and directly he felt its reality he was beset by an insane temptation to grip that exposed throat and squeeze the breath out of that body, lest it should escape his custody, leaving only a phantom behind.

Haldin did not stir a limb, but his overshadowed eyes moving a little gazed upwards at Razumov with wistful gratitude for this manifestation of feeling.

Razumov turned away and strode up and down the room. "It would have been possibly a kindness," he muttered to himself, and was appalled by the nature of that apology for a murderous intention his mind had found somewhere within him. And all the same he could not give it up. He became lucid about it. "What can he expect?" he thought. "The halter—in the end. And I . . ."

This argument was interrupted by Haldin's voice.

"Why be anxious for me? They can kill my body, but they cannot exile my soul from this world. I tell you what —[I believe in this world so much that I cannot conceive eternity otherwise than as a very long life.] That is perhaps the reason I am so ready to die."

"H'm," muttered Razumov, and biting his lower lip he

continued to walk up and down and to carry on his strange argument.

Yes, to a man in such a situation—of course it would be an act of kindness. The question, however, was not how to be kind, but how to be firm. He was a slippery customer . . .

"I too, Victor Victorovitch, believe in this world of ours," he said with force. "I too, while I live. . . . But you seem determined to haunt it. You can't seriously mean . . ."

The voice of the motionless Haldin began—

"Haunt it! Truly, the oppressors of thought which quickens the world, the destroyers of souls which aspire to perfection of human dignity, they shall be haunted. As to the destroyers of my mere body, I have forgiven them beforehand."

Razumov had stopped apparently to listen, but at the same time he was observing his own sensations. He was vexed with himself for attaching so much importance to what Haldin said.

"The fellow's mad," he thought firmly, but this opinion did not mollify him towards Haldin. It was a particularly impudent form of lunacy—and when it got loose in the sphere of public life of a country, it was obviously the duty of every good citizen . . .

This train of thought broke off short there and was succeeded by a paroxysm of silent hatred towards Haldin, so intense that Razumov hastened to speak at random.

"Yes. Eternity, of course. I, too, can't very well represent it to myself. . . . I imagine it, however, as something quiet and dull. There would be nothing unexpected—don't you see? The element of time would be wanting."

He pulled out his watch and gazed at it. Haldin turned over on his side and looked on intently.

Razumov got frightened at this movement. A slippery customer this fellow with a phantom. It was not midnight yet. He hastened on—

"And unfathomable mysteries! Can you conceive secret places in Eternity? Impossible. Whereas life is full of

them. There are secrets of birth, for instance. One carries
them on to the grave. There is something comical . . . but
never mind. And there are secret motives of conduct. A
man's most open actions have a secret side to them. That
is interesting and so unfathomable! For instance, a man
goes out of a room for a walk. Nothing more trivial in appearance. And yet it may be momentous. He comes back—
he has seen perhaps a drunken brute, taken particular
notice of the snow on the ground—and behold he is no
longer the same man. The most unlikely things have a secret power over one's thoughts—the grey whiskers of a
particular person—the goggle eyes of another."

Razumov's forehead was moist. He took a turn or two
in the room, his head low and smiling to himself viciously,

"Have you ever reflected on the power of goggle eyes
and grey whiskers? Excuse me. You seem to think I must
be crazy to talk in this vein at such a time. But I am not
talking lightly. I have seen instances. It has happened to
me once to be talking to a man whose fate was affected
by physical facts of that kind. And the man did not know
it. Of course, it was a case of conscience, but the material
facts such as these brought about the solution. . . . And
you tell me, Victor Victorovitch, not to be anxious! Why!
I am responsible for you," Razumov almost shrieked.

He avoided with difficulty a burst of Mephistophelian
laughter. Haldin, very pale, raised himself on his elbow.

"And the surprises of life," went on Razumov, after
glancing at the other uneasily. "Just consider their astonishing nature. A mysterious impulse induces you to come
here. I don't say you have done wrong. Indeed, from a
certain point of view you could not have done better. You
might have gone to a man with affections and family ties.
You have such ties yourself. As to me, you know I have
been brought up in an educational institute where they
did not give us enough to eat. To talk of affection in such
a connexion—you perceive yourself. . . . As to ties, the
only ties I have in the world are social. I must get acknowledged in some way before I can act at all. I sit here
working. . . . And don't you think I am working for

progress too? I've got to find my own ideas of the true way. . . . Pardon me," continued Razumov, after drawing breath and with a short, throaty laugh, "but I haven't inherited a revolutionary inspiration together with a resemblance from an uncle."

He looked again at his watch and noticed with sickening disgust that there were yet a good many minutes to midnight. He tore watch and chain off his waistcoat and laid them on the table well in the circle of bright lamplight. Haldin, reclining on his elbow, did not stir. Razumov was made uneasy by this attitude. "What move is he meditating over so quietly?" he thought. "He must be prevented. I must keep on talking to him."

He raised his voice.

"You are a son, a brother, a nephew, a cousin—I don't know what—to no end of people. I am just a man. Here I stand before you. A man with a mind. Did it ever occur to you how a man who had never heard a word of warm affection or praise in his life would think on matters on which you would think first with or against your class, your domestic tradition—your fireside prejudices? . . . Did you ever consider how a man like that would feel? I have no domestic tradition. I have nothing to think against. My tradition is historical. What have I to look back to but that national past from which you gentlemen want to wrench away your future? Am I to let my intelligence, my aspirations towards a better lot, be robbed of the only thing it has to go upon at the will of violent enthusiasts? You come from your province, but all this land is mine— or I have nothing. No doubt you shall be looked upon as a martyr some day—a sort of hero—a political saint. But I beg to be excused. I am content in fitting myself to be a worker. And what can you people do by scattering a few drops of blood on the snow? On this Immensity. On this unhappy Immensity! I tell you," he cried, in a vibrating, subdued voice, and advancing one step nearer the bed, "that what it needs is not a lot of haunting phantoms that I could walk through—but a man!"

Haldin threw his arms forward as if to keep him off in horror.

"I understand it all now," he exclaimed, with awe-struck dismay. "I understand—at last."

Razumov staggered back against the table. His forehead broke out in perspiration while a cold shudder ran down his spine.

"What have I been saying?" he asked himself. "Have I let him slip through my fingers after all?"

He felt his lips go stiff like buckram, and instead of a reassuring smile only achieved an uncertain grimace.

"What will you have?" he began in a conciliating voice which got steady after the first trembling word or two. "What will you have? Consider—a man of studious, retired habits—and suddenly like this. . . . I am not practised in talking delicately. But . . ."

He felt anger, a wicked anger, get hold of him again.

"What were we to do together till midnight? Sit here opposite each other and think of your—your—shambles?"

Haldin had a subdued, heartbroken attitude. He bowed his head; his hands hung between his knees. His voice was low and pained but calm.

"I see now how it is, Razumov—brother. You are a magnanimous soul, but my action is abhorrent to you—alas . . ."

Razumov stared. From fright he had set his teeth so hard that his whole face ached. It was impossible for him to make a sound.

"And even my person, too, is loathsome to you perhaps," Haldin added mournfully, after a short pause, looking up for a moment, then fixing his gaze on the floor. "For indeed, unless one . . ."

He broke off, evidently waiting for a word. Razumov remained silent. Haldin nodded his head dejectedly twice.

"Of course. Of course," he murmured. . . . "Ah!—weary work!"

He remained perfectly still for a moment, then made Razumov's leaden heart strike a ponderous blow by springing up briskly.

"So be it," he cried sadly in a low, distinct tone. "Farewell then."

Razumov started forward, but the sight of Haldin's raised hand checked him before he could get away from the table. He leaned on it heavily, listening to the faint sounds of some town clock tolling the hour. Haldin, already at the door, tall and straight as an arrow, with his pale face and a hand raised attentively, might have posed for the statue of a daring youth listening to an inner voice. Razumov mechanically glanced down at his watch. When he looked towards the door again Haldin had vanished. There was a faint rustling in the outer room, the feeble click of a bolt drawn back lightly. He was gone—almost as noiseless as a vision.

Razumov ran forward unsteadily, with parted, voiceless lips. The outer door stood open. Staggering out on the landing, he leaned far over the banister. Gazing down into the deep black shaft with a tiny glimmering flame at the bottom, he traced by ear the rapid spiral descent of somebody running down the stairs on tiptoe. It was a light, swift, pattering sound, which sank away from him into the depths: a fleeting shadow passed over the glimmer—a wink of the tiny flame. Then stillness.

Razumov hung over, breathing the cold raw air tainted by the evil smells of the unclean staircase. All quiet.

He went back into his room slowly, shutting the doors after him. The peaceful steady light of his reading-lamp shone on the watch. Razumov stood looking down at the little white dial. It wanted yet three minutes to midnight. He took the watch into his hand fumblingly.

"Slow," he muttered, and a strange fit of nervelessness came over him. His knees shook, the watch and chain slipped through his fingers in an instant and fell on the floor. He was so startled that he nearly fell himself. When at last he regained enough confidence in his limbs to stoop for it he held it to his ear at once. After a while he growled—

"Stopped," and paused for quite a long time before he muttered sourly—

"It's done. . . . And now to work."

He sat down, reached haphazard for a book, opened it in the middle and began to read; but after going conscientiously over two lines he lost his hold on the print completely and did not try to regain it. He thought—

"There was to a certainty a police agent of some sort watching the house across the street."

He imagined him lurking in a dark gateway, goggle-eyed, muffled up in a cloak to the nose and with a General's plumed, cocked hat on his head. This absurdity made him start in the chair convulsively. He literally had to shake his head violently to get rid of it. The man would be disguised perhaps as a peasant . . . a beggar. . . . Perhaps he would be just buttoned up in a dark overcoat and carrying a loaded stick—a shifty-eyed rascal, smelling of raw onions and spirits.

This evocation brought on positive nausea. "Why do I want to bother about this?" thought Razumov with disgust. "Am I a gendarme? Moreover, it is done."

He got up in great agitation. It was not done. Not yet. Not till half-past twelve. And the watch had stopped. This reduced him to despair. Impossible to know the time! The landlady and all the people across the landing were asleep. How could he go and . . . God knows what they would imagine, or how much they would guess. He dared not go into the streets to find out. "I am a suspect now. There's no use shirking that fact," he said to himself bitterly. If Haldin from some cause or another gave them the slip and failed to turn up in the Karabelnaya the police would be invading his lodging. And if he were not in he could never clear himself. Never. Razumov looked wildly about as if for some means of seizing upon time which seemed to have escaped him altogether. He had never, as far as he could remember, heard the striking of that town clock in his rooms before this night. And he was not even sure now whether he had heard it really on this night.

He went to the window and stood there with slightly bent head on the watch for the faint sound. "I will stay here till I hear something," he said to himself. He stood still, his ear turned to the panes. An atrocious aching numbness with shooting pains in his back and legs tortured him. He did not budge. His mind hovered on the borders of delirium. He heard himself suddenly saying, "I confess," as a person might do on the rack. "I am on the rack," he thought. He felt ready to swoon. The faint deep boom of the distant clock seemed to explode in his head— he heard it so clearly. . . . One!

If Haldin had not turned up the police would have been already here ransacking the house. No sound reached him. This time it was done.

He dragged himself painfully to the table and dropped into the chair. He flung the book away and took a square sheet of paper. It was like the pile of sheets covered with his neat minute handwriting, only blank. He took a pen brusquely and dipped it with a vague notion of going on with the writing of his essay—but his pen remained poised over the sheet. It hung there for some time before it came down and formed long scrawly letters.

Still-faced and his lips set hard, Razumov began to write. When he wrote a large hand his neat writing lost its character altogether—became unsteady, almost childish. He wrote five lines one under the other.

> History not Theory.
> Patriotism not Internationalism.
> Evolution not Revolution.
> Direction not Destruction.
> Unity not Disruption.

He gazed at them dully. Then his eyes strayed to the bed and remained fixed there for a good many minutes, while his right hand groped all over the table for the penknife.

He rose at last, and walking up with measured steps stabbed the paper with the penknife to the lath and plaster wall at the head of the bed. This done he stepped back a pace and flourished his hand with a glance round the room.

After that he never looked again at the bed. He took

his big cloak down from its peg and, wrapping himself
up closely, went to lie down on the hard horse-hair sofa at
the other side of his room. A leaden sleep closed his eyelids at once. Several times that night he woke up shivering
from a dream of walking through drifts of snow in a Russia where he was as completely alone as any betrayed
autocrat could be; an immense, wintry Russia which,
somehow, his view could embrace in all its enormous ex-
panse as if it were a map. But after each shuddering start
his heavy eyelids fell over his glazed eyes and he slept
again.

III

Approaching this part of Mr. Razumov's story, my mind,
the decent mind of an old teacher of languages, feels more
and more the difficulty of the task.

The task is not in truth the writing in the narrative form
a précis of a strange human document, but the rendering
—I perceive it now clearly—of the moral conditions ruling
over a large portion of this earth's surface; conditions not
easily to be understood, much less discovered in the limits
of a story, till some key-word is found; a word that could
stand at the back of all the words covering the pages, a
word which, if not truth itself, may perchance hold truth
enough to help the moral discovery which should be the
object of every tale.

I turn over for the hundredth time the leaves of Mr.
Razumov's record, I lay it aside, I take up the pen—and
the pen being ready for its office of setting down black on
white I hesitate. For the word that persists in creeping
under its point is no other word than "cynicism."

For that is the mark of Russian autocracy and of Russian revolt. In its pride of numbers, in its strange pretensions of sanctity, and in the secret readiness to abase itself
in suffering, the spirit of Russia is the spirit of cynicism. It
informs the declarations of her statesmen, the theories of
her revolutionists, and the mystic vaticinations of prophets
to the point of making freedom look like a form of de-

bauch, and the Christian virtues themselves appear actually indecent. . . . But I must apologize for the digression. It proceeds from the consideration of the course taken by the story of Mr. Razumov after his conservative convictions, diluted in a vague liberalism natural to the ardour of his age, had become crystallized by the shock of his contact with Haldin.

Razumov woke up for the tenth time perhaps with a heavy shiver. Seeing the light of day in his window, he resisted the inclination to lay himself down again. He did not remember anything, but he did not think it strange to find himself on the sofa in his cloak and chilled to the bone. The light coming through the window seemed strangely cheerless, containing no promise as the light of each new day should for a young man. It was the awakening of a man mortally ill, or of a man ninety years old. He looked at the lamp which had burnt itself out. It stood there, the extinguished beacon of his labours, a cold object of brass and porcelain, amongst the scattered pages of his notes and small piles of books—a mere litter of blackened paper—dead matter—without significance or interest.

He got on his feet, and divesting himself of his cloak hung it on the peg, going through all the motions mechanically. An incredible dullness, a ditch-water stagnation was sensible to his perceptions as though life had withdrawn itself from all things and even from his own thoughts. There was not a sound in the house.

Turning away from the peg, he thought in that same lifeless manner that it must be very early yet; but when he looked at the watch on his table he saw both hands arrested at twelve o'clock.

"Ah! yes," he mumbled to himself, and as if beginning to get roused a little he took a survey of his room. The paper stabbed to the wall arrested his attention. He eyed it from the distance without approval or perplexity; but when he heard the servant-girl beginning to bustle about in the outer room with the *samovar* for his morning tea, he walked up to it and took it down with an air of profound indifference.

While doing this he glanced down at the bed on which he had not slept that night. The hollow in the pillow made by the weight of Haldin's head was very noticeable.

Even his anger at this sign of the man's passage was dull. He did not try to nurse it into life. He did nothing all that day; he neglected even to brush his hair. The idea of going out never occurred to him—and if he did not start a connected train of thought it was not because he was unable to think. It was because he was not interested enough.

He yawned frequently. He drank large quantities of tea, he walked about aimlessly, and when he sat down he did not budge for a long time. He spent some time drumming on the window with his finger-tips quietly. In his listless wanderings round about the table he caught sight of his own face in the looking-glass and that arrested him. The eyes which returned his stare were the most unhappy eyes he had ever seen. And this was the first thing which disturbed the mental stagnation of that day.

He was not affected personally. He merely thought that life without happiness is impossible. What was happiness? He yawned and went on shuffling about and about between the walls of his room. Looking forward was happiness—that's all—nothing more. To look forward to the gratification of some desire, to the gratification of some passion, love, ambition, hate—hate too indubitably. Love and hate. And to escape the dangers of existence, to live without fear, was also happiness. There was nothing else. Absence of fear—looking forward. "Oh! the miserable lot of humanity!" he exclaimed mentally; and added at once in his thought, "I ought to be happy enough as far as that goes." But he was not excited by that assurance. On the contrary, he yawned again as he had been yawning all day. He was mildly surprised to discover himself being overtaken by night. The room grew dark swiftly though time had seemed to stand still. How was it that he had not noticed the passing of that day? Of course, it was the watch being stopped. . . .

He did not light his lamp, but went over to the bed and

threw himself on it without any hesitation. Lying on his
back, he put his hands under his head and stared upward.
After a moment he thought, "I am lying here like that man.
I wonder if he slept while I was struggling with the blizzard in the streets. No, he did not sleep. But why should I
not sleep?" and he felt the silence of the night press upon
all his limbs like a weight.

In the calm of the hard frost outside, the clear-cut
strokes of the town clock counting off midnight penetrated
the quietness of his suspended animation.

Again he began to think. It was twenty-four hours since
that man left his room. Razumov had a distinct feeling that
Haldin in the fortress was sleeping that night. It was a
certitude which made him angry because he did not want
to think of Haldin, but he justified it to himself by physio-
logical and psychological reasons. The fellow had hardly
slept for weeks on his own confession, and now every incertitude was at an end for him. No doubt he was looking
forward to the consummation of his martyrdom. A man
who resigns himself to kill need not go very far for resignation to die. Haldin slept perhaps more soundly than General T——, whose task—weary work too—was not done,
and over whose head hung the sword of revolutionary
vengeance.

Razumov, remembering the thick-set man with his
heavy jowl resting on the collar of his uniform, the cham-
pion of autocracy, who had let no sign of surprise, incredulity, or joy escape him, but whose goggle eyes could
express a mortal hatred of all rebellion—Razumov moved
uneasily on the bed.

"He suspected me," he thought. "I suppose he must
suspect everybody. He would be capable of suspecting his
own wife, if Haldin had gone to her boudoir with his confession."

Razumov sat up in anguish. Was he to remain a
political suspect all his days? Was he to go through life
as a man not wholly to be trusted—with a bad secret police
note tacked on to his record? What sort of future could he
look forward to?

"I am now a suspect," he thought again; but the habit of reflection and that desire of safety, of an ordered life, which was so strong in him came to his assistance as the night wore on. His quiet, steady, and laborious existence would vouch at length for his loyalty. There were many permitted ways to serve one's country. There was an activity that made for progress without being revolutionary. The field of influence was great and infinitely varied—once one had conquered a name.

His thought like a circling bird reverted after four-and-twenty hours to the silver medal, and as it were poised itself there.

When the day broke he had not slept, not for a moment, but he got up not very tired and quite sufficiently self-possessed for all practical purposes.

He went out and attended three lectures in the morning. But the work in the library was a mere dumb show of research. He sat with many volumes open before him trying to make notes and extracts. His new tranquillity was like a flimsy garment, and seemed to float at the mercy of a casual word. Betrayal! Why! the fellow had done all that was necessary to betray himself. Precious little had been needed to deceive him.

"I have said no word to him that was not strictly true. Not one word," Razumov argued with himself.

Once engaged on this line of thought there could be no question of doing useful work. The same ideas went on passing through his mind, and he pronounced mentally the same words over and over again. He shut up all the books and rammed all his papers into his pocket with convulsive movements, raging inwardly against Haldin.

As he was leaving the library a long bony student in a threadbare overcoat joined him, stepping moodily by his side. Razumov answered his mumbled greeting without looking at him at all.

"What does he want with me?" he thought with a strange dread of the unexpected which he tried to shake off lest it should fasten itself upon his life for good and all. And the other, muttering cautiously with downcast

eyes, supposed that his comrade had seen the news of de
P——'s executioner—that was the expression he used—having been arrested the night before last. . . .

"I've been ill—shut up in my rooms," Razumov mumbled through his teeth.

The tall student, raising his shoulders, shoved his hands
deep into his pockets. He had a hairless, square, tallowy
chin which trembled slightly as he spoke, and his nose
nipped bright red by the sharp air looked like a false nose
of painted cardboard between the sallow cheeks. His whole
appearance was stamped with the mark of cold and hunger. He stalked deliberately at Razumov's elbow with his
eyes on the ground.

"It's an official statement," he continued in the same
cautious mutter. "It may be a lie. But there was somebody
arrested between midnight and one in the morning on
Tuesday. This is certain."

And talking rapidly under the cover of his downcast
air, he told Razumov that this was known through an inferior Government clerk employed at the Central Secretariat. That man belonged to one of the revolutionary
circles. "The same, in fact, I am affiliated to," remarked
the student.

They were crossing a wide quadrangle. An infinite distress possessed Razumov, annihilated his energy, and before his eyes everything appeared confused and as if evanescent. He dared not leave the fellow there. "He may be
affiliated to the police," was the thought that passed
through his mind. "Who could tell?" But eyeing the miserable frost-nipped, famine-struck figure of his companion
he perceived the absurdity of his suspicion.

"But I—you know—I don't belong to any circle. I . . ."

He dared not say any more. Neither dared he mend
his pace. The other, raising and setting down his lamentably shod feet with exact deliberation, protested in a low
tone that it was not necessary for everybody to belong to
an organization. The most valuable personalities remained
outside. Some of the best work was done outside the organization. Then very fast, with whispering, feverish lips—

"The man arrested in the street was Haldin."

And accepting Razumov's dismayed silence as natural enough, he assured him that there was no mistake. That Government clerk was on night duty at the Secretariat. Hearing a great noise of footsteps in the hall and aware that political prisoners were brought over sometimes at night from the fortress, he opened the door of the room in which he was working, suddenly. Before the gendarme on duty could push him back and slam the door in his face, he had seen a prisoner being partly carried, partly dragged along the hall by a lot of policemen. He was being used very brutally. And the clerk had recognized Haldin perfectly. Less than half an hour afterwards General T—— arrived at the Secretariat to examine that prisoner personally.

"Aren't you astonished?" concluded the gaunt student.

"No," said Razumov roughly—and at once regretted his answer.

"Everybody supposed Haldin was in the provinces—with his people. Didn't you?"

The student turned his big hollow eyes upon Razumov, who said unguardedly—

"His people are abroad."

He could have bitten his tongue out with vexation. The student pronounced in a tone of profound meaning—

"So! You alone were aware . . ." and stopped.

"They have sworn my ruin," thought Razumov. "Have you spoken of this to any one else?" he asked with bitter curiosity.

The other shook his head.

"No, only to you. Our circle thought that as Haldin had been often heard expressing a warm appreciation of your character . . ."

Razumov could not restrain a gesture of angry despair which the other must have misunderstood in some way, because he ceased speaking and turned away his black, lack-lustre eyes.

They moved side by side in silence. Then the gaunt student began to whisper again, with averted gaze—

"As we have at present no one affiliated inside the fortress so as to make it possible to furnish him with a packet of poison, we have considered already some sort of retaliatory action—to follow very soon . . ."

Razumov trudging on interrupted—

"Were you acquainted with Haldin? Did he know where you live?"

"I had the happiness to hear him speak twice," his companion answered in the feverish whisper contrasting with the gloomy apathy of his face and bearing. "He did not know where I live. . . . I am lodging poorly . . . with an artisan family. . . . I have just a corner in a room. It is not very practicable to see me there but if you should need me for anything I am ready. . . ."

Razumov trembled with rage and fear. He was beside himself, but kept his voice low.

"You are not to come near me. You are not to speak to me. Never address a single word to me. I forbid you."

"Very well," said the other submissively, showing no surprise whatever at this abrupt prohibition. "You don't wish for secret reasons . . . perfectly . . . I understand."

He edged away at once, not looking up even; and Razumov saw his gaunt, shabby, famine-stricken figure cross the street obliquely with lowered head and that peculiar exact motion of the feet.

He watched him as one would watch a vision out of a nightmare, then he continued on his way, trying not to think. On his landing the landlady seemed to be waiting for him. She was a short, thick, shapeless woman with a large yellow face wrapped up everlastingly in a black woollen shawl. When she saw him come up the last flight of stairs she flung both her arms up excitedly, then clasped her hands before her face.

"Kirylo Sidorovitch—little father—what have you been doing? And such a quiet young man, too! The police are just gone this moment after searching your rooms."

Razumov gazed down at her with silent, scrutinizing attention. Her puffy yellow countenance was working with emotion. She screwed up her eyes at him entreatingly.

"Such a sensible young man! Anybody can see you are

sensible. And now—like this—all at once. . . . What is the good of mixing yourself up with these Nihilists? Do give over, little father. They are unlucky people."

Razumov moved his shoulders slightly.

"Or is it that some secret enemy has been calumniating you, Kirylo Sidorovitch? The world is full of black hearts and false denunciations nowadays. There is much fear about."

"Have you heard that I have been denounced by someone?" asked Razumov, without taking his eyes off her quivering face.

But she had not heard anything. She had tried to find out by asking the police captain while his men were turning the room upside down. The police captain of the district had known her for the last eleven years and was a humane person. But he said to her on the landing looking very black and vexed—

"My good woman, do not ask questions. I don't know anything myself. The order comes from higher quarters."

And indeed there had appeared, shortly after the arrival of the policemen of the district, a very superior gentleman in a fur coat and a shiny hat, who sat down in the room and looked through all the papers himself. He came alone and went away by himself, taking nothing with him. She had been trying to put things straight a little since they left.

Razumov turned away brusquely and entered his rooms.

All his books had been shaken and thrown on the floor. His landlady followed him, and stooping painfully began to pick them up into her apron. His papers and notes which were kept always neatly sorted (they all related to his studies) had been shuffled up and heaped together into a ragged pile in the middle of the table.

This disorder affected him profoundly, unreasonably. He sat down and stared. He had a distinct sensation of his very existence being undermined in some mysterious manner, of his moral supports falling away from him one by one. He even experienced a slight physical giddiness and made a movement as if to reach for something to steady himself with.

The old woman, rising to her feet with a low groan, shot all the books she had collected in her apron on to the sofa and left the room muttering and sighing.

It was only then that he noticed that the sheet of paper which for one night had remained stabbed to the wall above his empty bed was lying on top of the pile.

When he had taken it down the day before he had folded it in four, absent-mindedly, before dropping it on the table. And now he saw it lying uppermost, spread out, smoothed out even and covering all the confused pile of pages, the record of his intellectual life for the last three years. It had not been flung there. It had been placed there —smoothed out, too! He guessed in that an intention of profound meaning—or perhaps some inexplicable mockery.

He sat staring at the piece of paper till his eyes began to smart. He did not attempt to put his papers in order, either that evening or the next day—which he spent at home in a state of peculiar irresolution. This irresolution bore upon the question whether he should continue to live—neither more nor less. But its nature was very far removed from the hesitation of a man contemplating suicide. The idea of laying violent hands upon his body did not occur to Razumov. The unrelated organism bearing that label, walking, breathing, wearing these clothes, was of no importance to any one, unless maybe to the landlady. [The true Razumov had his being in the willed, in the determined future—in that future menaced by the lawlessness of autocracy—for autocracy knows no law—and the lawlessness of revolution. The feeling that his moral personality was at the mercy of these lawless forces was so strong that he asked himself seriously if it were worth while to go on accomplishing the mental functions of that existence which seemed no longer his own.]

"What is the good of exerting my intelligence, of pursuing the systematic development of my faculties and all my plans of work?" he asked himself. "I want to guide my conduct by reasonable convictions, but what security have

I against something—some destructive horror—walking in
upon me as I sit here? . . ."

Razumov looked apprehensively towards the door of the
outer room as if expecting some shape of evil to turn the
handle and appear before him silently.

"A common thief," he said to himself, "finds more guar-
antees in the law he is breaking, and even a brute like
Ziemianitch has his consolation." Razumov envied the ma-
terialism of the thief and the passion of the incorrigible
lover. The consequences of their actions were always clear
and their lives remained their own.

But he slept as soundly that night as though he had
been consoling himself in the manner of Ziemianitch. He
dropped off suddenly, lay like a log, remembered no dream
on waking. But it was as if his soul had gone out in the
night to gather the flowers of wrathful wisdom. He got up
in a mood of grim determination and as if with a new
knowledge of his own nature. He looked mockingly on the
heap of papers on his table; and left his room to attend
the lectures, muttering to himself, "We shall see."

He was in no humour to talk to anybody or hear himself questioned as to his absence from lectures the day before. But it was difficult to repulse rudely a very good
comrade with a smooth pink face and fair hair, bearing
the nickname amongst his fellow-students of "Madcap
Kostia." He was the idolized only son of a very wealthy
and illiterate Government contractor, and attended the
lectures only during the periodical fits of contrition following upon tearful paternal remonstrances. Noisily blundering like a retriever puppy, his elated voice and great
gestures filled the bare academy corridors with the joy of
thoughtless animal life, provoking indulgent smiles at a
great distance. His usual discourses treated of trotting
horses, wine-parties in expensive restaurants, and the
merits of persons of easy virtue, with a disarming artlessness of outlook. He pounced upon Razumov about midday,
somewhat less uproariously than his habit was, and led
him aside.

"Just a moment, Kirylo Sidorovitch. A few words here in this quiet corner."

He felt Razumov's reluctance, and insinuated his hand under his arm caressingly.

"No—pray do. I don't want to talk to you about any of my silly scrapes. What are my scrapes? Absolutely nothing. Mere childishness. The other night I flung a fellow out of a certain place where I was having a fairly good time. A tyrannical little beast of a quill-driver from the Treasury department. . . . He was bullying the people of the house. I rebuked him. 'You are not behaving humanely to God's creatures that are a jolly sight more estimable than yourself,' I said. I can't bear to see any tyranny, Kirylo Sidorovitch. Upon my word I can't. He didn't take it in good part at all. 'Who's that impudent puppy?' he begins to shout. I was in excellent form as it happened, and he went through the closed window very suddenly. He flew quite a long way into the yard. I raged like—like a—minotaur. The women clung to me and screamed, the fiddlers got under the table. . . . Such fun! My dad had to put his hand pretty deep into his pocket, I can tell you."

He chuckled.

"My dad is a very useful man. Jolly good thing it is for me, too. I do get into unholy scrapes."

His elation fell. That was just it. What was his life? Insignificant; no good to any one; a mere festivity. It would end some fine day in his getting his skull split with a champagne bottle in a drunken brawl. At such times, too, when men were sacrificing themselves to ideas. But he could never get any ideas into his head. His head wasn't worth anything better than to be split by a champagne bottle.

Razumov, protesting that he had no time, made an attempt to get away. The other's tone changed to confidential earnestness.

"For God's sake, Kirylo, my dear soul, let me make some sort of sacrifice. It would not be a sacrifice really. I have my rich dad behind me. There's positively no getting to the bottom of his pocket."

And rejecting indignantly Razumov's suggestion that this

was drunken raving, he offered to lend him some money to escape abroad with. He could always get money from his dad. He had only to say that he had lost it at cards or something of that sort, and at the same time promise solemnly not to miss a single lecture for three months on end. That would fetch the old man; and he, Kostia, was quite equal to the sacrifice. Though he really did not see what was the good for him to attend the lectures. It was perfectly hopeless.

"Won't you let me be of some use?" he pleaded to the silent Razumov, who with his eyes on the ground and utterly unable to penetrate the real drift of the other's intention, felt a strange reluctance to clear up the point.

"What makes you think I want to go abroad?" he asked at last very quietly.

Kostia lowered his voice.

"You had the police in your rooms yesterday. There are three or four of us who have heard of that. Never mind how we know. It is sufficient that we do. So we have been consulting together."

"Ah! You got to know that so soon," muttered Razumov negligently.

"Yes. We did. And it struck us that a man like you . . ."

"What sort of a man do you take me to be?" Razumov interrupted him.

"A man of ideas—and a man of action too. But you are very deep, Kirylo. There's no getting to the bottom of your mind. Not for fellows like me. But we all agreed that you must be preserved for our country. Of that we have no doubt whatever—I mean all of us who have heard Haldin speak of you on certain occasions. A man doesn't get the police ransacking his rooms without there being some devilry hanging over his head. . . . And so if you think that it would be better for you to bolt at once . . ."

Razumov tore himself away and walked down the corridor, leaving the other motionless with his mouth open. But almost at once he returned and stood before the amazed Kostia, who shut his mouth slowly. Razumov looked him straight in the eyes, before saying with marked deliberation and separating his words—

"I thank—you—very—much."

He went away again rapidly. Kostia, recovering from his surprise at these manœuvres, ran up behind him pressingly.

"No! Wait! Listen. I really mean it. It would be like giving your compassion to a starving fellow. Do you hear, Kirylo? And any disguise you may think of, that too I could procure from a costumier, a Jew I know. Let a fool be made serviceable according to his folly. Perhaps also a false beard or something of that kind may be needed."

Razumov turned at bay.

"There are no false beards needed in this business, Kostia—you good-hearted lunatic, you. What do you know of my ideas? My ideas may be poison to you."

The other began to shake his head in energetic protest.

"What have you got to do with ideas? Some of them would make an end of your dad's money-bags. Leave off meddling with what you don't understand. Go back to your trotting horses and your girls, and then you'll be sure at least of doing no harm to anybody, and hardly any to yourself."

The enthusiastic youth was overcome by this disdain.

"You're sending me back to my pig's trough, Kirylo. That settles it. I am an unlucky beast—and I shall die like a beast too. But mind—it's your contempt that has done for me."

Razumov went off with long strides. That this simple and grossly festive soul should have fallen too under the revolutionary curse affected him as an ominous symptom of the time. He reproached himself for feeling troubled. Personally he ought to have felt reassured. There was an obvious advantage in this conspiracy of mistaken judgment taking him for what he was not. But was it not strange?

Again he experienced that sensation of his conduct being taken out of his hands by Haldin's revolutionary tyranny. [His solitary and laborious existence had been destroyed—

the only thing he could call his own on this earth. By what right? he asked himself furiously. In what name?⟩

What infuriated him most was to feel that the "thinkers" of the University were evidently connecting him with Haldin—as a sort of confidant in the background apparently. A mysterious connexion! Ha! ha!

He had been made a personage without knowing anything about it. How that wretch Haldin must have talked about him! Yet it was likely that Haldin had said very little. The fellow's casual utterances were caught up and treasured and pondered over by all these imbeciles. And was not all secret revolutionary action based upon folly, self-deception, and lies?

"Impossible to think of anything else," muttered Razumov to himself. "I'll become an idiot if this goes on. The scoundrels and the fools are murdering my intelligence."

He lost all hope of saving his future, which depended on the free use of his intelligence.

He reached the doorway of his house in a state of mental discouragement which enabled him to receive with apparent indifference an official-looking envelope from the dirty hand of the dvornik.

"A gendarme brought it," said the man. "He asked if you were at home. I told him 'No, he's not at home.' So he left it. 'Give it into his own hands,' says he. Now you've got it—eh?"

He went back to his sweeping, and Razumov climbed his stairs, envelope in hand. Once in his room he did not hasten to open it. Of course this official missive was from the superior direction of the police. A suspect! A suspect!

He stared in dreary astonishment at the absurdity of his position. He thought with a sort of dry, unemotional melancholy; three years of good work gone, the course of forty more perhaps jeopardized—turned from hope to terror, because events started by human folly link themselves into a sequence which no sagacity can foresee and no courage can break through. Fatality enters your rooms while your landlady's back is turned; you come home and find it in possession bearing a man's name, clothed in flesh

—wearing a brown cloth coat and long boots—lounging against the stove. It asks you, "Is the outer door closed?"—and you don't know enough to take it by the throat and fling it downstairs. You don't know. You welcome the crazy fate. "Sit down," you say. And it is all over. You cannot shake it off any more. It will cling to you for ever. Neither halter nor bullet can give you back the freedom of your life and the sanity of your thought. . . . It was enough to make one dash one's head against a wall.

Razumov looked slowly all round the walls as if to select a spot to dash his head against. Then he opened the letter. It directed the student Kirylo Sidorovitch Razumov to present himself without delay at the General Secretariat.

Razumov had a vision of General T——'s goggle eyes waiting for him—the embodied power of autocracy, grotesque and terrible. He embodied the whole power of autocracy because he was its guardian. He was the incarnate suspicion, the incarnate anger, the incarnate ruthlessness of a political and social régime on its defence. He loathed rebellion by instinct. And Razumov reflected that the man was simply unable to understand a reasonable adherence to the doctrine of absolutism.

"What can he want with me precisely—I wonder?" he asked himself.

As if that mental question had evoked the familiar phantom, Haldin stood suddenly before him in the room with an extraordinary completeness of detail. Though the short winter day had passed already into the sinister twilight of a land buried in snow, Razumov saw plainly the narrow leather strap round the Tcherkess coat. The illusion of that hateful presence was so perfect that he half expected it to ask, "Is the outer door closed?" He looked at it with hatred and contempt. Souls do not take a shape of clothing. Moreover, Haldin could not be dead yet. Razumov stepped forward menacingly; the vision vanished—and turning short on his heel he walked out of his room with infinite disdain.

But after going down the first flight of stairs it occurred to him that perhaps the superior authorities of police meant to confront him with Haldin in the flesh. This thought struck him like a bullet, and had he not clung with both hands to the banister he would have rolled down to the next landing most likely. His legs were of no use for a considerable time. . . . But why? For what conceivable reason? To what end?

There could be no rational answer to these questions; but Razumov remembered the promise made by the General to Prince K——. His action was to remain unknown.

He got down to the bottom of the stairs, lowering himself as it were from step to step, by the banister. Under the gate he regained much of his firmness of thought and limb. He went out into the street without staggering visibly. Every moment he felt steadier mentally. And yet he was saying to himself that General T—— was perfectly capable of shutting him up in the fortress for an indefinite time. His temperament fitted his remorseless task, and his omnipotence made him inaccessible to reasonable argument.

But when Razumov arrived at the Secretariat he discovered that he would have nothing to do with General T——. It is evident from Mr. Razumov's diary that this dreaded personality was to remain in the background. A civilian of superior rank received him in a private room after a period of waiting in outer offices where a lot of scribbling went on at many tables in a heated and stuffy atmosphere.

The clerk in uniform who conducted him said in the corridor—

"You are going before Gregory Matvieitch Mikulin."

There was nothing formidable about the man bearing that name. His mild, expectant glance was turned on the door already when Razumov entered. At once, with the penholder he was holding in his hand, he pointed to a deep sofa between two windows. He followed Razumov with his eyes while that last crossed the room and sat down. The mild gaze rested on him, not curious, not inquisitive— certainly not suspicious—almost without expression. In its passionless persistence there was something resembling sympathy.

Razumov, who had prepared his will and his intelligence to encounter General T—— himself, was profoundly troubled. All the moral bracing up against the possible excesses of power and passion went for nothing before this sallow man, who wore a full unclipped beard. It was fair, thin, and very fine. The light fell in coppery gleams on the protuberances of a high, rugged forehead. And the aspect of the broad, soft physiognomy was so homely and rustic that the careful middle parting of the hair seemed a pretentious affectation.

The diary of Mr. Razumov testifies to some irritation on his part. I may remark here that the diary proper consisting of the more or less daily entries seems to have been begun on that very evening after Mr. Razumov had returned home.

Mr. Razumov, then, was irritated. His strung-up individuality had gone to pieces within him very suddenly.

"I must be very prudent with him," he warned himself in the silence during which they sat gazing at each other. It lasted some little time, and was characterized (for silences have their character) by a sort of sadness imparted to it perhaps by the mild and thoughtful manner of the bearded official. Razumov learned later that he was the chief of a department in the General Secretariat, with a rank in the civil service equivalent to that of a colonel in the army.

Razumov's mistrust became acute. The main point was, not to be drawn into saying too much. He had been called there for some reason. What reason? To be given to understand that he was a suspect—and also no doubt to be pumped. As to what precisely? There was nothing. Or perhaps Haldin had been telling lies. . . . Every alarming uncertainty beset Razumov. He could bear the silence no longer, and cursing himself for his weakness spoke first, though he had promised himself not to do so on any account.

"I haven't lost a moment's time," he began in a hoarse, provoking tone; and then the faculty of speech seemed to leave him and enter the body of Councillor Mikulin, who chimed in approvingly—

"Very proper. Very proper. Though as a matter of fact . . ."

But the spell was broken, and Razumov interrupted him boldly, under a sudden conviction that this was the safest attitude to take. With a great flow of words he complained of being totally misunderstood. Even as he talked with a perception of his own audacity he thought that the word "misunderstood" was better than the word "mistrusted," and he repeated it again with insistence. Suddenly he ceased, being seized with fright before the attentive immobility of the official. "What am I talking about?" he thought, eyeing him with a vague gaze. Mistrusted—not misunderstood—was the right symbol of these people. Misunderstood was the other kind of curse. Both had been brought on his head by that fellow Haldin. And his head ached terribly. He passed his hand over his brow—an involuntary gesture of suffering, which he was too careless to restrain.

At that moment Razumov beheld his own brain suffering on the rack—a long, pale figure drawn asunder horizontally with terrific force in the darkness of a vault, whose face he failed to see. It was as though he had dreamed for an infinitesimal fraction of time of some dark print of the Inquisition. . . .

It is not to be seriously supposed that Razumov had actually dozed off and had dreamed in the presence of Councillor Mikulin, of an old print of the Inquisition. He was indeed extremely exhausted, and he records a remarkably dream-like experience of anguish at the circumstance that there was no one whatever near the pale and extended figure. The solitude of the racked victim was particularly horrible to behold. The mysterious impossibility to see the face, he also notes, inspired a sort of terror. All these characteristics of an ugly dream were present. Yet he is certain that he never lost the consciousness of himself on the sofa, leaning forward with his hands between his knees and turning his cap round and round in his fingers. But everything vanished at the voice of Councillor Mikulin. Razumov felt profoundly grateful for the even simplicity of its tone.

"Yes. I have listened with interest. I comprehend in a measure your . . . But, indeed, you are mistaken in what you . . ." Councillor Mikulin uttered a series of broken sentences. Instead of finishing them he glanced down his beard. It was a deliberate curtailment which somehow made the phrases more impressive. But he could talk fluently enough as became apparent when changing his tone to persuasiveness he went on: "By listening to you as I did, I think I have proved that I do not regard our intercourse as strictly official. In fact, I don't want it to have that character at all. . . . Oh yes! I admit that the request for your presence here had an official form. But I put it to you whether it was a form which would have been used to secure the attendance of a . . ."

"Suspect," exclaimed Razumov, looking straight into the official's eyes. They were big with heavy eyelids, and met his boldness with a dim, steadfast gaze. "A suspect." The open repetition of that word which had been haunting all his waking hours gave Razumov a strange sort of satisfaction. Councillor Mikulin shook his head slightly. "Surely you do know that I've had my rooms searched by the police?"

"I was about to say a 'misunderstood person,' when you interrupted me," insinuated quietly Councillor Mikulin.

Razumov smiled without bitterness. The renewed sense of his intellectual superiority sustained him in the hour of danger. He said a little disdainfully—

"I know I am but a reed. But I beg you to allow me the superiority of the thinking reed over the unthinking forces that are about to crush him out of existence. Practical thinking in the last instance is but criticism. I may perhaps be allowed to express my wonder at this action of the police being delayed for two full days during which, of course, I could have annihilated everything compromising by burning it—let us say—and getting rid of the very ashes, for that matter."

"You are angry," remarked the official, with an unutterable simplicity of tone and manner. "Is that reasonable?"

Razumov felt himself colouring with annoyance.

"I am reasonable. I am even—permit me to say—a thinker, though to be sure, this name nowadays seems to be the monopoly of hawkers of revolutionary wares, the slaves of some French or German thought—devil knows what foreign notions. But I am not an intellectual mongrel. I think like a Russian. I think faithfully—and I take the liberty to call myself a thinker. It is not a forbidden word, as far as I know."

"No. Why should it be a forbidden word?" Councillor Mikulin turned in his seat with crossed legs and resting his elbow on the table propped his head on the knuckles of a half-closed hand. Razumov noticed a thick forefinger clasped by a massive gold band set with a blood-red stone —a signet ring that, looking as if it could weigh half a pound, was an appropriate ornament for that ponderous man with the accurate middle-parting of glossy hair above a rugged Socratic forehead.

"Could it be a wig?" Razumov detected himself wondering with an unexpected detachment. His self-confidence was much shaken. He resolved to chatter no more. Reserve! Reserve! All he had to do was to keep the Ziemianitch episode secret with absolute determination, when the questions came. Keep Ziemianitch strictly out of all the answers.

Councillor Mikulin looked at him dimly. Razumov's self-confidence abandoned him completely. It seemed impossible to keep Ziemianitch out. Every question would lead to that, because, of course, there was nothing else. He made an effort to brace himself up. It was a failure. But Councillor Mikulin was surprisingly detached too.

"Why should it be forbidden?" he repeated. "I too consider myself a thinking man, I assure you. The principal condition is to think correctly. I admit it is difficult sometimes at first for a young man abandoned to himself—with his generous impulses undisciplined, so to speak—at the

mercy of every wild wind that blows. Religious belief, of
course, is a great . . ."

Councillor Mikulin glanced down his beard, and Razumov, whose tension was relaxed by that unexpected and
discursive turn, murmured with gloomy discontent—

"That man, Haldin, believed in God."

"Ah! You are aware," breathed out Councillor Mikulin,
making the point softly, as if with discretion, but making it
nevertheless plainly enough, as if he too were put off his
guard by Razumov's remark. The young man preserved
an impassive, moody countenance, though he reproached
himself bitterly for a pernicious fool, to have given thus an
utterly false impression of intimacy. He kept his eyes on the
floor. "I must positively hold my tongue unless I am obliged
to speak," he admonished himself. And at once against his
will the question, "Hadn't I better tell him everything?"
presented itself with such force that he had to bite his
lower lip. Councillor Mikulin could not, however, have
nourished any hope of confession. He went on—

"You tell me more than his judges were able to get out
of him. He was judged by a commission of three. He would
tell them absolutely nothing. I have the report of the interrogatories here, by me. After every question there
stands 'Refuses to answer—refuses to answer.' It's like that
page after page. You see, I have been entrusted with some
further investigations around and about this affair. He has
left me nothing to begin my investigations on. A hardened
miscreant. And so, you say, he believed in . . ."

Again Councillor Mikulin glanced down his beard with
a faint grimace; but he did not pause for long. Remarking
with a shade of scorn that blasphemers also had that sort
of belief, he concluded by supposing that Mr. Razumov
had conversed frequently with Haldin on the subject.

"No," said Razumov loudly, without looking up. "He
talked and I listened. That is not a conversation."

"Listening is a great art," observed Mikulin parenthetically.

"And getting people to talk is another," mumbled
Razumov.

"Well, no—that is not very difficult," Mikulin said innocently, "except, of course, in special cases. For instance, this Haldin. Nothing could induce him to talk. He was brought four times before the delegated judges. Four secret interrogatories—and even during the last, when your personality was put forward . . ."

"My personality put forward?" repeated Razumov, raising his head brusquely. "I don't understand."

Councillor Mikulin turned squarely to the table, and taking up some sheets of grey foolscap dropped them one after another, retaining only the last in his hand. He held it before his eyes while speaking.

"It was—you see—judged necessary. In a case of that gravity no means of action upon the culprit should be neglected. You understand that yourself, I am certain."

Razumov stared with enormous wide eyes at the side view of Councillor Mikulin, who now was not looking at him at all.

"So it was decided (I was consulted by General T——) that a certain question should be put to the accused. But in deference to the earnest wishes of Prince K—— your name has been kept out of the documents and even from the very knowledge of the judges themselves. Prince K—— recognized the propriety, the necessity of what we proposed to do, but he was concerned for your safety. Things do leak out—that we can't deny. One cannot always answer for the discretion of inferior officials. There was, of course, the secretary of the special tribunal—one or two gendarmes in the room. Moreover, as I have said, in deference to Prince K—— even the judges themselves were to be left in ignorance. The question ready framed was sent to them by General T—— (I wrote it out with my own hand) with instructions to put it to the prisoner the very last of all. Here it is."

Councillor Mikulin threw back his head into proper focus and went on reading monotonously: "Question—Has the man well known to you, in whose rooms you remained for several hours on Monday and on whose information you have been arrested—has he had any previous knowledge of your intention to commit a political murder? . . . Prisoner refuses to reply.

"Question repeated. Prisoner preserves the same stubborn silence.

"The venerable Chaplain of the Fortress being then admitted and exhorting the prisoner to repentance, entreating him also to atone for his crime by an unreserved and full confession which should help to liberate from the sin of rebellion against the Divine laws and the sacred Majesty of the Ruler of our Christ-loving land—the prisoner opens his lips for the first time during this morning's audience and in a loud, clear voice rejects the venerable Chaplain's ministrations.

"At eleven o'clock the Court pronounces in summary form the death sentence.

"The execution is fixed for four o'clock in the afternoon, subject to further instructions from superior authorities."

Councillor Mikulin dropped the page of foolscap, glanced down his beard, and turning to Razumov, added in an easy, explanatory tone—

"We saw no object in delaying the execution. The order to carry out the sentence was sent by telegraph at noon. I wrote out the telegram myself. He was hanged at four o'clock this afternoon."

The definite information of Haldin's death gave Razumov the feeling of general lassitude which follows a great exertion or a great excitement. He kept very still on the sofa, but a murmur escaped him—

"He had a belief in a future existence."

Councillor Mikulin shrugged his shoulders slightly, and Razumov got up with an effort. There was nothing now to stay for in that room. Haldin had been hanged at four o'clock. There could be no doubt of that. He had, it seemed, entered upon his future existence, long boots, Astrakhan fur cap and all, down to the very leather strap round his waist. A flickering, vanishing sort of existence. It was not his soul, it was his mere phantom he had left behind on this earth—thought Razumov, smiling caustically to himself while he crossed the room, utterly forgetful of where he was and of Councillor Mikulin's existence. The official could have set a lot of bells ringing all over the building without leaving his chair. He let Razumov go quite up to the door before he spoke.

"Come, Kirylo Sidorovitch—what are you doing?"

Razumov turned his head and looked at him in silence. He was not in the least disconcerted. Councillor Mikulin's arms were stretched out on the table before him and his body leaned forward a little with an effort of his dim gaze.

"Was I actually going to clear out like this?" Razumov wondered at himself with an impassive countenance. And he was aware of this impassiveness concealing a lucid astonishment.

"Evidently I was going out if he had not spoken," he thought. "What would he have done then? I must end this affair one way or another. I must make him show his hand."

For a moment longer he reflected behind the mask as it were, then let go the door-handle and came back to the middle of the room.

"I'll tell you what you think," he said explosively, but not raising his voice. "You think that you are dealing with a secret accomplice of that unhappy man. No, I do not know that he was unhappy. He did not tell me. He was a wretch from my point of view, because to keep alive a false idea is a greater crime than to kill a man. I suppose you will not deny that? I hated him! Visionaries work everlasting evil on earth. Their Utopias inspire in the mass of mediocre minds a disgust of reality and a contempt for the secular logic of human development."

Razumov shrugged his shoulders and stared. "What a tirade!" he thought. The silence and immobility of Councillor Mikulin impressed him. The bearded bureaucrat sat at his post, mysteriously self-possessed like an idol with dim, unreadable eyes. Razumov's voice changed involuntarily.

"If you were to ask me where is the necessity of my hate for such as Haldin, I would answer you—there is nothing sentimental in it. I did not hate him because he had com-

mitted the crime of murder. Abhorrence is not hate. I
hated him simply because I am sane. It is in that character
that he outraged me. His death . . ."

Razumov felt his voice growing thick in his throat. The
dimness of Councillor Mikulin's eyes seemed to spread all
over his face and made it indistinct to Razumov's sight.
He tried to disregard these phenomena.

"Indeed," he pursued, pronouncing each word carefully,
"what is his death to me? If he were lying here on the floor
I could walk over his breast. . . . The fellow is a mere
phantom. . . ."

Razumov's voice died out very much against his will.
Mikulin behind the table did not allow himself the slightest movement. The silence lasted for some little time before Razumov could go on again.

"He went about talking of me. . . . Those intellectual
fellows sit in each other's rooms and get drunk on foreign
ideas in the same way young Guards' officers treat each
other with foreign wines. Merest debauchery. . . . Upon
my word,"—Razumov, enraged by a sudden recollection of
Ziemianitch, lowered his voice forcibly,—"upon my word,
we Russians are a drunken lot. Intoxication of some sort we
must have: to get ourselves wild with sorrow or maudlin
with resignation; to lie inert like a log or set fire to the
house. What is a sober man to do, I should like to know?
To cut oneself entirely from one's kind is impossible. To
live in a desert one must be a saint. But if a drunken man
runs out of the grog-shop, falls on your neck and kisses
you on both cheeks because something about your appearance has taken his fancy, what then—kindly tell me? You
may break, perhaps, a cudgel on his back and yet not
succeed in beating him off. . . ."

Councillor Mikulin raised his hand and passed it down
his face deliberately.

"That's . . . of course," he said in an undertone.

The quiet gravity of that gesture made Razumov pause.
It was so unexpected, too. What did it mean? It had an
alarming aloofness. Razumov remembered his intention of
making him show his hand.

"I have said all this to Prince K——," he began with assumed indifference, but lost it on seeing Councillor Mikulin's slow nod of assent. "You know it? You've heard . . . Then why should I be called here to be told of Haldin's execution? Did you want to confront me with his silence now that the man is dead? What is his silence to me? This is incomprehensible. You want in some way to shake my moral balance."

"No. Not that," murmured Councillor Mikulin, just audibly. "The service you have rendered is appreciated . . ."

"Is it?" interrupted Razumov ironically.

". . . and your position too." Councillor Mikulin did not raise his voice. "But only think! You fall into Prince K——'s study as if from the sky with your startling information. . . . You are studying yet, Mr. Razumov, but we are serving already—don't forget that. . . . And naturally some curiosity was bound to . . ."

Councillor Mikulin looked down his beard. Razumov's lips trembled.

"An occurrence of that sort marks a man," the homely murmur went on. "I admit I was curious to see you. General T—— thought it would be useful, too. . . . Don't think I am incapable of understanding your sentiments. When I was young like you I studied . . ."

"Yes—you wished to see me," said Razumov in a tone of profound distaste. "Naturally you have the right—I mean the power. It all amounts to the same thing. But it is perfectly useless, if you were to look at me and listen to me for a year. I begin to think there is something about me which people don't seem able to make out. It's unfortunate. I imagine, however, that Prince K—— understands. He seems to."

Councillor Mikulin moved slightly and spoke.

"Prince K—— is aware of everything that is being done, and I don't mind informing you that he approved my intention of becoming personally acquainted with you."

Razumov concealed an immense disappointment under the accents of railing surprise.

"So he is curious too! . . . Well—after all, Prince K——

knows me very little. It is really very unfortunate for me, but—it is not exactly my fault."

Councillor Mikulin raised a hasty deprecatory hand and inclined his head slightly over his shoulder.

"Now, Mr. Razumov—is it necessary to take it in that way? Everybody I am sure can . . ."

He glanced rapidly down his beard, and when he looked up again there was for a moment an interested expression in his misty gaze. Razumov discouraged it with a cold, repellent smile.

"No. That's of no importance to be sure—except that in respect of all this curiosity being aroused by a very simple matter. . . . What is to be done with it? It is unappeasable. I mean to say there is nothing to appease it with. I happen to have been born a Russian with patriotic instincts —whether inherited or not I am not in a position to say."

Razumov spoke consciously with elaborate steadiness.

"Yes, patriotic instincts developed by a faculty of independent thinking—of detached thinking. In that respect I am more free than any social democratic revolution could make me. It is more than probable that I don't think exactly as you are thinking. Indeed, how could it be? You would think most likely at this moment that I am elaborately lying to cover up the track of my repentance."

Razumov stopped. His heart had grown too big for his breast. Councillor Mikulin did not flinch.

"Why so?" he said simply. "I assisted personally at the search of your rooms. I looked through all the papers myself. I have been greatly impressed by a sort of political confession of faith. A very remarkable document. Now may I ask for what purpose . . ."

"To deceive the police naturally," said Razumov savagely. . . . "What is all this mockery? Of course, you can send me straight from this room to Siberia. That would be intelligible. To what is intelligible I can submit. But I protest against this comedy of persecution. The whole affair is becoming too comical altogether for my taste. A comedy of errors, phantoms, and suspicions. It's positively indecent . . ."

Councillor Mikulin turned an attentive ear.

"Did you say phantoms?" he murmured.

"I could walk over dozens of them." Razumov, with an impatient wave of his hand, went on headlong, "But, really, I must claim the right to be done once for all with that man. And in order to accomplish this I shall take the liberty . . ."

Razumov on his side of the table bowed slightly to the seated bureaucrat.

". . . To retire—simply to retire," he finished with great resolution.

He walked to the door, thinking, "Now he must show his hand. He must ring and have me arrested before I am out of the building, or he must let me go. And either way . . ."

An unhurried voice said—

"Kirylo Sidorovitch."

Razumov at the door turned his head.

"To retire," he repeated.

"Where to?" asked Councillor Mikulin softly.

PART SECOND

I

In the conduct of an invented story there are, no doubt, certain proprieties to be observed for the sake of clearness and effect. A man of imagination, however inexperienced in the art of narrative, has his instinct to guide him in the choice of his words, and in the development of the action. A grain of talent excuses many mistakes. But this is not a work of imagination; I have no talent; my excuse for this undertaking lies not in its art, but in its artlessness. Aware of my limitations and strong in the sincerity of my purpose, I would not try (were I able) to invent anything. I push my scruples so far that I would not even invent a transition.

Dropping then Mr. Razumov's record at the point where Councillor Mikulin's question "Where to?" comes in with the force of an insoluble problem, I shall simply say that I made the acquaintance of these ladies about six months before that time. By "these ladies" I mean, of course, the mother and the sister of the unfortunate Haldin.

By what arguments he had induced his mother to sell their little property and go abroad for an indefinite time, I cannot tell precisely. I have an idea that Mrs. Haldin, at her son's wish, would have set fire to her house and emigrated to the moon without any sign of surprise or apprehension; and that Miss Haldin—Nathalie, caressingly Natalka—would have given her assent to the scheme.

Their proud devotion to that young man became clear to me in a very short time. Following his directions they went straight to Switzerland—to Zürich—where they re-

mained the best part of a year. From Zurich, which they
did not like, they came to Geneva. A friend of mine in
Lausanne, a lecturer in history at the University (he had
married a Russian lady, a distant connection of Mrs. Hal-
din's), wrote to me suggesting I should call on these ladies.
It was a very kindly meant business suggestion. Miss
Haldin wished to go through a course of reading the best
English authors with a competent teacher.

Mrs. Haldin received me very kindly. Her bad French,
of which she was smilingly conscious, did away with the
formality of the first interview. She was a tall woman in a
black silk dress. A wide brow, regular features, and delicately cut lips, testified to her past beauty. She sat upright
in an easy chair and in a rather weak, gentle voice told me
that her Natalka simply thirsted after knowledge. Her thin
hands were lying on her lap, her facial immobility had in
it something monachal. "In Russia," she went on, "all
knowledge was tainted with falsehood. Not chemistry and
all that, but education generally," she explained. The Government corrupted the teaching for its own purposes. Both
her children felt that. Her Natalka had obtained a diploma
of a Superior School for Women and her son was a student at the St. Petersburg University. He had a brilliant
intellect, a most noble unselfish nature, and he was the
oracle of his comrades. Early next year, she hoped he
would join them and they would then go to Italy together.
In any other country but their own she would have been
certain of a great future for a man with the extraordinary
abilities and the lofty character of her son—but in
Russia . . .

The young lady sitting by the window turned her head
and said—

"Come, mother. Even with us things change with years."

Her voice was deep, almost harsh, and yet caressing in
its harshness. She had a dark complexion, with red lips and
a full figure. She gave the impression of strong vitality.
The old lady sighed.

"You are both young—you two. It is easy for you to

hope. But I, too, am not hopeless. Indeed, how could I be with a son like this?"

I addressed Miss Haldin, asking her what authors she wished to read. She directed upon me her grey eyes shaded by black eyelashes, and I became aware, notwithstanding my years, how attractive physically her personality could be to a man capable of appreciating in a woman something else than the mere grace of femininity. Her glance was as direct and trustful as that of a young man yet unspoiled by the world's wise lessons. And it was intrepid, but in this intrepidity there was nothing aggressive. A naïve yet thoughtful assurance is a better definition. She had reflected already (in Russia the young begin to think early), but she had never known deception as yet because obviously she had never yet fallen under the sway of passion. She was—to look at her was enough—very capable of being roused by an idea or simply by a person. At least, so I judged with I believe an unbiassed mind; for clearly my person could not be the person—and as to my ideas! . . .

We became excellent friends in the course of our reading. It was very pleasant. Without fear of provoking a smile, I shall confess that I became very much attached to that young girl. At the end of four months I told her that now she could very well go on reading English by herself. It was time for the teacher to depart. My pupil looked unpleasantly surprised.

Mrs. Haldin, with her immobility of feature and kindly expression of the eyes, uttered from her armchair in her uncertain French, *"Mais l'ami reviendra."* And so it was settled. I returned—not four times a week as before, but pretty frequently. In the autumn we made some short excursions together in company with other Russians. My friendship with these ladies gave me a standing in the Russian colony which otherwise I could not have had.

The day I saw in the papers the news of Mr. de P——'s assassination—it was a Sunday—I met the two ladies in the street and walked with them for some distance. Mrs. Haldin wore a heavy grey cloak, I remember, over her black silk dress, and her fine eyes met mine with a very quiet expression.

"We have been to the late service," she said. "Natalka came with me. Her girl-friends, the students here, of course don't. . . . With us in Russia the church is so identified with oppression, that it seems almost necessary when one wishes to be free in this life, to give up all hope of a future existence. But I cannot give up praying for my son."

She added with a sort of stony grimness, colouring slightly, and in French, *"Ce n'est peut être qu'une habitude."* ("It may be only habit.")

Miss Haldin was carrying the prayer-book. She did not glance at her mother.

"You and Victor are both profound believers," she said.

I communicated to them the news from their country which I had just read in a café. For a whole minute we walked together fairly briskly in silence. Then Mrs. Haldin murmured—

"There will be more trouble, more persecutions for this. They may be even closing the University. There is neither peace nor rest in Russia for one but in the grave."

"Yes. The way is hard," came from the daughter, looking straight before her at the Chain of Jura covered with snow, like a white wall closing the end of the street. "But concord is not so very far off."

"That is what my children think," observed Mrs. Haldin to me.

I did not conceal my feeling that these were strange times to talk of concord. Nathalie Haldin surprised me by saying, as if she had thought very much on the subject, that the occidentals did not understand the situation. She was very calm and youthfully superior.

"You think it is a class conflict, or a conflict of interests, as social contests are with you in Europe. But it is not that at all. It is something quite different."

"It is quite possible that I don't understand," I admitted.

That propensity of lifting every problem from the plane of the understandable by means of some sort of mystic expression, is very Russian. I knew her well enough to have discovered her scorn for all the practical forms of political liberty known to the western world. I suppose one must be a Russian to understand Russian simplicity, a terrible corroding simplicity in which mystic phrases clothe a naïve and hopeless cynicism. I think sometimes that the psychological secret of the profound difference of that people consists in this, that <u>they detest life</u>, the irremediable life of the earth as it is, <u>whereas we westerners cherish it with perhaps an equal exaggeration of its sentimental value.</u> But this is a digression indeed. . . .

I helped these ladies into the tramcar and they asked me to call in the afternoon. At least Mrs. Haldin asked me as she climbed up, and her Natalka smiled down at the dense westerner indulgently from the rear platform of the moving car. The light of the clear wintry forenoon was softened in her grey eyes.

Mr. Razumov's record, like the open book of fate, revives for me the memory of that day as something startlingly pitiless in its freedom from all forebodings. Victor Haldin was still with the living, but with the living whose only contact with life is the expectation of death. He must have been already referring to the last of his earthly affections, the hours of that obstinate silence, which for him was to be prolonged into eternity. That afternoon the ladies entertained a good many of their compatriots—more than was usual for them to receive at one time; and the drawing-room on the ground floor of a large house on the Boulevard des Philosophes was very much crowded.

I outstayed everybody; and when I rose Miss Haldin stood up too. I took her hand and was moved to revert to that morning's conversation in the street.

"Admitting that we occidentals do not understand the character of your people . . ." I began.

It was as if she had been prepared for me by some mysterious foreknowledge. She checked me gently—

"Their impulses—their . . ." she sought the proper expression and found it, but in French . . . "their *mouvements d'âme.*"

Her voice was not much above a whisper.

"Very well," I said. "But still we are looking at a conflict. You say it is not a conflict of classes and not a conflict of interests. Suppose I admitted that. Are antagonistic ideas then to be reconciled more easily—can they be cemented with blood and violence into that concord which you proclaim to be so near?"

She looked at me searchingly with her clear grey eyes, without answering my reasonable question—my obvious, my unanswerable question.

"It is inconceivable," I added, with something like annoyance.

"Everything is inconceivable," she said. "The whole world is inconceivable to the strict logic of ideas. And yet the world exists to our senses, and we exist in it. There must be a necessity superior to our conceptions. It is a very miserable and a very false thing to belong to the majority. We Russians shall find some better form of national freedom than an artificial conflict of parties—which is wrong because it is a conflict and contemptible because it is artificial. It is left for us Russians to discover a better way."

Mrs. Haldin had been looking out of the window. She turned upon me the almost lifeless beauty of her face, and the living benign glance of her big dark eyes.

"That's what my children think," she declared.

"I suppose," I addressed Miss Haldin, "that you will be shocked if I tell you that I haven't understood—I won't say a single word; I've understood all the words. . . . But what can be this era of disembodied concord you are looking forward to? Life is a thing of form. It has its plastic shape and a definite intellectual aspect. The most idealistic conceptions of love and forbearance must be clothed in flesh as it were before they can be made understandable."

I took my leave of Mrs. Haldin, whose beautiful lips never stirred. She smiled with her eyes only. Nathalie Haldin went with me as far as the door, very amiable.

"Mother imagines that I am the slavish echo of my brother Victor. It is not so. He understands me better than I can understand him. When he joins us and you come to know him you will see what an exceptional soul it is." She paused. "He is not a strong man in the conventional sense, you know," she added. "But his character is without a flaw."

"I believe that it will not be difficult for me to make friends with your brother Victor."

"Don't expect to understand him quite," she said, a little maliciously. "He is not at all—at all—western at bottom."

And on this unnecessary warning I left the room with another bow in the doorway to Mrs. Haldin in her armchair by the window. The shadow of autocracy all unperceived by me had already fallen upon the Boulevard des Philosophes, in the free, independent and democratic city of Geneva, where there is a quarter called "La Petite Russie." Whenever two Russians come together, the shadow of autocracy is with them, tinging their thoughts, their views, their most intimate feelings, their private life, their public utterances—haunting the secret of their silences.

What struck me next in the course of a week or so was the silence of these ladies. I used to meet them walking in the public garden near the University. They greeted me with their usual friendliness, but I could not help noticing their taciturnity. By that time it was generally known that the assassin of Mr. de P—— had been caught, judged, and executed. So much had been declared officially to the news agencies. But for the world at large he remained anonymous. The official secrecy had withheld his name from the public. I really cannot imagine for what reason.

One day I saw Miss Haldin walking alone in the main valley of the Bastions under the naked trees.

"Mother is not very well," she explained.

As Mrs. Haldin had, it seemed, never had a day's illness in her life, this indisposition was disquieting. It was nothing definite, too.

"I think she is fretting because we have not heard from my brother for rather a long time."

"No news—good news," I said cheerfully, and we began to walk slowly side by side.

"Not in Russia," she breathed out so low that I only just caught the words. I looked at her with more attention.

"You too are anxious?"

She admitted after a moment of hesitation that she was. "It is really such a long time since we heard . . ."

And before I could offer the usual banal suggestions she confided in me.

"Oh! But it is much worse than that. I wrote to a family we know in Petersburg. They had not seen him for more than a month. They thought he was already with us. They were even offended a little that he should have left Petersburg without calling on them. The husband of the lady went at once to his lodgings. Victor had left there and they did not know his address."

I remember her catching her breath rather pitifully. Her brother had not been seen at lectures for a very long time either. He only turned up now and then at the University gate to ask the porter for his letters. And the gentleman friend was told that the student Haldin did not come to claim the last two letters for him. But the police came to inquire if the student Haldin ever received any correspondence at the University and took them away.

"My two last letters," she said.

We faced each other. A few snow-flakes fluttered under the naked boughs. The sky was dark.

"What do you think could have happened?" I asked.

Her shoulders moved slightly.

"One can never tell—in Russia."

I saw then the shadow of autocracy lying upon Russian lives in their submission or their revolt. I saw it touch her handsome open face nestled in a fur collar and darken her clear eyes that shone upon me brilliantly grey in the murky light of a beclouded, inclement afternoon.

"Let us move on," she said. "It is cold standing to-day."

She shuddered a little and stamped her little feet. We moved briskly to the end of the alley and back to the great gates of the garden.

"Have you told your mother?" I ventured to ask.

"No. Not yet. I came out to walk off the impression of this letter."

I heard a rustle of paper somewhere. It came from her muff. She had the letter with her in there.

"What is it that you are afraid of?" I asked.

To us Europeans of the West, all ideas of political plots and conspiracies seem childish, crude inventions for the theatre or a novel. I did not like to be more definite in my inquiry.

"For us—for my mother specially, what I am afraid of is incertitude. People do disappear. Yes, they do disappear. I leave you to imagine what it is—the cruelty of the dumb weeks—months—years! This friend of ours has abandoned his inquiries when he heard of the police getting hold of the letters. I suppose he was afraid of compromising himself. He has a wife and children—and why should he, after all . . . Moreover, he is without influential *connexions* and not rich. What could he do? . . . Yes, I am afraid of silence—for my poor mother. She won't be able to bear it. For my brother I am afraid of . . ." she became almost indistinct, "of anything."

We were now near the gate opposite the theatre. She raised her voice.

"But lost people do turn up even in Russia. Do you know what my last hope is? Perhaps the next thing we know, we shall see him walking into our rooms."

I raised my hat and she passed out of the gardens, graceful and strong, after a slight movement of the head to me, her hands in the muff, crumpling the cruel Petersburg letter.

On returning home I opened the newspaper I receive from London, and glancing down the correspondence from Russia—not the telegrams but the correspondence—the first thing that caught my eye was the name of Haldin. Mr. de P——'s death was no longer an actuality, but the enterprising correspondent was proud of having ferreted out some unofficial information about that fact of modern history. He had got hold of Haldin's name, and had picked

up the story of the midnight arrest in the street. But the
sensation from a journalistic point of view was already
well in the past. He did not allot to it more than twenty
lines out of a full column. It was quite enough to give me
a sleepless night. I perceived that it would have been a
sort of treason to let Miss Haldin come without prepara-
tion upon that journalistic discovery which would infallibly
be reproduced on the morrow by French and Swiss newspapers. I had a very bad time of it till the morning, wake-
ful with nervous worry and night-marish with the feeling
of being mixed up with something theatrical and morbidly
affected. The incongruity of such a complication in those
two women's lives was sensible to me all night in the form
of absolute anguish. It seemed due to their refined simplicity that it should remain concealed from them for
ever. Arriving at an unconscionably early hour at the door
of their apartment, I felt as if I were about to commit an
act of vandalism. . . .   *q. and of Heart of Darkness*

The middle-aged servant woman led me into the drawing-room where there was a duster on a chair and a broom
leaning against the centre table. The motes danced in the
sunshine; I regretted I had not written a letter instead of
coming myself, and was thankful for the brightness of the
day. Miss Haldin in a plain black dress came lightly out
of her mother's room with a fixed uncertain smile on her
lips.

I pulled the paper out of my pocket. I did not imagine
that a number of the *Standard* could have the effect of
Medusa's head. Her face went stony in a moment—her
eyes—her limbs. The most terrible thing was that being
stony she remained alive. One was conscious of her pal-
pitating heart. I hope she forgave me the delay of my
clumsy circumlocution. It was not very prolonged; she
could not have kept so still from head to foot for more
than a second or two; and then I heard her draw a breath.
As if the shock had paralysed her moral resistance, and
affected the firmness of her muscles, the contours of her
face seemed to have given way. She was frightfully al-

tered. She looked aged—ruined. But only for a moment.
She said with decision—

"I am going to tell my mother at once."

"Would that be safe in her state?" I objected.

"What can be worse than the state she has been in for
the last month? We understand this in another way. The
crime is not at his door. Don't imagine I am defending
him before you."

She went to the bedroom door, then came back to ask
me in a low murmur not to go till she returned. For twenty
interminable minutes not a sound reached me. At last
Miss Haldin came out and walked across the room with
her quick light step. When she reached the armchair she
dropped into it heavily as if completely exhausted.

Mrs. Haldin, she told me, had not shed a tear. She was
sitting up in bed, and her immobility, her silence, were
very alarming. At last she lay down gently and had motioned her daughter away.

"She will call me in presently," added Miss Haldin. "I
left a bell near the bed."

I confess that my very real sympathy had no stand-
point. The Western readers for whom this story is written will understand what I mean. It was, if I may say so,
the want of experience. Death is a remorseless spoliator.
The anguish of irreparable loss is familiar to us all. There
is no life so lonely as to be safe against that experience.
But the grief I had brought to these two ladies had grue-
some associations. It had the associations of bombs and
gallows—a lurid, Russian colouring which made the complexion of my sympathy uncertain.

I was grateful to Miss Haldin for not embarrassing me
by an outward display of deep feeling. I admired her for
that wonderful command over herself, even while I was
a little frightened at it. It was the stillness of a great tension. What if it should suddenly snap? Even the door of
Mrs. Haldin's room, with the old mother alone in there,
had a rather awful aspect.

Nathalie Haldin murmured sadly—

"I suppose you are wondering what my feelings are?"

Essentially that was true. It was that very wonder which unsettled my sympathy of a dense Occidental. I could get hold of nothing but of some commonplace phrases, those futile phrases that give the measure of our impotence before each other's trials. I mumbled something to the effect that, for the young, life held its hopes and compensations. It held duties too—but of that I was certain it was not necessary to remind her.

She had a handkerchief in her hands and pulled at it nervously.

"I am not likely to forget my mother," she said. "We used to be three. Now we are two—two women. She's not so very old. She may live quite a long time yet. What have we to look for in the future? For what hope and what consolation?"

"You must take a wider view," I said resolutely, thinking that with this exceptional creature this was the right note to strike. She looked at me steadily for a moment, and then the tears she had been keeping down flowed unrestrained. She jumped up and stood in the window with her back to me.

I slipped away without attempting even to approach her. Next day I was told at the door that Mrs. Haldin was better. The middle-aged servant remarked that a lot of people—Russians—had called that day, but Miss Haldin had not seen anybody. A fortnight later, when making my daily call, I was asked in and found Mrs. Haldin sitting in her usual place by the window.

At first one would have thought that nothing was changed. I saw across the room the familiar profile, a little sharper in outline and overspread by a uniform pallor as might have been expected in an invalid. But no disease could have accounted for the change in her black eyes, smiling no longer with gentle irony. She raised them as she gave me her hand. I observed the three weeks' old number of the *Standard* folded with the correspondence from Russia uppermost, lying on a little table by the side of the arm-chair. Mrs. Haldin's voice was startlingly weak and colourless. Her first words to me framed a question.

"Has there been anything more in your newspapers?"

I released her long emaciated hand, shook my head negatively, and sat down.

"The English press is wonderful. Nothing can be kept secret from it, and all the world must hear. Only our Russian news is not always easy to understand. Not always easy. . . . But English mothers do not look for news like that . . ."

She laid her hand on the newspaper and took it away again. I said—

"We too have had tragic times in our history."

"A long time ago. A very long time ago."

"Yes."

"There are nations that have made their bargain with fate," said Miss Haldin, who had approached us. "We need not envy them."

"Why this scorn?" I asked gently. "It may be that our bargain was not a very lofty one. But the terms men and nations obtain from Fate are hallowed by the price."

Mrs. Haldin turned her head away and looked out of the window for a time, with that new, sombre, extinct gaze of her sunken eyes which so completely made another woman of her.

"That Englishman, this correspondent," she addressed me suddenly, "do you think it is possible that he knew my son?"

To this strange question I could only say that it was possible of course. She saw my surprise.

"If one knew what sort of man he was one could perhaps write to him," she murmured.

"Mother thinks," explained Miss Haldin, standing between us, with one hand resting on the back of my chair, "that my poor brother perhaps did not try to save himself."

I looked up at Miss Haldin in sympathetic consternation, but Miss Haldin was looking down calmly at her mother. The latter said—

"We do not know the address of any of his friends. Indeed, we know nothing of his Petersburg comrades. He

had a multitude of young friends, only he never spoke
much of them. One could guess that they were his disciples and that they idolized him. But he was so modest.
One would think that with so many devoted . . ."

She averted her head again and looked down the Boulevard des Philosophes, a singularly arid and dusty thoroughfare, where nothing could be seen at the moment but
two dogs, a little girl in a pinafore hopping on one leg,
and in the distance a workman wheeling a bicycle.

"Even amongst the Apostles of Christ there was found
a Judas," she whispered as if to herself, but with the evident intention to be heard by me.

The Russian visitors assembled in little knots, conversed
amongst themselves meantime, in low murmurs, and with
brief glances in our direction. It was a great contrast to the
usual loud volubility of these gatherings. Miss Haldin
followed me into the ante-room.

"People will come," she said. "We cannot shut the door
in their faces."

While I was putting on my overcoat she began to talk
to me of her mother. Poor Mrs. Haldin was fretting after
more news. She wanted to go on hearing about her unfortunate son. She could not make up her mind to abandon
him quietly to the dumb unknown. She would persist in
pursuing him in there through the long days of motionless
silence face to face with the empty Boulevard des Philosophes. She could not understand why he had not
escaped—as so many other revolutionists and conspirators
had managed to escape in other instances of that kind. It
was really inconceivable that the means of secret revolutionary organizations should have failed so inexcusably to
preserve her son. But in reality the inconceivable that
staggered her mind was nothing but the cruel audacity of
Death passing over her head to strike at that young and
precious heart.

Miss Haldin mechanically, with an absorbed look,
handed me my hat. I understood from her that the poor
woman was possessed by the sombre and simple idea that
her son must have perished because he did not want to be

saved. It could not have been that he despaired of his country's future. That was impossible. Was it possible that his mother and sister had not known how to merit his confidence; and that, after having done what he was compelled to do, his spirit became crushed by an intolerable doubt, his mind distracted by a sudden mistrust?

I was very much shocked by this piece of ingenuity.

"Our three lives were like that!" Miss Haldin twined the fingers of both her hands together in demonstration, then separated them slowly, looking straight into my face. "That's what poor mother found to torment herself and me with, for all the years to come," added the strange girl. At that moment her indefinable charm was revealed to me in the conjunction of passion and stoicism. I imagined what her life was likely to be by the side of Mrs. Haldin's terrible immobility, inhabited by that fixed idea. But my concern was reduced to silence by my ignorance of her modes of feeling. Difference of nationality is a terrible obstacle for our complex Western natures. But Miss Haldin probably was too simple to suspect my embarrassment. She did not wait for me to say anything, but as if reading my thoughts on my face she went on courageously—

"At first poor mother went numb, as our peasants say; then she began to think and she will go on now thinking and thinking in that unfortunate strain. You see yourself how cruel that is. . . ."

I never spoke with greater sincerity than when I agreed with her that it would be deplorable in the highest degree. She took an anxious breath.

"But all these strange details in the English paper," she exclaimed suddenly. "What is the meaning of them? I suppose they are true? But is it not terrible that my poor brother should be caught wandering alone, as if in despair, about the streets at night. . . ."

We stood so close to each other in the dark ante-room that I could see her biting her lower lip to suppress a dry sob. After a short pause she said—

"I suggested to mother that he may have been betrayed by some false friend or simply by some cowardly creature. It may be easier for her to believe that."

I understood now the poor woman's whispered allusion to Judas.

"It may be easier," I admitted, admiring inwardly the directness and the subtlety of the girl's outlook. She was dealing with life as it was made for her by the political conditions of her country. [She faced cruel realities, not morbid imaginings of her own making] I could not defend myself from a certain feeling of respect when she added simply—

"Time they say can soften every sort of bitterness. But I cannot believe that it has any power over remorse. It is better that mother should think some person guilty of Victor's death, than that she should connect it with a weakness of her son or a shortcoming of her own."

"But you, yourself, don't suppose that . . ." I began.

She compressed her lips and shook her head. She harboured no evil thoughts against any one, she declared— and perhaps nothing that happened was unnecessary. On these words, pronounced low and sounding mysterious in the half obscurity of the ante-room, we parted with an expressive and warm handshake. The grip of her strong, shapely hand had a seductive frankness, a sort of exquisite virility. I do not know why she should have felt so friendly to me. It may be that she thought I understood her much better than I was able to do. The most precise of her sayings seemed always to me to have enigmatical prolongations vanishing somewhere beyond my reach. I am reduced to suppose that she appreciated my attention and my silence. The attention she could see was quite sincere, so that the silence could not be suspected of coldness. It seemed to satisfy her. And it is to be noted that if she confided in me it was clearly not with the expectation of receiving advice, for which, indeed, she never asked.

II

Our daily relations were interrupted at this period for something like a fortnight. I had to absent myself unexpectedly from Geneva. On my return I lost no time in directing my steps up the Boulevard des Philosophes.

Through the open door of the drawing-room I was annoyed to hear a visitor holding forth steadily in an unctuous deep voice.

Mrs. Haldin's armchair by the window stood empty. On the sofa, Nathalie Haldin raised her charming grey eyes in a glance of greeting accompanied by the merest hint of a welcoming smile. But she made no movement. With her strong white hands lying inverted in the lap of her mourning dress she faced a man who presented to me a robust back covered with black broadcloth, and well in keeping with the deep voice. He turned his head sharply over his shoulder, but only for a moment.

"Ah! your English friend. I know. I know. That's nothing."

He wore spectacles with smoked glasses, a tall silk hat stood on the floor by the side of his chair. Flourishing slightly a big soft hand he went on with his discourse, precipitating his delivery a little more.

"I have never changed the faith I held while wandering in the forests and bogs of Siberia. It sustained me then—it sustains me now. The great Powers of Europe are bound to disappear—and the cause of their collapse will be very simple. They will exhaust themselves struggling against their proletariat. In Russia it is different. In Russia we have no classes to combat each other, one holding the power of wealth, and the other mighty with the strength of numbers. We have only an unclean bureaucracy in the face of a people as great and as incorruptible as the ocean. No, we have no classes. But we have the Russian woman. The admirable Russian woman! I receive most remarkable letters signed by women. So elevated in tone, so courageous, breathing such a noble ardour of service!

The greatest part of our hopes rests on women. I behold their thirst for knowledge. It is admirable. Look how they absorb, how they are making it their own. It is miraculous. But what is knowledge? . . . I understand that you have not been studying anything especially—medicine for instance. No? That's right. Had I been honoured by being asked to advise you on the use of your time when you arrived here I would have been strongly opposed to such a course. Knowledge in itself is mere dross."

He had one of those bearded Russian faces without shape, a mere appearance of flesh and hair with not a single feature having any sort of character. His eyes being hidden by the dark glasses there was an utter absence of all expression. I knew him by sight. He was a Russian refugee of mark. All Geneva knew his burly black-coated figure. At one time all Europe was aware of the story of his life written by himself and translated into seven or more languages. In his youth he had led an idle, dissolute life. Then a society girl he was about to marry died suddenly and thereupon he abandoned the world of fashion, and began to conspire in a spirit of repentance, and, after that, his native autocracy took good care that the usual things should happen to him. He was imprisoned in fortresses, beaten within an inch of his life, and condemned to work in mines, with common criminals. The great success of his book, however, was the chain.

I do not remember now the details of the weight and length of the fetters riveted on his limbs by an "Administrative" order, but it was in the number of pounds and the thickness of links an appalling assertion of the divine right of autocracy. Appalling and futile too, because this big man managed to carry off that simple engine of government with him into the woods. The sensational clink of these fetters is heard all through the chapters describing his escape—a subject of wonder to two continents. He had begun by concealing himself successfully from his guard in a hole on a river bank. It was the end of the day; with infinite labour he managed to free one of his legs. Meantime night fell. He was going to begin on his other leg when he was overtaken by a terrible misfortune. He dropped his file.

All this is precise yet symbolic; and the file had its pathetic history. It was given to him unexpectedly one evening, by a quiet, pale-faced girl. The poor creature had come out to the mines to join one of his fellow convicts, a delicate young man, a mechanic and a social democrat, with broad cheekbones and large staring eyes. She had worked her way across half Russia and nearly the whole of Siberia to be near him, and, as it seems, with the hope of helping him to escape. But she arrived too late. Her lover had died only a week before.

Through that obscure episode, as he says, in the history of ideas in Russia, the file came into his hands, and inspired him with an ardent resolution to regain his liberty. When it slipped through his fingers it was as if it had gone straight into the earth. He could by no manner of means put his hand on it again in the dark. He groped systematically in the loose earth, in the mud, in the water; the night was passing meantime, the precious night on which he counted to get away into the forests, his only chance of escape. For a moment he was tempted by despair to give up; but recalling the quiet, sad face of the heroic girl, he felt profoundly ashamed of his weakness. She had selected him for the gift of liberty and he must show himself worthy of the favour conferred by her feminine, indomitable soul. It appeared to be a sacred trust. To fail would have been a sort of treason against the sacredness of self-sacrifice and womanly love.

There are in his book whole pages of self-analysis whence emerges like a white figure from a dark confused sea the conviction of woman's spiritual superiority—his new faith confessed since in several volumes. His first tribute to it, the great act of his conversion, was his extraordinary existence in the endless forest of the Okhotsk Province, with the loose end of the chain wound about his waist. A strip torn off his convict shirt secured the end firmly. Other strips fastened it at intervals up his left leg to deaden the clanking and to prevent the slack links from getting hooked in the bushes. He became very fierce. He developed an unsuspected genius for the arts of a wild and hunted existence. He learned to creep into villages without betraying his presence by anything more than an occasional faint jingle. He broke into outhouses with an axe he managed to purloin in a wood-cutters' camp. In the deserted tracts of country he lived on wild berries and hunted for honey. His clothing dropped off him gradually. His naked tawny figure glimpsed vaguely through the bushes with a cloud of mosquitoes and flies hovering about the shaggy head, spread tales of terror through whole districts. His temper grew savage as the days went by, and he was glad to discover that there was so much of a brute in him. He had nothing else to put his trust in. For it was as though there had been two human beings indissolubly joined in that enterprise. The civilized man, the enthusiast of advanced humanitarian ideals thirsting for the triumph of spiritual love and political liberty; and the stealthy, primeval savage, pitilessly cunning in the preservation of his freedom from day to day, like a tracked wild beast.

The wild beast was making its way instinctively eastward to the Pacific coast, and the civilized humanitarian in fearful anxious dependence watched the proceedings with awe. Through all these weeks he could never make up his mind to appeal to human compassion. In the wary primeval savage this shyness might have been natural, but the other too, the civilized creature, the thinker, the escaping "political" had developed an absurd form of morbid pessimism, a form of temporary insanity, originating perhaps in the physical worry and discomfort of the chain. These links, he fancied, made him odious to the rest of mankind. It was a repugnant and suggestive load. Nobody could feel any pity at the disgusting sight of a man escaping with a broken chain. His imagination became affected by his fetters in a precise, matter-of-fact manner. It seemed to him impossible that people could resist the temptation of fastening the loose end to a staple in the wall while they went for the nearest police official. Crouch-

ing in holes or hidden in thickets, he had tried to read the
faces of unsuspecting free settlers working in the clearings
or passing along the paths within a foot or two of his eyes.
His feeling was that no man on earth could be trusted
with the temptation of the chain.

One day, however, he chanced to come upon a solitary woman. It was on an open slope of rough grass outside the forest. She sat on the bank of a narrow stream; she
had a red handkerchief on her head and a small basket
was lying on the ground near her hand. At a little distance could be seen a cluster of log cabins, with a water-
mill over a dammed pool shaded by birch trees and looking bright as glass in the twilight. He approached her
silently, his hatchet stuck in his iron belt, a thick cudgel in
his hand; there were leaves and bits of twig in his tangled
hair, in his matted beard; bunches of rags he had wound
round the links fluttered from his waist. A faint clink of his
fetters made the woman turn her head. Too terrified by
this savage apparition to jump up or even to scream, she
was yet too stout-hearted to faint. . . . Expecting nothing
less than to be murdered on the spot she covered her eyes
with her hands to avoid the sight of the descending axe.
When at last she found courage to look again, she saw the
shaggy wild man sitting on the bank six feet away from
her. His thin, sinewy arms hugged his naked legs; the
long beard covered the knees on which he rested his chin;
all these clasped, folded limbs, the bare shoulders, the
wild head with red staring eyes, shook and trembled violently while the bestial creature was making efforts to
speak. It was six weeks since he had heard the sound of
his own voice. It seemed as though he had lost the faculty
of speech. He had become a dumb and despairing brute,
till the woman's sudden, unexpected cry of profound pity,
the insight of her feminine compassion discovering the
complex misery of the man under the terrifying aspect of
the monster, restored him to the ranks of humanity. This
point of view is presented in his book, with a very effective
eloquence. She ended, he says, by shedding tears over
him, sacred, redeeming tears, while he also wept with joy

in the manner of a converted sinner. Directing him to hide in the bushes and wait patiently (a police patrol was expected in the Settlement) she went away towards the houses, promising to return at night.

As if providentially appointed to be the newly wedded wife of the village blacksmith, the woman persuaded her husband to come out with her, bringing some tools of his trade, a hammer, a chisel, a small anvil. . . . "My fetters" —the books says—"were struck off on the banks of the stream, in the starlight of a calm night by an athletic, taciturn young man of the people, kneeling at my feet, while the woman like a liberating genius stood by with clasped hands." Obviously a symbolic couple. At the same time they furnished his regained humanity with some decent clothing, and put heart into the new man by the information that the sea-coast of the Pacific was only a very few miles away. It could be seen, in fact, from the top of the next ridge. . . .

The rest of his escape does not lend itself to mystic treatment and symbolic interpretation. He ended by finding his way to the West by the Suez Canal route in the usual manner. Reaching the shores of South Europe he sat down to write his autobiography—the great literary success of its year. This book was followed by other books written with the declared purpose of elevating humanity. In these works he preached generally the cult of the woman. For his own part he practised it under the rites of special devotion to the transcendental merits of a certain Madame de S——, a lady of advanced views, no longer very young, once upon a time the intriguing wife of a now dead and forgotten diplomat. Her loud pretensions to be one of the leaders of modern thought and of modern sentiment, she sheltered (like Voltaire and Mme. de Staël) on the republican territory of Geneva. Driving through the streets in her big landau she exhibited to the indifference of the natives and the stares of the tourists a long-waisted, youthful figure of hieratic stiffness, with a pair of big gleaming eyes, rolling restlessly behind a short veil of black lace, which, coming down no further than her vividly red lips, resembled a mask. Usually the "heroic fugitive" (this name was bestowed upon him in a review of the English edition of his book)—the "heroic fugitive" accompanied her, sitting, portentously bearded and darkly bespectacled, not by her side, but opposite her, with his back to the horses. Thus, facing each other, with no one else in the roomy carriage, their airings suggested a conscious public manifestation. Or it may have been unconscious. Russian simplicity often marches innocently on the edge of cynicism for some lofty purpose. But it is a vain enterprise for sophisticated Europe to try and understand these doings. Considering the air of gravity extending even to the physiognomy of the coachman and the action of the showy horses, this quaint display might have possessed a mystic significance, but to the corrupt frivolity of a Western mind, like my own, it seemed hardly decent.

However, it is not becoming for an obscure teacher of languages to criticize a "heroic fugitive" of world-wide celebrity. I was aware from hearsay that he was an industrious busy-body, hunting up his compatriots in hotels, in private lodgings, and—I was told—conferring upon them the honour of his notice in public gardens when a suitable opening presented itself. I was under the impression that after a visit or two, several months before, he had given up the ladies Haldin—no doubt reluctantly, for there could be no question of his being a determined person. It was perhaps to be expected that he should reappear again on this terrible occasion, as a Russian and a revolutionist, to say the right thing, to strike the true, perhaps a comforting, note. But I did not like to see him sitting there. I trust that an unbecoming jealousy of my privileged position had nothing to do with it. I made no claim to a special standing for my silent friendship. Removed by the difference of age and nationality as if into the sphere of another existence, I produced, even upon myself, the effect of a dumb helpless ghost, of an anxious immaterial thing that could only hover about without the power to protect or guide by as much as a whisper. Since Miss

Haldin with her sure instinct had refrained from introducing me to the burly celebrity, I would have retired quietly and returned later on, had I not met a peculiar expression in her eyes which I interpreted as a request to stay, with the view, perhaps, of shortening an unwelcome visit.

He picked up his hat, but only to deposit it on his knees.

"We shall meet again, Natalia Victorovna. To-day I have called only to mark those feelings towards your honoured mother and yourself, the nature of which you cannot doubt. I needed no urging, but Eleanor—Madame de S—— herself has in a way sent me. She extends to you the hand of feminine fellowship. There is positively in all the range of human sentiments no joy and no sorrow that woman cannot understand, elevate, and spiritualize by her interpretation. That young man newly arrived from St. Petersburg, I have mentioned to you, is already under the charm."

At this point Miss Haldin got up abruptly. I was glad. He did not evidently expect anything so decisive and, at first, throwing his head back, he tilted up his dark glasses with bland curiosity. At last, recollecting himself, he stood up hastily, seizing his hat off his knees with great adroitness.

"How is it, Natalia Victorovna, that you have kept aloof so long, from what after all is—let disparaging tongues say what they like—a unique centre of intellectual freedom and of effort to shape a high conception of our future? In the case of your honoured mother I understand in a measure. At her age new ideas—new faces are not perhaps. . . . But you! Was it mistrust—or indifference? You must come out of your reserve. We Russians have no right to be reserved with each other. In our circumstances it is almost a crime against humanity. The luxury of private grief is not for us. Nowadays the devil is not combated by prayers and fasting. And what is fasting after all but starvation? You must not starve yourself, Natalia Victorovna. Strength is what we want. Spiritual strength, I mean. As to the other kind, what could withstand us Russians if we only put it forth? Sin is different in our day, and the way of salvation for pure souls is different too. It is no longer to be found in monasteries but in the world, in the . . ."

The deep sound seemed to rise from under the floor, and one felt steeped in it to the lips. Miss Haldin's interruption resembled the effort of a drowning person to keep above water. She struck in with an accent of impatience—

"But, Peter Ivanovitch, I don't mean to retire into a monastery. Who would look for salvation there?"

"I spoke figuratively," he boomed.

"Well, then, I am speaking figuratively too. But sorrow is sorrow and pain is pain in the old way. They make their demands upon people. One has got to face them the best way one can. I know that the blow which has fallen upon us so unexpectedly is only an episode in the fate of a people. You may rest assured that I don't forget that. But just now I have to think of my mother. How can you expect me to leave her to herself . . . ?"

"That is putting it in a very crude way," he protested in his great effortless voice.

Miss Haldin did not wait for the vibration to die out.

"And run about visiting amongst a lot of strange people? The idea is distasteful for me; and I do not know what else you may mean."

He towered before her, enormous, deferential, cropped as close as a convict; and this big pinkish poll evoked for me the vision of a wild head with matted locks peering through parted bushes, glimpses of naked, tawny limbs slinking behind the masses of sodden foliage under a cloud of flies and mosquitoes. It was an involuntary tribute to the vigour of his writing. Nobody could doubt that he had wandered in Siberian forests, naked and girt with a chain. The black broadcloth coat invested his person with a character of austere decency—something recalling a missionary.

"Do you know what I want, Natalia Victorovna?" he uttered solemnly. "I want you to be a fanatic."

"A fanatic?"

"Yes. Faith alone won't do."

His voice dropped to a still lower tone. He raised for a

moment one thick arm; the other remained hanging down against his thigh, with the fragile silk hat at the end.

"I shall tell you now something which I entreat you to ponder over carefully. Listen, we need a force that would move heaven and earth—nothing less."

The profound, subterranean note of this "nothing less" made one shudder, almost like the deep muttering of wind in the pipes of an organ.

"And are we to find that force in the salon of Madame de S——? Excuse me, Peter Ivanovitch, if I permit myself to doubt it. Is not that lady a woman of the great world, an aristocrat?"

"Prejudice!" he cried. "You astonish me. And suppose she was all that! She is also a woman of flesh and blood. There is always something to weigh down the spiritual side in all of us. But to make of it a reproach is what I did not expect from you. No! I did not expect that. One would think you have listened to some malevolent scandal."

"I have heard no gossip, I assure you. In our province how could we? But the world speaks of her. What can there be in common in a lady of that sort and an obscure country girl like me?"

"She is a perpetual manifestation of a noble and peerless spirit," he broke in. "Her charm—no, I shall not speak of her charm. But, of course, everybody who approaches her falls under the spell. . . . Contradictions vanish, trouble falls away from one. . . . Unless I am mistaken—but I never make a mistake in spiritual matters—you are troubled in your soul, Natalia Victorovna."

Miss Haldin's clear eyes looked straight at his soft enormous face; I received the impression that behind these dark spectacles of his he could be as impudent as he chose.

"Only the other evening walking back to town from Château Borel with our latest interesting arrival from Petersburg, I could notice the powerful soothing influence —I may say reconciling influence. . . . There he was, all these kilometres along the shores of the lake, silent, like a man who has been shown the way of peace. I could feel the leaven working in his soul, you understand. For one thing he listened to me patiently. I myself was inspired that evening by the firm and exquisite genius of Eleanor— Madame de S——, you know. It was a full moon and I could observe his face. I cannot be deceived. . . ."

Miss Haldin, looking down, seemed to hesitate.

"Well! I will think of what you said, Peter Ivanovitch. I shall try to call as soon as I can leave mother for an hour or two safely."

Coldly as these words were said I was amazed at the concession. He snatched her right hand with such fervour that I thought he was going to press it to his lips or his breast. But he only held it by the finger-tips in his great paw and shook it a little up and down while he delivered his last volley of words.

"That's right. That's right. I haven't obtained your full confidence as yet, Natalia Victorovna, but that will come. All in good time. The sister of Victor Haldin cannot be without importance. . . . It's simply impossible. And no woman can remain sitting on the steps. Flowers, tears, applause—that has had its time; it's a mediæval conception. The arena, the arena itself is the place for women!"

He relinquished her hand with a flourish, as if giving it to her for a gift, and remained still, his head bowed in dignified submission before her femininity.

"The arena! . . . You must descend into the arena, Natalia."

He made one step backwards, inclined his enormous body, and was gone swiftly. The door fell to behind him. But immediately the powerful resonance of his voice was heard addressing in the ante-room the middle-aged servant woman who was letting him out. Whether he exhorted her too to descend into the arena I cannot tell. The thing sounded like a lecture, and the slight crash of the outer door cut it short suddenly.

III

We remained looking at each other for a time.

"Do you know who he is?"

Miss Haldin, coming forward, put this question to me in English.

I took her offered hand.

"Everybody knows. He is a revolutionary feminist, a great writer, if you like, and—how shall I say it—the—the familiar guest of Madame de S——'s mystic revolutionary salon."

Miss Haldin passed her hand over her forehead.

"You know, he was with me for more than an hour before you came in. I was so glad mother was lying down. She has many nights without sleep, and then sometimes in the middle of the day she gets a rest of several hours. It is sheer exhaustion—but still, I am thankful. . . . If it were not for these intervals. . . ."

She looked at me and, with that extraordinary penetration which used to disconcert me, shook her head.

"No. She would not go mad."

"My dear young lady," I cried, by way of protest, the more shocked because in my heart I was far from thinking Mrs. Haldin quite sane.

"You don't know what a fine, lucid intellect mother had," continued Nathalie Haldin, with her calm, clear-eyed simplicity, which seemed to me always to have a quality of heroism.

"I am sure . . ." I murmured.

"I darkened mother's room and came out here. I've wanted for so long to think quietly."

She paused, then, without giving any sign of distress, added, "It's so difficult," and looked at me with a strange fixity, as if watching for a sign of dissent or surprise.

I gave neither. I was irresistibly impelled to say—

"The visit from that gentleman has not made it any easier, I fear."

Miss Haldin stood before me with a peculiar expression in her eyes.

"I don't pretend to understand Peter Ivanovitch completely. Some guide one must have, even if one does not wholly give up the direction of one's conduct to him. I am an inexperienced girl, but I am not slavish. There has been too much of that in Russia. Why should I not listen to him? There is no harm in having one's thoughts directed. But I don't mind confessing to you that I have not been completely candid with Peter Ivanovitch. I don't quite know what prevented me at the moment . . ."

She walked away suddenly from me to a distant part of the room; but it was only to open and shut a drawer in a bureau. She returned with a piece of paper in her hand. It was thin and blackened with close handwriting. It was obviously a letter.

"I wanted to read you the very words," she said. "This is one of my poor brother's letters. He never doubted. How could he doubt? They make only such a small handful, these miserable oppressors, before the unanimous will of our people."

"Your brother believed in the power of a people's will to achieve anything?"

"It was his religion," declared Miss Haldin.

I looked at her calm face and her animated eyes.

"Of course the will must be awakened, inspired, concentrated," she went on. "That is the true task of real agitators. One has got to give up one's life to it. The degradation of servitude, the absolutist lies must be uprooted and swept out. Reform is impossible. There is nothing to reform. There is no legality, there are no institutions. There are only arbitrary decrees. There is only a handful of cruel—perhaps blind—officials against a nation."

The letter rustled slightly in her hand. I glanced down at the flimsy blackened pages whose very handwriting seemed cabalistic, incomprehensible to the experience of Western Europe.

"Stated like this," I confessed, "the problem seems simple enough. But I fear I shall not see it solved. And if you go back to Russia I know that I shall not see you again. Yet once more I say: go back! Don't suppose that I am thinking of your preservation. No! I know that you will not be returning to personal safety. But I had much rather think of you in danger there than see you exposed to what may be met here."

"I tell you what," said Miss Haldin, after a moment of reflection. "I believe that you hate revolution; you fancy it's not quite honest. You belong to a people which has made a bargain with fate and wouldn't like to be rude to it. But we have made no bargain. It was never offered to us—so much liberty for so much hard cash. You shrink from the idea of revolutionary action for those you think well of as if it were something—how shall I say it—not quite decent."

I bowed my head.

"You are quite right," I said. "I think very highly of you."

"Don't suppose I do not know it," she began hurriedly. "Your friendship has been very valuable."

"I have done little else but look on."

She was a little flushed under the eyes.

"There is a way of looking on which is valuable. I have felt less lonely because of it. It's difficult to explain."

"Really? Well, I too have felt less lonely. That's easy to explain, though. But it won't go on much longer. The last thing I want to tell you is this: in a real revolution—not a simple dynastic change or a mere reform of institutions—in a real revolution the best characters do not come to the front. A violent revolution falls into the hands of narrow-minded fanatics and of tyrannical hypocrites at first. Afterwards comes the turn of all the pretentious intellectual failures of the time. Such are the chiefs and the leaders. You will notice that I have left out the mere rogues. The scrupulous and the just, the noble, humane, and devoted natures; the unselfish and the intelligent may begin a movement—but it passes away from them. They are not the leaders of a revolution. They are its victims: the victims of disgust, of disenchantment—often of remorse. Hopes grotesquely betrayed, ideals caricatured—that is the definition of revolutionary success. There have been in every revolution hearts broken by such successes. But enough of that. My meaning is that I don't want you to be a victim."

"If I could believe all you have said I still wouldn't think of myself," protested Miss Haldin. "I would take lib-

erty from any hand as a hungry man would snatch at a
piece of bread. The true progress must begin after. And
for that the right men shall be found. They are already
amongst us. One comes upon them in their obscurity,
unknown, preparing themselves. . . ."

She spread out the letter she had kept in her hand all
the time, and looking down at it—

"Yes! One comes upon such men!" she repeated, and
then read out the words, "Unstained, lofty, and solitary
existences."

Folding up the letter, while I looked at her interrogatively, she explained—

"These are the words which my brother applies to a
young man he came to know in St. Petersburg. An intimate friend, I suppose. It must be. His is the only name
my brother mentions in all his correspondence with me.
Absolutely the only one, and—would you believe it?—the
man is here. He arrived recently in Geneva."

"Have you seen him?" I inquired. "But, of course, you
must have seen him."

"No! No! I haven't! I didn't know he was here. It's Peter
Ivanovitch himself who told me. You have heard him yourself mentioning a new arrival from Petersburg. . . . Well,
that is the man of 'unstained, lofty, and solitary existence.'
My brother's friend!"

"Compromised politically, I suppose," I remarked.

"I don't know. Yes. It must be so. Who knows! Perhaps
it was this very friendship with my brother which . . .
But no! It is scarcely possible. Really, I know nothing except what Peter Ivanovitch told me of him. He has brought
a letter of introduction from Father Zosim—you know, the
priest-democrat; you have heard of Father Zosim?"

"Oh yes. The famous Father Zosim was staying here in
Geneva for some two months about a year ago," I said.
"When he left here he seems to have disappeared from
the world."

"It appears that he is at work in Russia again. Somewhere in the centre," Miss Haldin said, with animation.
"But please don't mention that to any one—don't let it slip

from you, because if it got into the papers it would be dangerous for him."

"You are anxious, of course, to meet that friend of your brother?" I asked.

Miss Haldin put the letter into her pocket. Her eyes looked beyond my shoulder at the door of her mother's room.

"Not here," she murmured. "Not for the first time, at least."

After a moment of silence I said good-bye, but Miss Haldin followed me into the ante-room, closing the door behind us carefully.

"I suppose you guess where I mean to go to-morrow?"

"You have made up your mind to call on Madame de S——."

"Yes. I am going to the Château Borel. I must."

"What do you expect to hear there?" I asked, in a low voice.

I wondered if she were not deluding herself with some impossible hope. It was not that, however.

"Only think—such a friend. The only man mentioned in his letters. He would have something to give me, if nothing more than a few poor words. It may be something said and thought in those last days. Would you want me to turn my back on what is left of my poor brother—a friend?"

"Certainly not," I said. "I quite understand your pious curiosity."

"—Unstained, lofty, and solitary existences," she murmured to herself. "There are! There are! Well, let me question one of them about the loved dead."

"How do you know, though, that you will meet him there? Is he staying in the Château as a guest—do you suppose?"

"I can't really tell," she confessed. "He brought a written introduction from Father Zosim—who, it seems, is a friend of Madame de S—— too. She can't be such a worthless woman after all."

"There were all sorts of rumours afloat about Father Zosim himself," I observed.

She shrugged her shoulders.

"Calumny is a weapon of our government too. It's well known. Oh yes! It is a fact that Father Zosim had the protection of the Governor-General of a certain province. We talked on the subject with my brother two years ago, I remember. But his work was good. And now he is proscribed. What better proof can one require. But no matter what that priest was or is. All that cannot affect my brother's friend. If I don't meet him there I shall ask these people for his address. And, of course, mother must see him too, later on. There is no guessing what he may have to tell us. It would be a mercy if mamma could be soothed. You know what she imagines. Some explanation perhaps may be found, or—or even made up, perhaps. It would be no sin."

"Certainly," I said, "it would be no sin. It may be a mistake, though."

"I want her only to recover some of her old spirit. While she is like this I cannot think of anything calmly."

"Do you mean to invent some sort of (pious fraud) for your mother's sake?" I asked.

"Why fraud? Such a friend is sure to know something of my brother in these last days. He could tell us. . . . There is something in the facts which will not let me rest. I am certain he meant to join us abroad—that he had some plans—some great patriotic action in view; not only for himself, but for both of us. I trusted in that. I looked forward to the time! Oh! with such hope and impatience. . . . I could have helped. And now suddenly this appearance of recklessness—as if he had not cared. . . ."

She remained silent for a time, then obstinately she concluded—

"I want to know . . ."

Thinking it over, later on, while I walked slowly away from the Boulevard des Philosophes, I asked myself critically, what precisely was it that she wanted to know? What I had heard of her history was enough to give me a clue. In the educational establishment for girls where Miss Haldin finished her studies she was looked upon rather un-

favourably. She was suspected of holding independent /
views on matters settled by official teaching. Afterwards,
when the two ladies returned to their country place, both
mother and daughter, by speaking their minds openly on
public events, had earned for themselves a reputation of
liberalism. The three-horse trap of the district police-cap-
tain began to be seen frequently in their village. "I must
keep an eye on the peasants"—so he explained his visits up
at the house. "Two lonely ladies must be looked after a
little." He would inspect the walls as though he wanted to
pierce them with his eyes, peer at the photographs, turn
over the books in the drawing-room negligently, and after
the usual refreshments, would depart. But the old priest
of the village came one evening in the greatest distress and
agitation, to confess that he—the priest—had been ordered
to watch and ascertain in other ways too (such as using
his spiritual power with the servants) all that was going
on in the house, and especially in respect of the visitors
these ladies received, who they were, the length of their
stay, whether any of them were strangers to that part of
the country, and so on. The poor, simple old man was in
an agony of humiliation and terror. "I came to warn you.
Be cautious in your conduct, for the love of God. I am
burning with shame, but there is no getting out from under the net. I shall have to tell them what I see, because
if I did not there is my deacon. He would make the worst
of things to curry favour. And then my son-in-law, the
husband of my Parasha, who is a writer in the Government
Domain office, they would soon kick him out—and maybe
send him away somewhere." The old man lamented the
necessities of the times—"when people do not agree somehow"—and wiped his eyes. He did not wish to spend the
evening of his days with a shaven head in the penitent's
cell of some monastery—"and subjected to all the severities
of ecclesiastical discipline; for they would show no mercy
to an old man," he groaned. He became almost hysterical,
and the two ladies, full of commiseration, soothed him the
best they could before they let him go back to his cottage.
But, as a matter of fact, they had very few visitors. The

neighbours—some of them old friends—began to keep away;
a few from timidity, others with marked disdain, being
grand people that came only for the summer—Miss Haldin
explained to me—aristocrats, reactionaries. It was a solitary
existence for a young girl. Her relations with her mother
were of the tenderest and most open kind; but Mrs. Haldin
had seen the experiences of her own generation, its sufferings, its deceptions, its apostasies too. Her affection for her
children was expressed by the suppression of all signs of
anxiety. She maintained a heroic reserve. To Nathalie Haldin, her brother with his Petersburg existence, not enigmatical in the least (there could be no doubt of what he
felt or thought) but conducted a little mysteriously, was
the only visible representative of a proscribed liberty. All
the significance of freedom, its indefinite promises, lived in
their long discussions, which breathed the loftiest hope of
action and faith in success. Then, suddenly, the action, the
hopes, came to an end with the details ferreted out by the
English journalist. The concrete fact, the fact of his death
remained; but it remained obscure in its deeper causes.
She felt herself abandoned without explanation. But she
did not suspect him. What she wanted was to learn almost
at any cost how she could remain faithful to his departed
spirit.

IV

Several days elapsed before I met Nathalie Haldin again.
I was crossing the place in front of the theatre when I
made out her shapely figure in the very act of turning
between the gate pillars of the unattractive public promenade of the Bastions. She walked away from me, but I knew
we should meet as she returned down the main alley—
unless, indeed, she were going home. In that case, I don't
think I should have called on her yet. My desire to keep
her away from these people was as strong as ever, but I
had no illusions as to my power. I was but a Westerner, and
it was clear that Miss Haldin would not, could not listen
to my wisdom; and as to my desire of listening to her voice,

it were better, I thought, not to indulge overmuch in that pleasure. No, I should not have gone to the Boulevard des Philosophes; but when at about the middle of the principal alley I saw Miss Haldin coming towards me, I was too curious, and too honest, perhaps, to run away.

There was something of the spring harshness in the air. The blue sky was hard, but the young leaves clung like soft mist about the uninteresting range of trees; and the clear sun put little points of gold into the grey of Miss Haldin's frank eyes, turned to me with a friendly greeting.

I inquired after the health of her mother.

She gave a slight movement of the shoulders and a little sad sigh.

"But, you see, I did come out for a walk . . . for exercise, as you English say."

I smiled approvingly, and she added an unexpected remark—

"It is a glorious day."

Her voice, slightly harsh, but fascinating with its masculine and bird-like quality, had the accent of spontaneous conviction. I was glad of it. It was as though she had become aware of her youth—for there was but little of springlike glory in the rectangular railed space of grass and trees, framed visibly by the orderly roof-slopes of that town, comely without grace, and hospitable without sympathy. In the very air through which she moved there was but little warmth; and the sky, the sky of a land without horizons, swept and washed clean by the April showers, extended a cold cruel blue, without elevation, narrowed suddenly by the ugly, dark wall of the Jura where, here and there, lingered yet a few miserable trails and patches of snow. All the glory of the season must have been within herself—and I was glad this feeling had come into her life, if only for a little time.

"I am pleased to hear you say these words."

She gave me a quick look. Quick, not stealthy. If there was one thing of which she was absolutely incapable, it was stealthiness. Her sincerity was expressed in the very rhythm of her walk. It was I who was looking at her covertly—if I may say so. I knew where she had been, but I did not know what she had seen and heard in that nest of aristocratic conspiracies. I use the word 'aristocratic' for want of a better term. The Château Borel, embowered in the trees and thickets of its neglected grounds, had its fame in our day, like the residence of that other dangerous and exiled woman, Madame de Staël, in the Napoleonic era. Only the Napoleonic despotism, the booted heir of the Revolution, which counted that intellectual woman for an enemy worthy to be watched, was something quite unlike the autocracy in mystic vestments, engendered by the slavery of a Tartar conquest. And Madame de S—— was very far from resembling the gifted author of *Corinne*. She made a great noise about being persecuted. I don't know if she were regarded in certain circles as dangerous. As to being watched, I imagine that the Château Borel could be subjected only to a most distant observation. It was in its exclusiveness an ideal abode for hatching superior plots—whether serious or futile. But all this did not interest me. I wanted to know the effect its extraordinary inhabitants and its special atmosphere had produced on a girl like Miss Haldin, so true, so honest, but so dangerously inexperienced! Her unconsciously lofty ignorance of the baser instincts of mankind left her disarmed before her own impulses. And there was also that friend of her brother, the significant new arrival from Russia . . . I wondered whether she had managed to meet him.

We walked for some time, slowly and in silence.

"You know," I attacked her suddenly, "if you don't intend telling me anything, you must say so distinctly, and then, of course, it shall be final. But I won't play at delicacy. I ask you point-blank for all the details."

She smiled faintly at my threatening tone.

"You are as curious as a child."

"No. I am only an anxious old man," I replied earnestly.

She rested her glance on me as if to ascertain the degree of my anxiety or the number of my years. My physiognomy has never been expressive, I believe, and as to my years I am not ancient enough as yet to be strikingly decrepit.

I have no long beard like the good hermit of a romantic ballad; my footsteps are not tottering, my aspect not that of a slow, venerable sage. Those picturesque advantages are not mine. I am old, alas, in a brisk, commonplace way. And it seemed to me as though there were some pity for me in Miss Haldin's prolonged glance. She stepped out a little quicker.

"You ask for all the details. Let me see. I ought to remember them. It was novel enough for a—a village girl like me."

After a moment of silence she began by saying that the Château Borel was almost as neglected inside as outside. It was nothing to wonder at. A Hamburg banker, I believe, retired from business, had it built to cheer his remaining days by the view of that lake whose precise, orderly, and well-to-do beauty must have been attractive to the unromantic imagination of a business man. But he died soon. His wife departed too (but only to Italy), and this house of moneyed ease, presumably unsaleable, had stood empty for several years. One went to it up a gravel drive, round a large, coarse grass-plot, with plenty of time to observe the degradation of its stuccoed front. Miss Haldin said that the impression was unpleasant. It grew more depressing as one came nearer.

She observed green stains of moss on the steps of the terrace. The front door stood wide open. There was no one about. She found herself in a wide, lofty, and absolutely empty hall, with a good many doors. These doors were all shut. A broad, bare stone staircase faced her, and the effect of the whole was of an untenanted house. She stood still, disconcerted by the solitude, but after a while she became aware of a voice speaking continuously somewhere.

"You were probably being observed all the time," I suggested. "There must have been eyes."

"I don't see how that could be," she retorted. "I haven't seen even a bird in the grounds. I don't remember hearing a single twitter in the trees. The whole place appeared utterly deserted except for the voice."

She could not make out the language—Russian, French,

or German. No one seemed to answer it. It was as though the voice had been left behind by the departed inhabitants to talk to the bare walls. It went on volubly, with a pause now and then. It was lonely and sad. The time seemed very long to Miss Haldin. An invincible repugnance prevented her from opening one of the doors in the hall. It was so hopeless. No one would come, the voice would never stop. She confessed to me that she had to resist an impulse to turn round and go away unseen, as she had come.

"Really? You had that impulse?" I cried, full of regret. "What a pity you did not obey it."

She shook her head.

"What a strange memory it would have been for one. Those deserted grounds, that empty hall, that impersonal, voluble voice, and—nobody, nothing, not a soul."

The memory would have been unique and harmless. But she was not a girl to run away from an intimidating impression of solitude and mystery. "No, I did not run away," she said. "I stayed where I was—and I did see a soul. Such a strange soul."

As she was gazing up the broad staircase, and had concluded that the voice came from somewhere above, a rustle of dress attracted her attention. She looked down and saw a woman crossing the hall, having issued apparently through one of the many doors. Her face was averted, so that at first she was not aware of Miss Haldin.

On turning her head and seeing a stranger, she appeared very much startled. From her slender figure Miss Haldin had taken her for a young girl; but if her face was almost childishly round, it was also sallow and wrinkled, with dark rings under the eyes. A thick crop of dusty brown hair was parted boyishly on the side with a lateral wave above the dry, furrowed forehead. After a moment of dumb blinking, she suddenly squatted down on the floor.

"What do you mean by squatted down?" I asked, astonished. "This is a very strange detail."

Miss Haldin explained the reason. This person when first seen was carrying a small bowl in her hand. She had squatted down to put it on the floor for the benefit of a large cat, which appeared then from behind her skirts, and hid its head into the bowl greedily. She got up, and approaching Miss Haldin asked with nervous bluntness—

"What do you want? Who are you?"

Miss Haldin mentioned her name and also the name of Peter Ivanovitch. The girlish, elderly woman nodded and puckered her face into a momentary expression of sympathy. Her black silk blouse was old and even frayed in places; the black serge skirt was short and shabby. She continued to blink at close quarters, and her eyelashes and eyebrows seemed shabby too. Miss Haldin, speaking gently to her, as if to an unhappy and sensitive person, explained how it was that her visit could not be an altogether unexpected event to Madame de S——.

"Ah! Peter Ivanovitch brought you an invitation. How was I to know? A *dame de compagnie* is not consulted, as you may imagine."

The shabby woman laughed a little. Her teeth, splendidly white and admirably even, looked absurdly out of place, like a string of pearls on the neck of a ragged tramp. "Peter Ivanovitch is the greatest genius of the century perhaps, but he is the most inconsiderate man living. So if you have an appointment with him you must not be surprised to hear that he is not here."

Miss Haldin explained that she had no appointment with Peter Ivanovitch. She became interested at once in that bizarre person.

"Why should he put himself out for you or any one else? Oh! these geniuses. If you only knew! Yes! And their books—I mean, of course, the books that the world admires, the inspired books. But you have not been behind the scenes. Wait till you have to sit at a table for a half a day with a pen in your hand. He can walk up and down his rooms for hours and hours. I used to get so stiff and numb that I was afraid I would lose my balance and fall off the chair all at once."

She kept her hands folded in front of her, and her eyes, fixed on Miss Haldin's face, betrayed no animation whatever. Miss Haldin, gathering that the lady who called herself a *dame de compagnie* was proud of having acted as secretary to Peter Ivanovitch, made an amiable remark.

"You could not imagine a more trying experience," declared the lady. "There is an Anglo-American journalist interviewing Madame de S—— now, or I would take you up," she continued in a changed tone and glancing towards the staircase. "I act as master of ceremonies."

It appeared that Madame de S—— could not bear Swiss servants about her person; and, indeed, servants would not stay for very long in the Château Borel. There were always difficulties. Miss Haldin had already noticed that the hall was like a dusty barn of marble and stucco with cobwebs in the corners and faint tracks of mud on the black and white tessellated floor.

"I look also after this animal," continued the *dame de compagnie*, keeping her hands folded quietly in front of her; and she bent her worn gaze upon the cat. "I don't mind a bit. Animals have their right; though, strictly speaking, I see no reason why they should not suffer as well as human beings. Do you? But of course they never suffer so much. That is impossible. Only, in their case it is more pitiful because they cannot make a revolution. I used to be a Republican. I suppose you are a Republican?"

Miss Haldin confessed to me that she did not know what to say. But she nodded slightly, and asked in her turn—

"And are you no longer a Republican?"

"After taking down Peter Ivanovitch from dictation for two years, it is difficult for me to be anything. First of all, you have to sit perfectly motionless. The slightest movements you make puts to flight the ideas of Peter Ivanovitch. You hardly dare to breathe. And as to coughing— God forbid. Peter Ivanovitch changed the position of the table to the wall because at first I could not help raising my eyes to look out of the window, while waiting for him to go on with his dictation. That was not allowed. He said I stared so stupidly. I was likewise not permitted to look at him over my shoulder. Instantly Peter Ivanovitch stamped his foot, and would roar, 'Look down on the paper!' It seems my expression, my face, put him off. Well,

I know that I am not beautiful, and that my expression is not hopeful either. He said that my air of unintelligent expectation irritated him. These are his own words."

Miss Haldin was shocked, but admitted to me that she was not altogether surprised.

"Is it possible that Peter Ivanovitch could treat any woman so rudely?" she cried.

The *dame de compagnie* nodded several times with an air of discretion, then assured Miss Haldin that she did not mind in the least. The trying part of it was to have the secret of the composition laid bare before her; to see the great author of the revolutionary gospels grope for words as if he were in the dark as to what he meant to say.

"I am quite willing to be the blind instrument of higher ends. To give one's life for the cause is nothing. But to have one's illusions destroyed—that is really almost more than one can bear. I really don't exaggerate," she insisted. "It seemed to freeze my very beliefs in me—the more so that when we worked in winter Peter Ivanovitch, walking up and down the room, required no artificial heat to keep himself warm. Even when we move to the South of France there are bitterly cold days, especially when you have to sit still for six hours at a stretch. The walls of these villas on the Riviera are so flimsy. Peter Ivanovitch did not seem to be aware of anything. It is true that I kept down my shivers from fear of putting him out. I used to set my teeth till my jaws felt absolutely locked. In the moments when Peter Ivanovitch interrupted his dictation, and sometimes these intervals were very long—often twenty minutes, no less, while he walked to and fro behind my back muttering to himself—I felt I was dying by inches, I assure you. Perhaps if I had let my teeth rattle Peter Ivanovitch might have noticed my distress, but I don't think it would have had any practical effect. He's very miserly in such matters."

The *dame de compagnie* glanced up the staircase. The big cat had finished the milk and was rubbing its whiskered cheek sinuously against her skirt. She dived to snatch it up from the floor.

"Miserliness is rather a quality than otherwise, you

know," she continued, holding the cat in her folded arms.
"With us it is misers who can spare money for worthy objects—not the so-called generous natures. But pray don't
think I am a sybarite. My father was a clerk in the Ministry of Finances with no position at all. You may guess by
this that our home was far from luxurious, though of
course we did not actually suffer from cold. I ran away
from my parents, you know, directly I began to think by
myself. It is not very easy, such thinking. One has got to
be put in the way of it, awakened to the truth. I am in-
debted for my salvation to an old apple-woman, who had
her stall under the gateway of the house we lived in. She
had a kind wrinkled face, and the most friendly voice
imaginable. One day, casually, we began to talk about a
child, a ragged little girl we had seen begging from men
in the streets at dusk; and from one thing to another my
eyes began to open gradually to the horrors from which
innocent people are made to suffer in this world, only in
order that governments might exist. After I once understood the crime of the upper classes, I could not go on
living with my parents. Not a single charitable word was
to be heard in our home from year's end to year's end;
there was nothing but the talk of vile office intrigues, and
of promotion and of salaries, and of courting the favour
of the chiefs. [The mere idea of marrying one day such
another man as my father made me shudder.] I don't mean
that there was any one wanting to marry me. There was
not the slightest prospect of anything of the kind. But was
it not sin enough to live on a Government salary while
half Russia was dying of hunger? The Ministry of Finances! What a grotesque horror it is! What does the
starving, ignorant people want with a Ministry of Finances? I kissed my old folks on both cheeks, and went
away from them to live in cellars, with the proletariat. I
tried to make myself useful to the utterly hopeless. I suppose you understand what I mean? I mean the people
who have nowhere to go and nothing to look forward to
in this life. Do you understand how frightful that is—nothing to look forward to! Sometimes I think that it is only in

Russia that there are such people and such a depth of misery can be reached. Well, I plunged into it, and—do you know—there isn't much that one can do in there. No, indeed—at least as long as there are Ministries of Finances and such like grotesque horrors to stand in the way. I suppose I would have gone mad there just trying to fight the vermin, if it had not been for a man. It was my old friend and teacher, the poor saintly apple-woman, who discovered him for me, quite accidentally. She came to fetch me late one evening in her quiet way. I followed her where she would lead; that part of my life was in her hand altogether, and without her my spirit would have perished miserably. The man was a young workman, a lithographer by trade, and he had got into trouble in connexion with that affair of temperance tracts—you remember. There was a lot of people put in prison for that. The Ministry of Finances again! What would become of it if the poor folk ceased making beasts of themselves with drink? Upon my word, I would think that finances and all the rest of it are an invention of the devil; only that a belief in a supernatural source of evil is not necessary; men alone are quite capable of every wickedness. Finances indeed!"

Hatred and contempt hissed in her utterance of the word "finances," but at the very moment she gently stroked the cat reposing in her arms. She even raised them slightly, and inclining her head rubbed her cheek against the fur of the animal, which received this caress with the complete detachment so characteristic of its kind. Then looking at Miss Haldin she excused herself once more for not taking her upstairs to Madame de S——. The interview could not be interrupted. Presently the journalist would be seen coming down the stairs. The best thing was to remain in the hall; and besides, all these rooms (she glanced all round at the many doors), all these rooms on the ground floor were unfurnished.

"Positively there is no chair down here to offer you," she continued. "But if you prefer your own thoughts to my

chatter, I will sit down on the bottom step here and keep
silent."

Miss Haldin hastened to assure her that, on the contrary, she was very much interested in the story of the
journeyman lithographer. He was a revolutionist, of course.

"A martyr, a simple man," said the *dame de compagnie*
with a faint sigh, and gazing through the open front door
dreamily. She turned her misty brown eyes on Miss
Haldin.

"I lived with him for four months. It was like a nightmare."

As Miss Haldin looked at her inquisitively she began to
describe the emaciated face of the man, his fleshless limbs,
his destitution. The room into which the apple-woman
had led her was a tiny garret, a miserable den under the
roof of a sordid house. The plaster fallen off the walls covered the floor, and when the door was opened a horrible
tapestry of black cobwebs waved in the draught. He had
been liberated a few days before—flung out of prison into
the streets. And Miss Haldin seemed to see for the first
time, a name and a face upon the body of that suffering
people whose hard fate had been the subject of so many
conversations, between her and her brother, in the garden
of their country house.

He had been arrested with scores and scores of other
people in that affair of the lithographed temperance tracts.
Unluckily, having got hold of a great many suspected
persons, the police thought they could extract from some
of them other information relating to the revolutionist
propaganda.

"They beat him so cruelly in the course of investigation," went on the *dame de compagnie*, "that they injured
him internally. When they had done with him he was
doomed. He could do nothing for himself. I beheld him
lying on a wooden bedstead without any bedding, with
his head on a bundle of dirty rags, lent to him out of charity by an old rag-picker, who happened to live in the
basement of the house. There he was, uncovered, burning
with fever, and there was not even a jug in the room for

the water to quench his thirst with. There was nothing whatever—just that bedstead and the bare floor."

"Was there no one in all that great town amongst the liberals and revolutionaries, to extend a helping hand to a brother?" asked Miss Haldin indignantly.

"Yes. But you do not know the most terrible part of that man's misery. Listen. It seems that they ill-used him so atrociously that, at last, his firmness gave way, and he did let out some information. Poor soul, the flesh is weak, you know. What it was he did not tell me. There was a crushed spirit in that mangled body. Nothing I found to say could make him whole. When they let him out, he crept into that hole, and bore his remorse stoically. He would not go near any one he knew. I would have sought assistance for him, but, indeed, where could I have gone looking for it? Where was I to look for any one who had anything to spare or any power to help? The people living round us were all starving and drunken. They were the victims of the Ministry of Finances. Don't ask me how we lived. I couldn't tell you. It was like a miracle of wretchedness. I had nothing to sell, and I assure you my clothes were in such a state that it was impossible for me to go out in the daytime. I was indecent. I had to wait till it was dark before I ventured into the streets to beg for a crust of bread, or whatever I could get, to keep him and me alive. Often I got nothing, and then I would crawl back and lie on the floor by the side of his couch. Oh yes, I can sleep quite soundly on bare boards. That is nothing, and I am only mentioning it to you so that you should not think I am a sybarite. It was infinitely less killing than the task of sitting for hours at a table in a cold study to take the books of Peter Ivanovitch from dictation. But you shall see yourself what that is like, so I needn't say any more about it."

"It is by no means certain that I will ever take Peter Ivanovitch from dictation," said Miss Haldin.

"No!" cried the other incredulously. "Not certain? You mean to say that you have not made up your mind?"

When Miss Haldin assured her that there never had been any question of that between her and Peter Ivanovitch, the woman with the cat compressed her lips tightly for a moment.

"Oh, you will find yourself settled at the table before you know that you have made up your mind. Don't make a mistake, it is disenchanting to hear Peter Ivanovitch dictate, but at the same time there is a fascination about it. He is a man of genius. Your face is certain not to irritate him; you may perhaps even help his inspiration, make it easier for him to deliver his message. As I look at you, I feel certain that you are the kind of woman who is not likely to check the flow of his inspiration."

Miss Haldin thought it useless to protest against all these assumptions.

"But this man—this workman—did he die under your care?" she said, after a short silence.

The *dame de compagnie*, listening up the stairs where now two voices were alternating with some animation, made no answer for a time. When the loud sounds of the discussion had sunk into an almost inaudible murmur, she turned to Miss Haldin.

"Yes, he died, but not, literally speaking, in my arms, as you might suppose. As a matter of fact, I was asleep when he breathed his last. So even now I cannot say I have seen anybody die. A few days before the end, some young men found us out in our extremity. They were revolutionists, as you might guess. He ought to have trusted in his political friends when he came out of prison. He had been liked and respected before, and nobody would have dreamed of reproaching him with his indiscretion before the police. Everybody knows how they go to work, and the strongest man has his moments of weakness before pain. Why even hunger alone is enough to give one queer ideas as to what may be done. A doctor came, our lot was alleviated as far as physical comforts go, but otherwise he could not be consoled—poor man. I assure you, Miss Haldin, that he was very lovable, but I had not the strength to weep. I was nearly dead myself. But there were kind hearts to take care of me. A dress was found to clothe my nakedness. I tell you, I was not decent—and after a time the revolutionists placed me with a Jewish family going abroad, as governess. Of course I could teach the children, I finished the sixth class of the Lyceum; but the real object was, that I should carry some important papers across the frontier. I was entrusted with a packet which I carried next my heart. The gendarmes at the station did not suspect the governess of a Jewish family, busy looking after three children. I don't suppose those Hebrews knew what I had on me, for I had been introduced to them in a very round-about way by persons who did not belong to the revolu-tionary movement, and naturally I had been instructed to accept a very small salary. When we reached Germany I left that family and delivered my papers to a revolutionist in Stuttgart; after this I was employed in various ways. But you do not want to hear all that. I have never felt that I was very useful, but I live in hopes of seeing all the Ministries destroyed, finances and all. The greatest joy of my life has been to hear what your brother has done."

She directed her round eyes again to the sunshine out-side, while the cat reposed within her folded arms in lordly beatitude and sphinx-like meditation.

"Yes! I rejoiced," she began again. "For me there is a heroic ring about the very name of Haldin. They must have been trembling with fear in their Ministries—all those men with fiendish hearts. Here I stand talking to you, and when I think of all the cruelties, oppressions, and in-justices that are going on at this very moment, my head begins to swim. I have looked closely at what would seem inconceivable if one's own eyes had not to be trusted. I have looked at things that made me hate myself for my helplessness. I hated my hands that had no power, my voice that could not be heard, my very mind that would not become unhinged. Ah! I have seen things. And you?"

Miss Haldin was moved. She shook her head slightly.

"No, I have seen nothing for myself as yet," she mur-mured. "We have always lived in the country. It was my brother's wish."

"It is a curious meeting—this—between you and me," continued the other. "Do you believe in chance, Miss

Haldin? How could I have expected to see you, his sister, with my own eyes? Do you know that when the news came the revolutionaries here were as much surprised as pleased, every bit? No one seemed to know anything about your brother. Peter Ivanovitch himself had not foreseen that such a blow was going to be struck. I suppose your brother was simply inspired. I myself think that such deeds should be done by inspiration. It is a great privilege to have the inspiration and the opportunity. Did he resemble you at all? Don't you rejoice, Miss Haldin?"

"You must not expect too much from me," said Miss Haldin, repressing an inclination to cry which came over her suddenly. She succeeded, then added calmly, "I am not a heroic person!"

"You think you couldn't have done such a thing yourself, perhaps?"

"I don't know. I must not even ask myself till I have lived a little longer, seen more. . . ."

The other moved her head appreciatively. The purring of the cat had a loud complacency in the empty hall. No sound of voices came from upstairs. Miss Haldin broke the silence.

"What is it precisely that you heard people say about my brother? You said that they were surprised. Yes, I supposed they were. Did it not seem strange to them that my brother should have failed to save himself after the most difficult part—that is, getting away from the spot—was over? Conspirators should understand these things well. There are reasons why I am very anxious to know how it is he failed to escape."

The *dame de compagnie* had advanced to the open hall-door. She glanced rapidly over her shoulder at Miss Haldin, who remained within the hall.

"Failed to escape," she repeated absently. "Didn't he make the sacrifice of his life? Wasn't he just simply inspired? Wasn't it an act of abnegation? Aren't you certain?"

"What I am certain of," said Miss Haldin, "is that it was not an act of despair. Have you not heard some opinion expressed here upon his miserable capture?"

The *dame de compagnie* mused for a while in the door-way.

"Did I hear? Of course, everything is discussed here. Has not all the world been speaking about your brother? For my part, the mere mention of his achievement plunges me into an envious ecstasy. Why should a man certain of immortality think of his life at all?"

She kept her back turned to Miss Haldin. Upstairs from behind a great dingy white and gold door, visible behind the balustrade of the first floor landing, a deep voice began to drone formally, as if reading over notes or something of the sort. It paused frequently, and then ceased altogether.

"I don't think I can stay any longer now," said Miss Haldin. "I may return another day."

She waited for the *dame de compagnie* to make room for her exit; but the woman appeared lost in the contemplation of sunshine and shadows, sharing between themselves the stillness of the deserted grounds. She concealed the view of the drive from Miss Haldin. Suddenly she said—

"It will not be necessary; here is Peter Ivanovitch himself coming up. But he is not alone. He is seldom alone now."

Hearing that Peter Ivanovitch was approaching, Miss Haldin was not so pleased as she might have been expected to be. Somehow she had lost the desire to see either the heroic captive or Madame de S——, and the reason of that shrinking which came upon her at the very last minute is accounted for by the feeling that those two people had not been treating the woman with the cat kindly.

"Would you please let me pass?" said Miss Haldin at last, touching lightly the shoulder of the *dame de compagnie*.

But the other, pressing the cat to her breast, did not budge.

"I know who is with him," she said, without even looking back.

More unaccountably than ever Miss Haldin felt a strong impulse to leave the house.

"Madame de S—— may be engaged for some time yet,

and what I have got to say to Peter Ivanovitch is just a simple question which I might put to him when I meet him in the grounds on my way down. I really think I must go. I have been some time here, and I am anxious to get back to my mother. Will you let me pass, please?"

The *dame de compagnie* turned her head at last.

"I never supposed that you really wanted to see Madame de S——," she said, with unexpected insight. "Not for a moment." There was something confidential and mysterious in her tone. She passed through the door, with Miss Haldin following her, on to the terrace, and they descended side by side the moss-grown stone steps. There was no one to be seen on the part of the drive visible from the front of the house.

"They are hidden by the trees over there," explained Miss Haldin's new acquaintance, "but you shall see them directly. I don't know who that young man is to whom Peter Ivanovitch has taken such a fancy. He must be one of us, or he would not be admitted here when the others come. You know what I mean by the others. But I must say that he is not at all mystically inclined. I don't know that I have made him out yet. Naturally I am never for very long in the drawing-room. There is always something to do for me, though the establishment here is not so extensive as the villa on the Riviera. But still there are plenty of opportunities for me to make myself useful."

To the left, passing by the ivy-grown end of the stables, appeared Peter Ivanovitch and his companion. They walked very slowly, conversing with some animation. They stopped for a moment, and Peter Ivanovitch was seen to gesticulate, while the young man listened motionless, with his arms hanging down and his head bowed a little. He was dressed in a dark brown suit and a black hat. The round eyes of the *dame de compagnie* remained fixed on the two figures, which had resumed their leisurely approach.

"An extremely polite young man," she said. "You shall see what a bow he will make; and it won't altogether be so exceptional either. He bows in the same way when he meets me alone in the hall."

She moved on a few steps, with Miss Haldin by her side, and things happened just as she had foretold. The young man took off his hat, bowed and fell back, while Peter Ivanovitch advanced quicker, his black, thick arms extended heartily, and seized hold of both Miss Haldin's hands, shook them, and peered at her through his dark glasses.

"That's right, that's right!" he exclaimed twice, approvingly. "And so you have been looked after by . . ." He frowned slightly at the *dame de compagnie*, who was still nursing the cat. "I conclude Eleanor—Madame de S—— is engaged. I know she expected somebody to-day. So the newspaper man did turn up, eh? She is engaged?"

For all answer the *dame de compagnie* turned away her head.

"It is very unfortunate—very unfortunate indeed. I very much regret that you should have been . . ." He lowered suddenly his voice. "But what is it—surely you are not departing, Natalia Victorovna? You got bored waiting, didn't you?"

"Not in the least," Miss Haldin protested. "Only I have been here some time, and I am anxious to get back to my mother."

"The time seemed long, eh? I am afraid our worthy friend here" (Peter Ivanovitch suddenly jerked his head sideways towards his right shoulder and jerked it up again),—"our worthy friend here has not the art of shortening the moments of waiting. No, distinctly she has not the art; and in that respect good intentions alone count for nothing."

The *dame de compagnie* dropped her arms, and the cat found itself suddenly on the ground. It remained quite still after alighting, one hind leg stretched backwards. Miss Haldin was extremely indignant on behalf of the lady companion.

"Believe me, Peter Ivanovitch, that the moments I have passed in the hall of this house have been not a little interesting, and very instructive too. They are memorable. I do not regret the waiting, but I see that the object of my call here can be attained without taking up Madame de S——'s time."

At this point I interrupted Miss Haldin. The above relation is founded on her narrative, which I have not so much dramatized as might be supposed. She had rendered, with extraordinary feeling and animation, the very accent almost of the disciple of the old apple-woman, the irreconcilable hater of Ministries, the voluntary servant of the poor. Miss Haldin's true and delicate humanity had been extremely shocked by the uncongenial fate of her new acquaintance, that lady companion, secretary, whatever she was. For my own part, I was pleased to discover in it one more obstacle to intimacy with Madame de S——. I had a positive abhorrence for the painted, bedizened, dead-faced, glassy-eyed Egeria of Peter Ivanovitch. I do not know what was her attitude to the unseen, but I know that in the affairs of this world she was avaricious, greedy, and unscrupulous. It was within my knowledge that she had been worsted in a sordid and desperate quarrel about money matters with the family of her late husband, the diplomatist. Some very august personages indeed (whom in her fury she had insisted upon scandalously involving in her affairs) had incurred her animosity. I find it perfectly easy to believe that she had come to within an ace of being spirited away, for reasons of state, into some discreet *maison de santé*—a madhouse of sorts, to be plain. It appears, however, that certain high-placed personages opposed it for reasons which . . .

But it's no use to go into details.

Wonder may be expressed at a man in the position of a teacher of languages knowing all this with such definiteness. A novelist says this and that of his personages, and if only he knows how to say it earnestly enough he may not be questioned upon the inventions of his brain in which his own belief is made sufficiently manifest by a telling phrase, a poetic image, the accent of emotion. Art is great! But I have no art, and not having invented Madame de S——, I feel bound to explain how I came to know so much about her.

My informant was the Russian wife of a friend of mine already mentioned, the professor of Lausanne University. It was from her that I learned the last fact of Madame de S——'s history, with which I intend to trouble my readers. She told me, speaking positively, as a person who trusts her sources, of the cause of Madame de S——'s flight from Russia, some years before. It was neither more nor less than this: that she became suspect to the police in connexion with the assassination of the Emperor Alexander. The ground of this suspicion was either some unguarded expressions that escaped her in public, or some talk overheard in her *salon*. Overheard, we must believe, by some guest, perhaps a friend, who hastened to play the informer, I suppose. At any rate, the overheard matter seemed to imply her foreknowledge of that event, and I think she was wise in not waiting for the investigation of such a charge. Some of my readers may remember a little book from her pen, published in Paris, a mystically bad-tempered, declamatory, and frightfully disconnected piece of writing, in which she all but admits the foreknowledge, more than hints at its supernatural origin, and plainly suggests in venomous innuendoes that the guilt of the act was not with the terrorists, but with a palace intrigue. When I observed to my friend, the professor's wife, that the life of Madame de S——, with its unofficial diplomacy, its intrigues, lawsuits, favours, disgrace, expulsions, its atmosphere of scandal, occultism, and charlatanism, was more fit for the eighteenth century than for the conditions of our own time, she assented with a smile, but a moment after went on in a reflective tone: "Charlatanism?—yes, in a certain measure. Still, times are changed. There are forces now which were non-existent in the eighteenth century. I should not be surprised if she were more dangerous than an Englishman would be willing to believe. And what's more, she is looked upon as really dangerous by certain people—*chez nous*."

Chez nous in this connexion meant Russia in general, and the Russian political police in particular. The object of my digression from the straight course of Miss Haldin's

relation (in my own words) of her visit to the Château
Borel, was to bring forward that statement of my friend,
the professor's wife. I wanted to bring it forward simply
to make what I have to say presently of Mr. Razumov's
presence in Geneva, a little more credible—for this is a
Russian story for Western ears, which, as I have observed
already, are not attuned to certain tones of cynicism and
cruelty, of moral negation, and even of moral distress already silenced at our end of Europe. And this I state as
my excuse for having left Miss Haldin standing, one of the
little group of two women and two men who had come
together below the terrace of the Château Borel.

The knowledge which I have just stated was in my
mind when, as I have said, I interrupted Miss Haldin. I
interrupted her with the cry of profound satisfaction—

"So you never saw Madame de S——, after all?"

Miss Haldin shook her head. It was very satisfactory to
me. She had not seen Madame de S——! That was excellent, excellent! I welcomed the conviction that she would
never know Madame de S—— now. I could not explain the
reason of the conviction but by the knowledge that Miss
Haldin was standing face to face with her brother's wonderful friend. I preferred him to Madame de S—— as the
companion and guide of that young girl abandoned to her
inexperience by the miserable end of her brother. But, at
any rate, that life now ended had been sincere, and perhaps its thoughts might have been lofty, its moral sufferings profound, its last act a true sacrifice. It is not for us,
the staid lovers calmed by the possession of a conquered
liberty, to condemn without appeal the fierceness of
thwarted desire.

I am not ashamed of the warmth of my regard for Miss
Haldin. It was, it must be admitted, an unselfish sentiment,
being its own reward. The late Victor Haldin—in the light
of that sentiment—appeared to me not as a sinister conspirator, but as a pure enthusiast. I did not wish indeed
to judge him, but the very fact that he did not escape, that
fact which brought so much trouble to both his mother
and his sister, spoke to me in his favour. Meantime, in my

fear of seeing the girl surrender to the influence of the Château Borel revolutionary feminism, I was more than willing to put my trust in that friend of the late Victor Haldin. He was nothing but a name, you will say. Exactly! A name! And what's more, the only name; the only name to be found in the correspondence between brother and sister. The young man had turned up; they had come face to face, and, fortunately, without the direct interference of Madame de S——. What will come of it? what will she tell me presently? I was asking myself.

It was only natural that my thought should turn to the young man, the bearer of the only name uttered in all the dream-talk of a future to be brought about by a revolution. And my thought took the shape of asking myself why this young man had not called upon these ladies. He had been in Geneva for some days before Miss Haldin heard of him first in my presence from Peter Ivanovitch. I regretted that last's presence at their meeting. I would rather have had it happen somewhere out of his spectacled sight. But I supposed that, having both these young people there, he introduced them to each other.

I broke the silence by beginning a question on that point—

"I suppose Peter Ivanovitch . . ."

Miss Haldin gave vent to her indignation. Peter Ivanovitch directly he had got his answer from her had turned upon the *dame de compagnie* in a shameful manner.

"Turned upon her?" I wondered. "What about? For what reason?"

"It was unheard of; it was shameful," Miss Haldin pursued, with angry eyes. "*Il lui a fait une scène*—like this, before strangers. And for what? You would never guess. For some eggs. . . . Oh!"

I was astonished. "Eggs, did you say?"

"For Madame de S——. That lady observes a special diet, or something of the sort. It seems she complained the day before to Peter Ivanovitch that the eggs were not rightly prepared. Peter Ivanovitch suddenly remembered this against the poor woman, and flew out at her. It was most astonishing. I stood as if rooted."

"Do you mean to say that the great feminist allowed himself to be abusive to a woman?" I asked.

"Oh, not that! It was something you have no conception of. It was an odious performance. Imagine, he raised his hat to begin with. He made his voice soft and deprecatory. 'Ah! you are not kind to us—you will not deign to remember . . .' This sort of phrases, that sort of tone. The poor creature was terribly upset. Her eyes ran full of tears. She did not know where to look. I shouldn't wonder if she would have preferred abuse, or even a blow."

I did not remark that very possibly she was familiar with both on occasions when no one was by. Miss Haldin walked by my side, her head up in scornful and angry silence.

"Great men have their surprising peculiarities," I observed inanely. "Exactly like men who are not great. But that sort of thing cannot be kept up for ever. How did the great feminist wind up this very characteristic episode?"

Miss Haldin, without turning her face my way, told me that the end was brought about by the appearance of the interviewer, who had been closeted with Madame de S——.

He came up rapidly, unnoticed, lifted his hat slightly, and paused to say in French: "The Baroness has asked me, in case I met a lady on my way out, to desire her to come in at once."

After delivering this message, he hurried down the drive. The *dame de compagnie* flew towards the house, and Peter Ivanovitch followed her hastily, looking uneasy. In a moment Miss Haldin found herself alone with the young man, who undoubtedly must have been the new arrival from Russia. She wondered whether her brother's friend had not already guessed who she was.

I am in a position to say that, as a matter of fact, he had guessed. It is clear to me that Peter Ivanovitch, for some reason or other, had refrained from alluding to these ladies' presence in Geneva. But Razumov had guessed. The trustful girl! Every word uttered by Haldin lived in Razumov's memory. They were like haunting shapes; they could not be exorcised. The most vivid amongst them was the mention of the sister. The girl had existed for him ever since. But he did not recognize her at once. Coming up with Peter Ivanovitch, he did observe her; their eyes had met, even. He had responded, as no one could help responding, to the harmonious charm of her whole person, its strength, its grace, its tranquil frankness—and then he had turned his gaze away. He said to himself that all this was not for him; the beauty of women and the friendship of men were not for him. He accepted that feeling with a purposeful sternness, and tried to pass on. It was only her outstretched hand which brought about the recognition. It stands recorded in the pages of his self-confession, that it nearly suffocated him physically with an emotional reaction of hate and dismay, as though her appearance had been a piece of accomplished treachery.

He faced about. The considerable elevation of the terrace concealed them from any one lingering in the doorway of the house; and even from the upstairs windows they could not have been seen. Through the thickets run wild, and the trees of the gently sloping grounds, he had cold, placid glimpses of the lake. A moment of perfect privacy had been vouchsafed to them at this juncture. I wondered to myself what use they had made of that fortunate circumstance.

"Did you have time for more than a few words?" I asked.

That animation with which she had related to me the incidents of her visit to the Château Borel had left her completely. Strolling by my side, she looked straight before her; but I noticed a little colour on her cheek. She did not answer me.

After some little time I observed that they could not have hoped to remain forgotten for very long, unless the other two had discovered Madame de S—— swooning with fatigue, perhaps, or in a state of morbid exaltation after the long interview. Either would require their devoted ministrations. I could depict to myself Peter Ivanovitch rushing busily out of the house again, bareheaded, perhaps, and on across the terrace with his swinging gait, the black skirts of the frock-coat floating clear of his stout light grey legs. I confess to having looked upon these young people as the quarry of the "heroic fugitive." I had the notion that they would not be allowed to escape capture. But of that I said nothing to Miss Haldin, only as she still remained uncommunicative, I pressed her a little.

"Well—but you can tell me at least your impression."

She turned her head to look at me, and turned away again.

"Impression?" she repeated slowly, almost dreamily; then in a quicker tone—

"He seems to be a man who has suffered more from his thoughts than from evil fortune."

"From his thoughts, you say?"

"And that is natural enough in a Russian," she took me up. "In a young Russian; so many of them are unfit for action, and yet unable to rest."

"And you think he is that sort of man?"

"No, I do not judge him. How could I, so suddenly? You asked for my impression—I explain my impression. I —I—don't know the world, nor yet the people in it; I have been too solitary—I am too young to trust my own opinions."

"Trust your instinct," I advised her. "Most women trust to that, and make no worse mistakes than men. In this case you have your brother's letter to help you."

She drew a deep breath like a light sigh.

"Unstained, lofty, and solitary existences," she quoted as if to herself. But I caught the wistful murmur distinctly.

"High praise," I whispered to her.

"The highest possible."

"So high that, like the award of happiness, it is more fit to come only at the end of a life. But still no common or altogether unworthy personality could have suggested such a confident exaggeration of praise and . . ."

"Ah!" She interrupted me ardently. "And if you had

only known the heart from which that judgment has come!"

She ceased on that note, and for a space I reflected on the character of the words which I perceived very well must tip the scale of the girl's feeling in that young man's favour. They had not the sound of a casual utterance. Vague they were to my Western mind and to my Western sentiment, but I could not forget that, standing by Miss Haldin's side, I was like a traveller in a strange country. It had also become clear to me that Miss Haldin was unwilling to enter into the details of the only material part of their visit to the Château Borel. But I was not hurt. Somehow I didn't feel it to be a want of confidence. It was some other difficulty—a difficulty I could not resent. And it was without the slightest resentment that I said—

"Very well. But on that high ground, which I will not dispute, you, like any one else in such circumstances, you must have made for yourself a representation of that exceptional friend, a mental image of him, and—please tell me—you were not disappointed?"

"What do you mean? His personal appearance?"

"I don't mean precisely his good looks, or otherwise."

We turned at the end of the alley and made a few steps without looking at each other.

"His appearance is not ordinary," said Miss Haldin at last.

"No, I should have thought not—from the little you've said of your first impression. After all, one has to fall back on that word. Impression! What I mean is that something indescribable which is likely to mark a 'not ordinary' person."

I perceived that she was not listening. There was no mistaking her expression; and once more I had the sense of being out of it—not because of my age, which at any rate could draw inferences—but altogether out of it, on another plane whence I could only watch her from afar. And so ceasing to speak I watched her stepping out by my side.

"No," she exclaimed suddenly, "I could not have been disappointed with a man of such strong feeling."

"Aha! Strong feeling," I muttered, thinking to myself censoriously: like this, at once, all in a moment!

"What did you say?" inquired Miss Haldin innocently.

"Oh, nothing. I beg your pardon. Strong feeling. I am not surprised."

"And you don't know how abruptly I behaved to him!" she cried remorsefully.

I suppose I must have appeared surprised, for, looking at me with a still more heightened colour, she said she was ashamed to admit that she had not been sufficiently collected; she had failed to control her words and actions as the situation demanded. She lost the fortitude worthy of both the men, the dead and the living; the fortitude which should have been the note of the meeting of Victor Haldin's sister with Victor Haldin's only known friend. He was looking at her keenly, but said nothing, and she was—she confessed—painfully affected by his want of comprehension. All she could say was: "You are Mr. Razumov." A slight frown passed over his forehead. After a short, watchful pause, he made a little bow of assent, and waited.

At the thought that she had before her the man so highly regarded by her brother, the man who had known his value, spoken to him, understood him, had listened to his confidences, perhaps had encouraged him—her lips trembled, her eyes ran full of tears; she put out her hand, made a step towards him impulsively, saying with an effort to restrain her emotion, "Can't you guess who I am?" He did not take the proffered hand. He even recoiled a pace, and Miss Haldin imagined that he was unpleasantly affected. Miss Haldin excused him, directing her displeasure at herself. She had behaved unworthily, like an emotional French girl. A manifestation of that kind could not be welcomed by a man of stern, self-contained character.

He must have been stern indeed, or perhaps very timid with women, not to respond in a more human way to the advances of a girl like Nathalie Haldin—I thought to myself. Those lofty and solitary existences (I remembered the

words suddenly) make a young man shy and an old man
savage—often.

"Well," I encouraged Miss Haldin to proceed.

She was still very dissatisfied with herself.

"I went from bad to worse," she said, with an air of discouragement very foreign to her. "I did everything foolish
except actually bursting into tears. I am thankful to say
I did not do that. But I was unable to speak for quite a
long time."

She had stood before him speechless, swallowing her
sobs, and when she managed at last to utter something, it
was only her brother's name—"Victor—Victor Haldin!" she
gasped out, and again her voice failed her.

"Of course," she commented to me, "this distressed him.
He was quite overcome. I have told you my opinion that
he is a man of deep feeling—it is impossible to doubt it. You
should have seen his face. He positively reeled. He leaned
against the wall of the terrace. Their friendship must have
been the very brotherhood of souls! I was grateful to him
for that emotion, which made me feel less ashamed of my
own lack of self-control. Of course I had regained the
power of speech at once, almost. All this lasted not more
than a few seconds. 'I am his sister,' I said. 'Maybe you
have heard of me.'"

"And had he?" I interrupted.

"I don't know. How could it have been otherwise? And
yet . . . But what does that matter? I stood there before
him, near enough to be touched and surely not looking like
an impostor. All I know is, that he put out both his hands
then to me, I may say flung them out at me, with the
greatest readiness and warmth, and that I seized and
pressed them, feeling that I was finding again a little of
what I thought was lost to me for ever, with the loss of
my brother—some of that hope, inspiration, and support
which I used to get from my dear dead . . ."

I understood quite well what she meant. We strolled
on slowly. I refrained from looking at her. And it was as
if answering my own thoughts that I murmured—

"No doubt it was a great friendship—as you say. And

that young man ended by welcoming your name, so to speak, with both hands. After that, of course, you would understand each other. Yes, you would understand each other quickly."

It was a moment before I heard her voice.

"Mr. Razumov seems to be a man of few words. A reserved man—even when he is strongly moved."

Unable to forget—or even to forgive—the bass-toned expansiveness of Peter Ivanovitch, the Arch-Patron of revolutionary parties, I said that I took this for a favourable trait of character. It was associated with sincerity—in my mind.

"And, besides, we had not much time," she added.

"No, you would not have, of course." My suspicion and even dread of the feminist and his Egeria was so ineradicable that I could not help asking with real anxiety, which I made smiling—

"But you escaped all right?"

She understood me, and smiled too, at my uneasiness.

"Oh yes! I escaped, if you like to call it that. I walked away quickly. There was no need to run. I am neither frightened nor yet fascinated, like that poor woman who received me so strangely."

"And Mr.—Mr. Razumov . . . ?"

"He remained there, of course. I suppose he went into the house after I left him. You remember that he came here strongly recommended to Peter Ivanovitch—possibly entrusted with important messages for him."

"Ah yes! From that priest who . . ."

"Father Zosim—yes. Or from others, perhaps."

"You left him, then. But have you seen him since, may I ask?"

For some time Miss Haldin made no anwer to this very direct question, then—

"I have been expecting to see him here to-day," she said quietly.

"You have! Do you meet, then, in this garden? In that case I had better leave you at once."

"No, why leave me? And we don't meet in this garden.

I have not seen Mr. Razumov since that first time. Not once. But I have been expecting him . . ."

She paused. I wondered to myself why that young revolutionist should show so little alacrity.

"Before we parted I told Mr. Razumov that I walked here for an hour every day at this time. I could not explain to him then why I did not ask him to come and see us at once. Mother must be prepared for such a visit. And then, you see, I do not know myself what Mr. Razumov has to tell us. He, too, must be told first how it is with poor mother. All these thoughts flashed through my mind at once. So I told him hurriedly that there was a reason why I could not ask him to see us at home, but that I was in the habit of walking here. . . . This is a public place, but there are never many people about at this hour. I thought it would do very well. And it is so near our apartments. I don't like to be very far away from mother. Our servant knows where I am in case I should be wanted suddenly."

"Yes. It is very convenient from that point of view," I agreed.

In fact, I thought the Bastions a very convenient place, since the girl did not think it prudent as yet to introduce that young man to her mother. It was here, then, I thought, looking round at that plot of ground of deplorable banality, that their acquaintance will begin and go on in the exchange of generous indignations and of extreme sentiments, too poignant, perhaps, for a non-Russian mind to conceive. I saw these two, escaped out of four score of millions of human beings ground between the upper and nether millstone, walking under these trees, their young heads close together. Yes, an excellent place to stroll and talk in. It even occurred to me, while we turned once more away from the wide iron gates, that when tired they would have plenty of accommodation to rest themselves. There was a quantity of tables and chairs displayed between the restaurant chalet and the bandstand, a whole raft of painted deals spread out under the trees. In the very middle of it I observed a solitary Swiss couple, whose fate was made secure from the cradle to the grave by the perfected

mechanism of democratic institutions in a republic that
could almost be held in the palm of one's hand. The man,
colourlessly uncouth, was drinking beer out of a glittering
glass; the woman, rustic and placid, leaning back in the
rough chair, gazed idly around.

There is little logic to be expected on this earth, not
only in the matter of thought, but also of sentiment. I was
surprised to discover myself displeased with that unknown
young man. A week had gone by since they met. Was he
callous, or shy, or very stupid? I could not make it out.

"Do you think," I asked Miss Haldin, after we had gone
some distance up the great alley, "that Mr. Razumov understood your intention?"

"Understood what I meant?" she wondered. "He was
greatly moved. That I know! In my own agitation I could
see it. But I spoke distinctly. He heard me; he seemed, indeed, to hang on my words . . ."

Unconsciously she had hastened her pace. Her utterance,
too, became quicker.

I waited a little before I observed thoughtfully—

"And yet he allowed all these days to pass."

"How can we tell what work he may have to do here?
He is not an idler travelling for his pleasure. His time may
not be his own—nor yet his thoughts, perhaps."

She slowed her pace suddenly, and in a lowered voice
added—

"Or his very life"—then paused and stood still. "For all
I know, he may have had to leave Geneva the very day he
saw me."

"Without telling you!" I exclaimed incredulously.

"I did not give him time. I left him quite abruptly. I
behaved emotionally to the end. I am sorry for it. Even if
I had given him the opportunity he would have been justified in taking me for a person not to be trusted. An emotional, tearful girl is not a person to confide in. But even
if he has left Geneva for a time, I am confident that we
shall meet again."

"Ah! you are confident. . . . I dare say. But on what
ground?"

"Because I've told him that I was in great need of some-one, a fellow-countryman, a fellow-believer, to whom I could give my confidence in a certain matter."

"I see. I don't ask you what answer he made. I confess that this is good ground for your belief in Mr. Razumov's appearance before long. But he has not turned up to-day?"

"No," she said quietly, "not to-day;" and we stood for a time in silence, like people that have nothing more to say to each other and let their thoughts run widely asunder before their bodies go off their different ways. Miss Haldin glanced at the watch on her wrist and made a brusque movement. She had already overstayed her time, it seemed.

"I don't like to be away from mother," she murmured, shaking her head. "It is not that she is very ill now. But somehow when I am not with her I am more uneasy than ever."

Mrs. Haldin had not made the slightest allusion to her son for the last week or more. She sat, as usual, in the armchair by the window, looking out silently on that hopeless stretch of the Boulevard des Philosophes. When she spoke, a few lifeless words, it was of indifferent, trivial things.

"For any one who knows what the poor soul is thinking of, that sort of talk is more painful than her silence. But that is bad too; I can hardly endure it, and I dare not break it."

Miss Haldin sighed, refastening a button of her glove which had come undone. I knew well enough what a hard time of it she must be having. The stress, its causes, its nature, would have undermined the health of an Occidental girl; but Russian natures have a singular power of re-sistance against the unfair strains of life. Straight and supple, with a short jacket open on her black dress, which made her figure appear more slender and her fresh but colourless face more pale, she compelled my wonder and admiration.

"I can't stay a moment longer. You ought to come soon to see mother. You know she calls you '*L'ami.*' It is an excellent name, and she really means it. And now *au revoir*, I must run."

She glanced vaguely down the broad walk—the hand she put out to me eluded my grasp by an unexpected upward movement, and rested upon my shoulder. Her red lips were slightly parted, not in a smile, however, but expressing a sort of startled pleasure. She gazed towards the gates and said quickly, with a gasp—

"There! I knew it. Here he comes!"

I understood that she must mean Mr. Razumov. A young man was walking up the alley, without haste. His clothes were some dull shade of brown, and he carried a stick. When my eyes first fell on him, his head was hanging on his breast as if in deep thought. While I was looking at him he raised it sharply, and at once stopped. I am certain he did, but that pause was nothing more perceptible than a faltering check in his gait, instantaneously overcome. Then he continued his approach, looking at us steadily. Miss Haldin signed to me to remain, and advanced a step or two to meet him.

I turned my head away from that meeting, and did not look at them again till I heard Miss Haldin's voice uttering his name in the way of introduction. Mr. Razumov was informed, in a warm, low tone, that, besides being a wonderful teacher, I was a great support "in our sorrow and distress."

Of course I was described also as an Englishman. Miss Haldin spoke rapidly, faster than I have ever heard her speak, and that by contrast made the quietness of her eyes more expressive.

"I have given him my confidence," she added, looking all the time at Mr. Razumov. That young man did, indeed, rest his gaze on Miss Haldin, but certainly did not look into her eyes which were so ready for him. Afterwards he glanced backwards and forwards at us both, while the faint commencement of a forced smile, followed by the suspicion of a frown, vanished one after another; I detected them, though neither could have been noticed by a person less intensely bent upon divining him than myself. I don't know

what Nathalie Haldin had observed, but my attention
seized the very shades of these movements. The attempted
smile was given up, the incipient frown was checked, and
smoothed so that there should be no sign; but I imagined
him exclaiming inwardly—

"Her confidence! To this elderly person—this foreigner!"

I imagined this because he looked foreign enough to
me. I was upon the whole favourably impressed. He had
an air of intelligence and even some distinction quite above
the average of the students and other inhabitants of the
Petite Russie. His features were more decided than in the
generality of Russian faces; he had a line of the jaw, a
clean-shaven, sallow cheek; his nose was a ridge, and not a
mere protuberance. He wore the hat well down over his
eyes, his dark hair curled low on the nape of his neck; in
the ill-fitting brown clothes there were sturdy limbs; a
slight stoop brought out a satisfactory breadth of shoulders.
Upon the whole I was not disappointed. Studious—robust
—shy. . . .

Before Miss Haldin had ceased speaking I felt the grip
of his hand on mine, a muscular, firm grip, but unexpectedly hot and dry. Not a word or even a mutter assisted
this short and arid handshake.

I intended to leave them to themselves, but Miss Haldin
touched me lightly on the forearm with a significant contact, conveying a distinct wish. Let him smile who likes,
but I was only too ready to stay near Nathalie Haldin,
and I am not ashamed to say that it was no smiling matter
to me. I stayed, not as a youth would have stayed, uplifted, as it were poised in the air, but soberly, with my
feet on the ground and my mind trying to penetrate her
intention. She had turned to Razumov.

"Well. This is the place. Yes, it is here that I meant
you to come. I have been walking every day. . . . Don't
excuse yourself—I understand. I am grateful to you for coming to-day, but all the same I cannot stay now. It is impossible. I must hurry off home. Yes, even with you standing
before me, I must run off. I have been too long away. . . .
You know how it is?"

These last words were addressed to me. I noticed that Mr. Razumov passed the tip of his tongue over his lips just as a parched, feverish man might do. He took her hand in its black glove, which closed on his, and held it—detained it quite visibly to me against a drawing-back movement.

"Thank you once more for—for understanding me," she went on warmly. He interrupted her with a certain effect of roughness. I didn't like him speaking to this frank creature so much from under the brim of his hat, as it were. And he produced a faint, rasping voice quite like a man with a parched throat.

"What is there to thank me for? Understand you? . . . How did I understand you? . . . You had better know that I understand nothing. I was aware that you wanted to see me in this garden. I could not come before. I was hindered. And even to-day, you see . . . late."

She still held his hand.

"I can, at any rate, thank you for not dismissing me from your mind as a weak, emotional girl. No doubt I want sustaining. I am very ignorant. But I can be trusted. Indeed I can!"

"You are ignorant," he repeated thoughtfully. He had raised his head, and was looking straight into her face now, while she held his hand. They stood like this for a long moment. She released his hand.

"Yes. You did come late. It was good of you to come on the chance of me having loitered beyond my time. I was talking with this good friend here. I was talking of you. Yes, Kirylo Sidorovitch, of you. He was with me when I first heard of your being here in Geneva. He can tell you what comfort it was to my bewildered spirit to hear that news. He knew I meant to seek you out. It was the only object of my accepting the invitation of Peter Ivanovitch. . . ."

"Peter Ivanovitch talked to you of me?" he interrupted, in that wavering, hoarse voice which suggested a horribly dry throat.

"Very little. Just told me your name, and that you had

arrived here. Why should I have asked for more? What
could he have told me that I did not know already from
my brother's letter? Three lines! And how much they meant
to me! I will show them to you one day, Kirylo Sidorovitch.
But now I must go. The first talk between us cannot be a
matter of five minutes, so we had better not begin. . . ."

I had been standing a little aside, seeing them both in
profile. At that moment it occurred to me that Mr. Razumov's face was older than his age.

"If mother"—the girl had turned suddenly to me—
"were to wake up in my absence (so much longer than
usual) she would perhaps question me. She seems to miss
me more, you know, of late. She would want to know
what delayed me—and, you see, it would be painful for
me to dissemble before her."

I understood the point very well. For the same reason
she checked what seemed to be on Mr. Razumov's part a
movement to accompany her.

"No! No! I go alone, but meet me here as soon as possible." Then to me in a lower, significant tone—

"Mother may be sitting at the window at this moment,
looking down the street. She must not know anything of
Mr. Razumov's presence here till—till something is arranged." She paused before she added a little louder, but
still speaking to me, "Mr. Razumov does not quite understand my difficulty, but you know what it is."

V

With a quick inclination of the head for us both, and an
earnest, friendly glance at the young man, Miss Haldin left
us covering our heads and looking after her straight, supple
figure receding rapidly. Her walk was not that hybrid and
uncertain gliding affected by some women, but a frank,
strong, healthy movement forward. Rapidly she increased
the distance—disappeared with suddenness at last. I discovered only then that Mr. Razumov, after ramming his
hat well over his brow, was looking me over from head to
foot. I dare say I was a very unexpected fact for that

young Russian to stumble upon. I caught in his physiognomy, in his whole bearing, an expression compounded of curiosity and scorn, tempered by alarm—as though he had been holding his breath while I was not looking. But his eyes met mine with a gaze direct enough. I saw then for the first time that they were of a clear brown colour and fringed with thick black eyelashes. They were the youngest feature of his face. Not at all unpleasant eyes. He swayed slightly, leaning on his stick and generally hung in the wind. It flashed upon me that in leaving us together Miss Haldin had an intention—that something was entrusted to me, since, by a mere accident I had been found at hand. On this assumed ground I put all possible friendliness into my manner. I cast about for some right thing to say, and suddenly in Miss Haldin's last words I perceived the clue to the nature of my mission.

"No," I said gravely, if with a smile, "you cannot be expected to understand."

His clean-shaven lip quivered ever so little before he said, as if wickedly amused—

"But haven't you heard just now? I was thanked by that young lady for understanding so well."

I looked at him rather hard. Was there a hidden and inexplicable sneer in this retort? No. It was not that. It might have been resentment. Yes. But what had he to resent? He looked as though he had not slept very well of late. I could almost feel on me the weight of his unrefreshed, motionless stare, the stare of a man who lies unwinking in the dark, angrily passive in the toils of disastrous thoughts. Now, when I know how true it was, I can honestly affirm that this *was* the effect produced on me. It was painful in a curiously indefinite way—for, of course, the definition comes to me now while I sit writing in the fullness of my knowledge. But this is what the effect was at that time of absolute ignorance. This new sort of uneasiness which he seemed to be forcing upon me I attempted to put down by assuming a conversational, easy familiarity.

"That extremely charming and essentially admirable young girl (I am—as you see—old enough to be frank in my expressions) was referring to her own feelings. Surely you must have understood that much?"

He made such a brusque movement that he even tottered a little.

"Must understand this! Not expected to understand that! I may have other things to do. And the girl is charming and admirable. Well—and if she is! I suppose I can see that for myself."

This sally would have been insulting if his voice had not been practically extinct, dried up in his throat; and the rustling effort of his speech too painful to give real offence.

I remained silent, checked between the obvious fact and the subtle impression. It was open to me to leave him there and then; but the sense of having been entrusted with a mission, the suggestion of Miss Haldin's last glance, was strong upon me. After a moment of reflection I said—

"Shall we walk together a little?"

He shrugged his shoulders so violently that he tottered again. I saw it out of the corner of my eye as I moved on, with him at my elbow. He had fallen back a little and was practically out of my sight, unless I turned my head to look at him. I did not wish to indispose him still further by an appearance of marked curiosity. It might have been distasteful to such a young and secret refugee from under the pestilential shadow hiding the true, kindly face of his land. And the shadow, the attendant of his countrymen, stretching across the middle of Europe, was lying on him too, darkening his figure to my mental vision. "Without doubt," I said to myself, "he seems a sombre, even a desperate revolutionist; but he is young, he may be unselfish and humane, capable of compassion, of . . ."

I heard him clear gratingly his parched throat, and became all attention.

"This is beyond everything," were his first words. "It is beyond everything! I find you here, for no reason that I can understand, in possession of something I cannot be expected to understand! A confidant! A foreigner! Talking about an admirable Russian girl. Is the admirable girl a fool, I begin to wonder? What are you at? What is your object?"

He was barely audible, as if his throat had no more resonance than a dry rag, a piece of tinder. It was so pitiful that I found it extremely easy to control my indignation.

"When you have lived a little longer, Mr. Razumov, you will discover that no woman is an absolute fool. I am not a feminist, like that illustrious author, Peter Ivanovitch, who, to say the truth, is not a little suspect to me. . . ."

He interrupted me, in a surprising note of whispering astonishment.

"Suspect to you! Peter Ivanovitch suspect to you! To you! . . ."

"Yes, in a certain aspect he is," I said, dismissing my remark lightly. "As I was saying, Mr. Razumov, when you have lived long enough, you will learn to discriminate between the noble trustfulness of a nature foreign to every meanness and the flattered credulity of some women; though even the credulous, silly as they may be, unhappy as they are sure to be, are never absolute fools. It is my belief that no woman is ever completely deceived. Those that are lost leap into the abyss with their eyes open, if all the truth were known."

"Upon my word," he cried at my elbow, "what is it to me whether women are fools or lunatics? I really don't care what you think of them. I—I am not interested in them. I let them be. I am not a young man in a novel. How do you know that I want to learn anything about women? . . . What is the meaning of all this?"

"The object, you mean, of this conversation, which I admit I have forced upon you in a measure."

"Forced! Object!" he repeated, still keeping half a pace or so behind me. "You wanted to talk about women, apparently. That's a subject. But I don't care for it. I have never . . . In fact, I have had other subjects to think about."

"I am concerned here with one woman only—a young girl—the sister of your dead friend—Miss Haldin. Surely you can think a little of her. What I meant from the first was that there is a situation which you cannot be expected to understand."

I listened to his unsteady footfalls by my side for the space of several strides.

"I think that it may prepare the ground for your next interview with Miss Haldin if I tell you of it. I imagine that she might have had something of the kind in her mind when she left us together. I believe myself authorized to speak. The peculiar situation I have alluded to has arisen in the first grief and distress of Victor Haldin's execution. There was something peculiar in the circumstances of his arrest. You no doubt know the whole truth. . . ."

I felt my arm seized above the elbow, and next instant found myself swung so as to face Mr. Razumov.

"You spring up from the ground before me with this talk. Who the devil are you? This is not to be borne! Why! What for? What do you know what is or is not peculiar? What have you to do with any confounded circumstances, or with anything that happens in Russia, anyway?"

He leaned on his stick with his other hand, heavily; and when he let go my arm, I was certain in my mind that he was hardly able to keep on his feet.

"Let us sit down at one of these vacant tables," I proposed, disregarding this display of unexpectedly profound emotion. It was not without its effect on me, I confess. I was sorry for him.

"What tables? What are you talking about? Oh—the empty tables? The tables there. Certainly. I will sit at one of the empty tables."

I led him away from the path to the very centre of the raft of deals before the *chalet*. The Swiss couple were gone by that time. We were alone on the raft, so to speak. Mr. Razumov dropped into a chair, let fall his stick, and propped on his elbows, his head between his hands, stared at me persistently, openly, and continuously, while I signalled the waiter and ordered some beer. I could not quarrel with this silent inspection very well, because, truth to tell, I felt somewhat guilty of having been sprung on him with some abruptness—of having "sprung from the ground," as he expressed it.

While waiting to be served I mentioned that, born from parents settled in St. Petersburg, I had acquired the language as a child. The town I did not remember, having left it for good as a boy of nine, but in later years I had renewed my acquaintance with the language. He listened, without as much as moving his eyes the least little bit. He had to change his position when the beer came, and the instant draining of his glass revived him. He leaned back in his chair and, folding his arms across his chest, continued to stare at me squarely. It occurred to me that his clean-shaven, almost swarthy face was really of the very mobile sort, and that the absolute stillness of it was the acquired habit of a revolutionist, of a conspirator everlastingly on his guard against self-betrayal in a world of secret spies.

"But you are an Englishman—a teacher of English literature," he murmured, in a voice that was no longer issuing from a parched throat. "I have heard of you. People told me you have lived here for years."

"Quite true. More than twenty years. And I have been assisting Miss Haldin with her English studies."

"You have been reading English poetry with her," he said, immovable now, like another man altogether, a complete stranger to the man of the heavy and uncertain footfalls a little while ago—at my elbow.

"Yes, English poetry," I said. "But the trouble of which I speak was caused by an English newspaper."

He continued to stare at me. I don't think he was aware that the story of the midnight arrest had been ferreted out by an English journalist and given to the world. When I explained this to him he muttered contemptuously, "It may have been altogether a lie."

"I should think you are the best judge of that," I retorted, a little disconcerted. "I must confess that to me it looks to be true in the main."

"How can you tell truth from lies?" he queried in his new, immovable manner.

"I don't know how you do it in Russia," I began, rather nettled by his attitude. He interrupted me.

"In Russia, and in general everywhere—in a newspaper, for instance. The colour of the ink and the shapes of the letters are the same."

"Well, there are other trifles one can go by. The character of the publication, the general verisimilitude of the news, the consideration of the motive, and so on. I don't trust blindly the accuracy of special correspondents—but why should this one have gone to the trouble of concocting a circumstantial falsehood on a matter of no importance to the world?"

"That's what it is," he grumbled. "What's going on with us is of no importance—a mere sensational story to amuse the readers of the papers—the superior contemptuous Europe. It is hateful to think of. But let them wait a bit!"

He broke off on this sort of threat addressed to the Western world. Disregarding the anger in his stare, I pointed out that whether the journalist was well- or ill-informed, the concern of the friends of these ladies was with the effect the few lines of print in question had produced—the effect alone. And surely he must be counted as one of the friends—if only for the sake of his late comrade and intimate fellow-revolutionist. At that point I thought he was going to speak vehemently; but he only astounded me by the convulsive start of his whole body. He restrained himself, folded his loosened arms tighter across his chest, and sat back with a smile in which there was a twitch of scorn and malice.

"Yes, a comrade and an intimate. . . . Very well," he said.

"I ventured to speak to you on that assumption. And I cannot be mistaken. I was present when Peter Ivanovitch announced your arrival here to Miss Haldin, and I saw her relief and thankfulness when your name was mentioned. Afterwards she showed me her brother's letter, and read out the few words in which he alludes to you. What else but a friend could you have been?"

"Obviously. That's perfectly well known. A friend. Quite correct. . . . Go on. You were talking of some effect."

I said to myself: "He puts on the callousness of a stern revolutionist, the insensibility to common emotions of a man devoted to a destructive idea. He is young, and his sincerity assumes a pose before a stranger, a foreigner, an old man. Youth must assert itself. . . ." As concisely as possible I exposed to him the state of mind poor Mrs. Haldin had been thrown into by the news of her son's untimely end.

He listened—I felt it—with profound attention. His level stare deflected gradually downwards, left my face, and rested at last on the ground at his feet.

"You can enter into the sister's feelings. As you said, I have only read a little English poetry with her, and I won't make myself ridiculous in your eyes by trying to speak of her. But you have seen her. She is one of these rare human beings that do not want explaining. At least I think so. They had only that son, that brother, for a link with the wider world, with the future. The very groundwork of active existence for Nathalie Haldin is gone with him. Can you wonder then that she turns with eagerness to the only man her brother mentions in his letters. Your name is a sort of legacy."

"What could he have written of me?" he cried, in a low, exasperated tone.

"Only a few words. It is not for me to repeat them to you, Mr. Razumov; but you may believe my assertion that these words are forcible enough to make both his mother and his sister believe implicitly in the worth of your judgment and in the truth of anything you may have to say to them. It's impossible for you now to pass them by like strangers."

I paused, and for a moment sat listening to the footsteps of the few people passing up and down the broad central walk. While I was speaking his head had sunk upon his breast above his folded arms. He raised it sharply.

"Must I go then and lie to that old woman!"

It was not anger; it was something else, something more

poignant, and not so simple. I was aware of it sympathetically, while I was profoundly concerned at the nature of that exclamation.

"Dear me! Won't the truth do, then? I hoped you could have told them something consoling. I am thinking of the poor mother now. Your Russia *is* a cruel country."

He moved a little in his chair.

"Yes," I repeated. "I thought you would have had something authentic to tell."

The twitching of his lips before he spoke was curious.

"What if it is not worth telling?"

"Not worth—from what point of view? I don't understand."

"From every point of view."

I spoke with some asperity.

"I should think that anything which could explain the circumstances of that midnight arrest. . . ."

"Reported by a journalist for the amusement of the civilized Europe," he broke in scornfully.

"Yes, reported. . . . But aren't they true? I can't make out your attitude in this. Either the man is a hero to you, or . . ."

He approached his face with fiercely distended nostrils close to mine so suddenly that I had the greatest difficulty in not starting back.

"You ask me! I suppose it amuses you, all this. Look here! I am a worker. I studied. Yes, I studied very hard. There is intelligence here." (He tapped his forehead with his finger-tips.) "Don't you think a Russian may have sane ambitions? Yes—I had even prospects. Certainly! I had. And now you see me here, abroad, everything gone, lost, sacrificed. You see me here—and you ask! You see me, don't you?—sitting before you."

He threw himself back violently. I kept outwardly calm.

"Yes, I see you here; and I assume you are here on account of the Haldin affair?"

His manner changed.

"You call it the Haldin affair—do you?" he observed indifferently.

"I have no right to ask you anything," I said. "I wouldn't presume. But in that case the mother and the sister of him who must be a hero in your eyes cannot be indifferent to you. The girl is a frank and generous creature, having the noblest—well—illusions. You will tell her nothing —or you will tell her everything.) But speaking now of the object with which I've approached you: first, we have to deal with the morbid state of the mother. Perhaps something could be invented under your authority as a cure for a distracted and suffering soul filled with maternal affection."

His air of weary indifference was accentuated, I could not help thinking, wilfully.

"Oh yes. Something might," he mumbled carelessly.

He put his hand over his mouth to conceal a yawn. When he uncovered his lips they were smiling faintly.

"Pardon me. This has been a long conversation, and I have not had much sleep the last two nights."

This unexpected, somewhat insolent sort of apology had the merit of being perfectly true. He had had no nightly rest to speak of since that day when, in the grounds of the Château Borel, the sister of Victor Haldin had appeared before him. The perplexities and the complex terrors—I may say—of this sleeplessness are recorded in the document I was to see later—the document which is the main source of this narrative. At the moment he looked to me convincingly tired, gone slack all over, like a man who has passed through some sort of crisis.

"I have had a lot of urgent writing to do," he added.

I rose from my chair at once, and he followed my example, without haste, a little heavily.

"I must apologize for detaining you so long," I said.

"Why apologize? One can't very well go to bed before night. And you did not detain me. I could have left you at any time."

I had not stayed with him to be offended.

"I am glad you have been sufficiently interested," I said calmly. "No merit of mine, though—the commonest sort of regard for the mother of your friend was enough. . . . As to Miss Haldin herself, she at one time was disposed to think that her brother had been betrayed to the police in some way."

To my great surprise Mr. Razumov sat down again suddenly. I stared at him, and I must say that he returned my stare without winking for quite a considerable time.

"In some way," he mumbled, as if he had not understood or could not believe his ears.

"Some unforeseen event, a sheer accident might have done that," I went on. "Or, as she characteristically put it to me, the folly or weakness of some unhappy fellow-revolutionist."

"Folly or weakness," he repeated bitterly.

"She is a very generous creature," I observed after a time. The man admired by Victor Haldin fixed his eyes on the ground. I turned away and moved off, apparently unnoticed by him. I nourished no resentment of the moody brusqueness with which he had treated me. The sentiment I was carrying away from that conversation was that of hopelessness. Before I had got fairly clear of the raft of chairs and tables he had rejoined me.

"H'm, yes!" I heard him at my elbow again. "But what do you think?"

I did not look round even.

"I think that you people are under a curse."

He made no sound. It was only on the pavement outside the gate that I heard him again.

"I should like to walk with you a little."

After all, I preferred this enigmatical young man to his celebrated compatriot, the great Peter Ivanovitch. But I saw no reason for being particularly gracious.

"I am going now to the railway station, by the shortest way from here, to meet a friend from England," I said, for all answer to his unexpected proposal. I hoped that something informing could come of it. As we stood on the curbstone waiting for a tramcar to pass, he remarked gloomily—

"I like what you said just now."

"Do you?"

We stepped off the pavement together.

"The great problem," he went on, "is to understand thoroughly the nature of the curse."

"That's not very difficult, I think."

"I think so too," he agreed with me, and his readiness, strangely enough, did not make him less enigmatical in the least.

"A curse is an evil spell," I tried him again. "And the important, the great problem, is to find the means to break it."

"Yes. To find the means."

That was also an assent, but he seemed to be thinking of something else. We had crossed diagonally the open space before the theatre, and began to descend a broad, sparsely frequented street in the direction of one of the smaller bridges. He kept on by my side without speaking for a long time.

"You are not thinking of leaving Geneva soon?" I asked.

He was silent for so long that I began to think I had been indiscreet, and should get no answer at all. Yet on looking at him I almost believed that my question had caused him something in the nature of positive anguish. I detected it mainly in the clasping of his hands, in which he put a great force stealthily. Once, however, he had overcome that sort of agonizing hesitation sufficiently to tell me that he had no such intention, he became rather communicative—at least relatively to the former off-hand curtness of his speeches. The tone, too, was more amiable. He informed me that he intended to study and also to write. He went even so far as to tell me he had been to Stuttgart. Stuttgart, I was aware, was one of the revolutionary centres. The directing committee of one of the Russian parties (I can't tell now which) was located in that town. It was there that he got into touch with the active work of the revolutionists outside Russia.

"I have never been abroad before," he explained, in a rather inanimate voice now. Then, after a slight hesitation, altogether different from the agonizing irresolution my first simple question "whether he meant to stay in Geneva" had aroused, he made me an unexpected confidence—

"The fact is, I have received a sort of mission from them."

"Which will keep you here in Geneva?"

"Yes. Here. In this odious . . ."

I was satisfied with my faculty for putting two and two together when I drew the inference that the mission had something to do with the person of the great Peter Ivanovitch. But I kept that surmise to myself naturally, and Mr. Razumov said nothing more for some considerable time. It was only when we were nearly on the bridge we had been making for that he opened his lips again, abruptly—

"Could I see that precious article anywhere?"

I had to think for a moment before I saw what he was referring to.

"It has been reproduced in parts by the Press here. There are files to be seen in various places. My copy of the English newspaper I left with Miss Haldin, I remember, on the day after it reached me. I was sufficiently worried by seeing it lying on a table by the side of the poor mother's chair for weeks. Then it disappeared. It was a relief, I assure you."

He had stopped short.

"I trust," I continued, "that you will find time to see these ladies fairly often—that you will make time."

He stared at me so queerly that I hardly knew how to define his aspect. I could not understand it in this connexion at all. What ailed him? I asked myself. What strange thought had come into his head? What vision of all the horrors that can be seen in his hopeless country had come suddenly to haunt his brain? If it were anything connected with the fate of Victor Haldin, then I hoped earnestly he would keep it to himself for ever. I was, to speak plainly, so shocked that I tried to conceal my impression by—Heaven forgive me—a smile and the assumption of a light manner.

"Surely," I exclaimed, "that needn't cost you a great effort."

He turned away from me and leaned over the parapet of the bridge. For a moment I waited, looking at his back. And yet, I assure you, I was not anxious just then to look at his face again. He did not move at all. He did not mean to move. I walked on slowly on my way towards the station, and at the end of the bridge I glanced over my shoulder. No, he had not moved. He hung well over the parapet, as if captivated by the smooth rush of the blue water under the arch. The current there is swift, extremely swift; it makes some people dizzy; I myself can never look at it for any length of time without experiencing a dread of being suddenly snatched away by its destructive force. Some brains cannot resist the suggestion of irresistible power and of headlong motion.

It apparently had a charm for Mr. Razumov. I left him hanging far over the parapet of the bridge. The way he had behaved to me could not be put down to mere boorishness. There was something else under his scorn and impatience. Perhaps, I thought, with sudden approach to hidden truth, it was the same thing which had kept him over a week, nearly ten days indeed, from coming near Miss Haldin. But what it was I could not tell.

PART THIRD

I

The water under the bridge ran violent and deep. Its slightly undulating rush seemed capable of scouring out a channel for itself through solid granite while you looked. But had it flowed through Razumov's breast, it could not have washed away the accumulated bitterness the wrecking of his life had deposited there.

"What is the meaning of all this?" he thought, staring downwards at the headlong flow so smooth and clean that only the passage of a faint air-bubble, or a thin vanishing streak of foam like a white hair, disclosed its vertiginous rapidity, its terrible force. "Why has that meddlesome old Englishman blundered against me? And what is this silly tale of a crazy old woman?"

He was trying to think brutally on purpose, but he avoided any mental reference to the young girl. "A crazy old woman," he repeated to himself. "It is a fatality! Or ought I to despise all this as absurd? But no! I am wrong! I can't afford to despise anything. An absurdity may be the starting-point of the most dangerous complications. How is one to guard against it? It puts to rout one's intelligence. The more intelligent one is the less one suspects an absurdity."

A wave of wrath choked his thoughts for a moment. It even made his body leaning over the parapet quiver; then he resumed his silent thinking, like a secret dialogue with himself. And even in that privacy, his thought had some reservations of which he was vaguely conscious.

"After all, this is not absurd. It is insignificant. It is absolutely insignificant—absolutely. The craze of an old woman—the fussy officiousness of a blundering elderly Englishman. What devil put him in the way? Haven't I treated him cavalierly enough? Haven't I just? That's the way to treat these meddlesome persons. Is it possible that he still stands behind my back, waiting?"

Razumov felt a faint chill run down his spine. It was not fear. He was certain that it was not fear—not fear for himself—but it was, all the same, a sort of apprehension as if for another, for someone he knew without being able to put a name to the personality. But the recollection that the officious Englishman had a train to meet tranquillized him for a time. It was too stupid to suppose that he should be wasting his time in waiting. It was unnecessary to look round and make sure.

But what did the man mean by his extraordinary rigmarole about the newspaper, and that crazy old woman? he thought suddenly. It was a damnable presumption, anyhow, something that only an Englishman could be capable of. All this was a sort of sport for him—the sport of revolution—a game to look at from the height of his superiority. And what on earth did he mean by his exclamation, "Won't the truth do?"

Razumov pressed his folded arms to the stone coping over which he was leaning with force. "Won't the truth do? The truth for the crazy old mother of the——"

The young man shuddered again. Yes. The truth would do! Apparently it would do. Exactly. And receive thanks, he thought, formulating the unspoken words cynically. "Fall on my neck in gratitude, no doubt," he jeered mentally. But this mood abandoned him at once. He felt sad, as if his heart had become empty suddenly. "Well, I must be cautious," he concluded, coming to himself as though his brain had been awakened from a trance. "There is nothing, no one, too insignificant, too absurd to be disregarded," he thought wearily. "I must be cautious."

Razumov pushed himself with his hand away from the balustrade and, retracing his steps along the bridge, walked straight to his lodgings, where, for a few days, he led a solitary and retired existence. He neglected Peter Ivanovitch, to whom he was accredited by the Stuttgart group; he never went near the refugee revolutionists, to whom he had been introduced on his arrival. He kept out of that world altogether. And he felt that such conduct, causing surprise and arousing suspicion, contained an element of danger for himself.

This is not to say that during these few days he never went out. I met him several times in the streets, but he gave me no recognition. Once, going home after an evening call on the ladies Haldin, I saw him crossing the dark roadway of the Boulevard des Philosophes. He had a broad-brimmed soft hat, and the collar of his coat turned up. I watched him make straight for the house, but, instead of going in, he stopped opposite the still lighted windows, and after a time went away down a side-street.

I knew that he had not been to see Mrs. Haldin yet. Miss Haldin told me he was reluctant; moreover, the mental condition of Mrs. Haldin had changed. She seemed to think now that her son was living, and she perhaps awaited his arrival. Her immobility in the great armchair in front of the window had an air of expectancy, even when the blind was down and the lamps lighted.

For my part, I was convinced that she had received her death-stroke; Miss Haldin, to whom, of course, I said nothing of my forebodings, thought that no good would come from introducing Mr. Razumov just then, an opinion which I shared fully. I knew that she met the young man on the Bastions. Once or twice I saw them strolling slowly up the main alley. They met every day for weeks. I avoided passing that way during the hour when Miss Haldin took her exercise there. One day, however, in a fit of absent-mindedness, I entered the gates and came upon her walking alone. I stopped to exchange a few words. Mr. Razumov failed to turn up, and we began to talk about him—naturally.

"Did he tell you anything definite about your brother's activities—his end?" I ventured to ask.

"No," admitted Miss Haldin, with some hesitation. "Nothing definite."

I understood well enough that all their conversations must have been referred mentally to that dead man who had brought them together. That was unavoidable. But it was in the living man that she was interested. That was unavoidable too, I suppose. And as I pushed my inquiries I discovered that he had disclosed himself to her as a by no means conventional revolutionist, contemptuous of catch-words, of theories of men too. I was rather pleased at that —but I was a little puzzled.

"His mind goes forward, far ahead of the struggle," Miss Haldin explained. "Of course, he is an actual worker too," she added.

"And do you understand him?" I inquired point-blank.

She hesitated again. "Not altogether," she murmured.

I perceived that he had fascinated her by an assumption of mysterious reserve.

"Do you know what I think?" she went on, breaking through her reserved, almost reluctant attitude: "I think that he is observing, studying me, to discover whether I am worthy of his trust . . ."

"And that pleases you?"

She kept mysteriously silent for a moment. Then with energy, but in a confidential tone—

"I am convinced," she declared, "that this extraordinary man is meditating some vast plan, some great undertaking; he is possessed by it—he suffers from it—and from being alone in the world."

"And so he's looking for helpers?" I commented, turning away my head.

Again there was a silence.

"Why not?" she said at last.

The dead brother, the dying mother, the foreign friend, had fallen into a distant background. But, at the same time, Peter Ivanovitch was absolutely nowhere now. And this thought consoled me. Yet I saw the gigantic shadow of Russian life deepening around her like the darkness of an advancing night. It would devour her presently. I inquired after Mrs. Haldin—that other victim of the deadly shade.

A remorseful uneasiness appeared in her frank eyes. Mother seemed no worse, but if I only knew what strange fancies she had sometimes! Then Miss Haldin, glancing at her watch, declared that she could not stay a moment longer, and with a hasty hand-shake ran off lightly.

Decidedly, Mr. Razumov was not to turn up that day. Incomprehensible youth!

But less than an hour afterwards, while crossing the Place Mollard, I caught sight of him boarding a South Shore tramcar.

"He's going to the Château Borel," I thought.

After depositing Razumov at the gates of the Château Borel, some half a mile or so from the town, the car continued its journey between two straight lines of shady trees. Across the roadway in the sunshine a short wooden pier jutted into the shallow pale water, which farther out had an intense blue tint contrasting unpleasantly with the green orderly slopes on the opposite shore. The whole view, with the harbour jetties of white stone underlining lividly the dark front of the town to the left, and the expanding space of water to the right with jutting promontories of no particular character, had the uninspiring, glittering quality of a very fresh oleograph. Razumov turned his back on it with contempt. He thought it odious—oppressively odious—in its unsuggestive finish: the very perfection of mediocrity attained at last after centuries of toil and culture. And turning his back on it, he faced the entrance to the grounds of the Château Borel.

The bars of the central way and the wrought-iron arch between the dark weather-stained stone piers were very rusty; and, though fresh tracks of wheels ran under it, the gate looked as if it had not been opened for a very long time. But close against the lodge, built of the same grey stone as the piers (its windows were all boarded up), there was a small side entrance. The bars of that were rusty too; it stood ajar and looked as though it had not been closed for a long time. In fact, Razumov, trying to push it open a little wider, discovered it was immovable.

"Democratic virtue. There are no thieves here, apparently," he muttered to himself, with displeasure. Before advancing into the grounds he looked back sourly at an idle working man lounging on a bench in the clean, broad avenue. The fellow had thrown his feet up; one of his arms hung over the low back of the public seat; he was taking a day off in lordly repose, as if everything in sight belonged to him.

"Elector! Eligible! Enlightened!" Razumov muttered to himself. "A brute, all the same."

Razumov entered the grounds and walked fast up the wide sweep of the drive, trying to think of nothing—to rest his head, to rest his emotions too. But arriving at the foot of the terrace before the house he faltered, affected physically by some invisible interference. The mysteriousness of his quickened heart-beats startled him. He stopped short and looked at the brick wall of the terrace, faced with shallow arches, meagrely clothed by a few unthriving creepers, with an ill-kept narrow flower-bed along its foot.

"It is here!" he thought, with a sort of awe. "It is here— on this very spot . . ."

He was tempted to flight at the mere recollection of his first meeting with Nathalie Haldin. He confessed it to himself; but he did not move, and that not because he wished to resist an unworthy weakness, but because he knew that he had no place to fly to. Moreover, he could not leave Geneva. He recognized, even without thinking, that it was impossible. It would have been a fatal admission, an act of moral suicide. It would have been also physically dangerous. Slowly he ascended the stairs of the terrace, flanked by two stained greenish stone urns of funereal aspect.

Across the broad platform, where a few blades of grass sprouted on the discoloured gravel, the door of the house, with its ground-floor windows shuttered, faced him, wide open. He believed that his approach had been noted, because, framed in the doorway, without his tall hat, Peter Ivanovitch seemed to be waiting for his approach.

The ceremonious black frock-coat and the bared head of Europe's greatest feminist accentuated the dubiousness of his status in the house rented by Madame de S——, his Egeria. His aspect combined the formality of the caller with the freedom of the proprietor. Florid and bearded and masked by the dark blue glasses, he met the visitor, and at once took him familiarly under the arm.

Razumov suppressed every sign of repugnance by an effort which the constant necessity of prudence had rendered almost mechanical. And this necessity had settled his expression in a cast of austere, almost fanatical, aloofness. The "heroic fugitive," impressed afresh by the severe detachment of this new arrival from revolutionary Russia, took a conciliatory, even a confidential tone. Madame de S—— was resting after a bad night. She often had bad nights. He had left his hat upstairs on the landing and had come down to suggest to his young friend a stroll and a good open-hearted talk in one of the shady alleys behind the house. After voicing this proposal, the great man glanced at the unmoved face by his side, and could not restrain himself from exclaiming—

"On my word, young man, you are an extraordinary person."

"I fancy you are mistaken, Peter Ivanovitch. If I were really an extraordinary person, I would not be here, walking with you in a garden in Switzerland, Canton of Geneva, Commune of—what's the name of the Commune this place belongs to? . . . Never mind—the heart of democracy, anyhow. A fit heart for it; no bigger than a parched pea and about as much value. I am no more extraordinary than the rest of us Russians, wandering abroad."

But Peter Ivanovitch dissented emphatically—

"No! No! You are not ordinary. I have some experience of Russians who are—well—living abroad. You appear to me, and to others too, a marked personality."

"What does he mean by this?" Razumov asked himself,

turning his eyes fully on his companion. The face of Peter Ivanovitch expressed a meditative seriousness.

"You don't suppose, Kirylo Sidorovitch, that I have not heard of you from various points where you made yourself known on your way here? I have had letters."

"Oh, we are great in talking about each other," interjected Razumov, who had listened with great attention. "Gossip, tales, suspicions, and all that sort of thing, we know how to deal in to perfection. Calumny, even."

In indulging in this sally, Razumov managed very well to conceal the feeling of anxiety which had come over him. At the same time he was saying to himself that there could be no earthly reason for anxiety. He was relieved by the evident sincerity of the protesting voice.

"Heavens!" cried Peter Ivanovitch. "What are you talking about? What reason can *you* have to . . . ?"

The great exile flung up his arms as if words had failed him in sober truth. Razumov was satisfied. Yet he was moved to continue in the same vein.

"I am talking of the poisonous plants which flourish in the world of conspirators, like evil mushrooms in a dark cellar."

"You are casting aspersions," remonstrated Peter Ivanovitch, "which as far as you are concerned——"

"No!" Razumov interrupted without heat. "Indeed, I don't want to cast aspersions, but it's just as well to have no illusions."

Peter Ivanovitch gave him an inscrutable glance of his dark spectacles, accompanied by a faint smile.

"The man who says that he has no illusions has at least that one," he said, in a very friendly tone. "But I see how it is, Kirylo Sidorovitch. You aim at stoicism."

"Stoicism! That's a pose of the Greeks and the Romans. Let's leave it to them. We are Russians, that is—children; that is—sincere; that is—cynical, if you like. But that's not a pose."

A long silence ensued. They strolled slowly under the lime-trees. Peter Ivanovitch had put his hands behind his back. Razumov felt the ungravelled ground of the deeply shaded walk damp and as if slippery under his feet. He asked himself, with uneasiness, if he were saying the right things. The direction of the conversation ought to have been more under his control, he reflected. The great man appeared to be reflecting on his side too. He cleared his throat slightly, and Razumov felt at once a painful re-awakening of scorn and fear.

"I am astonished," began Peter Ivanovitch gently. "Supposing you are right in your indictment, how can you raise any question of calumny or gossip, in your case? It is unreasonable. The fact is, Kirylo Sidorovitch, there is not enough known of you to give hold to gossip or even calumny. Just now you are a man associated with a great deed, which had been hoped for, and tried for too, without success. People have perished for attempting that which you and Haldin have done at last. You come to us out of Russia, with that prestige. But you cannot deny that you have not been communicative, Kirylo Sidorovitch. People you have met imparted their impressions to me; one wrote this, another that, but I form my own opinions. I waited to see you first. You are a man out of the common. That's positively so. You are close, very close. This taciturnity, this severe brow, this something inflexible and secret in you, inspires hopes and a little wonder as to what you may mean. There is something of a Brutus . . ." or Marcus Brutus

"Pray spare me those classical allusions!" burst out Razumov nervously. "What comes Junius Brutus to do here? It is ridiculous! Do you mean to say," he added sarcastically, but lowering his voice, "that the Russian revolutionists are all patricians and that I am an aristo-crat?"

Peter Ivanovitch, who had been helping himself with a few gestures, clasped his hands again behind his back, and made a few steps, pondering.

"Not *all* patricians," he muttered at last. "But you, at any rate, are one of *us*."

Razumov smiled bitterly.

"To be sure my name is not Gugenheimer," he said in a sneering tone. "I am not a democratic Jew. How can I help it? Not everybody has such luck. I have no name, I have no . . ."

The European celebrity showed a great concern. He stepped back a pace and his arms flew in front of his person, extended, deprecatory, almost entreating. His deep bass voice was full of pain.

"But, my dear young friend!" he cried. "My dear Kirylo Sidorovitch . . ."

Razumov shook his head.

"The very patronymic you are so civil as to use when addressing me I have no legal right to—but what of that? I don't wish to claim it. I have no father. So much the better. But I will tell you what: my mother's grandfather was a peasant—a serf. See how much I am one of *you*. I don't want any one to claim me. But Russia *can't* disown me. She cannot!"

Razumov struck his breast with his fist.

"I am *it!*"

Peter Ivanovitch walked on slowly, his head lowered. Razumov followed, vexed with himself. That was not the right sort of talk. All sincerity was an imprudence. Yet one could not renounce truth altogether, he thought, with despair. Peter Ivanovitch, meditating behind his dark glasses, became to him suddenly so odious that if he had had a knife, he fancied he could have stabbed him not only without compunction, but with a horrible triumphant satisfaction. His imagination dwelt on that atrocity in spite of himself. It was as if he were becoming light-headed. "It is not what is expected of me," he repeated to himself. "It is not what is—— I could get away by breaking the fastening on the little gate I see there in the back wall. It is a flimsy lock. Nobody in the house seems to know he is here with me. Oh yes. The hat! These women would discover presently the hat he has left on the landing. They would come upon him, lying dead in this damp, gloomy shade—but I would be gone and no one could ever . . . Lord! Am I going mad?" he asked himself in a fright.

The great man was heard—musing in an undertone.

"H'm, yes! That—no doubt—in a certain sense . . ." He

raised his voice. "There is a deal of pride about you . . ."

The intonation of Peter Ivanovitch took on a homely, familiar ring, acknowledging, in a way, Razumov's claim to peasant descent.

"A great deal of pride, brother Kirylo. And I don't say that you have no justification for it. I have admitted you had. I have ventured to allude to the facts of your birth simply because I attach no mean importance to it. You are one of us—*un des nôtres*. I reflect on that with satisfaction."

"I attach some importance to it also," said Razumov quietly. "I won't even deny that it may have some importance for you too," he continued, after a slight pause and with a touch of grimness of which he was himself aware, with some annoyance. He hoped it had escaped the perception of Peter Ivanovitch. "But suppose we talk no more about it?"

"Well, we shall not—not after this one time, Kirylo Sidorovitch," persisted the noble arch-priest of Revolution. "This shall be the last occasion. You cannot believe for a moment that I had the slightest idea of wounding your feelings. You are clearly a superior nature—that's how I read you. Quite above the common—h'm—susceptibilities. But the fact is, Kirylo Sidorovitch, I don't know your susceptibilities. Nobody, out of Russia, knows much of you— as yet!"

"You have been watching me?" suggested Razumov.

"Yes."

The great man had spoken in a tone of perfect frankness, but as they turned their faces to each other Razumov felt baffled by the dark spectacles. Under their cover, Peter Ivanovitch hinted that he had felt for some time the need of meeting a man of energy and character, in view of a certain project. He said nothing more precise, however; and after some critical remarks upon the personalities of the various members of the committee of revolutionary action in Stuttgart, he let the conversation lapse for quite a long while. They paced the alley from end to end. Razumov, silent too, raised his eyes from time to time to cast a glance at the back of the house. It offered no sign of being in-

habited. With its grimy, weather-stained walls and all the
windows shuttered from top to bottom, it looked damp
and gloomy and deserted. It might very well have been
haunted in traditional style by some doleful, groaning,
futile ghost of a middle-class order. The shades evoked, as
worldly rumour had it, by Madame de S—— to meet statesmen, diplomatists, deputies of various European Parlia-
ments, must have been of another sort. Razumov had
never seen Madame de S—— but in the carriage.

Peter Ivanovitch came out of his abstraction.

"Two things I may say to you at once. I believe, first,
that neither a leader nor any decisive action can come out
of the dregs of a people. Now, if you ask me what are the
dregs of a people—h'm—it would take too long to tell. You
would be surprised at the variety of ingredients that for
me go to the making up of these dregs—of that which
ought, *must* remain at the bottom. Moreover, such a statement might be subject to discussion. But I can tell you
what is *not* the dregs. On that it is impossible for us to
disagree. The peasantry of a people is not the dregs; neither is its highest class—well—the nobility. Reflect on that,
Kirylo Sidorovitch! I believe you are well fitted for reflection. Everything in a people that is not genuine, not its
own by origin or development, is—well—dirt! Intelligence
in the wrong place is that. Foreign-bred doctrines are
that. Dirt! Dregs! The second thing I would offer to your
meditation is this: that for us at this moment there yawns
a chasm between the past and the future. It can never be
bridged by foreign liberalism. All attempts at it are either
folly or cheating. Bridged it can never be! It has to be
filled up."

A sort of sinister jocularity had crept into the tones of
the burly feminist. He seized Razumov's arm above the
elbow, and gave it a slight shake.

"Do you understand, enigmatical young man? It has got
to be just filled up."

Razumov kept an unmoved countenance.

"Don't you think that I have already gone beyond meditation on that subject?" he said, freeing his arm by a quiet

movement which increased the distance a little between himself and Peter Ivanovitch, as they went on strolling abreast. And he added that surely whole cartloads of words and theories could never fill that chasm. No meditation was necessary. A sacrifice of many lives could alone—— He fell silent without finishing the phrase.

Peter Ivanovitch inclined his big hairy head slowly. After a moment he proposed that they should go and see if Madame de S—— was now visible.

"We shall get some tea," he said, turning out of the shaded gloomy walk with a brisker step.

The lady companion had been on the lookout. Her dark skirt whisked into the doorway as the two men came in sight round the corner. She ran off somewhere altogether, and had disappeared when they entered the hall. In the crude light falling from the dusty glass skylight upon the black and white tessellated floor, covered with muddy tracks, their footsteps echoed faintly. The great feminist led the way up the stairs. On the balustrade of the first-floor landing a shiny tall hat reposed, rim upwards, opposite the double door of the drawing-room, haunted, it was said, by evoked ghosts, and frequented, it was to be supposed, by fugitive revolutionists. The cracked white paint of the panels, the tarnished gilt of the mouldings, permitted one to imagine nothing but dust and emptiness within. Before turning the massive brass handle, Peter Ivanovitch gave his young companion a sharp, partly critical, partly preparatory glance.

"No one is perfect," he murmured discreetly. Thus, the possessor of a rare jewel might, before opening the casket, warn the profane that no gem perhaps is flawless.

He remained with his hand on the door-handle so long that Razumov assented by a moody "No."

"Perfection itself would not produce that effect," pursued Peter Ivanovitch, "in a world not meant for it. But you shall find there a mind—no!—the quintessence of feminine intuition which will understand any perplexity you may be suffering from by the irresistible, enlightening force of sympathy. Nothing can remain obscure before that—that—inspired, yes, inspired penetration, this true light of femininity."

The gaze of the dark spectacles in its glossy steadfastness gave his face an air of absolute conviction. Razumov felt a momentary shrinking before that closed door.

"Penetration? Light," he stammered out. "Do you mean some sort of thought-reading?"

Peter Ivanovitch seemed shocked.

"I mean something utterly different," he retorted, with a faint, pitying smile.

Razumov began to feel angry, very much against his wish.

"This is very mysterious," he muttered through his teeth.

"You don't object to being understood, to being guided?" queried the great feminist.

Razumov exploded in a fierce whisper.

"In what sense? Be pleased to understand that I am a serious person. Who do you take me for?"

They looked at each other very closely. Razumov's temper was cooled by the impenetrable earnestness of the blue glasses meeting his stare. Peter Ivanovitch turned the handle at last.

"You shall know directly," he said, pushing the door open.

A low-pitched grating voice was heard within the room. *"Enfin. Vous voilà."*

In the doorway, his black-coated bulk blocking the view, Peter Ivanovitch boomed in a hearty tone with something boastful in it:

"Yes. Here I am!"

He glanced over his shoulder at Razumov, who waited for him to move on.

"And I am bringing you a proved conspirator—a real one this time. *Un vrai celui là.*"

This pause in the doorway gave the "proved conspirator" time to make sure that his face did not betray his angry curiosity and his mental disgust.

These sentiments stand confessed in Mr. Razumov's

memorandum of his first interview with Madame de S——.
The very words I use in my narrative are written where
their sincerity cannot be suspected. The record, which
could not have been meant for any one's eyes but his own,
was not, I think, the outcome of that strange impulse of
indiscretion common to men who lead secret lives, and
accounting for the invariable existence of "compromising
documents" in all the plots and conspiracies of history. Mr.
Razumov looked at it, I suppose, as a man looks at himself
in a mirror, with wonder, perhaps with anguish, with anger
or despair. Yes, as a threatened man may look fearfully at
his own face in the glass, formulating to himself reassuring
excuses for his appearance marked by the taint of some
insidious hereditary disease.

II

The Egeria of the "Russian Mazzini" produced, at first
view, a strong effect by the death-like immobility of an
obviously painted face. The eyes appeared extraordinarily
brilliant. The figure, in a close-fitting dress, admirably
made, but by no means fresh, had an elegant stiffness. The
rasping voice inviting him to sit down; the rigidity of the
upright attitude with one arm extended along the back of
the sofa, the white gleam of the big eyeballs setting off the
black, fathomless stare of the enlarged pupils, impressed
Razumov more than anything he had seen since his hasty
and secret departure from St. Petersburg. A witch in
Parisian clothes, he thought. A portent! He actually hesitated in his advance, and did not even comprehend, at
first, what the rasping voice was saying.

"Sit down. Draw your chair nearer me. There——"

He sat down. At close quarters the rouged cheek-bones,
the wrinkles, the fine lines on each side of the vivid lips,
astounded him. He was being received graciously, with a
smile which made him think of a grinning skull.

"We have been hearing about you for some time."

He did not know what to say, and murmured some disconnected words. The grinning skull effect vanished.

"And do you know that the general complaint is that you have shown yourself very reserved everywhere?"

Razumov remained silent for a time, thinking of his answer.

"I, don't you see, am a man of action," he said huskily, glancing upwards.

Peter Ivanovitch stood in portentous expectant silence by the side of his chair. A slight feeling of nausea came over Razumov. What could be the relations of these two people to each other? She like a galvanized corpse out of some Hoffman's Tale—he the preacher of feminist gospel for all the world, and a super-revolutionist besides! This ancient, painted mummy with unfathomable eyes, and this burly, bull-necked, deferential . . . what was it? Witchcraft, fascination. . . . "It's for her money," he thought. "She has millions!"

The walls, the floor of the room were bare like a barn. The few pieces of furniture had been discovered in the garrets and dragged down into service without even having been properly dusted. It was the refuse the banker's widow had left behind her. The windows without curtains had an indigent, sleepless look. In two of them the dirty yellowy-white blinds had been pulled down. All this spoke, not of poverty, but of sordid penuriousness.

The hoarse voice on the sofa uttered angrily—

"You are looking round, Kirylo Sidorovitch. I have been shamefully robbed, positively ruined."

A rattling laugh, which seemed beyond her control, interrupted her for a moment.

"A slavish nature would find consolation in the fact that the principal robber was an exalted and almost a sacrosanct person—a Grand Duke, in fact. Do you understand, Mr. Razumov? A Grand Duke—No! You have no idea what thieves those people are! Downright thieves!"

Her bosom heaved, but her left arm remained rigidly extended along the back of the couch.

"You will only upset yourself," breathed out a deep voice, which, to Razumov's startled glance, seemed to proceed from under the steady spectacles of Peter Ivanovitch, rather than from his lips, which had hardly moved.

"What of that? I say thieves! *Voleurs! Voleurs!*"

Razumov was quite confounded by this unexpected clamour, which had in it something of wailing and croaking, and more than a suspicion of hysteria.

"*Voleurs! Voleurs! Vol . . .*"

"No power on earth can rob you of your genius," shouted Peter Ivanovitch in an overpowering bass, but without stirring, without a gesture of any kind. A profound silence fell.

Razumov remained outwardly impassive. "What is the meaning of this performance?" he was asking himself. But with a preliminary sound of bumping outside some door behind him, the lady companion, in a threadbare black skirt and frayed blouse, came in rapidly, walking on her heels, and carrying in both hands a big Russian samovar, obviously too heavy for her. Razumov made an instinctive movement to help which startled her so much that she nearly dropped her hissing burden. She managed, however, to land it on the table, and looked so frightened that Razumov hastened to sit down. She produced then, from an adjacent room, four glass tumblers, a teapot, and a sugar-basin, on a black iron tray.

The rasping voice asked from the sofa abruptly—

"*Les gâteaux?* Have you remembered to bring the cakes?"

Peter Ivanovitch, without a word, marched out on to the landing, and returned instantly with a parcel wrapped up in white glazed paper, which he must have extracted from the interior of his hat. With imperturbable gravity he undid the string and smoothed the paper open on a part of the table within reach of Madame de S——'s hand. The lady companion poured out the tea, then retired into a distant corner out of everybody's sight. From time to time Madame de S—— extended a claw-like hand, glittering with costly rings, towards the paper of cakes, took up one and devoured it, displaying her big false teeth ghoulishly. Meantime she talked in a hoarse tone of the political situation in the Balkans. She built great hopes on some complication in the peninsula for arousing a great movement of national indignation in Russia against "these thieves—thieves—thieves."

"You will only upset yourself," Peter Ivanovitch interposed, raising his glassy gaze. He smoked cigarettes and drank tea in silence, continuously. When he had finished a glass, he flourished his hand above his shoulder. At that signal the lady companion, ensconced in her corner, with round eyes like a watchful animal, would dart out to the table and pour him out another tumblerful.

Razumov looked at her once or twice. She was anxious, tremulous, though neither Madame de S—— nor Peter Ivanovitch paid the slightest attention to her. "What have they done between them to that forlorn creature?" Razumov asked himself. "Have they terrified her out of her sense with ghosts, or simply have they only been beating her?" When she gave him his second glass of tea, he noticed that her lips trembled in the manner of a scared person about to burst into speech. But of course she said nothing, and retired into her corner, as if hugging to herself the smile of thanks he gave her.

"She may be worth cultivating," thought Razumov suddenly.

He was calming down, getting hold of the actuality into which he had been thrown—for the first time perhaps since Victor Haldin had entered his room . . . and had gone out again. He was distinctly aware of being the object of the famous—or notorious—Madame de S——'s ghastly graciousness.

Madame de S—— was pleased to discover that this young man was different from the other types of revolutionist members of committees, secret emissaries, vulgar and unmannerly fugitive professors, rough students, ex-cobblers with apostolic faces, consumptive and ragged enthusiasts, Hebrew youths, common fellows of all sorts that used to come and go around Peter Ivanovitch—fanatics, pedants, proletarians all. It was pleasant to talk to this young man of notably good appearance—for Madame de S—— was not always in a mystical state of mind. Razumov's taciturnity only excited her to a quicker, more voluble utterance. It still dealt with the Balkans. She knew all the statesmen of that region, Turks, Bulgarians, Montenegrins, Roumanians, Greeks, Armenians, and nondescripts young and old, the living and the dead. With some money an intrigue could be started which would set the Peninsula in a blaze and outrage the sentiment of the Russian people. A cry of abandoned brothers could be raised, and then, with the nation seething with indignation, a couple of regiments or so would be enough to begin a military revolution in St. Petersburg and make an end of these thieves. . . .

"Apparently I've got only to sit still and listen," the silent Razumov thought to himself. "As to that hairy and obscene brute" (in such terms did Mr. Razumov refer mentally to the popular expounder of a feministic conception of social state), "as to him, for all his cunning he too shall speak out some day."

Razumov ceased to think for a moment. Then a sombre-toned reflection formulated itself in his mind, ironical and bitter. "I have the gift of inspiring confidence." He heard himself laughing aloud. It was like a goad to the painted, shiny-eyed harridan on the sofa.

"You may well laugh!" she cried hoarsely. "What else can one do! Perfect swindlers—and what base swindlers at that! Cheap Germans—Holstein-Gottorps! Though, indeed, it's hardly safe to say who and what they are. A family that counts a creature like Catherine the Great in its ancestry—you understand!"

"You are only upsetting yourself," said Peter Ivanovitch, patiently but in a firm tone. This admonition had its usual effect on the Egeria. She dropped her thick, discoloured eyelids and changed her position on the sofa. All her angular and lifeless movements seemed completely automatic now that her eyes were closed. Presently she opened them very full. Peter Ivanovitch drank tea steadily, without haste.

"Well, I declare!" She addressed Razumov directly. "The

people who have seen you on your way here are right. You are very reserved. You haven't said twenty words altogether since you came in. You let nothing of your thoughts be seen in your face either."

"I have been listening, Madame," said Razumov, using French for the first time, hesitatingly, not being certain of his accent. But it seemed to produce an excellent impression. Madame de S—— looked meaningly into Peter Ivanovitch's spectacles, as if to convey her conviction of this young man's merit. She even nodded the least bit in his direction, and Razumov heard her murmur under her breath the words, "Later on in the diplomatic service," which could not but refer to the favourable impression he had made. The fantastic absurdity of it revolted him because it seemed to outrage his ruined hopes with the vision of a mock-career. Peter Ivanovitch, impassive as though he were deaf, drank some more tea. Razumov felt that he must say something.

"Yes," he began deliberately, as if uttering a meditated opinion. "Clearly. Even in planning a purely military revolution the temper of the people should be taken into account."

"You have understood me perfectly. The discontent should be spiritualized. That is what the ordinary heads of revolutionary committees will not understand. They aren't capable of it. For instance, Mordatiev was in Geneva last month. Peter Ivanovitch brought him here. You know Mordatiev? Well, yes—you have heard of him. They call him an eagle—a hero! He has never done half as much as you have. Never attempted—not half. . . ."

Madame de S—— agitated herself angularly on the sofa.

"We, of course, talked to him. And do you know what he said to me? 'What have we to do with Balkan intrigues? We must simply extirpate the scoundrels.' Extirpate is all very well—but what then? The imbecile! I screamed at him, 'But you must spiritualize—don't you understand? —spiritualize the discontent.' . . ."

She felt nervously in her pocket for a handkerchief; she pressed it to her lips.

"Spiritualize?" said Razumov interrogatively, watching her heaving breast. The long ends of an old black lace scarf she wore over her head slipped off her shoulders and hung down on each side of her ghastly rosy cheeks.

"An odious creature," she burst out again. "Imagine a man who takes five lumps of sugar in his tea. . . . Yes, I said spiritualize! How else can you make discontent effective and universal?"

"Listen to this, young man." Peter Ivanovitch made himself heard solemnly. "Effective and universal."

Razumov looked at him suspiciously.

"Some say hunger will do that," he remarked.

"Yes. I know. Our people are starving in heaps. But you can't make famine universal. And it is not despair that we want to create. There is no moral support to be got out of that. It is indignation. . . ."

Madame de S— let her thin, extended arm sink on her knees.

"I am not a Mordatiev," began Razumov.

"*Bien sûr!*" murmured Madame de S—.

"Though I too am ready to say extirpate, extirpate! But in my ignorance of political work, permit me to ask: A Balkan—well—intrigue, wouldn't that take a very long time?"

Peter Ivanovitch got up and moved off quietly, to stand with his face to the window. Razumov heard a door close; he turned his head and perceived that the lady companion had scuttled out of the room.

"In matters of politics I am a supernaturalist." Madame de S— broke the silence harshly.

Peter Ivanovitch moved away from the window and struck Razumov lightly on the shoulder. This was a signal for leaving, but at the same time he addressed Madame de S— in a peculiar reminding tone—

"Eleanor!"

Whatever it meant, she did not seem to hear him. She leaned back in the corner of the sofa like a wooden figure. The immovable peevishness of the face, framed in the limp, rusty lace, had a character of cruelty.

"As to extirpating," she croaked at the attentive Razumov, "there is only one class in Russia which must be extirpated. Only one. And that class consists of only one family. You understand me? That one family must be extirpated."

Her rigidity was frightful, like the rigour of a corpse galvanized into harsh speech and glittering stare by the force of murderous hate. The sight fascinated Razumov—yet he felt more self-possessed than at any other time since he had entered this weirdly bare room. He was interested. But the great feminist by his side again uttered his appeal—

"Eleanor!"

She disregarded it. Her carmine lips vaticinated with an extraordinary rapidity. The liberating spirit would use arms before which rivers would part like Jordan, and ramparts fall down like the walls of Jericho. The deliverance from bondage would be effected by plagues and by signs, by wonders and by war. The women . . .

"Eleanor!"

She ceased; she had heard him at last. She pressed her hand to her forehead.

"What is it? Ah yes! That girl—the sister of . . ."

It was Miss Haldin that she meant. That young girl and her mother had been leading a very retired life. They were provincial ladies—were they not? The mother had been very beautiful—traces were left yet. Peter Ivanovitch, when he called there for the first time, was greatly struck. . . . But the cold way they received him was really surprising.

"He is one of our national glories," Madame de S— cried out, with sudden vehemence. "All the world listens to him."

"I don't know these ladies," said Razumov loudly, rising from his chair.

"What are you saying, Kirylo Sidorovitch? I understand that she was talking to you here, in the garden, the other day."

"Yes, in the garden," said Razumov gloomily. Then, with an effort, "She made herself known to me."

"And then ran away from us all," Madame de S—— continued, with ghastly vivacity. "After coming to the very door! What a peculiar proceeding! Well, I have been a shy little provincial girl at one time. Yes, Razumov" (she fell into this familiarity intentionally, with an appalling grimace of graciousness. Razumov gave a perceptible start), "yes, that's my origin. A simple provincial family."

"You are a marvel," Peter Ivanovitch uttered in his deepest voice.

But it was to Razumov that she gave her death's-head smile. Her tone was quite imperious.

"You must bring the wild young thing here. She is wanted. I reckon upon your success—mind!"

"She is not a wild young thing," muttered Razumov, in a surly voice.

"Well, then—that's all the same. She may be one of these young conceited democrats. Do you know what I think? I think she is very much like you in character. There is a smouldering fire of scorn in you. You are darkly self-sufficient, but I can see your very soul."

Her shiny eyes had a dry, intense stare, which, missing Razumov, gave him an absurd notion that she was looking at something which was visible to her behind him. He cursed himself for an impressionable fool, and asked with forced calmness—

"What is it you see? Anything resembling me?"

She moved her rigidly set face from left to right, negatively.

"Some sort of phantom in my image?" pursued Razumov slowly. "For, I suppose, a soul when it is seen is just that. A vain thing. There are phantoms of the living as well as of the dead."

The tenseness of Madame de S——'s stare had relaxed, and now she looked at Razumov in a silence that became disconcerting.

"I myself have had an experience," he stammered out, as if compelled. "I've seen a phantom once."

The unnaturally red lips moved to frame a question harshly.

"Of a dead person?"

"No. Living."

"A friend?"

"No."

"An enemy?"

"I hated him."

"Ah! It was not a woman, then?"

"A woman!" repeated Razumov, his eyes looking straight into the eyes of Madame de S——. "Why should it have been a woman? And why this conclusion? Why should I not have been able to hate a woman?"

As a matter of fact, the idea of hating a woman was new to him. At that moment he hated Madame de S——. But it was not exactly hate. It was more like the abhorrence that may be caused by a wooden or plaster figure of a repulsive kind. She moved no more than if she were such a figure; even her eyes, whose unwinking stare plunged into his own, though shining, were lifeless, as though they were as artificial as her teeth. For the first time Razumov became aware of a faint perfume, but faint as it was it nauseated him exceedingly. Again Peter Ivanovitch tapped him slightly on the shoulder. Thereupon he bowed, and was about to turn away when he received the unexpected favour of a bony, inanimate hand extended to him, with the two words in hoarse French—

"*Au revoir!*"

He bowed over the skeleton hand and left the room, escorted by the great man, who made him go out first. The voice from the sofa cried after them—

"You remain here, *Pierre*."

"Certainly, *ma chère amie*."

But he left the room with Razumov, shutting the door behind him. The landing was prolonged into a bare corridor, right and left, desolate perspectives of white and gold decoration without a strip of carpet. The very light, pouring through a large window at the end, seemed dusty; and a solitary speck reposing on the balustrade of white marble—the silk top-hat of the great feminist—asserted itself extremely, black and glossy in all that crude whiteness.

Peter Ivanovitch escorted the visitor without opening his lips. Even when they had reached the head of the stairs Peter Ivanovitch did not break the silence. Razumov's impulse to continue down the flight and out of the house without as much as a nod abandoned him suddenly. He stopped on the first step and leaned his back against the wall. Below him the great hall with its chequered floor of black and white seemed absurdly large and like some public place where a great power of resonance awaits the provocation of footfalls and voices. As if afraid of awakening the loud echoes of that empty house, Razumov adopted a low tone.

"I really have no mind to turn into a dilettante spiritualist."

Peter Ivanovitch shook his head slightly, very serious.

"Or spend my time in spiritual ecstasies or sublime meditations upon the gospel of feminism," continued Razumov. "I made my way here for my share of action—action, most respected Peter Ivanovitch! It was not the great European writer who attracted me, here, to this odious town of liberty. It was somebody much greater. It was the idea of the chief which attracted me. There are starving young men in Russia who believe in you so much that it seems the only thing that keeps them alive in their misery. Think of that, Peter Ivanovitch! No! But only think of that!"

The great man, thus entreated, perfectly motionless and silent, was the very image of patient, placid respectability.

"Of course I don't speak of the people. They are brutes," added Razumov, in the same subdued but forcible tone. At this, a protesting murmur issued from the "heroic fugitive's" beard. A murmur of authority.

"Say—children."

"No! Brutes!" Razumov insisted bluntly.

"But they are sound, they are innocent," the great man pleaded in a whisper.

"As far as that goes, a brute is sound enough." Razumov raised his voice at last. "And you can't deny the natural innocence of a brute. But what's the use of disputing about names? You just try to give these children the power and stature of men and see what they will be like. You just give it to them and see. . . . But never mind. I tell you, Peter Ivanovitch, that half a dozen young men do not come together nowadays in a shabby student's room without your name being whispered, not as a leader of thought, but as a centre of revolutionary energies—the centre of action. What else has drawn me near you, do you think? It is not what all the world knows of you surely. It's precisely what the world at large does not know. I was irresistibly drawn—let us say impelled, yes, impelled; or, rather, compelled, driven—driven," repeated Razumov loudly, and ceased, as if startled by the hollow reverberation of the word "driven" along two bare corridors and in the great empty hall.

Peter Ivanovitch did not seem startled in the least. The young man could not control a dry, uneasy laugh. The great revolutionist remained unmoved with an effect of commonplace, homely superiority.

"Curse him," said Razumov to himself, "he is waiting behind his spectacles for me to give myself away." Then aloud, with a satanic enjoyment of the scorn prompting him to play with the greatness of the great man—

"Ah, Peter Ivanovitch, if you only knew the force which drew—no, which *drove* me towards you! The irresistible force."

He did not feel any desire to laugh now. This time Peter Ivanovitch moved his head sideways, knowingly, as much as to say, "Don't I?" This expressive movement was almost imperceptible. Razumov went on in secret derision—

"All these days you have been trying to read me, Peter Ivanovitch. That is natural. I have perceived it and I have been frank. Perhaps you may think I have not been very expansive? But with a man like you it was not needed; it would have looked like an impertinence, perhaps. And besides, we Russians are prone to talk too much as a rule. I have always felt that. And yet, as a nation, we are dumb.

I assure you that I am not likely to talk to you so much again—ha! ha!——"

Razumov, still keeping on the lower step, came a little nearer to the great man.

"You have been condescending enough. I quite understood it was to lead me on. You must render me the justice that I have not tried to please. I have been impelled, compelled, or rather sent—let us say sent—towards you for a work that no one but myself can do. You would call it a harmless delusion: a ridiculous delusion at which you don't even smile. It is absurd of me to talk like this, yet some day you will remember these words, I hope. Enough of this. Here I stand before you—confessed! But one thing more I must add to complete it: a mere blind tool I can never consent to be."

Whatever acknowledgment Razumov was prepared for, he was not prepared to have both his hands seized in the great man's grasp. The swiftness of the movement was aggressive enough to startle. The burly feminist could not have been quicker had his purpose been to jerk Razumov treacherously up on the landing and bundle him behind one of the numerous closed doors near by. This idea actually occurred to Razumov; his hands being released after a darkly eloquent squeeze, he smiled, with a beating heart, straight at the beard and the spectacles hiding that impenetrable man.

He thought to himself (it stands confessed in his handwriting), "I won't move from here till he either speaks or turns away. This is a duel." Many seconds passed without a sign or sound.

"Yes, yes," the great man said hurriedly, in subdued tones, as if the whole thing had been a stolen, breathless interview. "Exactly. Come to see us here in a few days. This must be gone into deeply—deeply, between you and me. Quite to the bottom. To the . . . And, by the by, you must bring along Natalia Victorovna—you know, the Haldin girl . . ."

"Am I to take this as my first instruction from you?" inquired Razumov stiffly.

Peter Ivanovitch seemed perplexed by this new attitude.

"Ah! h'm! You are naturally the proper person—*la personne indiquée*. Everyone shall be wanted presently. Everyone."

He bent down from the landing over Razumov, who had lowered his eyes.

"The moment of action approaches," he murmured.

Razumov did not look up. He did not move till he heard the door of the drawing-room close behind the greatest of feminists returning to his painted Egeria. Then he walked down slowly into the hall. The door stood open, and the shadow of the house was lying aslant over the greatest part of the terrace. While crossing it slowly, he lifted his hat and wiped his damp forehead, expelling his breath with force to get rid of the last vestiges of the air he had been breathing inside. He looked at the palms of his hands, and rubbed them gently against his thighs.

He felt, bizarre as it may seem, as though another self, an independent sharer of his mind, had been able to view his whole person very distinctly indeed. "This is curious," he thought. After a while he formulated his opinion of it in the mental ejaculation: "Beastly!" This disgust vanished before a marked uneasiness. "This is an effect of nervous exhaustion," he reflected with weary sagacity. "How am I to go on day after day if I have no more power of resistance—moral resistance?"

He followed the path at the foot of the terrace. "Moral resistance, moral resistance;" he kept on repeating these words mentally. Moral endurance. Yes, that was the necessity of the situation. An immense longing to make his way out of these grounds and to the other end of the town, of throwing himself on his bed and going to sleep for hours, swept everything clean out of his mind for a moment. "Is it possible that I am but a weak creature after all?" he asked himself in sudden alarm. "Eh! What's that?"

He gave a start as if awakened from a dream. He even swayed a little before recovering himself.

"Ah! You stole away from us quietly to walk about here," he said.

The lady companion stood before him, but how she came there he had not the slightest idea. Her folded arms were closely cherishing the cat.

"I have been unconscious as I walked, it's a positive fact," said Razumov to himself in wonder. He raised his hat with marked civility.

The sallow woman blushed duskily. She had her invariably scared expression, as if somebody had just disclosed to her some terrible news. But she held her ground, Razumov noticed, without timidity. "She is incredibly shabby," he thought. In the sunlight her black costume looked greenish, with here and there threadbare patches where the stuff seemed decomposed by age into a velvety, black, furry state. Her very hair and eyebrows looked shabby. Razumov wondered whether she were sixty years old. Her figure, though, was young enough. He observed that she did not appear starved, but rather as if she had been fed on unwholesome scraps and leavings of plates.

Razumov smiled amiably and moved out of her way. She turned her head to keep her scared eyes on him.

"I know what you have been told in there," she affirmed, without preliminaries. Her tone, in contrast with her manner, had an unexpectedly assured character which put Razumov at his ease.

"Do you? You must have heard all sorts of talk on many occasions in there."

She varied her phrase, with the same incongruous effect of positiveness.

"I know to a certainty what you have been told to do."

"Really?" Razumov shrugged his shoulders a little. He was about to pass on with a bow, when a sudden thought struck him. "Yes. To be sure! In your confidential position you are aware of many things," he murmured, looking at the cat.

That animal got a momentary convulsive hug from the lady companion.

"Everything was disclosed to me a long time ago," she said.

"Everything," Razumov repeated absently.

"Peter Ivanovitch is an awful despot," she jerked out.

Razumov went on studying the stripes on the grey fur of the cat.

"An iron will is an integral part of such a temperament. How else could he be a leader? And I think that you are mistaken in——"

"There!" she cried. "You tell me that I am mistaken. But I tell you all the same that he cares for no one." She jerked her head up. "Don't you bring that girl here. That's what you have been told to do—to bring that girl here. Listen to me; you had better tie a stone round her neck and throw her into the lake."

Razumov had a sensation of chill and gloom, as if a heavy cloud had passed over the sun.

"The girl?" he said. "What have I to do with her?"

"But you have been told to bring Nathalie Haldin here. Am I not right? Of course I am right. I was not in the room, but I know. I know Peter Ivanovitch sufficiently well. He is a great man. Great men are horrible. Well, that's it. Have nothing to do with her. That's the best you can do, unless you want her to become like me—disillusioned! Disillusioned!"

"Like you," repeated Razumov, glaring at her face, as devoid of all comeliness of feature and complexion as the most miserable beggar is of money. He smiled, still feeling chilly: a peculiar sensation which annoyed him. "Disillusioned as to Peter Ivanovitch! Is that all you have lost?"

She declared, looking frightened, but with immense conviction, "Peter Ivanovitch stands for everything." Then she added, in another tone, "Keep the girl away from this house."

"And are you absolutely inciting me to disobey Peter Ivanovitch just because—because you are disillusioned?"

She began to blink.

"Directly I saw you for the first time I was comforted. You took your hat off to me. You looked as if one could trust you. Oh!"

She shrank before Razumov's savage snarl of, "I have heard something like this before."

She was so confounded that she could do nothing but blink for a long time.

"It was your humane manner," she explained plaintively. "I have been starving for, I won't say kindness, but just for a little civility, for I don't know how long. And now you are angry . . ."

"But no, on the contrary," he protested. "I am very glad you trust me. It's possible that later on I may . . ."

"Yes, if you were to get ill," she interrupted eagerly, "or meet some bitter trouble, you would find I am not a useless fool. You have only to let me know. I will come to you. I will indeed. And I will stick to you. Misery and I are old acquaintances—but this life here is worse than starving."

She paused anxiously, then in a voice for the first time sounding really timid, she added—

"Or if you were engaged in some dangerous work. Sometimes a humble companion—I would not want to know anything. I would follow you with joy. I could carry out orders. I have the courage."

Razumov looked attentively at the scared round eyes, at the withered, sallow, round cheeks. They were quivering about the corners of the mouth.

"She wants to escape from here," he thought.

"Suppose I were to tell you that I am engaged in dangerous work?" he uttered slowly.

She pressed the cat to her threadbare bosom with a breathless exclamation. "Ah!" Then not much above a whisper: "Under Peter Ivanovitch?"

"No, not under Peter Ivanovitch."

He read admiration in her eyes, and made an effort to smile.

"Then—alone?"

He held up his closed hand with the index raised.

"Like this finger," he said.

She was trembling slightly. But it occurred to Razumov that they might have been observed from the house, and he became anxious to be gone. She blinked, raising up to him her puckered face, and seemed to beg mutely to be told something more, to be given a word of encouragement for her starving, grotesque, and pathetic devotion.

"Can we be seen from the house?" asked Razumov confidentially.

She answered, without showing the slightest surprise at the question—

"No, we can't, on account of this end of the stables." And she added, with an acuteness which surprised Razumov, "But anybody looking out of an upstairs window would know that you have not passed through the gates yet."

"Who's likely to spy out of the window?" queried Razumov. "Peter Ivanovitch?"

She nodded.

"Why should he trouble his head?"

"He expects somebody this afternoon."

"You know the person?"

"There's more than one."

She had lowered her eyelids. Razumov looked at her curiously.

"Of course. You hear everything they say."

She murmured without any animosity—

"So do the tables and chairs."

He understood that the bitterness accumulated in the heart of that helpless creature had got into her veins and, like some subtle poison, had decomposed her fidelity to that hateful pair. It was a great piece of luck for him, he reflected; because women are seldom venal after the manner of men, who can be bought for material considerations. She would be a good ally, though it was not likely that she was allowed to hear as much as the tables and chairs of the Château Borel. That could not be expected. But still . . . And, at any rate, she could be made to talk.

When she looked up her eyes met the fixed stare of Razumov, who began to speak at once.

"Well, well, dear . . . but upon my word, I haven't the pleasure of knowing your name yet. Isn't it strange?"

For the first time she made a movement of the shoulders.

"Is it strange? No one is told my name. No one cares. No one talks to me, no one writes to me. My parents don't even know if I'm alive. I have no use for a name, and I have almost forgotten it myself."

Razumov murmured gravely, "Yes, but still . . ."

She went on much slower, with indifference—

"You may call me Tekla, then. My poor Andrei called me so. I was devoted to him. He lived in wretchedness and suffering, and died in misery. That is the lot of all us Russians, nameless Russians. There is nothing else for us, and no hope anywhere, unless . . ."

"Unless what?"

"Unless all these people with names are done away with," she finished, blinking and pursing up her lips.

"It will be easier to call you Tekla, as you direct me," said Razumov, "if you consent to call me Kirylo, when we are talking like this—quietly—only you and me."

And he said to himself, "Here's a being who must be terribly afraid of the world, else she would have run away from this situation before." Then he reflected that the mere fact of leaving the great man abruptly would make her a suspect. She could expect no support or countenance from any one. This revolutionist was not fit for an independent existence.

She moved with him a few steps, blinking and nursing the cat with a small balancing movement of her arms.

"Yes—only you and I. That's how I was with my poor Andrei, only he was dying, killed by these official brutes—while you You are strong. You kill the monsters. You have done a great deed. Peter Ivanovitch himself must consider you. Well—don't forget me—especially if you are going back to work in Russia. I could follow you, carrying anything that was wanted—at a distance, you know. Or I could watch for hours at the corner of a street if necessary—in wet or snow—yes, I could—all day long. Or I could write for you dangerous documents, lists of names or instructions, so that in case of mischance the handwriting could not compromise you. And you need not be afraid if they were to catch me. I would know how to keep dumb.

We women are not so easily daunted by pain. I heard
Peter Ivanovitch say it is our blunt nerves or something.
We can stand it better. And it's true; I would just as soon
bite my tongue out and throw it at them as not. What's
the good of speech to me? Who would ever want to hear
what I could say? Ever since I closed the eyes of my poor
Andrei I haven't met a man who seemed to care for the
sound of my voice. I should never have spoken to you if
the very first time you appeared here you had not taken
notice of me so nicely. I could not help speaking of you
to that charming dear girl. Oh, the sweet creature! And
strong! One can see that at once. If you have a heart
don't let her set her foot in here. Good-bye!"

Razumov caught her by the arm. Her emotion at being
thus seized manifested itself by a short struggle, after
which she stood still, not looking at him.

"But you can tell me," he spoke in her ear, "why they
—these people in that house there—are so anxious to get
hold of her?"

She freed herself to turn upon him, as if made angry by
the question.

"Don't you understand that Peter Ivanovitch must direct, inspire, influence? It is the breath of his life. There
can never be too many disciples. He can't bear thinking of
any one escaping him. And a woman, too! There is nothing
to be done without women, he says. He has written it.
He——"

The young man was staring at her passion when she
broke off suddenly and ran away behind the stable.

III

Razumov, thus left to himself, took the direction of the
gate. But on this day of many conversations, he discovered
that very probably he could not leave the grounds without
having to hold another one.

Stepping in view from beyond the lodge appeared the
expected visitors of Peter Ivanovitch: a small party composed of two men and a woman. They noticed him too,

immediately, and stopped short as if to consult. But in a moment the woman, moving aside, motioned with her arm to the two men, who, leaving the drive at once, struck across the large neglected lawn, or rather grass-plot, and made directly for the house. The woman remained on the path waiting for Razumov's approach. She had recognized him. He, too, had recognized her at the first glance. He had been made known to her at Zürich, where he had broken his journey while on his way from Dresden. They had been much together for the two days of his stay.

She was wearing the very same costume in which he had seen her first. A blouse of crimson silk made her noticeable at a distance. With that she wore a short brown skirt and a leather belt. Her complexion was the colour of coffee and milk, but very clear; her eyes black and glittering, her figure erect. A lot of thick hair, nearly white, was done up loosely under a dusty Tyrolese hat of dark cloth, which seemed to have lost some of its trimmings.

The expression of her face was grave, intent; so grave that Razumov, after approaching her close, felt obliged to smile. She greeted him with a manly hand-grasp.

"What! Are you going away?" she exclaimed. "How is that, Razumov?"

"I am going away because I haven't been asked to stay," Razumov answered, returning the pressure of her hand with much less force than she had put into it.

She jerked her head sideways like one who understands. Meantime Razumov's eyes had strayed after the two men. They were crossing the grass-plot obliquely, without haste. The shorter of the two was buttoned up in a narrow overcoat of some thin grey material, which came nearly to his heels. His companion, much taller and broader, wore a short, close-fitting jacket and tight trousers tucked into shabby top-boots.

The woman, who had sent them out of Razumov's way apparently, spoke in a businesslike voice.

"I had to come rushing from Zürich on purpose to meet the train and take these two along here to see Peter Ivanovitch. I've just managed it."

"Ah! indeed," Razumov said perfunctorily, and very vexed at her staying behind to talk to him. "From Zürich—yes, of course. And these two, they come from . . ."

She interrupted, without emphasis—

"From quite another direction. From a distance, too. A considerable distance."

Razumov shrugged his shoulders. The two men from a distance, after having reached the wall of the terrace, disappeared suddenly at its foot as if the earth had opened to swallow them up.

"Oh, well, they have just come from America." The woman in the crimson blouse shrugged her shoulders too a little before making that statement. "The time is drawing near," she interjected, as if speaking to herself. "I did not tell them who you were. Yakovlitch would have wanted to embrace you."

"Is that he with the wisp of hair hanging from his chin, in the long coat?"

"You've guessed aright. That's Yakovlitch."

"And they could not find their way here from the station without you coming on purpose from Zürich to show it to them? Verily, without women we can do nothing. So it stands written, and apparently so it is."

He was conscious of an immense lassitude under his effort to be sarcastic. And he could see that she had detected it with those steady, brilliant black eyes.

"What is the matter with you?"

"I don't know. Nothing. I've had a devil of a day."

She waited, with her black eyes fixed on his face. Then—

"What of that? You men are so impressionable and self-conscious. One day is like another, hard, hard—and there's an end of it, till the great day comes. I came over for a very good reason. They wrote to warn Peter Ivanovitch of their arrival. But where from? Only from Cherbourg on a bit of ship's notepaper. Anybody could have done that. Yakovlitch has lived for years and years in America. I am the only one at hand who had known him well in the old days. I knew him very well indeed. So

Peter Ivanovitch telegraphed, asking me to come. It's natural enough, is it not?"

"You came to vouch for his identity?" inquired Razumov.

"Yes. Something of the kind. Fifteen years of a life like his make changes in a man. Lonely, like a crow in a strange country. When I think of Yakovlitch before he went to America——"

The softness of the low tone caused Razumov to glance at her sideways. She sighed; her black eyes were looking away; she had plunged the fingers of her right hand deep into the mass of nearly white hair, and stirred them there absently. When she withdrew her hand the little hat perched on the top of her head remained slightly tilted, with a queer inquisitive effect, contrasting strongly with the reminiscent murmur that escaped her.

"We were not in our first youth even then. But a man is a child always."

Razumov thought suddenly, "They have been living together." Then aloud—

"Why didn't you follow him to America?" he asked point-blank.

She looked up at him with a perturbed air.

"Don't you remember what was going on fifteen years ago? It was a time of activity. The Revolution has its history by this time. You are in it and yet you don't seem to know it. Yakovlitch went away then on a mission; I went back to Russia. It had to be so. Afterwards there was nothing for him to come back to."

"Ah! indeed," muttered Razumov, with affected surprise. "Nothing!"

"What are you trying to insinuate?" she exclaimed quickly. "Well, and what then if he did get discouraged a little . . ."

"He looks like a Yankee, with that goatee hanging from his chin. A regular Uncle Sam," growled Razumov. "Well, and you? You who went to Russia? You did not get discouraged."

"Never mind. Yakovlitch is a man who cannot be doubted. He, at any rate, is the right sort."

Her black, penetrating gaze remained fixed upon Razumov while she spoke, and for a moment afterwards.

"Pardon me," Razumov inquired coldly, "but does it mean that you, for instance, think that I am not the right sort?"

She made no protest, gave no sign of having heard the question; she continued looking at him in a manner which he judged not to be absolutely unfriendly. In Zürich when he passed through she had taken him under her charge, in a way, and was with him from morning till night during his stay of two days. She took him round to see several people. At first she talked to him a great deal and rather unreservedly, but always avoiding all reference to herself; towards the middle of the second day she fell silent, attending him zealously as before, and even seeing him off at the railway station, where she pressed his hand firmly through the lowered carriage window, and, stepping back without a word, waited till the train moved. He had noticed that she was treated with quiet regard. He knew nothing of her parentage, nothing of her private history or political record; he judged her from his own private point of view, as being a distinct danger in his path. "Judged" is not perhaps the right word. It was more of a feeling, the summing up of slight impressions aided by the discovery that he could not despise her as he despised all the others. He had not expected to see her again so soon.

No, decidedly; her expression was not unfriendly. Yet he perceived an acceleration in the beat of his heart. The conversation could not be abandoned at that point. He went on in accents of scrupulous inquiry—

"Is it perhaps because I don't seem to accept blindly every development of the general doctrine—such for instance as the feminism of our great Peter Ivanovitch? If that is what makes me suspect, then I can only say I would scorn to be a slave even to an idea."

She had been looking at him all the time, not as a listener looks at one, but as if the words he chose to say were only of secondary interest. When he finished she slipped her hand, by a sudden and decided movement, under his arm and impelled him gently towards the gate of the grounds. He felt her firmness and obeyed the impulsion at once, just as the other two men had, a moment before, obeyed unquestioningly the wave of her hand.

They made a few steps like this.

"No, Razumov, your ideas are probably all right," she said. "You may be valuable—very valuable. What's the matter with you is that you don't like us."

She released him. He met her with a frosty smile.

"Am I expected then to have love as well as convictions?"

She shrugged her shoulders.

"You know very well what I mean. People have been thinking you not quite whole-hearted. I have heard that opinion from one side and another. But I have understood you at the end of the first day . . ."

Razumov interrupted her, speaking steadily.

"I assure you that your perspicacity is at fault here."

"What phrases he uses!" she exclaimed parenthetically. "Ah! Kirylo Sidorovitch, you like other men are fastidious, full of self-love and afraid of trifles. Moreover, you had no training. What you want is to be taken in hand by some woman. I am sorry I am not staying here a few days. I am going back to Zürich to-morrow, and shall take Yakovlitch with me most likely."

This information relieved Razumov.

"I am sorry too," he said. "But, all the same, I don't think you understand me."

He breathed more freely; she did not protest, but asked, "And how did you get on with Peter Ivanovitch? You have seen a good deal of each other. How is it between you two?"

Not knowing what answer to make, the young man inclined his head slowly.

Her lips had been parted in expectation. She pressed them together, and seemed to reflect.

"That's all right."

This had a sound of finality, but she did not leave him. It was impossible to guess what she had in her mind. Razumov muttered—

"It is not of me that you should have asked that question. In a moment you shall see Peter Ivanovitch himself, and the subject will come up naturally. He will be curious to know what has delayed you so long in this garden."

"No doubt Peter Ivanovitch will have something to say to me. Several things. He may even speak of you—question me. Peter Ivanovitch is inclined to trust me generally."

"Question you? That's very likely."

She smiled, half serious.

"Well—and what shall I say to him?"

"I don't know. You may tell him of your discovery."

"What's that?"

"Why—my lack of love for . . ."

"Oh! That's between ourselves," she interrupted, it was hard to say whether in jest or earnest.

"I see that you want to tell Peter Ivanovitch something in my favour," said Razumov, with grim playfulness. "Well, then, you can tell him that I am very much in earnest about my mission. I mean to succeed."

"You have been given a mission!" she exclaimed quickly.

"It amounts to that. I have been told to bring about a certain event."

She looked at him searchingly.

"A mission," she repeated, very grave and interested all at once. "What sort of mission?"

"Something in the nature of propaganda work."

"Ah! Far away from here?"

"No. Not very far," said Razumov, restraining a sudden desire to laugh, though he did not feel joyous in the least.

"So!" she said thoughtfully. "Well, I am not asking questions. It's sufficient that Peter Ivanovitch should know what each of us is doing. Everything is bound to come right in the end."

"You think so?"

"I don't think, young man. I just simply believe it."

"And is it to Peter Ivanovitch that you owe that faith?"

She did not answer the question, and they stood idle, silent, as if reluctant to part with each other.

"That's just like a man," she murmured at last. "As if it were possible to tell how a belief comes to one." Her thin Mephistophelian eyebrows moved a little. "Truly there are millions of people in Russia who would envy the life of dogs in this country. It is a horror and a shame to confess this even between ourselves. One must believe for very pity. This can't go on. No! It can't go on. For twenty years I have been coming and going, looking neither to the left nor to the right. . . . What are you smiling to yourself for? You are only at the beginning. You have begun well, but you just wait till you have trodden every particle of yourself under your feet in your comings and goings. For that is what it comes to. You've got to trample down every particle of your own feelings; for stop you cannot, you must not. I have been young, too—but perhaps you think that I am complaining—eh?"

"I don't think anything of the sort," protested Razumov indifferently.

"I dare say you don't, you dear superior creature. You don't care."

She plunged her fingers into the bunch of hair on the left side, and that brusque movement had the effect of setting the Tyrolese hat straight on her head. She frowned under it without animosity, in the manner of an investigator. Razumov averted his face carelessly.

"You men are all alike. You mistake luck for merit. You do it in good faith too! I would not be too hard on you. It's masculine nature. You men are ridiculously pitiful in your aptitude to cherish childish illusions down to the very grave. There are a lot of us who have been at work for fifteen years—I mean constantly—trying one way after another, underground and above ground, looking neither to the right nor to the left! I can talk about it. I have been one of those that never rested. . . . There! What's the use of talking. . . . Look at my grey hairs! And here two babies come along—I mean you and Haldin—you come along and manage to strike a blow at the very first try."

At the name of Haldin falling from the rapid and energetic lips of the woman revolutionist, Razumov had the usual brusque consciousness of the irrevocable. But in all the months which had passed over his head he had become hardened to the experience. The consciousness was no longer accompanied by the blank dismay and the blind anger of the early days. He had argued himself into new beliefs; and he had made for himself a mental atmosphere of gloomy and sardonic reverie, a sort of murky medium through which the event appeared like a featureless shadow having vaguely the shape of a man; a shape extremely familiar, yet utterly inexpressive, except for its air of discreet waiting in the dusk. It was not alarming.

"What was *he* like?" the woman revolutionist asked unexpectedly.

"What was he like?" echoed Razumov, making a painful effort not to turn upon her savagely. But he relieved himself by laughing a little while he stole a glance at her out of the corners of his eyes. This reception of her inquiry disturbed her.

"How like a woman," he went on. "What is the good of concerning yourself with his appearance? Whatever it was, he is removed beyond all feminine influences now."

A frown, making three folds at the root of her nose, accentuated the Mephistophelian slant of her eyebrows.

"You suffer, Razumov," she suggested, in her low, confident voice.

"What nonsense!" Razumov faced the woman fairly. "But now I think of it, I am not sure that he is beyond the influence of one woman at least; the one over there—Madame de S——, you know. Formerly the dead were allowed to rest, but now it seems they are at the beck and call of a crazy old harridan. We revolutionists make wonderful discoveries. It is true that they are not exactly our own. We have nothing of our own. But couldn't the friend of Peter Ivanovitch satisfy your feminine curiosity? Couldn't she conjure him up for you?"—he jested like a man in pain.

Her concentrated frowning expression relaxed, and she said, a little wearily, "Let us hope she will make an effort and conjure up some tea for us. But that is by no means certain. I am tired, Razumov."

"You tired! What a confession! Well, there has been tea up there. I had some. If you hurry on after Yakovlitch, instead of wasting your time with such an unsatisfactory sceptical person as myself, you may find the ghost of it— the cold ghost of it—still lingering in the temple. But as to you being tired I can hardly believe it. We are not supposed to be. We mustn't. We can't. The other day I read in some paper or other an alarmist article on the tireless activity of the revolutionary parties. It impresses the world. It's our prestige."

"He flings out continually these flouts and sneers;" the woman in the crimson blouse spoke as if appealing quietly to a third person, but her black eyes never left Razumov's face. "And what for, pray? Simply because some of his conventional notions are shocked, some of his petty masculine standards. You might think he was one of those nervous sensitives that come to a bad end. And yet," she went on, after a short, reflective pause and changing the mode of her address, "and yet I have just learned something which makes me think that you are a man of character, Kirylo Sidorovitch. Yes! indeed—you are."

The mysterious positiveness of this assertion startled Razumov. Their eyes met. He looked away and, through the bars of the rusty gate, stared at the clean, wide road shaded by the leafy trees. An electric tramcar, quite empty, ran along the avenue with a metallic rustle. It seemed to him he would have given anything to be sitting inside all alone. He was inexpressibly weary, weary in every fibre of his body, but he had a reason for not being the first to break off the conversation. At any instant, in the visionary and criminal babble of revolutionists, some momentous words might fall on his ear; from her lips, from anybody's lips. As long as he managed to preserve a clear mind and to keep down his irritability there was nothing to fear. The only condition of success and safety was indomitable will-power, he reminded himself.

He longed to be on the other side of the bars, as though

he were actually a prisoner within the grounds of this
centre of revolutionary plots, of this house of folly, of
blindness, of villainy and crime. Silently he indulged his
wounded spirit in a feeling of immense moral and mental
remoteness. He did not even smile when he heard her repeat the words—

"Yes! A strong character."

He continued to gaze through the bars like a moody
prisoner, not thinking of escape, but merely pondering
upon the faded memories of freedom.

"If you don't look out," he mumbled, still looking away,
"you will certainly miss seeing as much as the mere ghost
of that tea."

She was not to be shaken off in such a way. As a matter
of fact he had not expected to succeed.

"Never mind, it will be no great loss. I mean the missing of her tea and only the ghost of it at that. As to the
lady, you must understand that she has her positive uses.
See *that*, Razumov."

He turned his head at this imperative appeal and saw
the woman revolutionist making the motions of counting
money into the palm of her hand.

"That's what it is. You see?"

Razumov uttered a slow "I see," and returned to his
prisoner-like gazing upon the neat and shady road.

"Material means must be obtained in some way, and
this is easier than breaking into banks. More certain too.
There! I am joking . . . What is he muttering to himself
now?" she cried under her breath.

"My admiration of Peter Ivanovitch's devoted self-sacrifice, that's all. It's enough to make one sick."

"Oh, you squeamish, masculine creature. Sick! Makes
him sick! And what do you know of the truth of it? There's
no looking into the secrets of the heart.) Peter Ivanovitch
knew her years ago, in his worldly days, when he was a
young officer in the Guards. It is not for us to judge an
inspired person. That's where you men have an advantage.
You are inspired sometimes both in thought and action. I
have always admitted that when you *are* inspired, when

you manage to throw off your masculine cowardice and prudishness you are not to be equalled by us. Only, how seldom . . . Whereas the silliest woman can always be made of use. And why? Because we have passion, unappeasable passion . . . I should like to know what he is smiling at?"

"I am not smiling," protested Razumov gloomily.

"Well! How is one to call it? You made some sort of face. Yes, I know! You men can love here and hate there and desire something or other—and you make a great to-do about it, and you call it passion! Yes! While it lasts. But we women are in love with love, and with hate, with these very things I tell you, and with desire itself. That's why we can't be bribed off so easily as you men. In life, you see, there is not much choice. You have either to rot or to burn. And there is not one of us, painted or unpainted, that would not rather burn than rot."

She spoke with energy, but in a matter-of-fact tone. Razumov's attention had wandered away on a track of its own—outside the bars of the gate—but not out of earshot. He stuck his hands into the pockets of his coat.

"Rot or burn! Powerfully stated. Painted or unpainted. Very vigorous. Painted or . . . Do tell me—she would be infernally jealous of him, wouldn't she?"

"Who? What? The Baroness? Eleanor Maximovna? Jealous of Peter Ivanovitch? Heavens! Are these the questions the man's mind is running on? Such a thing is not to be thought of."

"Why? Can't a wealthy old woman be jealous? Or, are they all pure spirits together?"

"But what put it into your head to ask such a question?" she wondered.

"Nothing. I just asked. Masculine frivolity, if you like."

"I don't like," she retorted at once. "It is not the time to be frivolous. What are you flinging your very heart against? Or, perhaps, you are only playing a part."

Razumov had felt that woman's observation of him like a physical contact, like a hand resting lightly on his shoulder. At that moment he received the mysterious impression of her having made up her mind for a closer grip. He stiffened himself inwardly to bear it without betraying himself.

"Playing a part," he repeated, presenting to her an unmoved profile. "It must be done very badly since you see through the assumption."

She watched him, her forehead drawn into perpendicular folds, the thin black eyebrows diverging upwards like the antennæ of an insect. He added hardly audibly—

"You are mistaken. I am doing it no more than the rest of us."

"Who is doing it?" she snapped out.

"Who? Everybody," he said impatiently. "You are a materialist, aren't you?"

"Eh! My dear soul, I have outlived all that nonsense."

"But you must remember the definition of Cabanis: 'Man is a digestive tube.' I imagine now . . ."

"I spit on him."

"What? On Cabanis? All right. But you can't ignore the importance of a good digestion. The joy of life—you know the joy of life?—depends on a sound stomach, whereas a bad digestion inclines one to scepticism, breeds black fancies and thoughts of death. These are facts ascertained by physiologists. Well, I assure you that ever since I came over from Russia I have been stuffed with indigestible foreign concoctions of the most nauseating kind—pah!"

"You are joking," she murmured incredulously. He assented in a detached way.

"Yes. It is all a joke. It's hardly worth while talking to a man like me. Yet for that very reason men have been known to take their own life."

"On the contrary, I think it *is* worth while talking to you."

He kept her in the corner of his eye. She seemed to be thinking out some scathing retort, but ended by only shrugging her shoulders slightly.

"Shallow talk! I suppose one must pardon this weakness in you," she said, putting a special accent on the last word. There was something anxious in her indulgent conclusion.

Razumov noted the slightest shades in this conversation, which he had not expected, for which he was not prepared. That was it. "I was not prepared," he said to himself. "It has taken me unawares." It seemed to him that if he only could allow himself to pant openly like a dog for a time this oppression would pass away. "I shall never be found prepared," he thought, with despair. He laughed a little, saying as lightly as he could—

"Thanks. I don't ask for mercy." Then affecting a playful uneasiness, "But aren't you afraid Peter Ivanovitch might suspect us of plotting something unauthorized together by the gate here?"

"No, I am not afraid. You are quite safe from suspicions while you are with me, my dear young man." The humorous gleam in her black eyes went out. "Peter Ivanovitch trusts me," she went on, quite austerely. "He takes my advice. I am his right hand, as it were, in certain most important things. . . . That amuses you—what? Do you think I am boasting?"

"God forbid. I was just only saying to myself that Peter Ivanovitch seems to have solved the woman question pretty completely."

Even as he spoke he reproached himself for his words, for his tone. All day long he had been saying the wrong things. It was folly, worse than folly. It was weakness; it was this disease of perversity overcoming his will. Was this the way to meet speeches which certainly contained the promise of future confidences from that woman who apparently had a great store of secret knowledge and so much influence? Why give her this puzzling impression? But she did not seem inimical. There was no anger in her voice. It was strangely speculative.

"One does not know what to think, Razumov. You must have bitten something bitter in your cradle."

Razumov gave her a sidelong glance.

"H'm! Something bitter? That's an explanation," he muttered. "Only it was much later. And don't you think,

Sophia Antonovna, that you and I come from the same cradle?"

The woman, whose name he had forced himself at last to pronounce (he had experienced a strong repugnance in letting it pass his lips), the woman revolutionist murmured, after a pause—

"You mean—Russia?"

He disdained even to nod. She seemed softened, her black eyes very still, as though she were pursuing the simile in her thoughts to all its tender association. But suddenly she knitted her brows in a Mephistophelian frown.

"Yes. Perhaps no wonder, then. Yes. One lies there lapped up in evils, watched over by beings that are worse than ogres, ghouls, and vampires. They must be driven away, destroyed utterly. In regard of that task nothing else matters if men and women are determined and faithful. That's how I came to feel in the end. The great thing is not to quarrel amongst ourselves about all sorts of conventional trifles. Remember that, Razumov."

Razumov was not listening. He had even lost the sense of being watched in a sort of heavy tranquillity. His uneasiness, his exasperation, his scorn were blunted at last by all these trying hours. It seemed to him that now they were blunted for ever. "I am a match for them all," he thought, with a conviction too firm to be exulting. The woman revolutionist had ceased speaking; he was not looking at her; there was no one passing along the road. He almost forgot that he was not alone. He heard her voice again, curt, businesslike, and yet betraying the hesitation which had been the real reason of her prolonged silence.

"I say, Razumov!"

Razumov, whose face was turned away from her, made a grimace like a man who hears a false note.

"Tell me: is it true that on the very morning of the deed you actually attended the lectures at the University?"

An appreciable fraction of a second elapsed before the real import of the question reached him, like a bullet which strikes some time after the flash of the fired shot.

Luckily his disengaged hand was ready to grip a bar of the gate. He held it with a terrible force, but his presence of mind was gone. He could make only a sort of gurgling, grumpy sound.

"Come, Kirylo Sidorovitch!" she urged him. "I know you are not a boastful man. *That* one must say for you. You are a silent man. Too silent, perhaps. You are feeding on some bitterness of your own. You are not an enthusiast. You are, perhaps, all the stronger for that. But you might tell me. One would like to understand you a little more. I was so immensely struck . . . Have you really done it?"

He got his voice back. The shot had missed him. It had been fired at random, altogether, more like a signal for coming to close quarters. It was to be a plain struggle for self-preservation. And she was a dangerous adversary too. But he was ready for battle; he was so ready that when he turned towards her not a muscle of his face moved.

"Certainly," he said, without animation, secretly strung up but perfectly sure of himself. "Lectures—certainly. But what makes you ask?"

It was she who was animated.

"I had it in a letter, written by a young man in Petersburg; one of us, of course. You were seen—you were observed with your notebook, impassible, taking notes . . ."

He enveloped her with his fixed stare.

"What of that?"

"I call such coolness superb—that's all. It is a proof of uncommon strength of character. The young man writes that nobody could have guessed from your face and manner the part you had played only some two hours before —the great, momentous, glorious part . . ."

"Oh no. Nobody could have guessed," assented Razumov gravely, "because, don't you see, nobody at that time . . ."

"Yes, yes. But all the same you are a man of exceptional fortitude, it seems. You looked exactly as usual. It was remembered afterwards with wonder . . ."

"It cost me no effort," Razumov declared, with the same staring gravity.

"Then it's almost more wonderful still!" she exclaimed, and fell silent while Razumov asked himself whether he had not said there something utterly unnecessary—or even worse.

She raised her head eagerly.

"Your intention was to stay in Russia? You had planned . . ."

"No," interrupted Razumov without haste. "I had made no plans of any sort."

"You just simply walked away?" she struck in.

He bowed his head in slow assent. "Simply—yes." He had gradually released his hold on the bar of the gate, as though he had acquired the conviction that no random shot could knock him over now. And suddenly he was inspired to add, "The snow was coming down very thick, you know."

She had a slight appreciative movement of the head, like an expert in such enterprises, very interested, capable of taking every point professionally. Razumov remembered something he had heard.

"I turned into a narrow side street, you understand," he went on negligently, and paused as if it were not worth talking about. Then he remembered another detail and dropped it before her, like a disdainful dole to her curiosity.

"I felt inclined to lie down and go to sleep there."

She clicked her tongue at that symptom, very struck indeed. Then—

"But the notebook! The amazing notebook, man. You don't mean to say you had put it in your pocket before-hand!" she cried.

Razumov gave a start. It might have been a sign of impatience.

"I went home. Straight home to my rooms," he said distinctly.

"The coolness of the man! You dared?"

"Why not? I assure you I was perfectly calm. Ha! Calmer than I am now perhaps."

"I like you much better as you are now than when you

indulge that bitter vein of yours, Razumov. And nobody in the house saw you return—eh? That might have appeared queer."

"No one," Razumov said firmly. "Dvornik, landlady, girl, all out of the way. I went up like a shadow. It was a murky morning. The stairs were dark. I glided up like a phantom. Fate? Luck? What do you think?"

"I just see it!" The eyes of the woman revolutionist snapped darkly. "Well—and then you considered . . ."

Razumov had it all ready in his head.

"No. I looked at my watch, since you want to know. There was just time. I took that notebook, and ran down the stairs on tiptoe. Have you ever listened to the pit-pat of a man running round and round the shaft of a deep staircase? They have a gaslight at the bottom burning night and day. I suppose it's gleaming down there now . . . The sound dies out—the flame winks . . ."

He noticed the vacillation of surprise passing over the steady curiosity of the black eyes fastened on his face as if the woman revolutionist received the sound of his voice into her pupils instead of her ears. He checked himself, passed his hand over his forehead, confused, like a man who has been dreaming aloud.

"Where could a student be running if not to his lectures in the morning? At night it's another matter. I did not care if all the house had been there to look at me. But I don't suppose there was any one. It's best not to be seen or heard. Aha! The people that are neither seen nor heard are the lucky ones—in Russia. Don't you admire my luck?"

"Astonishing," she said. "If you have luck as well as determination, then indeed you are likely to turn out an invaluable acquisition for the work in hand."

Her tone was earnest; and it seemed to Razumov that it was speculative, even as though she were already apportioning him, in her mind, his share of the work. Her eyes were cast down. He waited, not very alert now, but with the grip of the ever-present danger giving him an air of attentive gravity. Who could have written about him in that letter from Petersburg? A fellow-student, surely—

some imbecile victim of revolutionary propaganda, some foolish slave of foreign, subversive ideals. A long, famine-stricken red-nosed figure presented itself to his mental search. That must have been the fellow!

He smiled inwardly at the absolute wrong-headedness of the whole thing, the self-deception of a criminal idealist shattering his existence like a thunder-clap out of a clear sky, and re-echoing amongst the wreckage in the false assumptions of those other fools. Fancy that hungry and piteous imbecile furnishing to the curiosity of the revolutionist refugees this utterly fantastic detail! He appreciated it as by no means constituting a danger. On the contrary. As things stood it was for his advantage rather, a piece of sinister luck which had only to be accepted with proper caution.

"And yet, Razumov," he heard the musing voice of the woman, "you have not the face of a lucky man." She raised her eyes with renewed interest. "And so that was the way of it. After doing your work you simply walked off and made for your rooms. That sort of thing succeeds sometimes. I suppose it was agreed beforehand that, once the business over, each of you would go his own way?"

Razumov preserved the seriousness of his expression and the deliberate, if cautious, manner of speaking.

"Was not that the best thing to do?" he asked, in a dispassionate tone. "And anyway," he added, after waiting a moment, "we did not give much thought to what would come after. We never discussed formally any line of conduct. It was understood, I think."

She approved his statement with slight nods.

"You, of course, wished to remain in Russia?"

"In St. Petersburg itself," emphasized Razumov. "It was the only safe course for me. And, moreover, I had nowhere else to go."

"Yes! Yes! I know. Clearly. And the other—this wonderful Haldin appearing only to be regretted—you don't know what he intended?"

Razumov had foreseen that such a question would certainly come to meet him sooner or later. He raised his

hands a little and let them fall helplessly by his side—
nothing more.

It was the white-haired woman conspirator who was the
first to break the silence.

"Very curious," she pronounced slowly. "And you did
not think, Kirylo Sidorovitch, that he might perhaps wish
to get in touch with you again?"

Razumov discovered that he could not suppress the
trembling of his lips. But he thought that he owed it to
himself to speak. A negative sign would not do again.
Speak he must, if only to get at the bottom of what that
St. Petersburg letter might have contained.

"I stayed at home next day," he said, bending down a
little and plunging his glance into the black eyes of the
woman so that she should not observe the trembling of
his lips. "Yes, I stayed at home. As my actions are remembered and written about, then perhaps you are aware that
I was *not* seen at the lectures next day. Eh? You didn't
know? Well, I stopped at home—the live-long day."

As if moved by his agitated tone, she murmured a sympathetic "I see! It must have been trying enough."

"You seem to understand one's feelings," said Razumov
steadily. "It was trying. It was horrible; it was an atrocious
day. It was not the last."

"Yes, I understand. Afterwards, when you heard they
had got him. Don't I know how one feels after losing a
comrade in the good fight? One's ashamed of being left.
And I can remember so many. Never mind. They shall be
avenged before long. And what is death? At any rate, it is
not a shameful thing like some kinds of life."

Razumov felt something stir in his breast, a sort of feeble and unpleasant tremor.

"Some kinds of life?" he repeated, looking at her searchingly.

"The subservient, submissive life. Life? No! Vegetation
on the filthy heap of iniquity which the world is. Life,
Razumov, not to be vile must be a revolt—a pitiless protest
—all the time."

She calmed down, the gleam of suffused tears in her

eyes dried out instantly by the heat of her passion, and it was in her capable, businesslike manner that she went on—

"You understand me, Razumov. You are not an enthusiast, but there is an immense force of revolt in you. I felt it from the first, directly I set my eyes on you—you remember—in Zürich. Oh! You are full of bitter revolt. That is good. Indignation flags sometimes, revenge itself may become a weariness, but that uncompromising sense of necessity and justice which armed your and Haldin's hands to strike down that fanatical brute . . . for it was that—nothing but that! I have been thinking it out. It could have been nothing else but that."

Razumov made a slight bow, the irony of which was concealed by an almost sinister immobility of feature.

"I can't speak for the dead. As for myself, I can assure you that my conduct was dictated by necessity and by the sense of—well—retributive justice."

"Good, that," he said to himself, while her eyes rested upon him, black and impenetrable like the mental caverns where revolutionary thought should sit plotting the violent way of its dream of changes. As if anything could be changed! In this world of men nothing can be changed—neither happiness nor misery. They can only be displaced at the cost of corrupted consciences and broken lives—a futile game for arrogant philosophers and sanguinary triflers. Those thoughts darted through Razumov's head while he stood facing the old revolutionary hand, the respected, trusted, and influential Sophia Antonovna, whose word had such a weight in the "active" section of every party. She was much more representative than the great Peter Ivanovitch. Stripped of rhetoric, mysticism, and theories, she was the true spirit of destructive revolution. And she was the personal adversary he had to meet. It gave him a feeling of triumphant pleasure to deceive her out of her own mouth. The epigrammatic saying that speech has been given to us for the purpose of concealing our thoughts came into his mind. Of that cynical theory this was a very subtle and a very scornful application, flouting in its own words the very spirit of ruthless revolution, embodied in that woman with her white hair and black eyebrows, like slightly sinuous lines of Indian ink, drawn together by the perpendicular folds of a thoughtful frown.

"That's it. Retributive. No pity!" was the conclusion of her silence. And this once broken, she went on impulsively in short, vibrating sentences—

"Listen to my story, Razumov! . . ." Her father was a clever but unlucky artisan. No joy had lighted up his laborious days. He died at fifty; all the years of his life he had panted under the thumb of masters whose rapacity exacted from him the price of the water, of the salt, of the very air he breathed; taxed the sweat of his brow and claimed the blood of his sons. No protection, no guidance! What had society to say to him? Be submissive and be honest. If you rebel I shall kill you. If you steal I shall imprison you. But if you suffer I have nothing for you—nothing except perhaps a beggarly dole of bread—but no consolation for your trouble, no respect for your manhood, no pity for the sorrows of your miserable life.

And so he laboured, he suffered, and he died. He died in the hospital. Standing by the common grave she thought of his tormented existence—she saw it whole. She reckoned the simple joys of life, the birthright of the humblest, of which his gentle heart had been robbed by the crime of a society which nothing can absolve.

"Yes, Razumov," she continued, in an impressive, lowered voice, "it was like a lurid light in which I stood, still almost a child, and cursed not the toil, not the misery which had been his lot, but (the great social iniquity of the system resting on unrequited toil and unpitied sufferings. From that moment I was a revolutionist.")

Razumov, trying to raise himself above the dangerous weaknesses of contempt or compassion, had preserved an impassive countenance. She, with an unaffected touch of mere bitterness, the first he could notice since he had come in contact with the woman, went on—

"As I could not go to the Church where the priests of the system exhorted such unconsidered vermin as I to res-

ignation, I went to the secret societies as soon as I knew
how to find my way. I was sixteen years old—no more,
Razumov! And—look at my white hair."

In these last words there was neither pride nor sadness.
The bitterness too was gone.

"There is a lot of it. I had always magnificent hair, even
as a chit of a girl. Only at that time we were cutting it
short and thinking that there was the first step towards
crushing the social infamy. Crush the Infamy! A fine watch-
word! I would placard it on the walls of prisons and
palaces, carve it on hard rocks, hang it out in letters of
fire on that empty sky for a sign of hope and terror—a
portent of the end . . ."

"You are eloquent, Sophia Antonovna," Razumov interrupted suddenly. "Only, so far you seem to have been writing it in water . . ."

She was checked but not offended. "Who knows? Very
soon it may become a fact written all over that great land
of ours," she hinted meaningly. "And then one would have
lived long enough. White hair won't matter."

Razumov looked at her white hair: and this mark of so
many uneasy years seemed nothing but a testimony to
the invincible vigour of revolt. It threw out into an astonishing relief the unwrinkled face, the brilliant black glance, the
upright compact figure, the simple, brisk self-possession of
the mature personality—as though in her revolutionary
pilgrimage she had discovered the secret, not of everlasting
youth, but of everlasting endurance.

How un-Russian she looked, thought Razumov. Her
mother might have been a Jewess or an Armenian or—devil
knew what. He reflected that a revolutionist is seldom true
to the settled type. (All revolt is the expression of strong
individualism—ran his thought vaguely. One can tell
them a mile off in any society, in any surroundings. It was
astonishing that the police . . .)

"We shall not meet again very soon, I think," she was
saying. "I am leaving to-morrow."

"For Zürich?" Razumov asked casually, but feeling relieved, not from any distinct apprehension, but from a feeling of stress as if after a wrestling match.

"Yes, Zürich—and farther on, perhaps, much farther. Another journey. When I think of all my journeys! The last must come some day. Never mind, Razumov. We had to have a good long talk. I would have certainly tried to see you if we had not met. Peter Ivanovitch knows where you live? Yes. I meant to have asked him—but it's better like this. You see, we expect two more men; and I had much rather wait here talking with you than up there at the house with . . ."

Having cast a glance beyond the gate, she interrupted herself. "Here they are," she said rapidly. "Well, Kirylo Sidorovitch, we shall have to say good-bye, presently."

IV

In his incertitude of the ground on which he stood Razumov felt perturbed. Turning his head quickly, he saw two men on the opposite side of the road. Seeing themselves noticed by Sophia Antonovna, they crossed over at once, and passed one after another through the little gate by the side of the empty lodge. They looked hard at the stranger, but without mistrust, the crimson blouse being a flaring safety signal. The first, great white hairless face, double chin, prominent stomach, which he seemed to carry forward consciously within a strongly distended overcoat, only nodded and averted his eyes peevishly; his companion—lean, flushed cheek-bones, a military red moustache below a sharp, salient nose—approached at once Sophia Antonovna, greeting her warmly. His voice was very strong but inarticulate. It sounded like a deep buzzing. The woman revolutionist was quietly cordial. . . .

"This is Razumov," she announced in a clear voice.

The lean new-comer made an eager half-turn. "He will want to embrace me," thought our young man with a deep recoil of all his being, while his limbs seemed too heavy to move. But it was a groundless alarm. He had to do now with a generation of conspirators who did not kiss each other on both cheeks; and raising an arm that felt like lead he dropped his hand into a largely outstretched palm, fleshless and hot as if dried up by fever, giving a bony pressure, expressive, seeming to say, "Between us there's no need of words."

The man had big, wide-open eyes. Razumov fancied he could see a smile behind their sadness.

"This is Razumov," Sophia Antonovna repeated loudly for the benefit of the fat man, who at some distance displayed the profile of his stomach.

No one moved. Everything, sounds, attitudes, movements, and immobility seemed to be part of an experiment, the result of which was a thin voice piping with comic peevishness—

"Oh yes! Razumov. We have been hearing of nothing but Mr. Razumov for months. For my part, I confess I would rather have seen Haldin on this spot instead of Mr. Razumov."

The squeaky stress put on the name "Razumov—Mr. Razumov" pierced the ear ridiculously, like the falsetto of a circus clown beginning an elaborate joke. Astonishment was Razumov's first response, followed by sudden indignation.

"What's the meaning of this?" he asked in a stern tone.

"Tut! Silliness. He's always like that." Sophia Antonovna was obviously vexed. But she dropped the information, "Necator," from her lips just loud enough to be heard by Razumov. The abrupt squeaks of the fat man seemed to proceed from that thing like a balloon he carried under his overcoat. The stolidity of his attitude, the big feet, the lifeless, hanging hands, the enormous bloodless cheek, the thin wisps of hair straggling down the fat nape of the neck, fascinated Razumov into a stare on the verge of horror and laughter.

Nikita, nicknamed Necator, with a sinister aptness of alliteration! Razumov had heard of him. He had heard so much since crossing the frontier of these celebrities of the militant revolution; the legends, the stories, the authentic chronicle, which now and then peeps out before a half-incredulous world. Razumov had heard of him. He was supposed to have killed more gendarmes and police agents than any revolutionist living. He had been entrusted with executions.

The paper with the letters N. N., the very pseudonym of murder, found pinned on the stabbed breast of a certain notorious spy (this picturesque detail of a sensational murder case had got into the newspapers), was the mark of his handiwork. "By order of the Committee.—N. N." A corner of the curtain lifted to strike the imagination of the gaping world. He was said to have been innumerable times in and out of Russia, the Necator of bureaucrats, of provincial governors, of obscure informers. He lived between whiles, Razumov had heard, on the shores of the Lake of Como, with a charming wife, devoted to the cause, and two young children. But how could that creature, so grotesque as to set town dogs barking at its mere sight, go about on those deadly errands and slip through the meshes of the police?

"What now? what now?" the voice squeaked. "I am only sincere. It's not denied that the other was the leading spirit. Well, it would have been better if he had been the one spared to us. More useful. I am not a sentimentalist. Say what I think . . . only natural."

Squeak, squeak, squeak, without a gesture, without a stir —the horrible squeaky burlesque of professional jealousy— this man of a sinister alliterative nickname, this executioner of revolutionary verdicts, the terrifying N. N. exasperated like a fashionable tenor by the attention attracted to the performance of an obscure amateur. Sophia Antonovna shrugged her shoulders. The comrade with the martial red moustache hurried towards Razumov full of conciliatory intentions in his strong buzzing voice.

"Devil take it! And in this place, too, in the public street, so to speak. But you can see yourself how it is. One of his fantastic sallies. Absolutely of no consequence."

"Pray don't concern yourself," cried Razumov, going off into a long fit of laughter. "Don't mention it."

The other, his hectic flush like a pair of burns on his

cheek-bones, stared for a moment and burst out laughing too. Razumov, whose hilarity died out all at once, made a step forward.

"Enough of this," he began in a clear, incisive voice, though he could hardly control the trembling of his legs. "I will have no more of it. I shall not permit any one. . . . I can see very well what you are at with those allusions. . . . Inquire, investigate! I defy you but I will not be played with."

He had spoken such words before. He had been driven to cry them out in the face of other suspicions. It was an infernal cycle bringing round that protest like a fatal necessity of his existence. But it was no use. He would be always played with. Luckily life does not last for ever.

"I won't have it!" he shouted, striking his fist into the palm of his other hand.

"Kirylo Sidorovitch—what has come to you?" The woman revolutionist interfered with authority. They were all looking at Razumov now; the slayer of spies and gendarmes had turned about, presenting his enormous stomach in full, like a shield.

"Don't shout. There are people passing." Sophia Antonovna was apprehensive of another outburst. A steam-launch from Monrepos had come to the landing-stage opposite the gate, its hoarse whistle and the churning noise alongside all unnoticed, had landed a small bunch of local passengers who were dispersing their several ways. Only a specimen of early tourist in knickerbockers, conspicuous by a brand-new yellow leather glass-case, hung about for a moment, scenting something unusual about these four people within the rusty iron gates of what looked like the grounds run wild of an unoccupied private house. Ah! If he had only known what the chance of commonplace travelling had suddenly put in his way! But he was a well-bred person; he averted his gaze and moved off with short steps along the avenue, on the watch for a tramcar.

A gesture from Sophia Antonovna, "Leave him to me," had sent the two men away—the buzzing of the inarticulate voice growing fainter and fainter, and the thin pipe of

"What now? what's the matter?" reduced to the proportions of a squeaking toy by the distance. They had left him
to her. So many things could be left safely to the experience
of Sophia Antonovna. And at once, her black eyes turned
to Razumov, her mind tried to get at the heart of that
outburst. It had some meaning. No one is born an active
revolutionist. The change comes disturbingly, with the
force of a sudden vocation, bringing in its train agonizing
doubts, assertive violences, an unstable state of the soul,
till the final appeasement of the convert in the perfect
fierceness of conviction. She had seen—often had only
divined—scores of these young men and young women
going through an emotional crisis. This young man looked
like a moody egotist. And besides, it was a special—a
unique case. She had never met an individuality which
interested and puzzled her so much.

"Take care, Razumov, my good friend. If you carry on
like this you will go mad. You are angry with everybody
and bitter with yourself, and on the lookout for something
to torment yourself with."

"It's intolerable!" Razumov could only speak in gasps.
"You must admit that I can have no illusions on the attitude
which . . . it isn't clear . . . or rather . . . only too clear."

He made a gesture of despair. It was not his courage
that failed him. The choking fumes of falsehood had taken
him by the throat—the thought of being condemned to
struggle on and on in that tainted atmosphere without the
hope of ever renewing his strength by a breath of fresh air.

"A glass of cold water is what you want." Sophia
Antonovna glanced up the grounds at the house and
shook her head, then out of the gate at the brimful
placidity of the lake. With a half-comical shrug of the
shoulders, she gave the remedy up in the face of that
abundance.

"It is you, my dear soul, who are flinging yourself at
something which does not exist. What is it? Self-reproach,
or what? It's absurd. You couldn't have gone and given
yourself up because your comrade was taken."

She remonstrated with him reasonably, at some length

too. He had nothing to complain of in his reception. Every new-comer was discussed more or less. Everybody had to be thoroughly understood before being accepted. No one that she could remember had been shown from the first so much confidence. Soon, very soon, perhaps sooner than he expected, he would be given an opportunity of showing his devotion to the sacred task of crushing the Infamy.

Razumov, listening quietly, thought: "It may be that she is trying to lull my suspicions to sleep. On the other hand, it is obvious that most of them are fools." He moved aside a couple of paces and, folding his arms on his breast, leaned back against the stone pillar of the gate.

"As to what remains obscure in the fate of that poor Haldin," Sophia Antonovna dropped into a slowness of utterance which was to Razumov like the falling of molten lead drop by drop; "as to that—though no one ever hinted that either from fear or neglect your conduct has not been what it should have been—well, I have a bit of intelligence . . ."

Razumov could not prevent himself from raising his head, and Sophia Antonovna nodded slightly.

"I have. You remember that letter from St. Petersburg I mentioned to you a moment ago?"

"The letter? Perfectly. Some busybody has been reporting my conduct on a certain day. It's rather sickening. I suppose our police are greatly edified when they open these interesting and—and—superfluous letters."

"Oh dear no! The police do not get hold of our letters as easily as you imagine. The letter in question did not leave St. Petersburg till the ice broke up. It went by the first English steamer which left the Neva this spring. They have a fireman on board—one of us, in fact. It has reached me from Hull . . ."

She paused as if she were surprised at the sullen fixity of Razumov's gaze, but went on at once, and much faster.

"We have some of our people there who . . . but never mind. The writer of the letter relates an incident which he thinks may possibly be connected with Haldin's arrest.

I was just going to tell you when those two men came along."

"That also was an incident," muttered Razumov, "of a very charming kind—for me."

"Leave off that!" cried Sophia Antonovna. "Nobody cares for Nikita's barking. There's no malice in him. Listen to what I have to say. You may be able to throw a light. There was in St. Petersburg a sort of town peasant—a man who owned horses. He came to town years ago to work for some relation as a driver and ended by owning a cab or two."

She might well have spared herself the slight effort of the gesture: "Wait!" Razumov did not mean to speak; he could not have interrupted her now, not to save his life. The contraction of his facial muscles had been involuntary, a mere surface stir, leaving him sullenly attentive as before.

"He was not a quite ordinary man of his class—it seems," she went on. "The people of the house—my informant talked with many of them—you know, one of those enormous houses of shame and misery . . ."

Sophia Antonovna need not have enlarged on the character of the house. Razumov saw clearly, towering at her back, a dark mass of masonry veiled in snowflakes, with the long row of windows of the eating-shop shining greasily very near the ground. The ghost of that night pursued him. He stood up to it with rage and with weariness.

"Did the late Haldin ever by chance speak to you of that house?" Sophia Antonovna was anxious to know.

"Yes." Razumov, making that answer, wondered whether he were falling into a trap. It was so humiliating to lie to these people that he probably could not have said no. "He mentioned to me once," he added, as if making an effort of memory, "a house of that sort. He used to visit some workmen there."

"Exactly."

Sophia Antonovna triumphed. Her correspondent had discovered that fact quite accidentally from the talk of the people of the house, having made friends with a workman who occupied a room there. They described Haldin's appearance perfectly. He brought comforting words of hope into their misery. He came irregularly, but he came very often, and—her correspondent wrote—sometimes he spent a night in the house, sleeping, they thought, in a stable which opened upon the inner yard.

"Note that, Razumov! In a stable."

Razumov had listened with a sort of ferocious but amused acquiescence.

"Yes. In the straw. It was probably the cleanest spot in the whole house."

"No doubt," assented the woman with that deep frown which seemed to draw closer together her black eyes in a sinister fashion. No four-footed beast could stand the filth and wretchedness so many human beings were condemned to suffer from in Russia. The point of this discovery was that it proved Haldin to have been familiar with that horse-owning peasant—a reckless, independent, free-living fellow not much liked by the other inhabitants of the house. He was believed to have been the associate of a band of house-breakers. Some of these got captured. Not while he was driving them, however; but still there was a suspicion against the fellow of having given a hint to the police and . . .

The woman revolutionist checked herself suddenly.

"And you? Have you ever heard your friend refer to a certain Ziemianitch?"

Razumov was ready for the name. He had been looking out for the question. "When it comes I shall own up," he had said to himself. But he took his time.

"To be sure!" he began slowly. "Ziemianitch, a peasant owning a team of horses. Yes. On one occasion. Ziemianitch! Certainly! Ziemianitch of the horses. . . . How could it have slipped my memory like this? One of the last conversations we had together."

"That means,"—Sophia Antonovna looked very grave,—"that means, Razumov, it was very shortly before—eh?"

"Before what?" shouted Razumov, advancing at the woman, who looked astonished but stood her ground. "Be-

fore . . . Oh! Of course, it was before! How could it have
been after? Only a few hours before."

"And he spoke of him favourably?"

"With enthusiasm! The horses of Ziemianitch! The free
soul of Ziemianitch!"

Razumov took a savage delight in the loud utterance of
that name, which had never before crossed his lips audibly.
He fixed his blazing eyes on the woman till at last her
fascinated expression recalled him to himself.

"The late Haldin," he said, holding himself in, with
downcast eyes, "was inclined to take sudden fancies to
people, on—on—what shall I say—insufficient grounds."

"There!" Sophia Antonovna clapped her hands. "That, to
my mind, settles it. The suspicions of my correspondent
were aroused . . ."

"Aha! Your correspondent," Razumov said in an almost
openly mocking tone. "What suspicions? How aroused? By
this Ziemianitch? Probably some drunken, gabbling, plau-
sible . . ."

"You talk as if you had known him."

Razumov looked up.

"No. But I knew Haldin."

Sophia Antonovna nodded gravely.

"I see. Every word you say confirms to my mind the
suspicion communicated to me in that very interesting
letter. This Ziemianitch was found one morning hanging
from a hook in the stable—dead."

Razumov felt a profound trouble. It was visible, because
Sophia Antonovna was moved to observe vivaciously—

"Aha! You begin to see."

He saw it clearly enough—in the light of a lantern casting spokes of shadow in a cellar-like stable, the body in a
sheepskin coat and long boots hanging against the wall. A
pointed hood, with the ends wound about up to the eyes,
hid the face. "But that does not concern me," he reflected.
"It does not affect my position at all. He never knew who
had thrashed him. He could not have known." Razumov
felt sorry for the old lover of the bottle and women.

"Yes. Some of them end like that," he muttered. "What is your idea, Sophia Antonovna?"

It was really the idea of her correspondent, but Sophia Antonovna had adopted it fully. She stated it in one word—"Remorse." Razumov opened his eyes very wide at that. Sophia Antonovna's informant, by listening to the talk of the house, by putting this and that together, had managed to come very near to the truth of Haldin's relation to Ziemianitch.

"It is I who can tell you what you were not certain of—that your friend had some plan for saving himself afterwards, for getting out of St. Petersburg, at any rate. Perhaps that and no more, trusting to luck for the rest. And that fellow's horses were part of the plan."

"They have actually got at the truth," Razumov marvelled to himself, while he nodded judicially. "Yes, that's possible, very possible." But the woman revolutionist was very positive that it was so. First of all, a conversation about horses between Haldin and Ziemianitch had been partly overheard. Then there were the suspicions of the people in the house when their "young gentleman" (they did not know Haldin by his name) ceased to call at the house. Some of them used to charge Ziemianitch with knowing something of this absence. He denied it with exasperation; but the fact was that ever since Haldin's disappearance he was not himself, growing moody and thin. Finally, during a quarrel with some woman (to whom he was making up), in which most of the inmates of the house took part apparently, he was openly abused by his chief enemy, an athletic pedlar, for an informer, and for having driven "our young gentleman to Siberia, the same as you did those young fellows who broke into houses." In consequence of this there was a fight, and Ziemianitch got flung down a flight of stairs. Thereupon he drank and moped for a week, and then hanged himself.

Sophia Antonovna drew her conclusions from the tale. She charged Ziemianitch either with drunken indiscretion as to a driving job on a certain date, overheard by some spy in some low grog-shop—perhaps in the very eating-shop on the ground floor of the house—or, maybe, a downright denunciation, followed by remorse. A man like that would be capable of anything. People said he was a flighty old chap. And if he had been once before mixed up with the police—as seemed certain, though he always denied it—in connexion with these thieves, he would be sure to be acquainted with some police underlings, always on the look out for something to report. Possibly at first his tale was not made anything of till the day that scoundrel de P— got his deserts. Ah! But then every bit and scrap of hint and information would be acted on, and fatally they were bound to get Haldin.

Sophia Antonovna spread out her hands—"Fatally."

Fatality—chance! Razumov meditated in silent astonishment upon the queer verisimilitude of these inferences. They were obviously to his advantage.

"It is right now to make this conclusive evidence known generally." Sophia Antonovna was very calm and deliberate again. She had received the letter three days ago, but did not write at once to Peter Ivanovitch. She knew then that she would have the opportunity presently of meeting several men of action assembled for an important purpose.

"I thought it would be more effective if I could show the letter itself at large. I have it in my pocket now. You understand how pleased I was to come upon you."

Razumov was saying to himself, "She won't offer to show the letter to me. Not likely. Has she told me everything that correspondent of hers has found out?" He longed to see the letter, but he felt he must not ask.

"Tell me, please, was this an investigation ordered, as it were?"

"No, no," she protested. "There you are again with your sensitiveness. It makes you stupid. Don't you see, there was no starting-point for an investigation even if any one had thought of it. A perfect blank! That's exactly what some people were pointing out as the reason for receiving you cautiously. It was all perfectly accidental, arising from my informant striking an acquaintance with an intelligent skindresser lodging in that particular slum-house. A wonderful coincidence!"

"A pious person," suggested Razumov, with a pale smile, "would say that the hand of God has done it all."

"My poor father would have said that." Sophia Antonovna did not smile. She dropped her eyes. "Not that his God ever helped him. It's a long time since God has done anything for the people. Anyway, it's done."

"All this would be quite final," said Razumov, with every appearance of reflective impartiality, "if there was any certitude that the 'our young gentleman' of these people was Victor Haldin. Have we got that?"

"Yes. There's no mistake. My correspondent was as familiar with Haldin's personal appearance as with your own," the woman affirmed decisively.

"It's the red-nosed fellow beyond a doubt," Razumov said to himself, with reawakened uneasiness. Had his own visit to that accursed house passed unnoticed? It was barely possible. Yet it was hardly probable. It was just the right sort of food for the popular gossip that gaunt busybody had been picking up. But the letter did not seem to contain any allusion to that. Unless she had suppressed it. And, if so, why? If it had really escaped the prying of that hunger-stricken democrat with a confounded genius for recognizing people from description, it could only be for a time. He would come upon it presently and hasten to write another letter—and then!

For all the envenomed recklessness of his temper, fed on hate and disdain, Razumov shuddered inwardly. It guarded him from common fear, but it could not defend him from disgust at being dealt with in any way by these people. It was a sort of superstitious dread. Now, since his position had been made more secure by their own folly at the cost of Ziemianitch, he felt the need of perfect safety, with its freedom from direct lying, with its power of moving amongst them silent, unquestioning, listening, impenetrable, like the very fate of their crimes and their folly. Was this advantage his already? Or not yet? Or never would be?

"Well, Sophia Antonovna," his air of reluctant concession was genuine in so far that he was really loath to part
with her without testing her sincerity by a question it was
impossible to bring about in any way; "well, Sophia
Antonovna, if that is so, then——"

"The creature has done justice to himself," the woman
observed, as if thinking aloud.

"What? Ah yes! Remorse," Razumov muttered with
equivocal contempt.

"Don't be harsh, Kirylo Sidorovitch, if you have lost a
friend." There was no hint of softness in her tone, only
the black glitter of her eyes seemed detached for an instant
from vengeful visions. "He was a man of the people. The
simple Russian soul is never wholly impenitent. It's something to know that."

"Consoling?" insinuated Razumov, in a tone of inquiry.

"Leave off railing," she checked him explosively. "Remember, Razumov, that women, children, and revolutionists hate irony, which is the negation of all saving
instincts, of all faith, of all devotion, of all action. Don't
rail! Leave off. . . . I don't know how it is, but there are
moments when you are abhorrent to me. . . ."

She averted her face. A languid silence, as if all the
electricity of the situation had been discharged in this flash
of passion, lasted for some time. Razumov had not flinched.
Suddenly she laid the tips of her fingers on his sleeve.

"Don't mind."

"I don't mind," he said very quietly.

He was proud to feel that she could read nothing on his
face. He was really mollified, relieved, if only for a moment,
from an obscure oppression. And suddenly he asked himself, "Why the devil did I go to that house? It was an
imbecile thing to do."

A profound disgust came over him. Sophia Antonovna lingered, talking in a friendly manner with an evident
conciliatory intention. And it was still about the famous
letter, referring to various minute details given by her informant, who had never seen Ziemianitch. The "victim of
remorse" had been buried several weeks before her corre-

spondent began frequenting the house. It—the house—
contained very good revolutionary material. The spirit of
the heroic Haldin had passed through these dens of black
wretchedness with a promise of universal redemption from
all the miseries that oppress mankind. Razumov listened
without hearing, gnawed by the newborn desire of safety
with its independence from that degrading method of
direct lying which at times he found it almost impossible to
practice.

No. The point he wanted to hear about could never
come into this conversation. There was no way of bringing
it forward. He regretted not having composed a perfect
story for use abroad, in which his fatal connexion with the
house might have been owned up to. But when he left
Russia he did not know that Ziemianitch had hanged himself. And, anyway, who could have foreseen this woman's
"informant" stumbling upon that particular slum of all the
slums awaiting destruction in the purifying flame of social
revolution? Who could have foreseen? Nobody! "It's a perfect, diabolic surprise," thought Razumov, calm-faced in
his attitude of inscrutable superiority, nodding assent to
Sophia Antonovna's remarks upon the psychology of "the
people," "Oh yes—certainly," rather coldly, but with a nervous longing in his fingers to tear some sort of confession out
of her throat.

Then, at the very last, on the point of separating, the
feeling of relaxed tension already upon him he heard
Sophia Antonovna allude to the subject of his uneasiness.
How it came about he could only guess, his mind being
absent at the moment, but it must have sprung from Sophia
Antonovna's complaints of the illogical absurdity of the
people. For instance—that Ziemianitch was notoriously
irreligious, and yet, in the last weeks of his life, he suffered
from the notion that he had been beaten by the devil.

"The devil," repeated Razumov, as though he had not
heard aright.

"The actual devil. The devil in person. You may well
look astonished, Kirylo Sidorovitch. Early on the very night
poor Haldin was taken, a complete stranger turned up and

gave Ziemianitch a most fearful thrashing while he was
lying dead-drunk in the stable. The wretched creature's
body was one mass of bruises. He showed them to the
people in the house."

"But you, Sophia Antonovna, you don't believe in the
actual devil?"

"Do you?" retorted the woman curtly. "Not but that
there are plenty of men worse than devils to make a hell
of this earth," she muttered to herself.

Razumov watched her, vigorous and white-haired, with
the deep fold between her thin eyebrows, and her black
glance turned idly away. It was obvious that she did not
make much of the story—unless, indeed, this was the perfection of duplicity. "A dark young man," she explained
further. "Never seen there before, never seen afterwards.
Why are you smiling, Razumov?"

"At the devil being still young after all these ages," he
answered composedly. "But who was able to describe him,
since the victim, you say, was dead-drunk at the time?"

"Oh! The eating-house keeper has described him. An
overbearing, swarthy young man in a student's cloak, who
came rushing in, demanded Ziemianitch, beat him furiously, and rushed away without a word, leaving the eating-
house keeper paralysed with astonishment."

"Does he, too, believe it was the devil?"

"That I can't say. I am told he's very reserved on the
matter. Those sellers of spirits are great scoundrels generally. I should think he knows more of it than anybody."

"Well, and you, Sophia Antonovna, what's your theory?"
asked Razumov in a tone of great interest. "Yours and
your informant's, who is on the spot."

"I agree with him. Some police-hound in disguise. Who
else could beat a helpless man so unmercifully? As for the
rest, if they were out that day on every trail, old and new,
it is probable enough that they might have thought it just
as well to have Ziemianitch at hand for more information,
or for identification, or what not. Some scoundrelly detec-
tive was sent to fetch him along, and being vexed at finding him so drunk broke a stable fork over his ribs. Later

on, after they had the big game safe in the net, they troubled their heads no more about that peasant."

Such were the last words of the woman revolutionist in this conversation, keeping so close to the truth, departing from it so far in the verisimilitude of thoughts and conclusions as to give one the notion of the invincible nature of human error, a glimpse into the utmost depths of self-deception. Razumov, after shaking hands with Sophia Antonovna, left the grounds, crossed the road, and walking out on the little steamboat pier leaned over the rail.

His mind was at ease; ease such as he had not known for many days, ever since that night . . . the night. The conversation with the woman revolutionist had given him the view of his danger at the very moment this danger vanished, characteristically enough. "I ought to have foreseen the doubts that would arise in those people's minds," he thought. Then his attention being attracted by a stone of peculiar shape, which he could see clearly lying at the bottom, he began to speculate as to the depth of water in that spot. But very soon, with a start of wonder at this extraordinary instance of ill-timed detachment, he returned to his train of thought. "I ought to have told very circumstantial lies from the first," he said to himself, with a mortal distaste of the mere idea which silenced his mental utterance for quite a perceptible interval. "Luckily, that's all right now," he reflected, and after a time spoke to himself, half aloud, "Thanks to the devil," and laughed a little.

The end of Ziemianitch then arrested his wandering thoughts. He was not exactly amused at the interpretation, but he could not help detecting in it a certain piquancy. He owned to himself that, had he known of that suicide before leaving Russia, he would have been incapable of making such excellent use of it for his own purposes. He ought to be infinitely obliged to the fellow with the red nose for his patience and ingenuity, "A wonderful psychologist apparently," he said to himself sarcastically. Remorse, indeed! It was a striking example of your true conspirator's blindness, of the stupid subtlety of people with one idea. This was a drama of love, not of conscience, Razumov continued to himself mockingly. A woman the old fellow was making up to! A robust pedlar, clearly a rival, throwing him down a flight of stairs. . . . And at sixty, for a lifelong lover, it was not an easy matter to get over. That was a feminist of a different stamp from Peter Ivanovitch. Even the comfort of the bottle might conceivably fail him in this supreme crisis. At such an age nothing but a halter could cure the pangs of an unquenchable passion. And, besides, there was the wild exasperation aroused by the unjust aspersions and the contumely of the house, with the maddening impossibility to account for that mysterious thrashing, added to these simple and bitter sorrows. "Devil, eh?" Razumov exclaimed, with mental excitement, as if he had made an interesting discovery. "Ziemianitch ended by falling into mysticism. So many of our true Russian souls end in that way! Very characteristic." He felt pity for Ziemianitch, a large neutral pity, such as one may feel for an unconscious multitude, a great people seen from above—like a community of crawling ants working out its destiny. It was as if this Ziemianitch could not possibly have done anything else. And Sophia Antonovna's cocksure and contemptuous "some police-hound" was characteristically Russian in another way. But there was no tragedy there. This was a comedy of errors. It was as if the devil himself were playing a game with all of them in turn. First with him, then with Ziemianitch, then with those revolutionists. The devil's own game this. . . . He interrupted his earnest mental soliloquy with a jocular thought at his own expense. "Hallo! I am falling into mysticism too."

His mind was more at ease than ever. Turning about he put his back against the rail comfortably. "All this fits with marvellous aptness," he continued to think. "The brilliance of my reputed exploit is no longer darkened by the fate of my supposed colleague. The mystic Ziemianitch accounts for that. An incredible chance has served me. No more need of lies. I shall have only to listen and to keep my scorn from getting the upper hand of my caution."

He sighed, folded his arms, his chin dropped on his breast, and it was a long time before he started forward from that pose, with the recollection that he had made up his mind to do something important that day. What it was he could not immediately recall, yet he made no effort of memory, for he was uneasily certain that he would remember presently.

He had not gone more than a hundred yards towards the town when he slowed down, almost faltered in his walk, at the sight of a figure walking in the contrary direction, draped in a cloak, under a soft, broad-brimmed hat, picturesque but diminutive, as if seen through the big end of an opera-glass. It was impossible to avoid that tiny man, for there was no issue for retreat.

"Another one going to that mysterious meeting," thought Razumov. He was right in his surmise, only *this* one, unlike the others who came from a distance, was known to him personally. Still, he hoped to pass on with a mere bow, but it was impossible to ignore the little thin hand with hairy wrist and knuckles protruded in a friendly wave from under the folds of the cloak, wore Spanish-wise, in disregard of a fairly warm day, a corner flung over the shoulder.

"And how is Herr Razumov?" sounded the greeting in German, by that alone made more odious to the object of the affable recognition. At closer quarters the diminutive personage looked like a reduction of an ordinary-sized man, with a lofty brow bared for a moment by the raising of the hat, the great pepper-and-salt full beard spread over the proportionally broad chest. A fine bold nose jutted over a thin mouth hidden in the mass of fine hair. All this, accented features, strong limbs in their relative smallness, appeared delicate without the slightest sign of debility. The eyes alone, almond-shaped and brown, were too big, with the whites slightly bloodshot by much pen labour under a lamp. The obscure celebrity of the tiny man was well known to Razumov. Polyglot, of unknown parentage, of indefinite nationality, anarchist, with a pedantic and ferocious temperament, and an amazingly inflammatory capacity for invective, he was a power in the background, this violent pamphleteer clamouring for revolutionary justice, this Julius Laspara, editor of the *Living Word*, confidant of conspirators, inditer of sanguinary menaces and manifestos, suspected of being in the secret of every plot. Laspara lived in the old town in a sombre, narrow house presented to him by a naïve middle-class admirer of his humanitarian eloquence. With him lived his two daughters, who overtopped him head and shoulders, and a pasty-faced, lean boy of six, languishing in the dark rooms in blue cotton overalls and clumsy boots, who might have belonged to either one of them or to neither. No stranger could tell. Julius Laspara no doubt knew which of his girls it was who, after casually vanishing for a few years, had as casually returned to him possessed of that child; but, with admirable pedantry, he had refrained from asking her for details—no, not so much as the name of the father, because maternity should be an anarchist function. Razumov had been admitted twice to that suite of several small dark rooms on the top floor: dusty windowpanes, litter of all sorts of sweepings all over the place, half-full glasses of tea forgotten on every table, the two Laspara daughters prowling about enigmatically silent, sleepy-eyed, corsetless, and generally, in their want of shape and the disorder of their rumpled attire, resembling old dolls; the great but obscure Julius, his feet twisted round his three-legged stool, always ready to receive the visitors, the pen instantly dropped, the body screwed round with a striking display of the lofty brow and of the great austere beard. When he got down from his stool it was as though he had descended from the heights of Olympus. He was dwarfed by his daughters, by the furniture, by any caller of ordinary stature. But he very seldom left it, and still more rarely was seen walking in broad daylight.

It must have been some matter of serious importance which had driven him out in that direction that afternoon. Evidently he wished to be amiable to that young man whose arrival had made some sensation in the world of political refugees. In Russian now, which he spoke, as he spoke and wrote four or five other European languages, without distinction and without force (other than that of invective), he inquired if Razumov had taken his inscrip-

tions at the University as yet. And the young man, shaking
his head negatively—

"There's plenty of time for that. But, meantime, are you
not going to write something for us?"

He could not understand how any one could refrain
from writing on anything, social, economic, historical—
anything. Any subject could be treated in the right spirit,
and for the ends of social revolution. And, as it happened,
a friend of his in London had got in touch with a review
of advanced ideas. "We must educate, educate everybody
—develop the great thought of absolute liberty and of
revolutionary justice."

Razumov muttered rather surlily that he did not even
know English.

"Write in Russian. We'll have it translated. There can
be no difficulty. Why, without seeking further, there is
Miss Haldin. My daughters go to see her sometimes." He
nodded significantly. "She does nothing, has never done
anything in her life. She would be quite competent, with
a little assistance. Only write. You know you must. And so
good-bye for the present."

He raised his arm and went on. Razumov backed against
the low wall, looked after him, spat violently, and went on
his way with an angry mutter—

"Cursed Jew!"

He did not know anything about it. Julius Laspara
might have been a Transylvanian, a Turk, an Andalusian,
or a citizen of one of the Hanse towns for anything he
could tell to the contrary. But this is not a story of the
West, and this exclamation must be recorded, accompanied by the comment that it was merely an expression
of hate and contempt, best adapted to the nature of the
feelings Razumov suffered from at the time. He was boil-
ing with rage, as though he had been grossly insulted. He
walked as if blind, following instinctively the shore of the
diminutive harbour along the quay, through a pretty, dull
garden, where dull people sat on chairs under the trees,
till, his fury abandoning him, he discovered himself in the
middle of a long, broad bridge. He slowed down at once.

To his right, beyond the toy-like jetties, he saw the green slopes framing the Petit Lac in all the marvellous banality of the picturesque made of painted cardboard, with the more distant stretch of water inanimate and shining like a piece of tin.

He turned his head away from that view for the tourists, and walked on slowly, his eyes fixed on the ground. One or two persons had to get out of his way, and then turned round to give a surprised stare to his profound absorption. The insistence of the celebrated subversive journalist rankled in his mind strangely. Write. Must write! He! Write! A sudden light flashed upon him. To write was the very thing he had made up his mind to do that day. He had made up his mind irrevocably to that step and then had forgotten all about it. That incorrigible tendency to escape from the grip of the situation was fraught with serious danger. He was ready to despise himself for it. What was it? Levity, or deep-seated weakness? Or an unconscious dread?

"Is it that I am shrinking? It can't be! It's impossible. To shrink now would be worse than moral suicide; it would be nothing less than moral damnation," he thought. "Is it possible that I have a conventional conscience?"

He rejected that hypothesis with scorn, and, checked on the edge of the pavement, made ready to cross the road and proceed up the wide street facing the head of the bridge; and that for no other reason except that it was there before him. But at the moment a couple of carriages and a slow-moving cart interposed, and suddenly he turned sharp to the left, following the quay again, but now away from the lake.

"It may be just my health," he thought, allowing himself a very unusual doubt of his soundness; for, with the exception of a childish ailment or two, he had never been ill in his life. But that was a danger, too. Only, it seemed as though he were being looked after in a specially remarkable way. "If I believed in an active Providence," Razumov said to himself, amused grimly, "I would see here the working of an ironical finger. To have a Julius

Laspara put in my way as if expressly to remind me of my purpose is— Write, he had said. I must write—I must, indeed! I shall write—never fear. Certainly. That's why I am here. And for the future I shall have something to write about."

He was exciting himself by this mental soliloquy. But the idea of writing evoked the thought of a place to write in, of shelter, of privacy, and naturally of his lodgings, mingled with a distaste for the necessary exertion of getting there, with a mistrust as of some hostile influence awaiting him within those odious four walls.

"Suppose one of those revolutionists," he asked himself, "were to take a fancy to call on me while I am writing?" The mere prospect of such an interruption made him shudder. One could lock one's door, or ask the tobacconist downstairs (some sort of a refugee himself) to tell inquirers that one was not in. Not very good precautions these. The manner of his life, he felt, must be kept clear of every cause for suspicion or even occasion for wonder, down to such trifling occurrences as a delay in opening a locked door. "I wish I were in the middle of some field miles away from everywhere," he thought.

He had unconsciously turned to the left once more and now was aware of being on a bridge again. This one was much narrower than the other, and instead of being straight, made a sort of elbow or angle. At the point of that angle a short arm joined it to a hexagonal islet with a soil of gravel and its shores faced with dressed stone, a perfection of puerile neatness. A couple of tall poplars and a few other trees stood grouped on the clean, dark gravel, and under them a few garden benches and a bronze effigy of Jean Jacques Rousseau seated on its pedestal.

On setting his foot on it Razumov became aware that, except for the woman in charge of the refreshment chalet, he would be alone on the island. There was something of naïve, odious, and inane simplicity about that unfrequented tiny crumb of earth named after Jean Jacques Rousseau. Something pretentious and shabby, too. He asked for a glass of milk, which he drank standing, at one

draught (nothing but tea had passed his lips since the morning), and was going away with a weary, lagging step when a thought stopped him short. He had found precisely what he needed. If solitude could ever be secured in the open air in the middle of a town, he would have it there on this absurd island, together with the faculty of watching the only approach.

He went back heavily to a garden seat, dropped into it. This was the place for making a beginning of that writing which had to be done. The materials he had on him. "I shall always come here," he said to himself, and afterwards sat for quite a long time motionless, without thought and sight and hearing, almost without life. He sat long enough for the declining sun to dip behind the roofs of the town at his back, and throw the shadow of the houses on the lake front over the islet, before he pulled out of his pocket a fountain pen, opened a small notebook on his knee, and began to write quickly, raising his eyes now and then at the connecting arm of the bridge. These glances were needless; the people crossing over in the distance seemed unwilling even to look at the islet where the exiled effigy of the author of the *Social Contract* sat enthroned above the bowed head of Razumov in the sombre immobility of bronze. After finishing his scribbling, Razumov, with a sort of feverish haste, put away the pen, then rammed the notebook into his pocket, first tearing out the written pages with an almost convulsive brusqueness. But the folding of the flimsy batch on his knee was executed with thoughtful nicety. That done, he leaned back in his seat and remained motionless holding the papers in his left hand. The twilight had deepened. He got up and began to pace to and fro slowly under the trees.

"There can be no doubt that now I am safe," he thought. His fine ear could detect the faintly accentuated murmurs of the current breaking against the point of the island, and he forgot himself in listening to them with interest. But even to his acute sense of hearing the sound was too elusive.

"Extraordinary occupation I am giving myself up to," he

murmured. And it occurred to him that this was about
the only sound he could listen to innocently, and for his
own pleasure, as it were. Yes, the sound of water, the voice
of the wind—completely foreign to human passions. All
the other sounds of this earth brought contamination to
the solitude of a soul.

This was Mr. Razumov's feeling, the soul, of course, being his own, and the word being used not in the theologi-
cal sense, but standing, as far as I can understand it, for
that part of Mr. Razumov which was not his body, and
more specially in danger from the fires of this earth. And
it must be admitted that in Mr. Razumov's case the bitterness of solitude from which he suffered was not an altogether morbid phenomenon.

PART FOUR

I

That I should, at the beginning of this retrospect, mention again that Mr. Razumov's youth had no one in the world, as literally no one as it can be honestly affirmed of any human being, is but a statement of fact from a man who believes in the psychological value of facts. There is also, perhaps, a desire of punctilious fairness. Unidentified with any one in this narrative where the aspects of honour and shame are remote from the ideas of the Western world, and taking my stand on the ground of common humanity, it is for that very reason that I feel a strange reluctance to state baldly here what every reader has most likely already discovered himself. Such reluctance may appear absurd if it were not for the thought that because of the imperfection of language there is always something ungracious (and even disgraceful) in the exhibition of naked truth. But the time has come when Councillor of State Mikulin can no longer be ignored. His simple question "Where to?" on which we left Mr. Razumov in St. Petersburg, throws a light on the general meaning of this individual case.

"Where to?" was the answer in the form of a gentle question to what we may call Mr. Razumov's declaration of independence. The question was not menacing in the least and, indeed, had the ring of innocent inquiry. Had it been taken in a merely topographical sense, the only answer to it would have appeared sufficiently appalling to Mr. Razumov. Where to? Back to his rooms, where the

Revolution had sought him out to put to a sudden test his dormant instincts, his half-conscious thoughts and almost wholly unconscious ambitions, by the touch as of some furious and dogmatic religion, with its call to frantic sacrifices, its tender resignations, its dreams and hopes uplifting the soul by the side of the most sombre moods of despair. And Mr. Razumov had let go the door-handle and had come back to the middle of the room, asking Councillor Mikulin angrily, "What do you mean by it?"

As far as I can tell, Councillor Mikulin did not answer that question. He drew Mr. Razumov into familiar conversation. It is the peculiarity of Russian natures, that, however strongly engaged in the drama of action, they are still turning their ear to the murmur of abstract ideas. This conversation (and others later on) need not be recorded. Suffice it to say that it brought Mr. Razumov as we know him to the test of another faith. There was nothing official in its expression, and Mr. Razumov was led to defend his attitude of detachment. But Councillor Mikulin would have none of his arguments. "For a man like you," were his last weighty words in the discussion, "such a position is impossible. Don't forget that I have seen that interesting piece of paper. I understand your liberalism. I have an intellect of that kind myself. Reform for me is mainly a question of method. But the principle of revolt is a physical intoxication, a sort of hysteria which must be kept away from the masses. You agree to this without reserve, don't you? Because, you see, Kirylo Sidorovitch, abstention, reserve, in certain situations, come very near to political crime. The ancient Greeks understood that very well."

Mr. Razumov, listening with a faint smile, asked Councillor Mikulin point-blank if this meant that he was going to have him watched.

The high official took no offence at the cynical inquiry. "No, Kirylo Sidorovitch," he answered gravely. "I don't mean to have you watched."

Razumov, suspecting a lie, affected yet the greatest liberty of mind during the short remainder of that interview.

The older man expressed himself throughout in familiar terms, and with a sort of shrewd simplicity. Razumov concluded that to get to the bottom of that mind was an impossible feat. A great disquiet made his heart beat quicker. The high official, issuing from behind the desk, was actually offering to shake hands with him.

"Good-bye, Mr. Razumov. An understanding between intelligent men is always a satisfactory occurrence. Is it not? And, of course, these rebel gentlemen have not the monopoly of intelligence."

"I presume that I shall not be wanted any more?" Razumov brought out that question while his hand was still being grasped. Councillor Mikulin released it slowly.

"That, Mr. Razumov," he said with great earnestness, "is as it may be. God alone knows the future. But you may rest assured that I never thought of having you watched. You are a young man of great independence. Yes. You are going away free as air, but you will end by coming back to us."

"I! I!" Razumov exclaimed in an appalled murmur of protest. "What for?" he added feebly.

"Yes! You yourself, Kirylo Sidorovitch," the high police functionary insisted in a low, severe tone of conviction. "You will be coming back to us. Some of our greatest minds had to do that in the end."

"Our greatest minds," repeated Razumov in a dazed voice.

"Yes, indeed! Our greatest minds. . . . Good-bye."

Razumov, shown out of the room, walked away from the door. But before he got to the end of the passage he heard heavy footsteps, and a voice calling upon him to stop. He turned his head and was startled to see Councillor Mikulin pursuing him in person. The high functionary hurried up, very simple, slightly out of breath.

"One minute. As to what we were talking about just now, it shall be as God wills it. But I may have occasion to require you again. You look surprised, Kirylo Sidorovitch. Yes, again . . . to clear up any further point that may turn up."

"But I don't know anything," stammered out Razumov. "I couldn't possibly know anything."

"Who can tell? Things are ordered in a wonderful manner. Who can tell what *may* become disclosed to you before this day is out? You have been already the instrument of Providence. You smile, Kirylo Sidorovitch; you are an *esprit fort.*" (Razumov was not conscious of having smiled.) "But I believe firmly in Providence. Such a confession on the lips of an old hardened official like me may sound to you funny. But you yourself yet some day will recognize. . . . Or else what happened to you cannot be accounted for at all. Yes, decidedly I shall have occasion to see you again, but not here. This wouldn't be quite— h'm . . . Some convenient place shall be made known to you. And even the written communications between us in *that* respect or in any other had better pass through the intermediacy of our—if I may express myself so—common friend, Prince K— Now I beg you, Kirylo Sidorovitch— don't! I am certain he'll consent. You must give me the credit of being aware of what I am saying. You have no better friend than Prince K——, and as to myself it is a long time now since I've been honoured by his . . ."

He glanced down his beard.

"I won't detain you any longer. We live in difficult times, in times of monstrous chimeras and evil dreams and criminal follies. We shall certainly meet once more. It may be some little time, though, before we do. Till then may Heaven send you fruitful reflections!"

Once in the street, Razumov started off rapidly, without caring for the direction. At first he thought of nothing; but in a little while the consciousness of his position presented itself to him as something so ugly, dangerous, and absurd, the difficulty of ever freeing himself from the toils of that complication so insoluble, that the idea of going back and, as he termed it to himself, *confessing* to Councillor Mikulin flashed through his mind.

Go back! What for? Confess! To what? "I have been speaking to him with the greatest openness," he said to himself with perfect truth. "What else could I tell him?

That I have undertaken to carry a message to that brute Ziemianitch? Establish a false complicity and destroy what chance of safety I have won for nothing—what folly!"

Yet he could not defend himself from fancying that Councillor Mikulin was, perhaps, the only man in the world able to understand his conduct. To be understood appeared extremely fascinating.

On the way home he had to stop several times; all his strength seemed to run out of his limbs; and in the movement of the busy streets, isolated as if in a desert, he remained suddenly motionless for a minute or so before he could proceed on his way. He reached his rooms at last.

Then came an illness, something in the nature of a low fever, which all at once removed him to a great distance from the perplexing actualities, from his very room, even. He never lost consciousness; he only seemed to himself to be existing languidly somewhere very far away from everything that had ever happened to him. He came out of this state slowly, with an effect, that is to say, of extreme slowness, though the actual number of days was not very great. And when he had got back into the middle of things they were all changed, subtly and provokingly in their nature: inanimate objects, human faces, the landlady, the rustic servant-girl, the staircase, the streets, the very air. He tackled these changed conditions in a spirit of severity. He walked to and fro to the University, ascended stairs, paced the passages, listened to lectures, took notes, crossed courtyards in angry aloofness, his teeth set hard till his jaws ached.

He was perfectly aware of madcap Kostia gazing like a young retriever from a distance, of the famished student with the red drooping nose, keeping scrupulously away as desired; of twenty others, perhaps, he knew well enough to speak to. And they all had an air of curiosity and concern as if they expected something to happen. "This can't last much longer," thought Razumov more than once. On certain days he was afraid that any one addressing him suddenly in a certain way would make him scream out insanely a lot of filthy abuse. Often, after returning home, he would drop into a chair in his cap and cloak and remain still for hours holding some book he had got from the library in his hand; or he would pick up the little penknife and sit there scraping his nails endlessly and feeling furious all the time—simply furious. "This is impossible," he would mutter suddenly to the empty room.

Fact to be noted: this room might conceivably have become physically repugnant to him, emotionally intolerable, morally uninhabitable. But no. Nothing of the sort (and he had himself dreaded it at first), nothing of the sort happened. On the contrary, he liked his lodgings better than any other shelter he, who had never known a home, had ever hired before. He liked his lodgings so well that often, on that very account, he found a certain difficulty in making up his mind to go out. It resembled a physical seduction such as, for instance, makes a man reluctant to leave the neighbourhood of a fire on a cold day.

For as, at that time, he seldom stirred except to go to the University (what else was there to do?) it followed that whenever he went abroad he felt himself at once closely involved in the moral consequences of his act. It was there that the dark prestige of the Haldin mystery fell on him, clung to him like a poisoned robe it was impossible to fling off. He suffered from it exceedingly, as well as from the conversational, commonplace, unavoidable intercourse with the other kind of students. "They must be wondering at the change in me," he reflected anxiously. He had an uneasy recollection of having savagely told one or two innocent, nice enough fellows to go to the devil. Once a married professor he used to call upon formerly addressed him in passing: "How is it we never see you at our Wednesdays now, Kirylo Sidorovitch?" Razumov was conscious of meeting this advance with odious, muttering boorishness. The professor was obviously too astonished to be offended. All this was bad. And all this was Haldin, always Haldin—nothing but Haldin—everywhere Haldin: a moral spectre infinitely more effective than any visible apparition of the dead. It was only the room through which

that man had blundered on his way from crime to death
that his spectre did not seem to be able to haunt. Not, to
be exact, that he was ever completely absent from it, but
that there he had no sort of power. There it was Razumov
who had the upper hand, in a composed sense of his own
superiority. A vanquished phantom—nothing more. Often
in the evening, his repaired watch faintly ticking on the
table by the side of the lighted lamp, Razumov would look
up from his writing and stare at the bed with an expectant,
dispassionate attention. Nothing was to be seen there. He
never really supposed that anything ever could be seen
there. After a while he would shrug his shoulders slightly
and bend again over his work. For he had gone to work
and, at first, with some success. His unwillingness to leave
that place where he was safe from Haldin grew so strong
that at last he ceased to go out at all. From early morning
till far into the night he wrote, he wrote for nearly a week;
never looking at the time, and only throwing himself on
the bed when he could keep his eyes open no longer.
Then, one afternoon, quite casually, he happened to glance
at his watch. He laid down his pen slowly.

"At this very hour," was his thought, "the fellow stole
unseen into this room while I was out. And there he sat
quiet as a mouse—perhaps in this very chair."

Razumov got up and began to pace the floor steadily,
glancing at the watch now and then. "This is the time
when I returned and found him standing against the
stove," he observed to himself. When it grew dark he lit
his lamp. Later on he interrupted his tramping once more,
only to wave away angrily the girl who attempted to enter the room with tea and something to eat on a tray.
And presently he noted the watch pointing at the hour of
his own going forth into the falling snow on that terrible
errand.

"Complicity," he muttered faintly, and resumed his
pacing, keeping his eye on the hands as they crept on
slowly to the time of his return.

"And, after all," he thought suddenly, "I might have
been the chosen instrument of Providence. This is a man-

ner of speaking, but there may be truth in every manner of speaking. What if that absurd saying were true in its essence?"

He meditated for a while, then sat down, his legs stretched out, with stony eyes, and with his arms hanging down on each side of the chair like a man totally abandoned by Providence—desolate.

He noted the time of Haldin's departure and continued to sit still for another half-hour; then muttering, "And now to work," drew up to the table, seized the pen and instantly dropped it under the influence of a profoundly disquieting reflection: "There's three weeks gone by and no word from Mikulin."

What did it mean? Was he forgotten? Possibly. Then why not remain forgotten—creep in somewhere? Hide. But where? How? With whom? In what hole? And was it to be for ever, or what?

But a retreat was big with shadowy dangers. The eye of the social revolution was on him, and Razumov for a moment felt an unnamed and despairing dread, mingled with an odious sense of humiliation. Was it possible that he no longer belonged to himself? This was damnable. But why not simply keep on as before? Study. Advance. Work hard as if nothing had happened (and first of all win the Silver Medal), acquire distinction, become a great reforming servant of the greatest of States. Servant, too, of the mightiest homogeneous mass of mankind with a capability for logical, guided development in a brotherly solidarity of force and aim such as the world had never dreamt of . . . the Russian nation! . . .

Calm, resolved, steady in his great purpose, he was stretching his hand towards the pen when he happened to glance towards the bed. He rushed at it, enraged, with a mental scream: "It's you, crazy fanatic, who stand in the way!" He flung the pillow on the floor violently, tore the blankets aside. . . . Nothing there. And, turning away, he caught for an instant in the air, like a vivid detail in a dissolving view of two heads, the eyes of General T—— and of Privy-Councillor Mikulin side by side fixed upon him, quite different in character, but with the same unflinching and weary and yet purposeful expression . . . servants of the nation!

Razumov tottered to the washstand very alarmed about himself, drank some water and bathed his forehead. "This will pass and leave no trace," he thought confidently. "I am all right." But as to supposing that he had been forgotten it was perfect nonsense. He was a marked man on that side. And that was nothing. It was what that miserable phantom stood for which had to be got out of the way . . . "If one only could go and spit it all out at some of them—and take the consequences."

He imagined himself accosting the red-nosed student and suddenly shaking his fist in his face. "From that one, though," he reflected, "there's nothing to be got, because he has no mind of his own. He's living in a red democratic trance. Ah! you want to smash your way into universal happiness, my boy. I will give you universal happiness, you silly, hypnotized ghoul, you! And what about my own happiness, eh? Haven't I got any right to it, just because I can think for myself? . . ."

And again, but with a different mental accent, Razumov said to himself, "I am young. Everything can be lived down." At that moment he was crossing the room slowly, intending to sit down on the sofa and try to compose his thoughts. But before he had got so far everything abandoned him—hope, courage, belief in himself, trust in men. His heart had, as it were, suddenly emptied itself. It was no use struggling on. Rest, work, solitude, and the frankness of intercourse with his kind were alike forbidden to him. Everything was gone. His existence was a great cold blank, something like the enormous plain of the whole of Russia levelled with snow and fading gradually on all sides into shadows and mists.

He sat down, with swimming head, closed his eyes, and remained like that, sitting bolt upright on the sofa and perfectly awake for the rest of the night; till the girl bustling into the outer room with the samovar thumped with

her fist on the door, calling out "Kirylo Sidorovitch, please!
It is time for you to get up!"

Then, pale like a corpse obeying the dread summons of
judgment, Razumov opened his eyes and got up.

Nobody will be surprised to hear, I suppose, that when
the summons came he went to see Councillor Mikulin. It
came that very morning, while, looking white and shaky,
like an invalid just out of bed, he was trying to shave himself. The envelope was addressed in the little attorney's
handwriting. That envelope contained another, super-
scribed to Razumov, in Prince K——'s hand, with the request
"Please forward under cover at once" in a corner. The note
inside was an autograph of Councillor Mikulin. The writer
stated candidly that nothing had arisen which needed
clearing up, but nevertheless appointed a meeting with
Mr. Razumov at a certain address in town which seemed
to be that of an oculist.

Razumov read it, finished shaving, dressed, looked at the
note again, and muttered gloomily, "Oculist." He pondered
over it for a time, lit a match, and burned the two en-
velopes and the enclosure carefully. Afterwards he waited,
sitting perfectly idle and not even looking at anything in
particular till the appointed hour drew near—and then
went out.

Whether, looking at the unofficial character of the summons, he might have refrained from attending to it is hard
to say. Probably not. At any rate, he went; but, what's
more, he went with a certain eagerness, which may appear
incredible till it is remembered that Councillor Mikulin was
the only person on earth with whom Razumov could talk,
taking the Haldin adventure for granted. And Haldin,
when once taken for granted, was no longer a haunting,
falsehood-breeding spectre. Whatever troubling power he
exercised in all the other places of the earth, Razumov
knew very well that at this oculist's address he would be
merely the hanged murderer of Mr. de P—— and nothing
more. For the dead can live only with the exact intensity
and quality of the life imparted to them by the living. So

Mr. Razumov, certain of relief, went to meet Councillor Mikulin with the eagerness of a pursued person welcoming any sort of shelter.

This much said, there is no need to tell anything more of that first interview and of the several others. To the morality of a Western reader an account of these meetings would wear perhaps the sinister character of old legendary tales where the Enemy of Mankind is represented holding subtly mendacious dialogues with some tempted soul. It is not my part to protest. Let me but remark that the Evil One, with his single passion of satanic pride for the only motive, is yet, on a larger, modern view, allowed to be not quite so black as he used to be painted. With what greater latitude, then, should we appraise the exact shade of mere mortal man, with his many passions and his miserable ingenuity in error, always dazzled by the base glitter of mixed motives, everlastingly betrayed by a short-sighted wisdom.

Councillor Mikulin was one of those powerful officials who, in a position not obscure, not occult, but simply inconspicuous, exercise a great influence over the methods rather than over the conduct of affairs. A devotion to Church and Throne is not in itself a criminal sentiment; to prefer the will of one to the will of many does not argue the possession of a black heart or prove congenital idiocy. Councillor Mikulin was not only a clever but also a faithful official. Privately he was a bachelor with a love of comfort, living alone in an apartment of five rooms luxuriously furnished; and was known by his intimates to be an enlightened patron of the art of female dancing. Later on the larger world first heard of him in the very hour of his downfall, during one of those State trials which astonish and puzzle the average plain man who reads the newspapers, by a glimpse of unsuspected intrigues. And in the stir of vaguely seen monstrosities, in that momentary, mysterious disturbance of muddy waters, Councillor Mikulin went under, dignified, with only a calm, emphatic protest of his innocence—nothing more. No disclosures damaging to a harassed autocracy, complete fidelity to the secrets of the miserable *arcana imperii* deposited in his patriotic breast, a display of bureaucratic stocism in a Russian official's ineradicable, almost sublime contempt for truth; stoicism of silence understood only by the very few of the initiated, and not without a certain cynical grandeur of self-sacrifice on the part of a sybarite. For the terribly heavy sentence turned Councillor Mikulin civilly into a corpse, and actually into something very much like a common convict.

It seems that the savage autocracy, no more than the divine democracy, does not limit its diet exclusively to the bodies of its enemies. It devours its friends and servants as well. The downfall of His Excellency Gregory Gregorievitch Mikulin (which did not occur till some years later) completes all that is known of the man. But at the time of Mr. de P——'s murder (or execution) Councillor Mikulin, under the modest style of Head of Department at the General Secretariat, exercised a wide influence as the confidant and right-hand man of his former schoolfellow and lifelong friend, General T——. One can imagine them talking over the case of Mr. Razumov, with the full sense of their unbounded power over all the lives in Russia, with cursory disdain, like two Olympians glancing at a worm. The relationship with Prince K—— was enough to save Razumov from some carelessly arbitrary proceeding, and it is also very probable that after the interview at the Secretariat he would have been left alone. Councillor Mikulin would not have forgotten him (he forgot no one who ever fell under his observation), but would have simply dropped him for ever. Councillor Mikulin was a good-natured man and wished no harm to any one. Besides (with his own reforming tendencies) he was favourably impressed by that young student, the son of Prince K——, and apparently no fool.

But as fate would have it, while Mr. Razumov was finding that no way of life was possible to him, Councillor Mikulin's discreet abilities were rewarded by a very responsible post—nothing less than the direction of the general police supervision over Europe. And it was then, and then only, when taking in hand the perfecting of the service which watches the revolutionist activities abroad, that he thought again of Mr. Razumov. He saw great possibilities of special usefulness in that uncommon young man on whom he had a hold already, with his peculiar temperament, his unsettled mind and shaken conscience, struggling in the toils of a false position. . . . It was as if the revolutionists themselves had put into his hand that tool so much finer than the common base instruments, so perfectly fitted, if only vested with sufficient credit, to penetrate into places inaccessible to common informers. Providential! Providential! And Prince K——, taken into the secret, was ready enough to adopt that mystical view too. "It will be necessary, though, to make a career for him afterwards," he had stipulated anxiously. "Oh! absolutely. We shall make that our affair," Mikulin had agreed. Prince K——'s mysticism was of an artless kind; but Councillor Mikulin was astute enough for two.

Things and men have always a certain sense, a certain side by which they must be got hold of if one wants to obtain a solid grasp and a perfect command. The power of Councillor Mikulin consisted in the ability to seize upon that sense, that side in the men he used. It did not matter to him what it was—vanity, despair, love, hate, greed, intelligent pride or stupid conceit, it was all one to him as long as the man could be made to serve. The obscure, unrelated young student Razumov, in the moment of great moral loneliness, was allowed to feel that he was an object of interest to a small group of people of high position. Prince K—— was persuaded to intervene personally, and on a certain occasion gave way to a manly emotion which, all unexpected as it was, quite upset Mr. Razumov. The sudden embrace of that man, agitated by his loyalty to a throne and by suppressed paternal affection, was a revelation to Mr. Razumov of something within his own breast.

"So that was it!" he exclaimed to himself. A sort of contemptuous tenderness softened the young man's grim view of his position as he reflected upon that agitated interview with Prince K——. This simple-minded, worldly ex-Guards-man and senator whose soft grey official whiskers had brushed against his cheek, his aristocratic and convinced father, was he a whit less estimable or more absurd than that famine-stricken, fanatical revolutionist, the red-nosed student?

And there was some pressure, too, besides the persuasiveness. Mr. Razumov was always being made to feel that he had committed himself. There was no getting away from that feeling, from that soft, unanswerable, "Where to?" of Councillor Mikulin. But no susceptibilities were ever hurt. It was to be a dangerous mission to Geneva for obtaining, at a critical moment, absolutely reliable information from a very inaccessible quarter of the inner revolutionary circle. There were indications that a very serious plot was being matured. . . . The repose indispensable to a great country was at stake. . . . A great scheme of orderly reforms would be endangered. . . . The highest personages in the land were patriotically uneasy, and so on. In short, Councillor Mikulin knew what to say. This skill is to be inferred clearly from the mental and psychological self-confession, self-analysis of Mr. Razumov's written journal—the pitiful resource of a young man who had near him no trusted intimacy, no natural affection to turn to.

How all this preliminary work was concealed from observation need not be recorded. The expedient of the oculist gives a sufficient instance. Councillor Mikulin was resourceful, and the task not very difficult. Any fellow-student, even the red-nosed one, was perfectly welcome to see Mr. Razumov entering a private house to consult an oculist. Ultimate success depended solely on the revolutionary self-delusion which credited Razumov with a mysterious complicity in the Haldin affair. To be compromised in it was credit enough—and it was their own doing. It was precisely *that* which stamped Mr. Razumov as a providential man, wide as poles apart from the usual type of agent for "European supervision."

And it was *that* which the Secretariat set itself the task to foster by a course of calculated and false indiscretions.

It came at last to this, that one evening, Mr. Razumov

was unexpectedly called upon by one of the "thinking" students whom formerly, before the Haldin affair, he used to meet at various private gatherings; a big fellow with a quiet, unassuming manner and a pleasant voice.

Recognizing his voice raised in the ante-room, "May one come in?" Razumov, lounging idly on his couch, jumped up. "Suppose he were coming to stab me?" he thought sardonically, and, assuming a green shade over his left eye, said in a severe tone, "Come in."

The other was embarrassed; hoped he was not intruding. "You haven't been seen for several days, and I've wondered." He coughed a little. "Eye better?"

"Nearly well now."

oculist!

"Good. I won't stop a minute; but you see I, that is, we —anyway, I have undertaken the duty to warn you, Kirylo Sidorovitch, that you are living in false security maybe."

Razumov sat still with his head leaning on his hand, which nearly concealed the unshaded eye.

"I have that idea, too."

"That's all right, then. Everything seems quiet now, but those people are preparing some move of general repression. That's of course. But it isn't that I came to tell you." He hitched his chair closer, dropped his voice. "You will be arrested before long—we fear."

An obscure scribe in the Secretariat had overheard a few words of a certain conversation, and had caught a glimpse of a certain report. This intelligence was not to be neglected.

Razumov laughed a little, and his visitor became very anxious.

"Ah! Kirylo Sidorovitch, this is no laughing matter. They have left you alone for a while, but . . . ! Indeed, you had better try to leave the country, Kirylo Sidorovitch, while there's yet time."

Razumov jumped up and began to thank him for the advice with mocking effusiveness, so that the other, colouring up, took himself off with the notion that this mysterious Razumov was not a person to be warned or advised by inferior mortals.

Councillor Mikulin, informed the next day of the incident, expressed his satisfaction. "H'm. Ha! Exactly what was wanted to . . ." and glanced down his beard.

"I conclude," said Razumov, "that the moment has come for me to start on my mission."

"The psychological moment," Councillor Mikulin insisted softly—very gravely—as if awed.

All the arrangements to give verisimilitude to the appearance of a difficult escape were made. Councillor Mikulin did not expect to see Mr. Razumov again before his departure. These meetings were a risk, and there was nothing more to settle.

"We have said everything to each other by now, Kirylo Sidorovitch," said the high official feelingly, pressing Razumov's hand with that unreserved heartiness a Russian can convey in his manner. "There is nothing obscure between us. And I will tell you what! I consider myself fortunate in having—h'm—your . . ."

He glanced down his beard, and, after a moment of thoughtful silence, handed to Razumov a half-sheet of notepaper—an abbreviated note of matters already discussed, certain points of inquiry, the line of conduct agreed on, a few hints as to personalities, and so on. It was the only compromising document in the case, but, as Councillor Mikulin observed, "it could be easily destroyed. Mr. Razumov had better not see any one now—till on the other side of the frontier, when, of course, it will be just that . . . See and hear and . . ."

He glanced down his beard; but when Razumov declared his intention to see one person at least before leaving St. Petersburg, Councillor Mikulin failed to conceal a sudden uneasiness. The young man's studious, solitary, and austere existence was well known to him. It was the greatest guarantee of fitness. He became deprecatory. Had his dear Kirylo Sidorovitch considered whether, in view of such a momentous enterprise, it wasn't really advisable to sacrifice every sentiment? . . .

Razumov interrupted the remonstrance scornfully. It was not a young woman, it was a young fool he wished to see for a certain purpose. Councillor Mikulin was relieved, but surprised.

"Ah! And what for—precisely?"

"For the sake of improving the aspect of verisimilitude," said Razumov curtly, in a desire to affirm his independence. "I must be trusted in what I do."

Councillor Mikulin gave way tactfully, murmuring, "Oh, certainly, certainly. Your judgment . . ."

And with another handshake they parted.

The fool of whom Mr. Razumov had thought was the rich and festive student known as madcap Kostia. Featherheaded, loquacious, excitable, one could make certain of his utter and complete indiscretion. But that riotous youth, when reminded by Razumov of his offers of service some time ago, passed from his usual elation into boundless dismay.

"Oh, Kirylo Sidorovitch, my dearest friend—my saviour —what shall I do? I've blown last night every rouble I had from my dad the other day. Can't you give me till Thursday? I shall rush round to all the usurers I know . . . No, of course, you can't! Don't look at me like that. What shall I do? No use asking the old man. I tell you he's given me a fistful of big notes three days ago. Miserable wretch that I am."

He wrung his hands in despair. Impossible to confide in the old man. "They" had given him a decoration, a cross on the neck only last year, and he had been cursing the modern tendencies ever since. Just then he would see all the intellectuals in Russia hanged in a row rather than part with a single rouble.

"Kirylo Sidorovitch, wait a moment. Don't despise me. I have it. I'll, yes—I'll do it—I'll break into his desk. There's no help for it. I know the drawer where he keeps his plunder, and I can buy a chisel on my way home. He will be terribly upset, but, you know, the dear old duffer really loves me. He'll have to get over it—and I, too. Kirylo, my dear soul, if you can only wait for a few hours—till this evening—I shall steal all the blessed lot I can lay my hands on! You doubt me! Why? You've only to say the word."

"Steal, by all means," said Razumov, fixing him stonily.

"To the devil with the ten commandments!" cried the other, with the greatest animation. "It's the new future now."

But when he entered Razumov's room late in the evening it was with an unaccustomed soberness of manner, almost solemnly.

"It's done," he said.

Razumov sitting bowed, his clasped hands hanging between his knees, shuddered at the familiar sound of these words. Kostia deposited slowly in the circle of lamplight a small brown-paper parcel tied with a piece of string.

"As I've said—all I could lay my hands on. The old boy'll think the end of the world has come."

Razumov nodded from the couch, and contemplated the hare-brained fellow's gravity with a feeling of malicious pleasure.

"I've made my little sacrifice," sighed mad Kostia. "And I've to thank you, Kirylo Sidorovitch, for the opportunity."

"It has cost you something?"

"Yes, it has. You see, the dear old duffer really loves me. He'll be hurt."

"And you believe all they tell you of the new future and the sacred will of the people?"

"Implicitly. I would give my life . . . Only, you see I am like a pig at a trough. I am no good. It's my nature."

Razumov, lost in thought, had forgotten his existence till the youth's voice, entreating him to fly without loss of time, roused him unpleasantly.

"All right. Well—good-bye."

"I am not going to leave you till I've seen you out of St. Petersburg," declared Kostia unexpectedly, with calm determination. "You can't refuse me that now. For God's sake, Kirylo, my soul, the police may be here any moment, and when they get you they'll immure you somewhere for ages—till your hair turns grey. I have down there the best trotter of dad's stables and a light sledge. We shall do thirty miles before the moon sets, and find some roadside station . . ."

Razumov looked up amazed. The journey was decided —unavoidable. He had fixed the next day for his departure on the mission. And now he discovered suddenly that he had not believed in it. He had gone about listening, speaking, thinking, planning his simulated flight, with the growing conviction that all this was preposterous. As if anybody ever did such things! It was like a game of make-believe. And now he was amazed! Here was somebody who believed in it with desperate earnestness. "If I don't go now, at once," thought Razumov, with a start of fear, "I shall never go." He rose without a word, and the anxious Kostia thrust his cap on him, helped him into his cloak, or else he would have left the room bareheaded as he stood. He was walking out silently when a sharp cry arrested him.

"Kirylo!"

"What?" He turned reluctantly in the doorway. Upright, with a stiffly extended arm, Kostia, his face set and white, was pointing an eloquent forefinger at the brown little packet lying forgotten in the circle of bright light on the table. Razumov hesitated, came back for it under the severe eyes of his companion, at whom he tried to smile. But the boyish, mad youth was frowning. "It's a dream," thought Razumov, putting the little parcel into his pocket and descending the stairs; "nobody does such things." The other held him under the arm, whispering of dangers ahead, and of what he meant to do in certain contingencies. "Preposterous," murmured Razumov, as he was being tucked up in the sledge. He gave himself up to watching the development of the dream with extreme attention. It continued on foreseen lines, inexorably logical—the long drive, the wait at the small station sitting by a stove. They did not exchange half a dozen words altogether. Kostia, gloomy himself, did not care to break the silence. At parting they embraced twice—it had to be done; and then Kostia vanished out of the dream.

When dawn broke, Razumov, very still in a hot, stuffy railway-car full of bedding and of sleeping people in all its dimly lighted length, rose quietly, lowered the glass a few inches, and flung out on the great plain of snow a small brown-paper parcel. Then he sat down again muffled up and motionless. "For the people," he thought, staring out of the window. The great white desert of frozen, hard earth glided past his eyes without a sign of human habitation.

That had been a waking act; and then the dream had him again: Prussia, Saxony, Würtemberg, faces, sights, words—all a dream, observed with an angry, compelled attention. Zürich, Geneva—still a dream, minutely followed, wearing one into harsh laughter, to fury, to death—with the fear of awakening at the end. . . .

II

"Perhaps life is just that," reflected Razumov, pacing to and fro under the trees of the little island, all alone with the bronze statue of Rousseau. "A dream and a fear." The dusk deepened. The pages written over and torn out of his notebook were the first-fruit of his "mission." No dream that. They contained the assurance that he was on the eve of real discoveries. "I think there is no longer anything in the way of my being completely accepted."

He had resumed his impressions in those pages, some of the conversations. He even went so far as to write: "By the by, I have discovered the personality of that terrible N. N. A horrible, paunchy brute. If I hear anything of his future movements I shall send you warning."

The futility of all this overcame him like a curse. Even then he could not believe in the reality of his mission. He looked round despairingly, as if for some way to redeem his existence from that unconquerable feeling. He crushed angrily in his hand the pages of the notebook. "This must be posted," he thought.

He gained the bridge and returned to the north shore, where he remembered having seen in one of the narrower streets a little obscure shop stocked with cheap wood carvings, its walls lined with extremely dirty cardboard-bound volumes of a small circulating library. They sold stationery there, too. A morose, shabby old man dozed behind the counter. A thin woman in black, with a sickly face, produced the envelope he had asked for without even looking at him. Razumov thought that these people were safe to deal with because they no longer cared for anything in the world. He addressed the envelope on the counter with the German name of a certain person living in Vienna. But Razumov knew that this, his first communication for Councillor Mikulin, would find its way to the Embassy there, be copied in cypher by somebody trustworthy, and sent on to its destination, all safe, along with the diplomatic correspondence. That was the arrangement contrived to cover up the track of the information from all unfaithful eyes, from all indiscretions, from all mishaps and treacheries. It was to make him safe—absolutely safe.

He wandered out of the wretched shop and made for the post office. It was then that I saw him for the second time that day. He was crossing the Rue Mont Blanc with every appearance of an aimless stroller. He did not recognize me, but I made him out at some distance. He was very good-looking, I thought, this remarkable friend of Miss Haldin's brother. I watched him go up to the letter-box and then retrace his steps. Again he passed me very close, but I am certain he did not see me that time, either. He carried his head well up, but he had the expression of a somnambulist struggling with the very dream which drives him forth to wander in dangerous places. My thoughts reverted to Natalia Haldin, to her mother. He was all that was left to them of their son and brother.

The Westerner in me was discomposed. There was something shocking in the expression of that face. Had I been myself a conspirator, a Russian political refugee, I could have perhaps been able to draw some practical conclusion from this chance glimpse. As it was, it only discomposed me strongly, even to the extent of awakening an indefinite apprehension in regard to Natalia Haldin. All this is rather inexplicable, but such was the origin of the purpose I formed there and then to call on these ladies in the evening, after my solitary dinner. It was true that I

had met Miss Haldin only a few hours before, but Mrs.
Haldin herself I had not seen for some considerable time.
The truth is, I had shirked calling of late.

Poor Mrs. Haldin! I confess she frightened me a little.
She was one of those natures, rare enough, luckily, in
which one cannot help being interested, because they
provoke both terror and pity. One dreads their contact
for oneself, and still more for those one cares for, so clear
it is that they are born to suffer and to make others suffer,
too. It is strange to think that, I won't say liberty, but the
mere liberalism of outlook which for us is a matter of
words, of ambitions, of votes (and if of feeling at all, then
of the sort of feeling which leaves our deepest affections
untouched) may be for other beings very much like ourselves and living under the same sky, a heavy trial of fortitude, a matter of tears and anguish and blood. Mrs. Haldin had felt the pangs of her own generation. There was
that enthusiast brother of hers—the officer they shot under
Nicholas. A faintly ironic resignation is no armour for a
vulnerable heart. Mrs. Haldin, struck at through her children, was bound to suffer afresh from the past, and to feel
the anguish of the future. She was of those who do not
know how to heal themselves, of those who are too much
aware of their heart, who, neither cowardly nor selfish,
look passionately at its wounds—and count the cost.

Such thoughts as these seasoned my modest, lonely bachelor's meal. If anybody wishes to remark that this was a
roundabout way of thinking of Natalia Haldin, I can only
retort that she was well worth some concern. She had all
her life before her. Let it be admitted, then, that I was
thinking of Natalia Haldin's life in terms of her mother's
character, a manner of thinking about a girl permissible
for an old man, not too old yet to have become a stranger
to pity. There was almost all her youth before her; a youth
robbed arbitrarily of its natural lightness and joy, overshadowed by an un-European despotism; a terribly sombre youth given over to the hazards of a furious strife between equally ferocious antagonisms.

I lingered over my thoughts more than I should have

done. One felt so helpless, and even worse—so unrelated, in a way. At the last moment I hesitated as to going there at all. What was the good?

The evening was already advanced when, turning into the Boulevard des Philosophes, I saw the light in the window at the corner. The blind was down, but I could imagine behind it Mrs. Haldin seated in the chair, in her usual attitude, looking out for someone, which had lately acquired the poignant quality of mad expectation.

I thought that I was sufficiently authorized by the light to knock at the door. The ladies had not retired as yet. I only hoped they would not have any visitors of their own nationality. A broken-down, retired Russian official was to be found there sometimes in the evening. He was infinitely forlorn and wearisome by his mere dismal presence. I think these ladies tolerated his frequent visits because of an ancient friendship with Mr. Haldin, the father, or something of that sort. I made up my mind that if I found him prosing away there in his feeble voice I should remain but a very few minutes.

The door surprised me by swinging open before I could ring the bell. I was confronted by Miss Haldin, in hat and jacket, obviously on the point of going out. At that hour! For the doctor, perhaps?

Her exclamation of welcome reassured me. It sounded as if I had been the very man she wanted to see. My curiosity was awakened. She drew me in, and the faithful Anna, the elderly German maid, closed the door, but did not go away afterwards. She remained near it as if in readiness to let me out presently. It appeared that Miss Haldin had been on the point of going out to find me.

She spoke in a hurried manner very unusual with her. She would have gone straight and rung at Mrs. Ziegler's door, late as it was, for Mrs. Ziegler's habits . . .

Mrs. Ziegler, the widow of a distinguished professor who was an intimate friend of mine, lets me have three rooms out of her very large and fine apartment, which she didn't give up after her husband's death; but I have my own entrance opening on the same landing. It was an arrangement of at least ten years' standing. I said that I was very glad that I had the idea to . . .

Miss Haldin made no motion to take off her outdoor things. I observed her heightened colour, something pronouncedly resolute in her tone. Did I know where Mr. Razumov lived?

Where Mr. Razumov lived? Mr. Razumov? At this hour —so urgently? I threw my arms up in sign of utter ignorance. I had not the slightest idea where he lived. If I could have foreseen her question only three hours ago, I might have ventured to ask him on the pavement before the new post office building, and possibly he would have told me, but very possibly, too, he would have dismissed me rudely to mind my own business. And possibly, I thought, remembering that extraordinary hallucined, anguished, and absent expression, he might have fallen down in a fit from the shock of being spoken to. I said nothing of all this to Miss Haldin, not even mentioning that I had a glimpse of the young man so recently. The impression had been so extremely unpleasant that I would have been glad to forget it myself.

"I don't see where I could make inquiries," I murmured helplessly. I would have been glad to be of use in any way, and would have set off to fetch any man, young or old, for I had the greatest confidence in her common sense. "What made you think of coming to me for that information?" I asked.

"It wasn't exactly for that," she said, in a low voice. She had the air of someone confronted by an unpleasant task.

"Am I to understand that you must communicate with Mr. Razumov this evening?"

Natalia Haldin moved her head affirmatively; then after a glance at the door of the drawing-room, said in French—

"C'est maman," and remained perplexed for a moment. Always serious, not a girl to be put out by any imaginary difficulties, my curiosity was suspended on her lips, which remained closed for a moment. What was Mr. Razumov's connexion with this mention of her mother? Mrs. Haldin had not been informed of her son's friend's arrival in Geneva.

"May I hope to see your mother this evening?" I inquired.

Miss Haldin extended her hand as if to bar the way.

"She is in a terrible state of agitation. Oh, you would not be able to detect. . . . It's inward, but I who know mother, I am appalled. I haven't the courage to face it any longer. It's all my fault; I suppose I cannot play a part; I've never before hidden anything from mother. There has never been an occasion for anything of that sort between us. But you know yourself the reason why I refrained from telling her at once of Mr. Razumov's arrival here. You understand, don't you? Owing to her unhappy state. And—there—— I am no actress. My own feelings being strongly engaged, I somehow . . . I don't know. She noticed something in my manner. She thought I was concealing something from her. She noticed my longer absences, and, in fact, as I have been meeting Mr. Razumov daily, I used to stay away longer than usual when I went out. Goodness knows what suspicions arose in her mind. You know that she has not been herself ever since. . . . So this evening she—who has been so awfully silent for weeks—began to talk all at once. She said that she did not want to reproach me; that I had my character as she had her own; that she did not want to pry into my affairs or even into my thoughts; for her part, she had never had anything to conceal from her children . . . cruel things to listen to. And all this in her quiet voice, with that poor, wasted face as calm as a stone. It was unbearable."

Miss Haldin talked in an undertone and more rapidly than I had ever heard her speak before. That in itself was disturbing. The ante-room being strongly lighted, I could see under the veil the heightened colour of her face. She stood erect, her left hand was resting lightly on a small table. The other hung by her side without stirring. Now and then she caught her breath slightly.

"It was too startling. Just fancy! She thought that I was making preparations to leave her without saying anything.

I knelt by the side of her chair and entreated her to think of what she was saying! She put her hand on my head, but she persists in her delusion all the same. She had always thought that she was worthy of her children's confidence, but apparently it was not so. Her son could not trust her love nor yet her understanding—and now I was planning to abandon her in the same cruel and unjust manner, and so on, and so on. Nothing I could say. . . . It is morbid obstinacy. . . . She said that she felt there was something, some change in me. . . . If my convictions were calling me away, why this secrecy, as though she had been a coward or a weakling not safe to trust? 'As if my heart could play traitor to my children,' she said. . . . It was hardly to be borne. And she was smoothing my head all the time. . . . It was perfectly useless to protest. She is ill. Her very soul is . . ."

I did not venture to break the silence which fell between us. I looked into her eyes, glistening through the veil.

"I! Changed!" she exclaimed in the same low tone. "My convictions calling me away! It was cruel to hear this, because my trouble is that I am weak and cannot see what I ought to do. You know that. And to end it all I did a selfish thing. To remove her suspicions of myself I told her of Mr. Razumov. It was selfish of me. You know we were completely right in agreeing to keep the knowledge away from her. Perfectly right. Directly I told her of our poor Victor's friend being here I saw how right we have been. She ought to have been prepared; but in my distress I just blurted it out. Mother got terribly excited at once. How long has he been here? What did he know, and why did he not come to see us at once, this friend of her Victor? What did that mean? Was she not to be trusted even with such memories as there were left of her son? . . . Just think how I felt seeing her, white as a sheet, perfectly motionless, with her thin hands gripping the arms of the chair. I told her it was all my fault."

I could imagine the motionless dumb figure of the mother in her chair, there, behind the door, near which the daughter was talking to me. The silence in there seemed to call aloud for vengeance against an historical fact and the modern instances of its working. That view flashed through my mind, but I could not doubt that Miss Haldin had had an atrocious time of it. I quite understood when she said that she could not face the night upon the impression of that scene. Mrs. Haldin had given way to most awful imaginings, to most fantastic and cruel suspicions. All this had to be lulled at all costs and without loss of time. It was no shock to me to learn that Miss Haldin had said to her, "I will go and bring him here at once." There was nothing absurd in that cry, no exaggeration of sentiment. I was not even doubtful in my "Very well, but how?"

It was perfectly right that she should think of me, but what could I do in my ignorance of Mr. Razumov's quarters.

"And to think he may be living near by, within a stone's-throw, perhaps!" she exclaimed.

I doubted it; but I would have gone off cheerfully to fetch him from the other end of Geneva. I suppose she was certain of my readiness, since her first thought was to come to me. But the service she meant to ask of me really was to accompany her to the Château Borel.

I had an unpleasant mental vision of the dark road, of the sombre grounds, and the desolately suspicious aspect of that home of necromancy and intrigue and feminist adoration. I objected that Madame de S—— most likely would know nothing of what we wanted to find out. Neither did I think it likely that the young man would be found there. I remembered my glimpse of his face, and somehow gained the conviction that a man who looked worse than if he had seen the dead would want to shut himself up somewhere where he could be alone. I felt a strange certitude that Mr. Razumov was going home when I saw him.

"It is really of Peter Ivanovitch that I was thinking," said Miss Haldin quietly.

Ah! He, of course, would know. I looked at my watch. It was twenty minutes past nine only. . . . Still.

"I would try his hotel, then," I advised. "He has rooms at the Cosmopolitan, somewhere on the top floor."

I did not offer to go by myself, simply from mistrust of the reception I should meet with. But I suggested the faithful Anna, with a note asking for the information.

Anna was still waiting by the door at the other end of the room, and we two discussed the matter in whispers. Miss Haldin thought she must go herself. Anna was timid and slow. Time would be lost in bringing back the answer, and from that point of view it was getting late, for it was by no means certain that Mr. Razumov lived near by.

"If I go myself," Miss Haldin argued, "I can go straight to him from the hotel. And in any case I should have to go out, because I must explain to Mr. Razumov personally —prepare him in a way. You have no idea of mother's state of mind."

Her colour came and went. She even thought that both for her mother's sake and for her own it was better that they should not be together for a little time. Anna, whom her mother liked, would be at hand.

"She could take her sewing into the room," Miss Haldin continued, leading the way to the door. Then addressing in German the maid who opened it before us, "You may tell my mother that this gentleman called and is gone with me to find Mr. Razumov. She must not be uneasy if I am away for some length of time."

We passed out quickly into the street, and she took deep breaths of the cool night air. "I did not even ask you," she murmured.

"I should think not," I said, with a laugh. The manner of my reception by the great feminist could not be considered now. That he would be annoyed to see me, and probably treat me to some solemn insolence, I had no doubt, but I supposed that he would not absolutely dare to throw me out. And that was all I cared for. "Won't you take my arm?" I asked.

She did so in silence, and neither of us said anything worth recording till I let her go first into the great hall of the hotel. It was brilliantly lighted, and with a good many people lounging about.

"I could very well go up there without you," I suggested.

"I don't like to be left waiting in this place," she said in a low voice. "I will come too."

I led her straight to the lift then. At the top floor the attendant directed us to the right: "End of the corridor."

The walls were white, the carpet red, electric lights blazed in profusion, and the emptiness, the silence, the closed doors all alike and numbered, made me think of the perfect order of some severely luxurious model penitentiary on the solitary confinement principle. Up there under the roof of that enormous pile for housing travellers no sound of any kind reached us, the thick crimson felt muffled our footsteps completely. We hastened on, not looking at each other till we found ourselves before the very last door of that long passage. Then our eyes met, and we stood thus for a moment lending ear to a faint murmur of voices inside.

"I suppose this is it," I whispered unnecessarily. I saw Miss Haldin's lips move without a sound, and after my sharp knock the murmur of voices inside ceased. A profound stillness lasted for a few seconds, and then the door was brusquely opened by a short, black-eyed woman in a red blouse, with a lot of nearly white hair, done up negligently in an untidy and unpicturesque manner. Her thin, jetty eyebrows were drawn together. I learned afterwards with interest that she was the famous—or the notorious—Sophia Antonovna, but I was struck then by the quaint Mephistophelian character of her inquiring glance, because it was so curiously evil-less, so—I may say—undevilish. It got softened still more as she looked up at Miss Haldin, who stated, in her rich, even voice, her wish to see Peter Ivanovitch for a moment.

"I am Miss Haldin," she added.

At this, with her brow completely smoothed out now, but without a word in answer, the woman in the red blouse walked away to a sofa and sat down, leaving the door wide open.

And from the sofa, her hands lying on her lap, she watched us enter, with her black glittering eyes.

Miss Haldin advanced into the middle of the room; I, faithful to my part of mere attendant, remained by the door after closing it behind me. The room, quite a large one, but with a low ceiling, was scantily furnished, and an electric bulb with a porcelain shade pulled low down over a big table (with a very large map spread on it) left its distant parts in a dim, artificial twilight. Peter Ivanovitch was not to be seen, neither was Mr. Razumov present. But, on the sofa, near Sophia Antonovna, a bony-faced man with a goatee beard leaned forward with his hands on his knees, staring hard with a kindly expression. In a remote corner a broad, pale face and a bulky shape could be made out, uncouth, and as if insecure on the low seat on which it rested. The only person known to me was little Julius Laspara, who seemed to have been poring over the map, his feet twined tightly round the chair-legs. He got down briskly and bowed to Miss Haldin, looking absurdly like a hook-nosed boy with a beautiful false pepper-and-salt beard. He advanced, offering his seat, which Miss Haldin declined. She had only come in for a moment to say a few words to Peter Ivanovitch.

His high-pitched voice became painfully audible in the room.

"Strangely enough, I was thinking of you this very afternoon, Natalia Victorovna. I met Mr. Razumov. I asked him to write me an article on anything he liked. You could translate it into English—with such a teacher."

He nodded complimentarily in my direction. At the name of Razumov an indescribable sound, a sort of feeble squeak, as of some angry small animal, was heard in the corner occupied by the man who seemed much too large for the chair on which he sat. I did not hear what Miss Haldin said. Laspara spoke again.

"It's time to do something, Natalia Victorovna. But I suppose you have your own ideas. Why not write something yourself? Suppose you came to see us soon? We could talk it over. Any advice . . ."

Again I did not catch Miss Haldin's words. It was Laspara's voice once more.

"Peter Ivanovitch? He's retired for a moment into the other room. We are all waiting for him."

The great man, entering at that moment, looked bigger, taller, quite imposing in a long dressing-gown of some dark stuff. It descended in straight lines down to his feet. He suggested a monk or a prophet, a robust figure of some desert-dweller—something Asiatic; and the dark glasses in conjunction with this costume made him more mysterious than ever in the subdued light.

Little Laspara went back to his chair to look at the map, the only brilliantly lit object in the room. Even from my distant position by the door I could make out, by the shape of the blue part representing the water, that it was a map of the Baltic provinces. Peter Ivanovitch exclaimed slightly, advancing towards Miss Haldin, checked himself on perceiving me, very vaguely no doubt, and peered with his dark, bespectacled stare. He must have recognized me by my grey hair, because, with a marked shrug of his broad shoulders, he turned to Miss Haldin in benevolent indulgence. He seized her hand in his thick cushioned palm, and put his other big paw over it like a lid.

While those two standing in the middle of the floor were exchanging a few inaudible phrases no one else moved in the room: Laspara, with his back to us, kneeling on the chair, his elbows propped on the big-scale map, the shadowy enormity in the corner, the frankly staring man with the goatee on the sofa, the woman in the red blouse by his side—not one of them stirred. I suppose that really they had no time, for Miss Haldin withdrew her hand immediately from Peter Ivanovitch and before I was ready for her was moving to the door. A disregarded Westerner, I threw it open hurriedly and followed her out, my last glance leaving them all motionless in their varied poses: Peter Ivanovitch alone standing up, with his dark glasses like an enormous blind teacher, and behind him the vivid patch of light on the coloured map, pored over by the diminutive Laspara.

Later on, much later on, at the time of the newspaper rumours (they were vague and soon died out) of an abortive military conspiracy in Russia, I remembered the glimpse I had of that motionless group with its central figure. No details ever came out, but it was known that the revolutionary parties abroad had given their assistance, had sent emissaries in advance, that even money was found to dispatch a steamer with a cargo of arms and conspirators to invade the Baltic provinces. And while my eyes scanned the imperfect disclosures (in which the world was not much interested) I thought that the old, settled Europe had been given in my person attending that Russian girl something like a glimpse behind the scenes. A short, strange glimpse on the top floor of a great hotel of all places in the world: the great man himself; the motionless great bulk in the corner of the slayer of spies and gendarmes; Yakovlitch the veteran of ancient terrorist campaigns; the woman with her hair as white as mine and the lively black eyes, all in a mysterious half-light, with the strongly lighted map of Russia on the table. The woman I had the opportunity to see again. As we were waiting for the lift she came hurrying along the corridor, with her eyes fastened on Miss Haldin's face, and drew her aside as if for a confidential communication. It was not long. A few words only.

Going down in the lift, Natalia Haldin did not break the silence. It was only when out of the hotel and as we moved along the quay in the fresh darkness spangled by the quay lights, reflected in the black water of the little port on our left hand, and with lofty piles of hotels on our right, that she spoke.

"That was Sophia Antonovna—you know the woman? . . ."

"Yes, I know—the famous . . ."

"The same. It appears that after we went out Peter Ivanovitch told them why I had come. That was the reason she ran out after us. She named herself to me, and then she said, 'You are the sister of a brave man who shall be remembered. You may see better times.' I told her I hoped to see the time when all this would be forgotten, even if the name of my brother were to be forgotten too. Something moved me to say that, but you understand?"

"Yes," I said. "You think of the era of concord and justice."

"Yes. There is too much hate and revenge in that work. It must be done. It is a sacrifice—and so let it be all the greater. Destruction is the work of anger. Let the tyrants and the slayers be forgotten together, and only the reconstructors be remembered."

"And did Sophia Antonovna agree with you?" I asked sceptically.

"She did not say anything except, 'It is good for you to believe in love.' I should think she understood me. Then she asked me if I hoped to see Mr. Razumov presently. I said I trusted I could manage to bring him to see my mother this evening, as my mother had learned of his being here and was morbidly impatient to learn if he could tell us something of Victor. He was the only friend of my brother we knew of, and a great intimate. She said, 'Oh! Your brother—yes. Please tell Mr. Razumov that I have made public the story which came to me from St. Petersburg. It concerns your brother's arrest,' she added. 'He was betrayed by a man of the people who has since hanged himself. Mr. Razumov will explain it all to you. I gave him the full information this afternoon. And please tell Mr. Razumov that Sophia Antonovna sends him her greetings. I am going away early in the morning—far away.'"

And Miss Haldin added, after a moment of silence—

"I was so moved by what I heard so unexpectedly that I simply could not speak to you before. . . . A man of the people! Oh, our poor people!"

She walked slowly, as if tired out suddenly. Her head drooped; from the windows of a building with terraces and balconies came the banal sound of hotel music; before the low mean portals of the Casino two red posters blazed under the electric lamps, with a cheap provincial effect—and the emptiness of the quays, the desert aspect of the streets, had an air of hypocritical respectability and of inexpressible dreariness.

I had taken for granted she had obtained the address, and let myself be guided by her. On the Mont Blanc bridge, where a few dark figures seemed lost in the wide and long perspective defined by the lights, she said—

"It isn't very far from our house. I somehow thought it couldn't be. The address is Rue de Carouge. I think it must be one of those big new houses for artisans."

She took my arm confidingly, familiarly, and accelerated her pace. There was something primitive in our proceedings. We did not think of the resources of civilization. A late tramcar overtook us; a row of *fiacres* stood by the railing of the gardens. It never entered our heads to make use of these conveyances. She was too hurried, perhaps, and as to myself—well, she had taken my arm confidingly. As we were ascending the easy incline of the Corraterie, all the shops shuttered and no light in any of the windows (as if all the mercenary population had fled at the end of the day), she said tentatively—

"I could run in for a moment to have a look at mother. It would not be much out of the way."

I dissuaded her. If Mrs. Haldin really expected to see Razumov that night it would have been unwise to show herself without him. The sooner we got hold of the young man and brought him along to calm her mother's agitation the better. She assented to my reasoning, and we crossed diagonally the Place de Théâtre, bluish grey with its floor of slabs of stone, under the electric light, and the lonely equestrian statue all black in the middle. In the Rue de Carouge we were in the poorer quarters and approaching the outskirts of the town. Vacant building plots alternated with high, new houses. At the corner of a side street the crude light of a whitewashed shop fell into the night, fan-like, through a wide doorway. One could see from a distance the inner wall with its scantily furnished shelves, and the deal counter painted brown. That was the house. Approaching it along the dark stretch of a fence of tarred planks, we saw the narrow pallid face of the cut angle, five single windows high, without a gleam in them, and crowned by the heavy shadow of a jutting roof slope.

"We must inquire in the shop," Miss Haldin directed me.

A sallow, thinly whiskered man, wearing a dingy white collar and a frayed tie, laid down a newspaper, and, leaning familiarly on both elbows far over the bare counter, answered that the person I was inquiring for was indeed his *locataire* on the third floor, but that for the moment he was out.

"For the moment," I repeated, after a glance at Miss Haldin. "Does this mean that you expect him back at once?"

He was very gentle, with ingratiating eyes and soft lips. He smiled faintly as though he knew all about everything. Mr. Razumov, after being absent all day, had returned early in the evening. He was very surprised about half an hour or a little more ago to see him come down again. Mr. Razumov left his key, and in the course of some words which passed between them had remarked that he was going out because he needed air.

From behind the bare counter he went on smiling at us, his head held between his hands. Air. Air. But whether that meant a long or a short absence it was difficult to say. The night was very close, certainly.

After a pause, his ingratiating eyes turned to the door, he added—

"The storm will drive him in."

"There's going to be a storm?" I asked.

"Why, yes!"

As if to confirm his words we heard a very distant, deep rumbling noise.

Consulting Miss Haldin by a glance, I saw her so reluctant to give up her quest that I asked the shopkeeper, in case Mr. Razumov came home within half an hour, to beg him to remain downstairs in the shop. We would look in again presently.

For all answer he moved his head imperceptibly. The approval of Miss Haldin was expressed by her silence. We walked slowly down the street, away from the town; the low garden walls of the modest villas doomed to demolition were overhung by the boughs of trees and masses of foliage, lighted from below by gas lamps. The violent and monotonous noise of the icy waters of the Arve falling over a low dam swept towards us with a chilly draught of air across a great open space, where a double line of lamplights outlined a street as yet without houses. But on the other shore, overhung by the awful blackness of the thunder-cloud, a solitary dim light seemed to watch us with a weary stare. When we had strolled as far as the bridge, I said—

"We had better get back. . . ."

In the shop the sickly man was studying his smudgy newspaper, now spread out largely on the counter. He just raised his head when I looked in and shook it negatively, pursing up his lips. I rejoined Miss Haldin outside at once, and we moved off at a brisk pace. She remarked that she would send Anna with a note the first thing in the morning. I respected her taciturnity, silence being perhaps the best way to show my concern.

The semi-rural street we followed on our return changed gradually to the usual town thoroughfare, broad and deserted. We did not meet four people altogether, and the way seemed interminable, because my companion's natural anxiety had communicated itself sympathetically to me. At last we turned into the Boulevard des Philosophes, more wide, more empty, more dead—the very desolation of slumbering respectability. At the sight of the two lighted windows, very conspicuous from afar, I had the mental vision of Mrs. Haldin in her armchair keeping a dreadful, tormenting vigil under the evil spell of an arbitrary rule: a victim of tyranny and revolution, a sight at once cruel and absurd.

III

"You will come in for a moment?" said Natalia Haldin.

I demurred on account of the late hour. "You know mother likes you so much," she insisted.

"I will just come in to hear how your mother is."

She said, as if to herself, "I don't even know whether she will believe that I could not find Mr. Razumov, since she has taken it into her head that I am concealing something from her. You may be able to persuade her. . . ."

"Your mother may mistrust me too," I observed.

"You! Why? What could you have to conceal from her? You are not a Russian nor a conspirator."

I felt profoundly my European remoteness, and said nothing, but I made up my mind to play my part of helpless spectator to the end. The distant rolling of thunder in the valley of the Rhone was coming nearer to the sleeping town of prosaic virtues and universal hospitality. We crossed the street opposite the great dark gateway, and Miss Haldin rang at the door of the apartment. It was opened almost instantly, as if the elderly maid had been waiting in the ante-room for our return. Her flat physiognomy had an air of satisfaction. The gentleman was there, she declared, while closing the door.

Neither of us understood. Miss Haldin turned round brusquely to her. "Who?"

"Herr Razumov," she explained.

She had heard enough of our conversation before we left to know why her young mistress was going out. Therefore, when the gentleman gave his name at the door, she admitted him at once.

"No one could have foreseen that," Miss Haldin murmured, with her serious grey eyes fixed upon mine. And, remembering the expression of the young man's face seen not much more than four hours ago, the look of a haunted somnambulist, I wondered with a sort of awe.

"You asked my mother first?" Miss Haldin inquired of the maid.

"No. I announced the gentleman," she answered, surprised at our troubled faces.

"Still," I said in an undertone, "your mother was prepared."

"Yes. But he has no idea . . ."

It seemed to me she doubted his tact. To her question how long the gentleman had been with her mother, the maid told us that *der Herr* had been in the drawing-room no more than a short quarter of an hour.

She waited a moment, then withdrew, looking a little scared. Miss Haldin gazed at me in silence.

"As things have turned out," I said, "you happen to know exactly what your brother's friend has to tell your mother. And surely after that . . ."

"Yes," said Natalia Haldin slowly. "I only wonder, as I was not here when he came, if it wouldn't be better not to interrupt now."

We remained silent, and I suppose we both strained our ears, but no sound reached us through the closed door. The features of Miss Haldin expressed a painful irresolution; she made a movement as if to go in, but checked herself. She had heard footsteps on the other side of the door. It came open, and Razumov, without pausing, stepped out into the ante-room. The fatigue of that day and the struggle with himself had changed him so much that I would have hesitated to recognize that face which, only a few hours before, when he brushed against me in front of the post office, had been startling enough but quite different. It had been not so livid then, and its eyes not so sombre. They certainly looked more sane now, but there was upon them the shadow of something consciously evil.

I speak of that, because, at first, their glance fell on me, though without any sort of recognition or even comprehension. I was simply in the line of his stare. I don't know if he had heard the bell or expected to see anybody. He was going out, I believe, and I do not think that he saw Miss Haldin till she advanced towards him a step or two. He disregarded the hand she put out.

"It's you, Natalia Victorovna. . . . Perhaps you are surprised . . . at this late hour. But, you see, I remembered our conversations in that garden. I thought really it was your wish that I should—without loss of time . . . so I came. No other reason. Simply to tell . . ."

He spoke with difficulty. I noticed that, and remembered his declaration to the man in the shop that he was going out because he "needed air." If that was his object, then it was clear that he had miserably failed. With downcast eyes and lowered head he made an effort to pick up the strangled phrase.

"To tell what I have heard myself only to-day—to-day . . ."

Through the door he had not closed I had a view of the drawing-room. It was lighted only by a shaded lamp—Mrs. Haldin's eyes could not support either gas or electricity. It was a comparatively big room, and in contrast with the strongly lighted ante-room its length was lost in semi-transparent gloom backed by heavy shadows; and on that ground I saw the motionless figure of Mrs. Haldin, inclined slightly forward, with a pale hand resting on the arm of the chair.

She did not move. With the window before her she had no longer that attitude suggesting expectation. The blind was down; and outside there was only the night sky harbouring a thunder-cloud, and the town indifferent and hospitable in its cold, almost scornful, toleration—a respectable town of refuge to which all these sorrows and hopes were nothing. Her white head was bowed.

The thought that the real drama of autocracy is not played on the great stage of politics came to me as, fated to be a spectator, I had this other glimpse behind the scenes, something more profound than the words and gestures of the public play. I had the certitude that this mother refused in her heart to give her son up after all. It was more than Rachel's inconsolable mourning, it was something deeper, more inaccessible in its frightful tranquillity. Lost in the ill-defined mass of the high-backed chair, her white, inclined profile suggested the contemplation of something in her lap, as though a beloved head were resting there.

I had this glimpse behind the scenes, and then Miss Haldin, passing by the young man, shut the door. It was not done without hesitation. For a moment I thought that she would go to her mother, but she sent in only an anxious glance. Perhaps if Mrs. Haldin had moved . . . but no.

There was in the immobility of that bloodless face the dreadful aloofness of suffering without remedy.

Meantime the young man kept his eyes fixed on the floor. The thought that he would have to repeat the story he had told already was intolerable to him. He had expected to find the two women together. And then, he had said to himself, it would be over for all time—for all time. "It's lucky I don't believe in another world," he had thought cynically.

Alone in his room after having posted his secret letter, he had regained a certain measure of composure by writing in his secret diary. He was aware of the danger of that strange self-indulgence. He alludes to it himself, but he could not refrain. It calmed him—it reconciled him to his existence. He sat there scribbling by the light of a solitary candle, till it occurred to him that having heard the explanation of Haldin's arrest, as put forward by Sophia Antonovna, it behoved him to tell these ladies himself. They were certain to hear the tale through some other channel, and then his abstention would look strange, not only to the mother and sister of Haldin, but to other people also. Having come to this conclusion, he did not discover in himself any marked reluctance to face the necessity, and very soon an anxiety to be done with it began to torment him. He looked at his watch. No; it was not absolutely too late.

The fifteen minutes with Mrs. Haldin were like the revenge of the unknown: that white face, that weak, distinct voice; that head, at first turned to him eagerly, then, after a while, bowed again and motionless—in the dim, still light of the room in which his words which he tried to subdue resounded so loudly—had troubled him like some strange discovery. And there seemed to be a secret obstinacy in that sorrow, something he could not understand; at any rate, something he had not expected. Was it hostile? But it did not matter. Nothing could touch him now; in the eyes of the revolutionists there was now no shadow on his past. The phantom of Haldin had been indeed walked over, was left behind lying powerless and passive

on the pavement covered with snow. And this was the
phantom's mother consumed with grief and white as a
ghost. He had felt a pitying surprise. But that, of course,
was of no importance. Mothers did not matter. He could
not shake off the poignant impression of that silent, quiet,
white-haired woman, but a sort of sternness crept into
his thoughts. These were the consequences. Well, what of
it? "Am I then on a bed of roses?" he had exclaimed to
himself, sitting at some distance with his eyes fixed upon
that figure of sorrow. He had said all he had to say to her,
and when he had finished she had not uttered a word. She
had turned away her head while he was speaking. The
silence which had fallen on his last words had lasted for
five minutes or more. What did it mean? Before its incomprehensible character he became conscious of anger in
his stern mood, the old anger against Haldin reawakened
by the contemplation of Haldin's mother. And was it not
something like enviousness which gripped his heart, as if
of a privilege denied to him alone of all the men that had
ever passed through this world? It was the other who had
attained to repose and yet continued to exist in the affection of that mourning old woman, in the thoughts of all
these people posing for lovers of humanity. It was impossible to get rid of him. "It's myself whom I have given up to
destruction," thought Razumov. "He has induced me to
do it. I can't shake him off."

Alarmed by that discovery, he got up and strode out of
the silent, dim room with its silent old woman in the chair,
that mother! He never looked back. It was frankly a flight.
But on opening the door he saw his retreat cut off. There
was the sister. He had never forgotten the sister, only he
had not expected to see her then—or ever any more, perhaps. Her presence in the ante-room was as unforeseen
as the apparition of her brother had been. Razumov gave
a start as though he had discovered himself cleverly
trapped. He tried to smile, but could not manage it, and
lowered his eyes. "Must I repeat that silly story now?" he
asked himself, and felt a sinking sensation. Nothing solid
had passed his lips since the day before, but he was not in

a state to analyze the origins of his weakness. He meant to take up his hat and depart with as few words as possible, but Miss Haldin's swift movement to shut the door took him by surprise. He half turned after her, but without raising his eyes passively, just as a feather might stir in the disturbed air. The next moment she was back in the place she had started from, with another half-turn on his part, so that they came again into the same relative positions.

"Yes, yes," she said hurriedly. "I am very grateful to you, Kirylo Sidorovitch, for coming at once—like this. . . . Only, I wish I had . . . Did mother tell you?"

"I wonder what she could have told me that I did not know before," he said, obviously to himself, but perfectly audible. "Because I always *did* know it," he added louder, as if in despair.

He hung his head. He had such a strong sense of Natalia Haldin's presence that to look at her he felt would be a relief. It was she who had been haunting him now. He had suffered that persecution ever since she had suddenly appeared before him in the garden of the Villa Borel with an extended hand and the name of her brother on her lips. . . . The ante-room had a row of hooks on the wall nearest to the outer door, while against the wall opposite there stood a small dark table and one chair. The paper, bearing a very faint design, was all but white. The light of an electric bulb high up under the ceiling searched that clear square box into its four bare corners, crudely, without shadows—a strange stage for an obscure drama.

"What do you mean?" asked Miss Haldin. "What is it that you knew always?"

He raised his face, pale, full of unexpressed suffering. But that look in his eyes of dull, absent obstinacy, which struck and surprised everybody he was talking to, began to pass away. It was as though he were coming to himself in the awakened consciousness of that marvellous harmony of feature, of lines, of glances, of voice, which made of the girl before him a being so rare, outside, and, as it were, above the common notion of beauty. He looked at her so long that she coloured slightly.

"What is it that you knew?" she repeated vaguely.

That time he managed to smile.

"Indeed, if it had not been for a word of greeting or two, I would doubt whether your mother was aware at all of my existence. You understand?"

Natalia Haldin nodded; her hands moved slightly by her side.

"Yes. Is it not heart-breaking? She has not shed a tear yet—not a single tear."

"Not a tear! And you, Natalia Victorovna? You have been able to cry?"

"I have. And then I am young enough, Kirylo Sidorovitch, to believe in the future. But when I see my mother so terribly distracted, I almost forget everything. I ask myself whether one should feel proud—or only resigned. We had such a lot of people coming to see us. There were utter strangers who wrote asking for permission to call to present their respects. It was impossible to keep our door shut for ever. You know that Peter Ivanovitch himself . . . Oh yes, there was much sympathy, but there were persons who exulted openly at that death. Then, when I was left alone with poor mother, all this seemed so wrong in spirit, something not worth the price she is paying for it. But directly I heard you were here in Geneva, Kirylo Sidorovitch, I felt that you were the only person who could assist me . . ."

"In comforting a bereaved mother? Yes!" he broke in in a manner which made her open her clear unsuspecting eyes. "But there is a question of fitness. Has this occurred to you?"

There was a breathlessness in his utterance which contrasted with the monstrous hint of mockery in his intention.

"Why!" whispered Natalia Haldin with feeling. "Who more fit than you?"

He had a convulsive movement of exasperation, but controlled himself.

"Indeed! Directly you heard that I was in Geneva, be-

fore even seeing me? It is another proof of that confidence
which . . ."

All at once his tone changed, became more incisive and
more detached.

"Men are poor creatures, Natalia Victorovna. They have
no intuition of sentiment. In order to speak fittingly to a
mother of her lost son one must have had some experience
of the filial relation. It is not the case with me—if you must
know the whole truth. Your hopes have to deal here with
'a breast unwarmed by any affection,' as the poet says.
. . . That does not mean it is insensible," he added in a
lower tone.

"I am certain your heart is not unfeeling," said Miss
Haldin softly.

"No. It is not as hard as a stone," he went on in the
same introspective voice, and looking as if his heart were
lying as heavy as a stone in that unwarmed breast of
which he spoke. "No, not so hard. But how to prove what
you give me credit for—ah! that's another question. No
one has ever expected such a thing from me before. No
one whom my tenderness would have been of any use to.
And now you come. You! Now! No, Natalia Victorovna.
It's too late. You come too late. You must expect nothing
from me."

She recoiled from him a little, though he had made no
movement, as if she had seen some change in his face,
charging his words with the significance of some hidden
sentiment they shared together. To me, the silent spectator, they looked like two people becoming conscious of a
spell which had been lying on them ever since they first
set eyes on each other. Had either of them cast a glance
then in my direction, I would have opened the door quietly
and gone out. But neither did; and I remained, every fear
of indiscretion lost in the sense of my enormous remoteness from their captivity within the sombre horizon of
Russian problems, the boundary of their eyes, of their
feelings—the prison of their souls.

Frank, courageous, Miss Haldin controlled her voice in
the midst of her trouble.

"What can this mean?" she asked, as if speaking to herself.

"It may mean that you have given yourself up to vain imaginings while I have managed to remain amongst the truth of things and the realities of life—our Russian life—such as they are."

"They are cruel," she murmured.

"And ugly. Don't forget that—and ugly. Look where you like. Look near you, here abroad where you are, and then look back at home, whence you came."

"One must look beyond the present." Her tone had an ardent conviction.

"The blind can do that best. I have had the misfortune to be born clear-eyed. And if you only knew what strange things I have seen! What amazing and unexpected apparitions! . . . But why talk of all this?"

"On the contrary, I want to talk of all this with you," she protested with earnest serenity. The sombre humours of her brother's friend left her unaffected, as though that bitterness, that suppressed anger, were the signs of an indignant rectitude. She saw that he was not an ordinary person, and perhaps she did not want him to be other than he appeared to her trustful eyes. "Yes, with you especially," she insisted. "With you of all the Russian people in the world. . . ." A faint smile dwelt for a moment on her lips. "I am like poor mother in a way. I too seem unable to give up our beloved dead, who, don't forget, was all in all to us. I don't want to abuse your sympathy, but you must understand that it is in you that we can find all that is left of his generous soul."

I was looking at him; not a muscle of his face moved in the least. And yet, even at the time, I did not suspect him of insensibility. It was a sort of rapt thoughtfulness. Then he stirred slightly.

"You are going, Kirylo Sidorovitch?" she asked.

"I! Going? Where? Oh yes, but I must tell you first . . ." His voice was muffled and he forced himself to produce it with visible repugnance, as if speech were something disgusting or deadly. "That story, you know—the story I heard this afternoon. . . ."

"I know the story already," she said sadly.

"You know it! Have you correspondents in St. Petersburg too?"

"No. It's Sophia Antonovna. I have seen her just now. She sends you her greetings. She is going away to-morrow."

He had lowered at last his fascinated glance; she too was looking down, and standing thus before each other in the glaring light, between the four bare walls, they seemed brought out from the confused immensity of the Eastern borders to be exposed cruelly to the observation of my Western eyes. And I observed them. There was nothing else to do. My existence seemed so utterly forgotten by these two that I dared not now make a movement. And I thought to myself that, of course, they had to come to-gether, the sister and the friend of that dead man. The ideas, the hopes, the aspirations, the cause of Freedom, expressed in their common affection for Victor Haldin, the moral victim of autocracy,—all this must draw them to each other fatally. Her very ignorance and his loneliness to which he had alluded so strangely must work to that end. And, indeed, I saw that the work was done already. Of course. It was manifest that they must have been thinking of each other for a long time before they met. She had the letter from that beloved brother kindling her imagination by the severe praise attached to that one name; and for him to see that exceptional girl was enough. The only cause for surprise was his gloomy aloofness before her clearly expressed welcome. But he was young, and how-ever austere and devoted to his revolutionary ideals, he was not blind. The period of reserve was over; he was coming forward in his own way. I could not mistake the significance of this late visit, for in what he had to say there was nothing urgent. The true cause dawned upon me: he had discovered that he needed her—and she was moved by the same feeling. It was the second time that I saw them together, and I knew that next time they met I

would not be there, either remembered or forgotten.
I would have virtually ceased to exist for both these young
people.

I made this discovery in a very few moments. Meantime, Natalia Haldin was telling Razumov briefly of our
peregrinations from one end of Geneva to the other. While
speaking she raised her hands above her head to untie her
veil, and that movement displayed for an instant the seductive grace of her youthful figure, clad in the simplest
of mourning. In the transparent shadow the hat rim threw
on her face her grey eyes had an enticing lustre. Her
voice, with its unfeminine yet exquisite timbre, was steady,
and she spoke quickly, frank, unembarrassed. As she justified her action by the mental state of her mother, a spasm
of pain marred the generously confiding harmony of her
features. I perceived that with his downcast eyes he had
the air of a man who is listening to a strain of music rather
than to articulated speech. And in the same way, after
she had ceased, he seemed to listen yet, motionless, as if
under the spell of suggestive sound. He came to himself
muttering:

"Yes, yes. She has not shed a tear. She did not seem to
hear what I was saying. I might have told her anything.
She looked as if no longer belonging to this world."

Miss Haldin gave signs of profound distress. Her voice
faltered. "You don't know how bad it has come to be. She
expects now to *see him!*" The veil dropped from her fingers,
and she clasped her hands in anguish. "It will end by her
seeing him," she cried.

Razumov raised his head sharply and attached on her a
prolonged thoughtful glance.

"H'm. That's very possible," he muttered in a peculiar
tone, as if giving his opinion on a matter of fact. "I wonder
what . . ." He checked himself.

"That would be the end. Her mind will be gone then,
and her spirit will follow."

Miss Haldin unclasped her hands and let them fall by
her side.

"You think so?" he queried profoundly. Miss Haldin's

lips were slightly parted. Something unexpected and unfathomable in that young man's character had fascinated
her from the first. "No! There's neither truth nor consolation to be got from the phantoms of the dead," he added
after a weighty pause. "I might have told her something
true; for instance, that your brother meant to save his life
—to escape. There can be no doubt of that. But I did not."

"You did not! But why?"

"I don't know. Other thoughts came into my head," he
answered. He seemed to me to be watching himself inwardly, as though he were trying to count his own heart-
beats, while his eyes never for a moment left the face of
the girl. "You were not there," he continued. "I had made
up my mind never to see you again."

This seemed to take her breath away for a moment.

"You. . . . How is it possible?"

"You may well ask. . . . However, I think that I refrained from telling your mother from prudence. I might
have assured her that in the last conversation he held as
a free man he mentioned you both. . . ."

"That last conversation was with you," she struck in, in
her deep, moving voice. "Some day you must. . . ."

"It was with me. Of you he said that you had trustful
eyes. And why I have not been able to forget that phrase
I don't know. It meant that there is in you no guile, no
deception, no falsehood, no suspicion—nothing in your
heart that could give you a conception of a living, acting,
speaking lie, if ever it came in your way. That you are a
predestined victim. . . . Ha! what a devilish suggestion!"

The convulsive, uncontrolled tone of the last words disclosed the precarious hold he had over himself. He was
like a man defying his own dizziness in high places and
tottering suddenly on the very edge of the precipice. Miss
Haldin pressed her hand to her breast. The dropped black
veil lay on the floor between them. Her movement steadied
him. He looked intently on that hand till it descended
slowly, and then raised again his eyes to her face. But he
did not give her time to speak.

"No? You don't understand? Very well." He had recovered his calm by a miracle of will. "So you talked with Sophia Antonovna?"

"Yes. Sophia Antonovna told me. . . ." Miss Haldin stopped, wonder growing in her wide eyes.

"H'm. That's the respectable enemy," he muttered, as though he were alone.

"The tone of her references to you was extremely friendly," remarked Miss Haldin, after waiting for a while.

"Is that your impression? And she the most intelligent of the lot, too. Things then are going as well as possible. Everything conspires to. . . . Ah! these conspirators," he said slowly, with an accent of scorn; "they would get hold of you in no time! You know, Natalia Victorovna, I have the greatest difficulty in saving myself from the superstition of an active Providence. It's irresistible. . . . The alternative, of course, would be the personal Devil of our simple ancestors. But, if so, he has overdone it altogether —the old Father of Lies—our national patron—our domestic god, whom we take with us when we go abroad. He has overdone it. It seems that I am not simple enough. . . . That's it! I ought to have known. . . . And I did know it," he added in a tone of poignant distress which overcame my astonishment.

"This man is deranged," I said to myself, very much frightened.

The next moment he gave me a very special impression beyond the range of commonplace definitions. It was as though he had stabbed himself outside and had come in there to show it; and more than that—as though he were turning the knife in the wound and watching the effect. That was the impression, rendered in physical terms. One could not defend oneself from a certain amount of pity. But it was for Miss Haldin, already so tried in her deepest affections, that I felt a serious concern. Her attitude, her face, expressed compassion struggling with doubt on the verge of terror.

"What is it, Kirylo Sidorovitch?" There was a hint of tenderness in that cry. He only stared at her in that complete surrender of all his faculties which in a happy lover would have had the name of ecstasy.

"Why are you looking at me like this, Kirylo Sidorovitch? I have approached you frankly. I need at this time to see clearly in myself. . . ." She ceased for a moment as if to give him an opportunity to utter at last some word worthy of her exalted trust in her brother's friend. His silence became impressive, like a sign of a momentous resolution.

In the end Miss Haldin went on, appealingly—

"I have waited for you anxiously. But now that you have been moved to come to us in your kindness, you alarm me. You speak obscurely. It seems as if you were keeping back something from me."

"Tell me, Natalia Victorovna," he was heard at last in a strange unringing voice, "whom did you see in that place?"

She was startled, and as if deceived in her expectations.

"Where? In Peter Ivanovitch's rooms? There was Mr. Laspara and three other people."

"Ha! The vanguard—the forlorn hope of the great plot," he commented to himself. "Bearers of the spark to start an explosion which is meant to change fundamentally the lives of so many millions in order that Peter Ivanovitch should be the head of a State."

"You are teasing me," she said. "Our dear one told me once to remember that men serve always something greater than themselves—the idea."

"Our dear one," he repeated slowly. The effort he made to appear unmoved absorbed all the force of his soul. He stood before her like a being with hardly a breath of life. His eyes, even as under great physical suffering, had lost all their fire. "Ah! your brother. . . . But on your lips, in your voice, it sounds . . . and indeed in you everything is divine. . . . I wish I could know the innermost depths of your thoughts, of your feelings."

"But why, Kirylo Sidorovitch?" she cried, alarmed by these words coming out of strangely lifeless lips.

"Have no fear. It is not to betray you. So you went

there? . . . . And Sophia Antonovna, what did she tell you, then?"

"She said very little, really. She knew that I should hear everything from you. She had no time for more than a few words." Miss Haldin's voice dropped and she became silent for a moment. "The man, it appears, has taken his life," she said sadly.

"Tell me, Natalia Victorovna," he asked after a pause, "do you believe in remorse?"

"What a question!"

"What can *you* know of it?" he muttered thickly. "It is not for such as you . . . What I meant to ask was whether you believed in the efficacy of remorse?"

She hesitated as though she had not understood, then her face lighted up.

"Yes," she said firmly.

"So he is absolved. Moreover, that Ziemianitch was a brute, a drunken brute."

A shudder passed through Natalia Haldin.

"But a man of the people," Razumov went on, "to whom they, the revolutionists, tell a tale of sublime hopes. Well, the people must be forgiven. . . . And you must not believe all you've heard from that source, either," he added, with a sort of sinister reluctance.

"You are concealing something from me," she exclaimed. |

"Do you, Natalia Victorovna, believe in the duty of revenge?"

"Listen, Kirylo Sidorovitch. I believe that the future will be merciful to us all. Revolutionist and reactionary, victim and executioner, betrayer and betrayed, they shall all be pitied together when the light breaks on our black sky at last. Pitied and forgotten; for without that there can be no union and no love."

"I hear. No revenge for you, then? Never? Not the least bit?" He smiled bitterly with his colourless lips. "You yourself are like the very spirit of that merciful future. Strange that it does not make it easier. . . . No! But suppose that the real betrayer of your brother—Ziemianitch had a part in it too, but insignificant and quite involuntary—suppose that he was a young man, educated, an intellectual worker, thoughtful, a man your brother might have trusted lightly, perhaps, but still—suppose. . . . But there's a whole story there."

"And you know the story! But why, then——"

"I have heard it. There is a staircase in it, and even phantoms, but that does not matter if a man always serves something greater than himself—the idea. I wonder who is the greatest victim in that tale?"

"In that tale!" Miss Haldin repeated. She seemed turned into stone.

"Do you know why I came to you? It is simply because there is no one anywhere in the whole great world I could go to. Do you understand what I say? Not one to go to. Do you conceive the desolation of the thought—no one—to—go—to?"

Utterly misled by her own enthusiastic interpretation of two lines in the letter of a visionary, under the spell of her own dread of lonely days, in their overshadowed world of angry strife, she was unable to see the truth struggling on his lips. What she was conscious of was the obscure form of his suffering. She was on the point of extending her hand to him impulsively when he spoke again.

"An hour after I saw you first I knew how it would be. The terrors of remorse, revenge, confession, anger, hate, fear, are like nothing to the atrocious temptation which you put in my way the day you appeared before me with your voice, with your face, in the garden of that accursed villa."

She looked utterly bewildered for a moment; then, with a sort of despairing insight went straight to the point.

"The story, Kirylo Sidorovitch, the story!"

"There is no more to tell!" He made a movement forward, and she actually put her hand on his shoulder to push him away; but her strength failed her, and he kept his ground, though trembling in every limb. "It ends here —on this very spot." He pressed a denunciatory finger to his breast with force, and became perfectly still.

I ran forward, snatching up the chair, and was in time to catch hold of Miss Haldin and lower her down. As she

sank into it she swung half round on my arm, and remained averted from us both, drooping over the back. He
looked at her with an appalling expressionless tranquillity.
Incredulity, struggling with astonishment, anger, and disgust, deprived me for a time of the power of speech. Then
I turned on him, whispering from very rage—

"This is monstrous. What are you staying for? Don't let
her catch sight of you again. Go away! . . ." He did not
budge. "Don't you understand that your presence is intolerable—even to me? If there's any sense of shame in
you. . . ."

Slowly his sullen eyes moved in my direction. "How did
this old man come here?" he muttered, astounded.

Suddenly Miss Haldin sprang up from the chair, made
a few steps, and tottered. Forgetting my indignation, and
even the man himself, I hurried to her assistance. I took
her by the arm, and she let me lead her into the drawing-
room. Away from the lamp, in the deeper dusk of the distant end, the profile of Mrs. Haldin, her hands, her whole
figure had the stillness of a sombre painting. Miss Haldin
stopped, and pointed mournfully at the tragic immobility
of her mother, who seemed to watch a beloved head lying
in her lap.

That gesture had an unequalled force of expression, so
far-reaching in its human distress that one could not believe
that it pointed out merely the ruthless working of political
institutions. After assisting Miss Haldin to the sofa, I turned
round to go back and shut the door. Framed in the opening, in the searching glare of the white ante-room, my
eyes fell on Razumov, still there, standing before the empty
chair, as if rooted for ever to the spot of his atrocious confession. A wonder came over me that the mysterious force
which had torn it out of him had failed to destroy his
life, to shatter his body. It was there unscathed. I stared at
the broad line of his shoulders, his dark head, the amazing
immobility of his limbs. At his feet the veil dropped by
Miss Haldin looked intensely black in the white crudity
of the light. He was gazing at it spell-bound. Next moment,
stooping with an incredible, savage swiftness, he snatched

it up and pressed it to his face with both hands. Something, extreme astonishment perhaps, dimmed my eyes, so that he seemed to vanish before he moved.

The slamming of the outer door restored my sight, and I went on contemplating the empty chair in the empty ante-room. The meaning of what I had seen reached my mind with a staggering shock. I seized Natalia Haldin by the shoulder.

"That miserable wretch has carried off your veil!" I cried, in the scared, deadened voice of an awful discovery. "He . . ."

The rest remained unspoken. I stepped back and looked down at her, in silent horror. Her hands were lying lifelessly, palms upwards, on her lap. She raised her grey eyes slowly. Shadows seemed to come and go in them as if the steady flame of her soul had been made to vacillate at last in the cross-currents of poisoned air from the corrupted dark immensity claiming her for its own, where virtues themselves fester into crimes in the cynicism of oppression and revolt.

"It is impossible to be more unhappy. . . ." The languid whisper of her voice struck me with dismay. "It is impossible. . . . I feel my heart becoming like ice."

IV

Razumov walked straight home on the wet glistening pavement. A heavy shower passed over him; distant lightning played faintly against the fronts of the dumb houses with the shuttered shops all along the Rue de Carouge; and now and then, after the faint flash, there was a faint, sleepy rumble; but the main forces of the thunderstorm remained massed down the Rhone valley as if loath to attack the respectable and passionless abode of democratic liberty, the serious-minded town of dreary hotels, tendering the same indifferent hospitality to tourists of all nations and to international conspirators of every shade.

The owner of the shop was making ready to close when Razumov entered and without a word extended his hand for the key of his room. On reaching it for him, from a shelf, the man was about to pass a small joke as to taking the air in a thunderstorm, but, after looking at the face of his lodger, he only observed, just to say something—

"You've got very wet."

"Yes, I am washed clean," muttered Razumov, who was dripping from head to foot, and passed through the inner door towards the staircase leading to his room.

He did not change his clothes, but, after lighting the candle, took off his watch and chain, laid them on the table, and sat down at once to write. The book of his compromising record was kept in a locked drawer, which he pulled out violently, and did not even trouble to push back afterwards.

In this queer pedantism of a man who had read, thought, lived, pen in hand, there is the sincerity of the attempt to grapple by the same means with another profounder knowledge. After some passages which have been already made use of in the building up of this narrative, or add nothing new to the psychological side of this disclosure (there is even one more allusion to the silver medal in this last entry), comes a page and a half of incoherent writing where his expression is baffled by the novelty and the mysteriousness of that side of our emotional life to which his solitary existence had been a stranger. Then only he begins to address directly the reader he had in his mind, trying to express in broken sentences, full of wonder and awe, the sovereign (he uses that very word) power of her person over his imagination, in which lay the dormant seed of her brother's words.

". . . The most trustful eyes in the world—your brother said of you when he was as well as a dead man already. And when you stood before me with your hand extended, I remembered the very sound of his voice, and I looked into your eyes—and that was enough. I knew that something had happened, but I did not know then what. . . . But don't be deceived, Natalia Victorovna. I believed that I had in my breast nothing but an inexhaustible fund of anger and hate for you both. I remembered that he had looked to you for the perpetuation of his visionary soul. He, this man who had robbed me of my hard-working, purposeful existence. I, too, had my guiding idea; and remember that, amongst us, it is more difficult to lead a life of toil and self-denial than to go out in the street and kill from conviction. But enough of that. Hate or no hate, I felt at once that, while shunning the sight of you, I could never succeed in driving away your image. I would say, addressing that dead man, 'Is this the way you are going to haunt me?' It is only later on that I understood—only to-day, only a few hours ago. What could I have known of what was tearing me to pieces and dragging the secret for ever to my lips? You were appointed to undo the evil by making me betray myself back into truth and peace. You! And you have done it in the same way, too, in which he ruined me: by forcing upon me your confidence. Only what I detested him for, in you ended by appearing noble and exalted. But, I repeat, be not deceived. I was given up to evil. I exulted in having induced that silly innocent fool to steal his father's money. He was a fool, but not a thief. I made him one. It was necessary. I had to confirm myself in my contempt and hate for what I betrayed. I have suffered from as many vipers in my heart as any social democrat of them all—vanity, ambitions, jealousies, shameful desires, evil passions of envy and revenge. I had my security stolen from me, years of good work, my best hopes. Listen —now comes the true confession. The other was nothing. To save me, your trustful eyes had to entice my thought to the very edge of the blackest treachery. I could see them constantly looking at me with the confidence of your pure heart which had not been touched by evil things. Victor Haldin had stolen the truth of my life from me, who had nothing else in the world, and he boasted of living on through you on this earth where I had no place to lay my head. She will marry some day, he had said—and your eyes were trustful. And do you know what I said to myself? I shall steal his sister's soul from her. When we met that first morning in the gardens, and you spoke to me confidingly in the generosity of your spirit, I was thinking,

'Yes, he himself by talking of her trustful eyes has delivered her into my hands!' If you could have looked then into my heart, you would have cried out aloud with terror and disgust.

"Perhaps no one will believe the baseness of such an intention to be possible. It's certain that, when we parted that morning, I gloated over it. I brooded upon the best way. The old man you introduced me to insisted on walking with me. I don't know who he is. He talked of you, of your lonely, helpless state, and every word of that friend of yours was egging me on to the unpardonable sin of stealing a soul. Could he have been the devil himself in the shape of an old Englishman? Natalia Victorovna, I was possessed! I returned to look at you every day, and drink in your presence the poison of my infamous intention. But I foresaw difficulties. Then Sophia Antonovna, of whom I was not thinking—I had forgotten her existence—appears suddenly with that tale from St. Petersburg. . . . The only thing needed to make me safe—a trusted revolutionist for ever.

"It was as if Ziemianitch had hanged himself to help me on to further crime. The strength of falsehood seemed irresistible. These people stood doomed by the folly and the illusion that was in them—they being themselves the slaves of lies. Natalia Victorovna, I embraced the might of falsehood, I exulted in it—I gave myself up to it for a time. Who could have resisted! You yourself were the prize of it. I sat alone in my room, planning a life, the very thought of which makes me shudder now, like a believer who had been tempted to an atrocious sacrilege. But I brooded ardently over its images. The only thing was that there seemed to be no air in it. And also I was afraid of your mother. I never knew mine. I've never known any kind of love. There is something in the mere word. . . . Of you, I was not afraid—forgive me for telling you this. No, not of you. You were truth itself. You could not suspect me. As to your mother, you yourself feared already that her mind had given way from grief. Who could believe anything against me? Had not Ziemianitch hanged himself from remorse? I said to myself, 'Let's put it to the test, and be done with it once for all.' I trembled when I went in; but your mother hardly listened to what I was saying to her, and, in a little while, seemed to have forgotten my very existence. I sat looking at her. There was no longer anything between you and me. You were defenceless—and soon, very soon, you would be alone. . . . I thought of you. Defenceless. For days you have talked with me—opening your heart. I remembered the shadow of your eyelashes over your grey trustful eyes. And your pure forehead! It is low like the forehead of statues—calm, unstained. It was as if your pure brow bore a light which fell on me, searched my heart and saved me from ignominy, from ultimate undoing. And it saved you too. Pardon my presumption. But there was that in your glances which seemed to tell me that you . . . Your light! your truth! I felt that I must tell you that I had ended by loving you. And to tell you that I must first confess. Confess, go out —and perish.

"Suddenly you stood before me! You alone in all the world to whom I must confess. You fascinated me—you have freed me from the blindness of anger and hate—the truth shining in you drew the truth out of me. Now I have done it; and as I write here, I am in the depths of anguish, but there is air to breathe at last—air! And, by the by, that old man sprang up from somewhere as I was speaking to you, and raged at me like a disappointed devil. I suffer horribly, but I am not in despair. There is only one more thing to do for me. After that—if they let me—I shall go away and bury myself in obscure misery. In giving Victor Haldin up, it was myself, after all, whom I have betrayed most basely. You must believe what I say now, you can't refuse to believe this. Most basely. It is through you that I came to feel this so deeply. After all, it is they and not I who have the right on their side!—theirs is the strength of invisible powers. So be it. Only don't be deceived, Natalia Victorovna, I am not converted. Have I then the soul of a slave? No! I am independent—and therefore perdition is my lot."

On these words, he stopped writing, shut the book, and

wrapped it in the black veil he had carried off. He then ransacked the drawers for paper and string, made up a parcel which he addressed to Miss Haldin, Boulevard des Philosophes, and then flung the pen away from him into a distant corner.

This done, he sat down with the watch before him. He could have gone out at once, but the hour had not struck yet. The hour would be midnight. There was no reason for that choice except that the facts and the words of a certain evening in his past were timing his conduct in the present. The sudden power Natalia Haldin had gained over him he ascribed to the same cause. "You don't walk with impunity over a phantom's breast," he heard himself mutter. "Thus he saves me," he thought suddenly. "He himself, the betrayed man." The vivid image of Miss Haldin seemed to stand by him, watching him relentlessly. She was not disturbing. He had done with life, and his thought even in her presence tried to take an impartial survey. Now his scorn extended to himself. "I had neither the simplicity nor the courage nor the self-possession to be a scoundrel, or an exceptionally able man. For who, with us in Russia, is to tell a scoundrel from an exceptionally able man? . . ."

He was the puppet of his past, because at the very stroke of midnight he jumped up and ran swiftly downstairs as if confident that, by the power of destiny, the house door would fly open before the absolute necessity of his errand. And as a matter of fact, just as he got to the bottom of the stairs, it was opened for him by some people of the house coming home late—two men and a woman. He slipped out through them into the street, swept then by a fitful gust of wind. They were, of course, very much startled. A flash of lightning enabled them to observe him walking away quickly. One of the men shouted, and was starting in pursuit but the woman had recognized him. "It's all right. It's only that young Russian from the third floor." The darkness returned with a single clap of thunder, like a gun fired for a warning of his escape from the prison of lies.

He must have heard at some time or other and now

remembered unconsciously that there was to be a gathering of revolutionists at the house of Julius Laspara that
evening. At any rate, he made straight for the Laspara
house, and found himself without surprise ringing at its
street door, which, of course, was closed. By that time
the thunderstorm had attacked in earnest. The steep incline of the street ran with water, the thick fall of rain
enveloped him like a luminous veil in the play of lightning.
He was perfectly calm, and, between the crashes, listened
attentively to the delicate tinkling of the doorbell somewhere within the house.

There was some difficulty before he was admitted. His
person was not known to that one of the guests who had
volunteered to go downstairs and see what was the matter.
Razumov argued with him patiently. There could be no
harm in admitting a caller. He had something to communicate to the company upstairs.

"Something of importance?"

"That'll be for the hearers to judge."

"Urgent?"

"Without a moment's delay."

Meantime, one of the Laspara daughters descended the
stairs, small lamp in hand, in a grimy and crumpled gown,
which seemed to hang on her by a miracle, and looking
more than ever like an old doll with a dusty brown wig,
dragged from under a sofa. She recognized Razumov at
once.

"How do you do? Of course you may come in."

Following her light Razumov climbed two flights of
stairs from the lower darkness. Leaving the lamp on a
bracket on the landing, she opened a door, and went in,
accompanied by the sceptical guest. Razumov entered last.
He closed the door behind him, and stepping on one side,
put his back against the wall.

The three little rooms *en suite*, with low, smoky ceilings
and lit by paraffin lamps were crammed with people. Loud
talking was going on in all three, and tea-glasses, full,
half-full, and empty, stood everywhere, even on the floor.
The other Laspara girl sat, dishevelled and languid, behind

an enormous samovar. In the inner doorway Razumov had a glimpse of the protuberance of a large stomach, which he recognized. Only a few feet from him Julius Laspara was getting down hurriedly from his high stool.

The appearance of the midnight visitor caused no small sensation. Laspara is very summary in his version of that night's happenings. After some words of greeting, disregarded by Razumov, Laspara (ignoring purposely his guest's soaked condition and his extraordinary manner of presenting himself) mentioned something about writing an article. He was growing uneasy, and Razumov appeared absent-minded. "I have written already all I shall ever write," he said at last, with a little laugh.

The whole company's attention was riveted on the newcomer, dripping with water, deadly pale, and keeping his position against the wall. Razumov put Laspara gently aside, as though he wished to be seen from head to foot by everybody. By then the buzz of conversation had died down completely, even in the most distant of the three rooms. The doorway facing Razumov became blocked by men and women, who craned their necks and certainly seemed to expect something startling to happen.

A squeaky, insolent declaration was heard from that group.

"I know this ridiculously conceited individual."

"What individual?" asked Razumov, raising his bowed head, and searching with his eyes all the eyes fixed upon him. An intense surprised silence lasted for a time. "If it's me. . . ."

He stopped, thinking over the form of his confession, and found it suddenly, unavoidably suggested by the fateful evening of his life.

"I am come here," he began, in a clear voice, "to talk of an individual called Ziemianitch. Sophia Antonovna has informed me that she would make public a certain letter from St. Petersburg. . . ."

"Sophia Antonovna has left us early in the evening," said Laspara. "It's quite correct. Everybody here has heard. . . ."

"Very well," Razumov interrupted, with a shade of impatience, for his heart was beating strongly. Then mastering his voice so far that there was even a touch of irony in his clear, forcible enunciation—

"In justice to that individual, the much ill-used peasant, Ziemianitch, I now declare solemnly that the conclusions of that letter calumniate a man of the people—a bright Russian soul. Ziemianitch had nothing to do with the actual arrest of Victor Haldin."

Razumov dwelt on the name heavily, and then waited till the faint, mournful murmur which greeted it had died out.

"Victor Victorovitch Haldin," he began again, "acting with, no doubt, noble-minded imprudence, took refuge with a certain student of whose opinions he knew nothing but what his own illusions suggested to his generous heart. It was an unwise display of confidence. But I am not here to appreciate the actions of Victor Haldin. Am I to tell you of the feelings of that student, sought out in his obscure solitude, and menaced by the complicity forced upon him? Am I to tell you what he did? It's a rather complicated story. In the end the student went to General T—— himself, and said, 'I have the man who killed de P—— locked up in my room, Victor Haldin—a student like myself.'"

A great buzz arose, in which Razumov raised his voice.

"Observe—that man had certain honest ideals in view. But I didn't come here to explain him."

"No. But you must explain how you know all this," came in grave tones from somebody.

"A vile coward!" This simple cry vibrated with indignation. "Name him!" shouted other voices.

"What are you clamouring for?" said Razumov disdainfully, in the profound silence which fell on the raising of his hand. "Haven't you all understood that I am that man?"

Laspara went away brusquely from his side and climbed upon his stool. In the first forward surge of people towards him, Razumov expected to be torn to pieces, but they fell back without touching him, and nothing came of it but noise. It was bewildering. His head ached terribly. In the

confused uproar he made out several times the name of
Peter Ivanovitch, the word "judgment," and the phrase,
"But this is a confession," uttered by somebody in a desperate shriek. In the midst of the tumult, a young man,
younger than himself, approached him with blazing eyes.

"I must beg you," he said, with venomous politeness,
"to be good enough not to move from this spot till you are
told what you are to do."

Razumov shrugged his shoulders.

"I came in voluntarily."

"Maybe. But you won't go out till you are permitted,"
retorted the other.

He beckoned with his hand, calling out, "Louisa! Louisa!
come here, please"; and, presently, one of the Laspara girls
(they had been staring at Razumov from behind the
samovar) came along, trailing a bedraggled tail of dirty
flounces, and dragging with her a chair, which she set
against the door, and, sitting down on it, crossed her legs.
The young man thanked her effusively, and rejoined a
group carrying on an animated discussion in low tones.
Razumov lost himself for a moment.

A squeaky voice screamed, "Confession or no confession,
you are a police spy!"

The revolutionist Nikita had pushed his way in front of
Razumov, and faced him with his big, livid cheeks, his
heavy paunch, bull neck, and enormous hands. Razumov
looked at the famous slayer of gendarmes in silent disgust.

"And what are you?" he said, very low, then shut his
eyes, and rested the back of his head against the wall.

"It would be better for you to depart now." Razumov
heard a mild, sad voice, and opened his eyes. The gentle
speaker was an elderly man, with a great brush of fine hair
making a silvery halo all round his keen, intelligent face.
"Peter Ivanovitch shall be informed of your confession—
and you shall be directed . . ."

Then, turning to Nikita, nicknamed Necator, standing
by, he appealed to him in a murmur—

"What else can we do? After this piece of sincerity he
cannot be dangerous any longer."

The other muttered, "Better make sure of that before we let him go. Leave that to me. I know how to deal with such gentlemen."

He exchanged meaning glances with two or three men, who nodded slightly, then turning roughly to Razumov, "You have heard? You are not wanted here. Why don't you get out?"

The Laspara girl on guard rose, and pulled the chair out of the way unemotionally. She gave a sleepy stare to Razumov, who started, looked round the room and passed slowly by her as if struck by some sudden thought.

"I beg you to observe," he said, already on the landing, "that I had only to hold my tongue. To-day, of all days since I came amongst you, I was made safe, and to-day I made myself free from falsehood, from remorse—independent of every single human being on this earth."

He turned his back on the room, and walked towards the stairs, but, at the violent crash of the door behind him, he looked over his shoulder and saw that Nikita with three others, had followed him out. "They are going to kill me, after all," he thought.

Before he had time to turn round and confront them fairly, they set on him with a rush. He was driven headlong against the wall. "I wonder how," he completed his thought. Nikita cried, with a shrill laugh right in his face, "We shall make you harmless. You wait a bit."

Razumov did not struggle. The three men held him pinned against the wall, while Nikita, taking up a position a little on one side, deliberately swung off his enormous arm. Razumov, looking for a knife in his hand, saw it come at him open, unarmed, and received a tremendous blow on the side of his head over his ear. At the same time he heard a faint, dull detonating sound, as if someone had fired a pistol on the other side of the wall. A raging fury awoke in him at this outrage. The people in Laspara's rooms, holding their breath, listened to the desperate scuffling of four men all over the landing; thuds against the walls, a terrible crash against the very door, then all of them went down together with a violence which seemed to shake the whole house. Razumov, overpowered, breathless, crushed under the weight of his assailants, saw the monstrous Nikita squatting on his heels near his head, while the others held him down, kneeling on his chest, gripping his throat, lying across his legs.

"Turn his face the other way," the paunchy terrorist directed, in an excited, gleeful squeak.

Razumov could struggle no longer. He was exhausted; he had to watch passively the heavy open hand of the brute descend again in a degrading blow over his other ear. It seemed to split his head in two, and all at once the men holding him became perfectly silent—soundless as shadows. In silence they pulled him brutally to his feet, rushed with him noiselessly down the staircase, and, opening the door, flung him out into the street.

He fell forward, and at once rolled over and over helplessly, going down the short slope together with the rush of running rain water. He came to rest in the roadway of the street at the bottom, lying on his back, with a great flash of lightning over his face—a vivid, silent flash of lightning which blinded him utterly. He picked himself up, and put his arm over his eyes to recover his sight. Not a sound reached him from anywhere, and he began to walk, staggering, down a long, empty street. The lightning waved and darted round him its silent flames, the water of the deluge fell, ran, leaped, drove—noiseless like the drift of mist. In this unearthly stillness his footsteps fell silent on the pavement, while a dumb wind drove him on and on, like a lost mortal in a phantom world ravaged by a soundless thunderstorm. God only knows where his noiseless feet took him to that night, here and there, and back again without pause or rest. Of one place, at least, where they did lead him, we heard afterwards; and, in the morning, the driver of the first south-shore tramcar, clanging his bell desperately, saw a bedraggled, soaked man without a hat, and walking in the roadway unsteadily with his head down, step right in front of his car, and go under.

When they picked him up, with two broken limbs and a crushed side, Razumov had not lost consciousness. It was as though he had tumbled, smashing himself, into a world of mutes. Silent men, moving unheard, lifted him up, laid him on the sidewalk, gesticulating and grimacing round him their alarm, horror, and compassion. A red face with moustaches stooped close over him, lips moving, eyes rolling. Razumov tried hard to understand the reason of this dumb show. To those who stood around him, the features of that stranger, so grievously hurt, seemed composed in meditation. Afterwards his eyes sent out at them a look of fear and closed slowly. They stared at him. Razumov made an effort to remember some French words.

"*Je suis sourd,*" he had time to utter feebly, before he fainted.

"He is deaf," they exclaimed to each other. "That's why he did not hear the car."

They carried him off in that same car. Before it started on its journey, a woman in a shabby black dress, who had run out of the iron gate of some private grounds up the road, clambered on to the rear platform and would not be put off.

"I am a relation," she insisted, in bad French. "This young man is a Russian, and I am his relation."

On this plea they let her have her way. She sat down calmly, and took his head on her lap; her scared faded eyes avoided looking at his deathlike face. At the corner of a street, on the other side of the town, a stretcher met the car. She followed it to the door of the hospital, where they let her come in and see him laid on a bed. Razumov's new-found relation never shed a tear, but the officials had some difficulty in inducing her to go away. The porter observed her lingering on the opposite pavement for a long time. Suddenly, as though she had remembered something, she ran off.

The ardent hater of all Finance ministers, the slave of Madame de S——, had made up her mind to offer her resignation as lady companion to the Egeria of Peter Ivanovitch. She had found work to do after her own heart.

But hours before, while the thunderstorm still raged in the night, there had been in the rooms of Julius Laspara a great sensation. The terrible Nikita, coming in from the landing, uplifted his squeaky voice in horrible glee before all the company—

"Razumov! Mr. Razumov! The wonderful Razumov! He shall never be any use as a spy on any one. He won't talk, because he will never hear anything in his life—not a thing! I have burst the drums of his ears for him. Oh, you may trust me. I know the trick. Ha! Ha! Ha! I know the trick."

V

It was nearly a fortnight after her mother's funeral that I saw Natalia Haldin for the last time.

In those silent, sombre days the doors of the *appartement* on the Boulevard des Philosophes were closed to everyone but myself. I believe I was of some use, if only in this, that I alone was aware of the incredible part of the situation. Miss Haldin nursed her mother alone to the last moment. If Razumov's visit had anything to do with Mrs. Haldin's end (and I cannot help thinking that it hastened it considerably), it is because the man, trusted impulsively by the ill-fated Victor Haldin, had failed to gain the confidence of Victor Haldin's mother. What tale, precisely, he told her cannot be known—at any rate, I do not know it—but to me she seemed to die from the shock of an ultimate disappointment borne in silence. She had not believed him. Perhaps she could no longer believe any one, and consequently had nothing to say to any one—not even to her daughter. I suspect that Miss Haldin lived the heaviest hours of her life by that silent death-bed. I confess I was angry with the broken-hearted old woman passing away in the obstinacy of her mute distrust of her daughter.

When it was all over I stood aside. Miss Haldin had her compatriots round her then. A great number of them attended the funeral. I was there too, but afterwards managed to keep away from Miss Haldin, till I received a short note rewarding my self-denial. "It is as you would have it. I am going back to Russia at once. My mind is made up. Come and see me."

Verily, it was a reward of discretion. I went without delay to receive it. The *appartement* of the Boulevard des Philosophes presented the dreary signs of impending abandonment. It looked desolate and as if already empty to my eyes.

Standing, we exchanged a few words about her health, mine, remarks as to some people of the Russian colony, and then Natalia Haldin, establishing me on the sofa, began to talk openly of her future work, of her plans. It was all to be as I had wished it. And it was to be for life. We should never see each other again. Never!

I gathered this success to my breast. Natalia Haldin looked matured by her open and secret experiences. With her arms folded she walked up and down the whole length of the room, talking slowly, smooth-browed, with a resolute profile. She gave me a new view of herself, and I marvelled at that something grave and measured in her voice, in her movements, in her manner. It was the perfection of collected independence. The strength of her nature had come to surface because the obscure depths had been stirred.

"We two can talk of it now," she observed, after a silence and stopping short before me. "Have you been to inquire at the hospital lately?"

"Yes, I have." And as she looked at me fixedly, "He will live, the doctors say. But I thought that Tekla . . ."

"Tekla has not been near me for several days," explained Miss Haldin quickly. "As I never offered to go to the hospital with her, she thinks that I have no heart. She is disillusioned about me."

And Miss Haldin smiled faintly.

"Yes. She sits with him as long and as often as they will let her," I said. "She says she must never abandon him—never as long as she lives. He'll need somebody—a hopeless cripple, and stone deaf with that."

"Stone deaf? I didn't know," murmured Natalia Haldin.

"He is. It seems strange. I am told there were no apparent injuries to the head. They say, too, that it is not very likely that he will live so very long for Tekla to take care of him."

Miss Haldin shook her head.

"While there are travellers ready to fall by the way our Tekla will never be idle. She is a good Samaritan by an irresistible vocation. The revolutionists didn't understand her. Fancy a devoted creature like that being employed to carry about documents sewn in her dress, or made to write from dictation."

"There is not much perspicacity in the world." ——

No sooner uttered, I regretted that observation. Natalia Haldin, looking me straight in the face, assented by a slight movement of her head. She was not offended, but turning away began to pace the room again. To my Western eyes she seemed to be getting farther and farther from me, quite beyond my reach now, but undiminished in the increasing distance. I remained silent as though it were hopeless to raise my voice. The sound of hers, so close to me, made me start a little.

"Tekla saw him picked up after the accident. The good soul never explained to me really how it came about. She affirms that there was some understanding between them —some sort of compact—that in any sore need, in misfortune, or difficulty, or pain, he was to come to her."

"Was there?" I said. "It is lucky for him that there was, then. He'll need all the devotion of the good Samaritan."

It was a fact that Tekla, looking out of her window at five in the morning, for some reason or other, had beheld Razumov in the grounds of the Château Borel, standing stockstill, bare-headed in the rain, at the foot of the terrace. She had screamed out to him, by name, to know what was the matter. He never even raised his head. By the time she had dressed herself sufficiently to run downstairs he was gone. She started in pursuit, and rushing out into the road, came almost directly upon the arrested tramcar and the small knot of people picking up Razumov. That much Tekla had told me herself one afternoon we happened to meet at the door of the hospital, and without any kind of comment. But I did not want to meditate very long on the inwardness of this peculiar episode.

"Yes, Natalia Victorovna, he will need somebody when they dismiss him, on crutches and stone deaf from the hospital. But I do not think that when he rushed like an escaped madman into the grounds of the Château Borel it was to seek the help of that good Tekla."

"No," said Natalia, stopping short before me, "perhaps not." She sat down and leaned her head on her hand thoughtfully. The silence lasted for several minutes. During that time I remembered the evening of his atrocious confession—the plaint she seemed to have hardly enough life left in her to utter, "It is impossible to be more unhappy. . . ." The recollection would have given me a shudder if I had not been lost in wonder at her force and her tranquillity. There was no longer any Natalia Haldin, because she had completely ceased to think of herself. It was a great victory, a characteristically Russian exploit in self-suppression.

She recalled me to myself by getting up suddenly like a person who has come to a decision. She walked to the writing-table, now stripped of all the small objects associated with her by daily use—a mere piece of dead furniture; but it contained something living, still, since she took from a recess a flat parcel which she brought to me.

"It's a book," she said rather abruptly. "It was sent to me wrapped up in my veil. I told you nothing at the time, but now I've decided to leave it with you. I have the right to do that. It was sent to me. It is mine. You may preserve it, or destroy it after you have read it. And while you read it, please remember that I *was* defenceless. And that he . . ."

"Defenceless!" I repeated, surprised, looking hard at her.

"You'll find the very word written there," she whispered. "Well, it's true! I *was* defenceless—but perhaps you were able to see that for yourself." Her face coloured, then went deadly pale. "In justice to the man, I want you to remember that I was. Oh, I was, I was!"

I rose, a little shakily.

"I am not likely to forget anything you say at this our last parting."

Her hand fell into mine.

"It's difficult to believe that it must be good-bye with us."

She returned my pressure and our hands separated.

"Yes. I am leaving here to-morrow. My eyes are open at last and my hands are free now. As for the rest—which of us can fail to hear the stifled cry of our great distress? It may be nothing to the world."

"The world is more conscious of your discordant voices," I said. "It is the way of the world."

"Yes." She bowed her head in assent, and hesitated for a moment. "I must own to you that I shall never give up looking forward to the day when all discord shall be silenced. Try to imagine its dawn! the tempest of blows and of execrations is over; all is still; the new sun is rising, and the weary men united at last, taking count in their conscience of the ended contest, feel saddened by their victory, because so many ideas have perished for the triumph of one, so many beliefs have abandoned them without support. They feel alone on the earth and gather close together. Yes, there must be many bitter hours! But at last the anguish of hearts shall be extinguished in love."

And on this last word of her wisdom, a word so sweet, so bitter, so cruel sometimes, I said good-bye to Natalia Haldin. It is hard to think I shall never look any more into the trustful eyes of that girl—wedded to an invincible belief in the advent of loving concord springing like a heavenly flower from the soil of men's earth, soaked in blood, torn by struggles, watered with tears.

It must be understood that at that time I didn't know anything of Mr. Razumov's confession to the assembled revolutionists. Natalia Haldin might have guessed what was the "one thing more" which remained for him to do; but this my Western eyes had failed to see.

Tekla, the ex-lady companion of Madame de S——,

haunted his bedside at the hospital. We met once or twice at the door of that establishment, but on these occasions she was not communicative. She gave me news of Mr. Razumov as concisely as possible. He was making a slow recovery, but would remain a hopeless cripple all his life. Personally, I never went near him: I never saw him again, after the awful evening when I stood by, a watchful but ignored spectator of his scene with Miss Haldin. He was in due course discharged from the hospital, and his "relative" —so I was told—had carried him off somewhere.

My information was completed nearly two years later. The opportunity, certainly, was not of my seeking; it was quite accidentally that I met a much-trusted woman revolutionist at the house of a distinguished Russian gentleman of liberal convictions, who came to live in Geneva for a time.

He was quite a different sort of celebrity from Peter Ivanovitch—a dark-haired man with kind eyes, high-shouldered, courteous, and with something hushed and circumspect in his manner. He approached me, choosing the moment when there was no one near, followed by a grey-haired, alert lady in a crimson blouse.

"Our Sophia Antonovna wishes to be made known to you," he addressed me, in his guarded voice. "And so I leave you two to have a talk together."

"I would never have intruded myself upon your notice," the grey-haired lady began at once, "if I had not been charged with a message for you."

It was a message of a few friendly words from Natalia Haldin. Sophia Antonovna had just returned from a secret excursion into Russia, and had seen Miss Haldin. She lived in a town "in the centre," sharing her compassionate labours between the horrors of overcrowded jails, and the heartrending misery of bereaved homes. She did not spare herself in good service, Sophia Antonovna assured me.

"She has a faithful soul, an undaunted spirit and an indefatigable body," the woman revolutionist summed it all up, with a touch of enthusiasm.

A conversation thus engaged was not likely to drop from

want of interest on my side. We went to sit apart in a corner where no one interrupted us. In the course of our talk about Miss Haldin, Sophia Antonovna remarked suddenly—

"I suppose you remember seeing me before? That evening when Natalia came to ask Peter Ivanovitch for the address of a certain Razumov, that young man who . . ."

"I remember perfectly," I said. When Sophia Antonovna learned that I had in my possession that young man's journal given me by Miss Haldin she became intensely interested. She did not conceal her curiosity to see the document.

I offered to show it to her, and she at once volunteered to call on me next day for that purpose.

She turned over the pages greedily for an hour or more, and then handed me the book with a faint sigh. While moving about Russia, she had seen Razumov too. He lived, not "in the centre," but "in the south." She described to me a little two-roomed wooden house, in the suburb of some very small town, hiding within the high plank-fence of a yard overgrown with nettles. He was crippled, ill, getting weaker every day, and Tekla the Samaritan tended him unweariedly with the pure joy of unselfish devotion. There was nothing in that task to become disillusioned about.

I did not hide from Sophia Antonovna my surprise that she should have visited Mr. Razumov. I did not even understand the motive. But she informed me that she was not the only one.

"Some of *us* always go to see him when passing through. He is intelligent. He has ideas. . . . He talks well, too."

Presently I heard for the first time of Razumov's public confession in Laspara's house. Sophia Antonovna gave me a detailed relation of what had occurred there. Razumov himself had told her all about it, most minutely.

Then, looking hard at me with her brilliant black eyes—

"There are evil moments in every life. A false suggestion enters one's brain, and then fear is born—fear of oneself, fear for oneself. Or else a false courage—who knows?

Well, call it what you like; but tell me, how many of them would deliver themselves up deliberately to perdition (as he himself says in that book) rather than go on living, secretly debased in their own eyes? How many? . . . And please mark this—he was safe when he did it. It was just when he believed himself safe and more—infinitely more—when the possibility of being loved by that admirable girl first dawned upon him, that he discovered that his bitterest railings, the worst wickedness, the devil work of his hate and pride, could never cover up the ignominy of the existence before him. There's character in such a discovery."

I accepted her conclusion in silence. Who would care to question the grounds of forgiveness or compassion? However, it appeared later on, that there was some compunction, too, in the charity extended by the revolutionary world to Razumov the betrayer. Sophia Antonovna continued uneasily—

"And then, you know, he was the victim of an outrage. It was not authorized. Nothing was decided as to what was to be done with him. He had confessed voluntarily. And that Nikita who burst the drums of his ears purposely, out on the landing, you know, as if carried away by indignation—well, he has turned out to be a scoundrel of the worst kind—a traitor himself, a betrayer—a spy! Razumov told me he had charged him with it by a sort of inspiration . . ."

"I had a glimpse of that brute," I said. "How any of you could have been deceived for half a day passes my comprehension!"

She interrupted me.

"There! There! Don't talk of it. The first time I saw him, I, too, was appalled. They cried me down. We were always telling each other, 'Oh! you mustn't mind his appearance.' And then he was always ready to kill. There was no doubt of it. He killed—yes! in both camps. The fiend . . ."

Then Sophia Antonovna, after mastering the angry trembling of her lips, told me a very queer tale. It went that Councillor Mikulin, travelling in Germany (shortly after Razumov's disappearance from Geneva), happened to meet Peter Ivanovitch in a railway carriage. Being alone in the compartment, these two talked together half the night, and it was then that Mikulin the Police Chief gave a hint to the Arch-Revolutionist as to the true character of the arch-slayer of gendarmes. It looks as though Mikulin had wanted to get rid of that particular agent of his own! He might have grown tired of him, or frightened of him. It must also be said that Mikulin had inherited the sinister Nikita from his predecessor in office.

And this story, too, I received without comment in my character of a mute witness of things Russian, unrolling their Eastern logic under my Western eyes. But I permitted myself a question—

"Tell me, please, Sophia Antonovna, did Madame de S—— leave all her fortune to Peter Ivanovitch?"

"Not a bit of it." The woman revolutionist shrugged her shoulders in disgust. "She died without making a will. A lot of nephews and nieces came down from St. Petersburg, like a flock of vultures, and fought for her money amongst themselves. All beastly Kammerherrs and Maids of Honour—abominable court flunkeys. Tfui!"

"One does not hear much of Peter Ivanovitch now," I remarked, after a pause.

"Peter Ivanovitch," said Sophia Antonovna gravely, "has united himself to a peasant girl."

I was truly astonished.

"What! On the Riviera?"

"What nonsense! Of course not."

Sophia Antonovna's tone was slightly tart.

"Is he, then, living actually in Russia? It's a tremendous risk—isn't it?" I cried. "And all for the sake of a peasant girl. Don't you think it's very wrong of him?"

Sophia Antonovna preserved a mysterious silence for a while, then made a statement.

"He just simply adores her."

"Does he? Well, then, I hope that she won't hesitate to beat him."

Sophia Antonovna got up and wished me good-bye, as though she had not heard a word of my impious hope; but, in the very doorway, where I attended her, she turned round for an instant, and declared in a firm voice—

"Peter Ivanovitch is an inspired man."

THE END

ADDENDA: SUPPLEMENTARY NOTES

The numbers attached to these supplementary notes correspond with the numbers of the footnotes in the "Introduction" to this edition of *Under Western Eyes*.

4. The "shabby volume" in which Conrad said he found his clue to the story of Nostromo and the stealing "single-handed of a whole lighter-full of silver" has been identified as *On Many Seas: The Life and Exploits of a Yankee Sailor,* by Herbert Elliot Hamblen, writing under the pseudonym of Frederick Benton Williams, as edited by William Stone Booth, published in London and New York in 1897. See "The Original Nostromo: Conrad's Source," by John Halverson and Ian Watt, in *The Review of English Studies,* February 1959, pp. 45–52. The "piratical-looking" seaman Nicolo in Chapter XXXII of Hamblen's narrative, which is an account of his early sea voyages between 1864 and 1878, was evidently transformed into the silver-stealing episode in Conrad's novels. Where and how Conrad heard of this matter "in 1875 or '6" during his voyages on French ships to the West Indies has not been determined, and remains questionable in view of what seems to have been the fictitious basis of Nicolo's adventure. Further derivations in *Nostromo* from Edward B. Eastwick's *Venezuela: or, Sketches of Life in a South American Republic* (second edition, 1868), from George Frederick Masterman's *Seven Eventful Years in Paraguay* (1868), and from other possible sources have been traced by Edgar Wright in his University of London Master's thesis on *Joseph Conrad: His Expressed Views about Technique and the Principles Underlying Them* (London, March 1955); in Ivo Vidan's "One Source of Conrad's *Nostromo*," *The Review of English Studies,* June 1956; and in Jocelyn Baines' *Joseph Conrad: A Critical Biography* (1960), pp. 293–97. As noted here, Conrad's

own allusion, quoted in the Introduction, is in his "Author's Note" to *Nostromo*, written in 1917.

8. Conrad's most serious ambitions as a playwright concerned his tales of political subjects. (As early as 1905 his short play, *One Day More*, a dramatic version of the story "Tomorrow" in the *Typhoon* volume, was produced in London and among its admirers was Max Beerbohm, whose review is included in *Around Theatres;* fifteen years later he made another short play, *Laughing Anne,* from his story "Because of the Dollars" in the *Within the Tides* volume.) In 1919–20 he dramatized his novel *The Secret Agent* and it was produced for a short and unsuccessful run in London in November 1922. In 1920 he wrote a film scenario based on his tale of South American Revolution, "Gaspar Ruiz" (in *A Set of Six,* 1908); and earlier, in 1914, under the stimulus of the Huerta rising and dictatorship in Mexico, he planned to make a dramatic version of *Nostromo* with his Polish friend, J. H. Retinger, but this also was never completed. (*Cf.* Retinger's *Conrad and His Contemporaries* [London, 1941], pp. 120–25.) His plan to make a play out of *Under Western Eyes* in the last decade of his life was never realized.

Under Western Eyes eventually reached dramatic form in a film version, one of the most serious attempts thus far to put Conrad on the screen. This was produced in France in 1936 by André Daven, with direction by Marc Allegret, under the title *Razumov.* The cast was distinguished: Razumov was played by Pierre Fresnay, Haldin by Jean-Louis Barrault, Mikulin by Jacques Copeau, Mikulin's agent by Pierre Renoir, Laspara by Michel Simon, Nikita by Gabris, and Razumov's father, Prince K——, by Roger Karl. These parts were well played but the film—surprisingly so in view of Gide's possible hand in it—was largely a fiasco. The assassination was changed from a bombing to a shooting; the motive of Razumov's betrayal of Haldin was pointlessly altered; the part of Nathalie Haldin was abominably acted and misinterpreted by Danielle Parola (and badly handled by the scenarist); and after the action moved from St. Petersburg to Geneva Conrad's plot was reduced to ineptitude and distortion and became almost unrecognizable.

Conrad, who in his later years became interested in the cinema as a medium for his tales, has not been fortunate generally in the film versions of his work. There was a version of *Lord Jim* (with Percy Marmont) in 1925; one of *Nostromo,* under the title *The Silver Treasure,* in 1926; one of *Romance* in 1927; one of *The Rescue* in 1929; one of *The Secret Agent*, under the title *The Woman Alone* (later retitled *I Married a Murderer*), by Alfred Hitchcock in 1936, with an excellent Verloc by Oscar Homolka, several other good castings, and characteristic Hitchcock suspense, but with drastic changes in the plot and action; and three of *Victory* in 1919, 1930 (as *Dangerous Paradise*), and 1941 (scenario by John L. Balderston, direction by Anthony Veiller, with Heyst played by Fredric March, Lena by Betty Field, and the villains well acted by Cedric Hardwicke as Jones, Jerome Cowan as Ricardo, and Schomberg as Sig Rumann), but here again the point of the novel was watered down and became unrecognizable. The most successful films thus far have been Carol Reed's English production, severely truncated but filmed in the East, of *An Outcast of the Islands* in 1951 (Trevor Howard as Willems, Robert Morley as Almayer, Wendy Hiller as Almayer's wife); and a sensitive version of "The Secret Sharer" in the two-part film *Face to Face* of 1952 (adaptation by Aeneas Mackenzie, direction by John Brahm and Bretaigne Windust, the part of the captain played by James Mason), where it was coupled with a version by James Agee of Stephen Crane's "The Bride Comes to Yellow Sky."

9. Agnes Tobin, the American friend to whom Conrad dedicated *Under Western Eyes*, was born in San Francisco in 1864 and died there in 1939, but for many years from the 1880's onward she resided for long periods in England, France, and Italy. A poet and translator of Petrarch and Racine's *Phèdre*, she became the friend and benefactress of many writers and artists, among them Yeats, Wilfrid and Alice Meynell, Arthur Symons, Francis Thompson, Augustus John, Verlaine, Huysmans, Gide, Jammes, Vielé-Griffin, Stuart Merrill, Ada Negri, Nellie Melba, Mrs. Patrick Campbell (at whose request she made the *Phèdre* translation), as well as the Conrads. She figures in memoirs, diaries, and letters by Yeats, Gide, John, Huysmans, Jammes, Conrad, and others. Her earlier versions of Petrarch were published as *Love's Crucifix* in London in 1902; later versions in a privately printed volume, *Ave Maria: In Praise of the Blessed Virgin—Canzone of Petrarch* (San Francisco, n.d.). In 1958 there was published privately by the Grabhorn Press, San Francisco, a memorial volume, *Agnes Tobin: Letters, Translations, Poems*, with a memoir, as well as the *Phèdre* translation in a companion volume. Some sentences written by Conrad about

the writing of *Under Western Eyes*, quoted here, have been taken from her inscribed copy of the novel, kindly lent me by her sister, Mrs. Celia Tobin Clark, of San Mateo. (They closely resemble Conrad's inscription in Richard Curle's copy, included in *Notes by Joseph Conrad written in a Set of his First Editions, in the Possession of Richard Curle*, privately printed in 1925.) Agnes Tobin was one of the two Americans to whom Conrad dedicated books. The other was Frederic Courtland Penfield, last American ambassador to the Austrian Empire, to whom *The Rescue* was dedicated in 1920 in gratitude for the help he gave Conrad and his family in returning from Poland to England via Austria and Italy "in the world's great storm of the year 1914."

12. Investigations or accounts of Azeff and his activities that appeared while Conrad was working on *Under Western Eyes* were: L. Bernstein's *L'Affaire Azeff: histoire et documents* (Paris: Société des Amis du Peuple russe, 1909); L. G. Deutsch's *Der Lockspitzel Azew und die terroristische Taktik*, German translation by S. Gumbach (Frankfurt am Main: Maier Gesellschaft, 1909); and Jean Longuet's *Terroristes et Policiers: Azev, Harting, et Cie., Etude historique et critique*, with a preface by W.-L. Bourtsev (Paris: F. Juven, 1909). There is a large amount of writing on his career. Later accounts and documents are in *Azef: Choses vues* by Mark Aleksandrovitch Landau [the novelist Marc Aldanov] (Paris: *Oeuvres libres*, No. 113, 1930), and in *Der grosse Verräter* by Alexander Bauermeister (Dresden: Zwinger Verlag, 1937). A novel based on Azeff is Roman Borisovitch Gul's *Provocateur: A Historical Novel of the Russian Terror*, translated by Léonide Zarine, preface by Stephen Graham (New York: Harcourt, Brace, 1931). Another and relevant account is Boris Ivanovitch Nikolajewski's book *Aseff: The Russian Judas* (London: Hurst and Blackett, 1934), published in America as *Aseff the Spy: Russian Terrorist and Police Stool* (New York: Doubleday, Doran, 1934). This contains, among much interesting matter for readers of *Under Western Eyes*, an account of the Plehve assassination and a photograph of the wreckage of Plehve's carriage in the streets of St. Petersburg after the throwing of Sasonov's bomb. A valuable recent history of Russian radical and revolutionary developments to 1917 is Avrahm Yarmolinsky's *The Road to Revolution: A Century of Russian Radicalism* (New York: 1959, to be reissued in 1962). [Azeff's name will be found variously transliterated in indexes

and books as Azeff, Azef, or Azev, more incorrectly as Aseff or Asev, and his full name as Yevno (or Evno) Meiyer Fishelovitch Azeff or as Evgeni (Yevgenii) Filippovitch Azeff (Azef, Azev, Aseff). His dates are 1869–1918.]

It may be mentioned that Ford Madox Hueffer [Ford], in his *Return to Yesterday* (1931), gives a sketchy account of what he claims to have been Azeff's instigation of the attempted bombing of the Greenwich Observatory in 1894 ("the fantastic idea that an outrage in England might induce the British Government and British public opinion to decree the expulsion of all political exiles from their shores"), pp. 134–35—this being the event that Conrad incorporated into *The Secret Agent,* though Ford does not allude here to Conrad's novels. He goes on to tell that Azeff tried to get him to publish in *The English Review,* presumably sometime in 1908–10, "a volume of the diary of the late Tzar." Ford gives other details on his acquaintance with Stepniak, Kropotkin, Grumeisen, Magdalena Schabrowsky, and other Russians or Slavs, but his details on Azeff are undocumented and scarcely to be relied on.

20. Studies of Polish elements in Conrad's life and thought have appeared from many Polish critics and scholars in recent decades. Among the earlier were studies under various titles by Zbigniew Grabowski (1927), Roman Dyboski (1933), Piotr Grzegorczyk (1933), and Józef Ujejski's important volume *O Konradzie Korzeniowskim* of 1936, available in a French translation by Pierre Duméril as *Joseph Conrad* (Paris: Editions Edgar Malfère: Société Française d'Editions Littéraires et Techniques [Collection Polonaise], 1939). Among more recent students are Jan Józef Szczepański, Jacek Woźniakowski, Ivo Vidan, and Zdzisław Najder, whose volume of Conrad studies is to appear in Warsaw in 1962. Other valuable studies have been by Gustaw Herling-Grudziński ("W oczach Conrada" in *Kultura,* Paris, October 1957); by Wit Tarnawski in his introduction to a Polish translation of *Lord Jim* (Jerusalem: Interim Treasury Committee for the Polish Question, 1946) and in an essay "O Conradzie" in *Myśl Polska* (London, March 1948); and by the critic Maria Dąbrowska in her volume of essays *Szkice o Conradzie* (Warsaw, 1959). Of special importance is Czesław Miłosz's short biography of Conrad's father, "Apollo Nałęcz Korzeniowski," in *Kultura* (Paris), February 1956, with further valuable material in Miłosz's *The Captive* Mind, translated by Jane Zielonko (New York: Knopf, 1953). Two recent symposia

published outside Poland are the twenty-fifth Conrad anniversary issue of *Wiadomości Literackie* (London), October 10, 1949, and a collection of papers and documents edited by Wit Tarnawski, *Conrad Żywy* (London: 1957). Conrad's Polish origins and background were first recounted in French and English by G. Jean-Aubry in his *Life and Letters* (1927) and his *Vie de Conrad* (Paris: Gallimard, 1947, now translated as *The Sea Dreamer*, New York: Doubleday, 1957); but the first full treatment of these problems to appear in English was in Gustav Morf's *The Polish Heritage of Joseph Conrad* (London: Sampson, Low, Marston, n.d. [1930]), which, in spite of its excessive reading of Polish significances into Conrad's tales and its sometimes questionable psychological interpretation, was an important survey of the Polish elements in Conrad and remains a landmark in its field. A recent Polish biography of Conrad's father, *Apollo Korzeniowski: Ostatni Dramatopisarz Romantyczny*, published in Wrocław in 1957 by Roman Taborski, adds important material to Conrad's family and Polish background.

21. The elements of Polish history outlined in Part VI of the Introduction to this volume, admittedly a brief sketch of a large and complex subject, are derived from a fairly comprehensive reading in a voluminous literature. The most fully detailed account now available in English is the *Cambridge History of Poland*, edited by W. F. Reddaway, J. H. Penson, O. Halecki, and R. Dyboski, Vol. I: *From the Origins to Sobieski* [to 1696]; Vol. II: *From Augustus II to Piłsudski, 1697–1935* (Cambridge, England: University Press, 1941–). Among books in the early nineteenth century are *Tableau de la Pologne ancienne et moderne* by Conrad Malte-Brun (Paris, 1830) and *Lettres sur la Russie, la Finlande, et la Pologne* by Xavier Marmier (Paris, 1843). The Danish critic and historian Georg Brandes' *Poland: A Study of the Land, People, and Literature* was published in English translation in London in 1903. Among works available in English or French between 1920 and 1940 are: *Poland Old and New*, by Roman Dyboski (London, 1926); Vladimir Korostovets's *The Rebirth of Poland* (London, 1928); Edouard Krakowski's *Histoire de la Pologne: la Nation polonaise devant l'Europe*, with a preface by Paul Valéry (Paris, 1934); Robert Machray's *The Poland of Piłsudski* (London, 1936); and Raymond L. Buell's *Poland: Key to Europe* (New York, 1939); also *Joseph Piłsudski: the Memoirs of a Polish Revolutionary*, tr. by D. R. Gillie (London, 1931). Since 1940 have appeared

S-Wicz's Glasgow lecture on *Poland's Position in Central Europe* (Kilmarnock, 1941); Oskar Halecki's *The History of Poland: An Essay in Historical Synthesis* (London, 1942); James T. Shotwell's *Poland and Russia* (New York, 1945); Wacław Lednicki's *Life and Culture of Poland as Reflected in Polish Literature* (New York, 1944); Samuel Harrison Thomson's *The New Poland* (New York, 1947); Roman Umiastowski's *Poland, Russia and Great Britain, 1941–45: A Study of the Evidence* (London, 1946); Jan Ciechanowski's *Defeat in Victory* (New York, 1947); the anonymous work *The Dark Side of the Moon,* with a preface by T. S. Eliot, a study of Polish relations with the U. S. S. R., 1939–45 (London, 1946); a symposium edited by Zygmunt Wojciechowski, *Poland's Place in Europe* (Poznan: Instytut Zachodni, 1947); Stanislaw Mikołajczyk's *The Pattern of Soviet Domination* (London, 1948); Samuel L. Sharp's *Poland: White Eagle on a Red Field* (Cambridge, Mass., 1953); and Manfred Kridl's *A Survey of Polish Literature and Culture* (s'Gravenhage: Mouton, 1956). The studies of Conrad and his family listed here are important in this field also; and the bibliographies in the *Cambridge History of Poland* show the extent and range of this literature.

THE CONRAD ANCHOR

The following works of Joseph Conrad are published in Anchor Books editions and with introductions by Morton Dauwen Zabel:

The tales and short stories of Conrad:

[The remaining stories of Conrad will be published in two further Anchor Books as follows: *Falk, and Other Tales of the Sea* ("Falk: A Reminiscence," "The Partner," "The Brute," "Freya of the Seven Isles," and "The Black Mate"); and *Tales of Conflict* ("The Idiots," "The Return," "Amy Foster," "Tomorrow," and "Il Conde").]

The following novels by Conrad are also published in Anchor Books editions:

The Secret Agent.   A 8

Victory.   A 106

Chance.   A 113

The Rescue.   A 199

The Rover.   A 240

Other novels and works by Conrad will be published as Anchor Books in the future.

ANCHOR BOOKS

BRITISH FICTION

CONRAD, JOSEPH   The Secret Agent, A8
——   The Shadow-Line, Typhoon and The Secret Sharer, A178
——   Under Western Eyes, ed. Zabel, A323
——   Victory, A106
——   Youth, Heart of Darkness and The End of the Tether, A173
KIPLING, RUDYARD   The English in England: Short Stories by Rudyard Kipling, ed. Jarrell, A362
——   In the Vernacular: The English in India, ed. Jarrell, A363
MISH, CHARLES C., ed.   Anchor Anthology of Short Fiction of the Seventeenth Century, AC1
SNOW, C. P.   The Masters, A162
WEINTRAUB, STANLEY, ed.   The Yellow Book: Quintessence of the Nineties, A421

CONTINENTAL FICTION

ALAIN-FOURNIER, HENRI   The Wanderer, A14
CHEKHOV, ANTON   Ward No. 6 Six Russian Short Novels, ed. Jarrell, A348
COLETTE   My Mother's House and The Vagabond, A62
DOSTOEVSKY   Three Short Novels of Dostoevsky, A193
FLORES, ANGEL, ed.   Nineteenth Century German Tales, A184
GOGOL, NIKOLAI   The Overcoat Six Russian Short Novels, ed. Jarrell, A348
JARRELL, RANDALL, ed.   Six Russian Short Novels, A348
LERMONTOV, MIHAIL   A Hero of Our Time, A133
LESKOV, NIKOLAI   The Lady Macbeth of the Mtsensk District Six Russian Short Novels, ed. Jarrell, A348
MERWIN, W. S., trans.   The Life of Lazarillo de Tormes, A316
SERGE, VICTOR   The Case of Comrade Tulayev, A349
TOLSTOY, LEO   The Death of Ivan Ilych and Master and Man Six Russian Short Novels, ed. Jarrell, A348
TURGENEV, IVAN   A Lear of the Steppes Six Russian Short Novels, ed. Jarrell, A348

ORIENTAL LITERATURE

KAI-YU, HSU, trans. & ed.   Twentieth Century Chinese Poetry—An Anthology, A413
KANG-HU, KIANG   The Jade Mountain—Being Three Hundred Poems of the T'ang Dynasty 618–906, trans. Bynner, A411
MURASAKI, LADY   The Tale of Genji, trans. Waley
   Vol. I—A55
SCOTT, A. C.   Literature and the Arts in Twentieth Century China, A343
TSAO HSUEH-CHIN   Dream of the Red Chamber, trans. Wang, A159

ANCHOR BOOKS

EUROPEAN HISTORY

MARX, KARL, & ENGELS, FRIEDRICH Basic Writings on Politics and Philosophy, A185

MEYERHOFF, HANS, ed. The Philosophy of History in Our Time, A164

MILL, JOHN STUART John Stuart Mill: Essays on Politics and Culture, ed. Himmelfarb, A373

MUELLER, WILLIAM A. Church and State in Luther and Calvin, A454

NAMIER, LEWIS 1848: The Revolution of the Intellectuals, A385

NEALE, J. E. Queen Elizabeth I, A105

NEVINS, ALLEN The Gateway to History, A314

OSTROGORSKI, M. Democracy and the Organization of Political Parties—
Vol. I: England, ed. Lipset, A388a

PIRENNE, HENRI A History of Europe
Vol. I—From the End of the Roman World in the West to the Beginnings of the Western States, A156a
Vol. II—From the Thirteenth Century to the Renaissance and Reformation, A156b
—— Medieval Cities, A82

SERGE, VICTOR The Case of Comrade Tulayev, A349

SHATTUCK, ROGER The Banquet Years, A238

STERN, FRITZ The Politics of Cultural Despair—A Study in the Rise of Germanic Ideology, A436

SYPHER, WYLIE Four Stages of Renaissance Style, A45

TOCQUEVILLE, ALEXIS DE The Old Regime and the French Revolution, A60

TREVELYAN, G. M. History of England
Vol. I—From the Earliest Times to the Reformation, A22a
Vol. II—The Tudors and the Stuart Era, A22b
Vol. III—From Utrecht to Modern Times, A22c

TROTSKY, LEON The Russian Revolution, A170

VICO, GIAMBATTISTA The New Science of Giambattista Vico, trans. Bergin & Fisch, A254

WADDELL, HELEN The Wandering Scholars, A63

WANDRUSZKA, ADAM The House of Habsburg, trans. Epstein, A453

WEDGWOOD, C. V. The Thirty Years War, A249

WILLEY, BASIL The Seventeenth Century Background, A19

WILSON, EDMUND To the Finland Station, A6

136 novel

material? 2nn 212

300. disappears from sight =
        failure of vision.
            cf. 256
                rendezvous as conflict
            as approp. here as
                time is to OMB
            (less exuberant)
                mother of Victor Expects
                    a Vision 293

310 - to make him harmless, thus
        deafen him.

315 - not much perspicacity
        in the world